DAVID FIDDIMORE was born in 1944 in Yorkshire and is married with two children. He worked for five years at the Royal Veterinary College before joining HM Customs and Excise, where his work included postings to the investigation and intelligence divisions.

A Blind Man's War is the sixth novel featuring Charlie Bassett.

DAVID FIDDIMORE

A Blind Man's War

PAN BOOKS

First published 2011 by Pan Books
an imprint of Pan Macmillan, a division of Macmillan Publishers Limited
Pan Macmillan, 20 New Wharf Road, London N1 9RR
Basingstoke and Oxford
Associated companies throughout the world
www.panmacmillan.com

ISBN 978-0-330-50583-3

1 3 5 7 9 8 6 4 2

A CIP catalogue record for this book is available from
the British Library.

Typeset by Set Systems Ltd, Saffron Walden, Essex
Printed in the UK by CPI Mackays, Chatham ME5 8TD

Visit **www.panmacmillan.com** to read more about all our books
and to buy them. You will also find features, author interviews and
news of any author events, and you can sign up for e-newsletters
so that you're always first to hear about our new releases.

How do you say 'thank you' . . . to Charlie's hard pressed editors, those who provide the word pictures and technical information which make these stories work, and the many readers who write to him with stories which are often stranger, funnier and altogether more interesting than those he could dream up alone?

The best I can come up with is to print it at the beginning of this book, and hope that you notice.

Bless you all.

A BLIND MAN'S WAR

Chapter One

Toast and Tizer

It had been a decent late-summer's day until Dieter said, 'Are you going to get married, Dad? Because I can't see how we're going to manage if you don't.'

'I hadn't planned on it.'

That was the sort of reply Hopalong Cassidy would have made before thumping a Red Indian and blowing on his knuckles.

Thinking back on it I must have been thirty-two by then, and Dieter about fifteen. We had met in Germany in 1945, when he was a little lost orphan boy. I hadn't intended to adopt him; it was something which had crept up on me. We were sitting in the bar of the Happy Return, a pub owned by my old Major and his woman Maggs. It was next door to my bungalow down on Bosham Bay.

Maggs always referred to herself as 'the Major's woman', and enjoyed the matrons clucking in the back pews every time she went to church.

'Explain,' I asked Dieter.

'I'm going to the Merchant Navy College: you agreed.'

'So I did.'

'So what happens to Carly? He can't live next door on his own, and even here with Mrs Maggs and the Major he'll be terribly lonely.' Carlo was my other son, although like Dieter he wasn't a biological connection: he was the result of the liaison between Grace, my lover, and an Italian deserter. In Carlo's case I had been left, literally, holding the baby when his mother and her Italian bailed out . . . But that's another story. I hadn't intended to adopt Carlo either. 'We haven't been separated since you brought us down here; I've been more like a father to him.'

'More like a father than me, you mean?'

'I didn't mean that, Dad, but you're not exactly here as often as other dads, are you?' He was right. The little bugger usually was. He added, 'Don't think we're not grateful to you for taking us on. It's just going to be tricky for Carly when I go away next year.'

I lit my pipe. He sipped his ginger beer. I sipped my pint of bitter and glanced at the bar clock, wondering when I could allow myself the first whisky of the night. James – the Major – had just restocked, and I was keen to start sampling.

'Did you have anyone particular in mind?' I asked Dieter. 'For me to marry I mean?'

He gnawed his lower lip. 'There was that red-headed girl you brought down here a few times after you got back from Egypt. You seemed to get on well; you certainly made enough noise after you went to bed for the night.' Whenever he came out with something like that I wondered whether he was really only fifteen. I'd collected him on a battlefield; holding onto the hand of a dead teenager he thought was his brother. 'And she got on well with Carly.'

'June. But she didn't get on well enough with me to stay, did she?'

'Did you ask her?'

He always put me under the cosh.

'I was getting round to it.' She had another boyfriend who

had slipped in when I was abroad. I still see her when I visit the company's head office, but she became engaged to marry this new guy, and couldn't see her way into letting him down when I got back. These things used to happen all the time in the war – we didn't have too much time then to fret about them. June was one of my boss's secretaries; our heady romance had been going well before the War Office jerked my chain in 1953 and sent me to Egypt. 'How long have we got before you go?'

'About six months . . .' He looked rather longingly I thought at my pint, swallowed the last of his ginger beer, and stood up, saying, 'I have to get back. Carly's struggling with his English homework, and I promised I'd help him.' A German boy helping an English boy with his English homework – you live and learn, I suppose. Despite his Eyetie name Carlo was as English as the icing-sugar primroses on a chocolate Easter egg.

There was a rush later, and I helped James behind the bar – between pulling pints I asked him, 'Are you giving Dieter beer when I'm not around?'

'Yes, Charlie. Someone has to teach him how to drink. He gets half a pint a day; usually when he gets back from school . . . and he keeps his mouth shut about it. Is that a problem?'

'No, James. I'm glad you're watching out for him.' It wasn't the first time I'd slipped up with the boys, and I was sure that it wasn't to be the last.

Maggs and the Major had built me a prefab alongside their pub in Bosham while we were still blessed by a Labour government. The boys lived there with me when I was away from where I worked – Lympne in Kent, a couple of hours along the coast. I managed a small commercial airline. Well, that's stretching the truth actually – it more or less managed itself these days.

I had formally adopted Dieter with the help of the Chichester

WVS. I think it went through because it was the easiest way out for the authorities.

But Carlo was another matter. I was his legal guardian for the time being.

His father was certainly dead because a mate of mine had shot him. His mother might have been still alive – nobody knew for certain – but if she was dead it was because I had killed her. Grace and I had exchanged loving gunshots with each other in a small town in Turkey in 1953. She had hit me twice, but was unable to make it stick. I thought I had hit her once – I saw her stagger – but no body had turned up. So you never know, do you?

The matter had become less pressing the next time I got down to see them – about a fortnight later – because James, the Major, was living in the bungalow with the boys. Usually they stayed in the pub with him and Maggs when I was away. We sat round the kitchen table just after I arrived, with plates of beans on toast. Carlo had a glass of Tizer, James and I pints of beer, and Dieter's half-pint was out in the open. He sipped it thoughtfully.

I asked James, 'What happened to you?'

Dieter didn't give him a chance. He said, 'Mrs Maggs threw him out. She caught him with Mrs Valentine on Mr Valentine's boat.'

Ho-hum. What goes around comes around. Mrs Valentine was a willing workhorse: I knew, because I'd taken a few equestrian lessons myself. I asked them, 'What does Mr Valentine think about it?'

'I don't know,' James muttered scornfully. 'We haven't seen him for months; he's resigned from the yacht club. Maybe they've separated: she didn't give me time to ask.'

'So Maggs, to whom you're not married, is living in your pub, and you are living in my house?'

'It's just a temporary arrangement . . .' I hadn't seen James look so uncomfortable for years. 'Just until she cools down.'

'She'll get over it,' Carlo told us, and belched. He still sang soprano, and had a squeaky voice. 'Women usually do.'

We all turned to look at him. The little sod was only eleven years old. Dieter was right in one way: someone had to take Carly in hand.

'Don't talk about your elders that way,' I told him – probably too tamely.

'Anyone who's not a friend of the Major's is not a friend of mine, Dad.'

'You'd better move in for good,' I said to James, 'and teach these wee buggers some manners.'

Mrs Valentine's front end was Evelyn. *Eve.* You should never name girl children Eve, Bathsheba or Salome: it puts ideas in their heads. I'm sure that James had known of my previous engagements with her. Later on we sat on either side of the fire, and toasted each other in Red Label Johnnie Walker.

'What was she like?' I asked him. 'Any good?'

'Very energetic. I thought we'd go through the bottom of the boat. It didn't occur to me that Maggs would be offended.'

'Why? Because of that brothel she kept in France?'

'I suppose so.'

'That was stupid, James. The brothel was business; you're *personal* as far as Maggs is concerned. How do you feel about her?'

'Haven't got a clue, old boy: I never think about it.'

'Then you'd better bloody start. Cheers.' I raised my glass to him. It was the first time in ten years I'd ever given him any advice – it was usually the other way round. I've said it before, haven't I? What goes around comes around. 'Do you think she'll forgive you?'

'She's told me she will; after a fortnight. How can she know that?'

'I dunno. It's a mystery – that's a phrase I learned in Egypt.' An Egyptian pal used it to block any question he didn't want to answer.

'When,' he asked me, 'are you going to open that bloody envelope?'

The envelope in question was brown manila, and bore those magic letters *OHMS*. It must have come from the place we were beginning to call Fairyland on account of all the southpaws that were floating to the top in the Home Civil Service. The postman had delivered it earlier in the week, and Dieter had put it on the mantelpiece above the fire for me. The microscopic *RTS* address on the reverse directed it back to the Foreign Office in London. I opened it, and read the two terse lines on the letter it contained.

'They want me to go up for some kind of interview next week,' I told James. 'And Old Man Halton wants to see me as well. What do you think?'

James held his glass towards the fire, and squinted at the flames through the whisky. After a big swallow he said, 'I think you're in the shit again, old son.'

Just like Dieter, my old Major was rarely wrong about these things.

There are two impressive things about the Foreign and Commonwealth Office building in London: they are *size* and *scale*. Absolute and comparative. The room I was escorted to was large enough to keep one of Halton Air's Avros in, and still have room for a tennis court. Halton Air was my employer, and the Avro was the York – a civilian development of the Lancaster Bombers I had flown in the war. I was admitted through a double door from a Cecil B. DeMille film, and had to walk four miles across a room whose tall, narrow windows stretched from floor to ceiling. As I walked across the room I moved continually from bands of light to bands of shadow. It was a vaguely disorienting experience.

The desk in the middle was so old it was probably made from Armada timbers. The man sitting behind it didn't look much younger. He didn't rise to greet me: I don't think he could. They call things like him Whitehall 'Mandarins' these days, and he looked as if he was welded to his seat. He smiled a thin smile that somehow conveyed the fact that it pained him to have to do so, and indicated an upright chair opposite him. I'd seen photographs of chairs like that in America – they wire them up to the mains, and kill people in them.

He said, 'Mr Bassett?'

'That's the name I write on my shirt tabs.' It didn't work. The smile became thinner. If I had had a violin bow I could have played a tune on it.

'Thank you for coming to see us.'

I quickly looked around. I couldn't see any *us*, only him.

'That's all right, squire. I had to come up to town to see my boss anyway.'

At the word *squire* he winced. One to me.

'Do you know why we've asked to see you?'

'Haven't a clue. Sorry. If that's all, can I go now?' I don't know why I was being such a tit: there was just something about this specimen that immediately annoyed me. I wanted to punch his lights out. I half rose to make my point.

'No. Sit down. The Foreign Secretary has asked us to discuss your record with you.'

'Which record?'

I actually had a point. There were two card files on the desk; one under his right hand and one under the left. The one under his left hand was my old blue RAF personal file. It was about three times as thick as the last time I had seen it: that seemed hardly fair. The one under his right hand had a buff card cover, and was slimmer. That would have been a relief if the hand over it hadn't been trembling, as if the file contained a violent animal straining to get out. He calmed his hand with an effort, and spread his fingers out, pinning the papers to the desk.

'This one: you're a damned disgrace.'

We went *mano-a-mano* – the old eye lock – and I said, 'Oh, that. I wouldn't worry about that. There's bound to have been a misunderstanding.'

He didn't fall for it. He didn't say, 'Pull the other one.' They don't say that in Eton and Oxford.

They say things like, 'Sit up, and damned well pay attention. This file contains letters to the Foreign Secretary from our embassies all over the world, concerning your behaviour in other sovereign countries. To be specific, it comprises a list of countries who don't ever want you back.' He flipped the file open, and lifted a number of sheets of paper one by one. 'France. The Netherlands. Belgium. France again. Germany. Germany again . . .' He lifted a further three sheets of paper, and added, '*Especially* Germany. East Germany. Egypt. Iraq. Persia . . . Need I go on?'

'If you like.' I was, I admit, a little taken aback. I didn't think I'd pissed folk off that badly.

'America . . . What have you done to the Americans? They're supposed to be our allies.'

'Nothing: I've never met an American I didn't like. They must be mixing me up with someone else.'

'Not a chance, Mr Bassett – the FBI has labelled you "an

undesirable alien" who consorts with terrorists, spies, black marketeers, smugglers and career criminals.'

I shrugged.

'I seriously haven't a clue. I don't know what you're talking about. They must mean someone else.'

He allowed himself his first proper smile of the morning. 'For your sake, I truly bloody well hope so. Would you like a cup of coffee?'

When had we swapped from mid-morning tea to coffee?

'Why not? Then you can tell me what you want.'

Mrs Bassett, you see, didn't have any stupid sons, and I wouldn't have been sitting there unless the spiny bastard wanted something.

Coffee came in a tall Georgian silver pot. The china cups and saucers were as fine as knife blades, and probably worth a king's ransom: these civil servants did all right for themselves. He played mother. The biscuits were sweet Abernethy. That was a social gaffe: you should always serve Abernethies with cheese. I think I read that in a John Buchan novel.

'I want you to go back to the RAF, as a civilian consultant, and do some radio work on Cyprus for them,' he told me.

I blew half an Abernethy biscuit all over him as I spluttered.

'And you can go and take a running jump.'

At least we understood each other from more or less the word go.

He smiled as he brushed his jacket down. It wasn't a smile I liked.

He said, 'Most men would be grateful of an offer of employment these days, even if it is temporary.'

'I already have a job. I run a perfectly respectable small airline from a perfectly respectable small airfield in Kent. Thank you for the offer, and I'll be going now.' Again I tried to move from my seat.

He waved me down. 'You haven't finished your coffee. I always think the coffee's rather good here, don't you?' Then he added, 'Your perfectly respectable airline is on the move – to Panshanger, I hear – where most of your kit will be put into mothballs. I expect that's what Halton wants to see you about. He indicated that you might be kicking your heels for a couple of months, and we thought you'd be pleased to have something to do.'

'Indicated to whom?' Although Lord God Almighty Halton was my employer, almost a patron you might say, I wasn't surprised he'd discussed my future with strangers: in his world there was *him*, and everybody else – the *everybody else* were pawns to be moved around in his chess game.

'One of the ministers, I expect. He moves in exalted circles, doesn't he? What's he like?'

'Almost as small as me and twice as nasty. He coughs kerosene.'

'He has a reputation for looking after his people; rather old-fashioned.'

'You're probably right.' It was a grudging admission I had to make. 'I just wish he'd tell us about it first . . . Did he know in advance about this job you're offering me?'

'No. You come recommended.'

'By whom?'

'A rather highly placed officer in RAF Intelligence. They were among the departments we canvassed when the need arose: she advised us to get you if we could . . . Apparently you ran an intercept station at Cheltenham before it went all *Cold War* on us, and became GCHQ. Correct?'

I paused for a few seconds before I answered: ran a few bars of music in my head – an aria from *Norma*.

'Yes. I was there for four or five months; but you must have checked up on that already.' *She* in RAF Intelligence was not

Ayesha. She was Dolly. The first time I had met her she had been Section Officer Dolly Wayne, a War Office driver. That's what I thought anyway. We'd knocked around with one another every now and again – in personal relationships she was as rootless as me. She'd even missed her own wedding because she was too hung-over to get to the altar: that takes a lot of beating.

'Of course we've checked; I just didn't want you thinking we'd pulled your name out of a hat.'

'I don't want your damned job – I'm finished with that sort of bullshit.' But then my nose got the better of me; I think they rely on that. I asked, 'Tell me how long it would have been for, anyway.'

'Four or five months I expect. Then your airline will be back in business.'

'How do you know that?'

'Can't tell you. Walls still have ears.'

'You're mad; the whole damned lot of you. Anyway, if I *had* agreed what would have been in it for me?'

'Civil Service pay at an undeservedly elevated level, and we'll look after those boys of yours if anything goes wrong this time.'

These drip-dry-shirted bastards have had me over all my life. Halfway through a conversation you think you have under control, you feel the fish hook go through your lip, and they've got you. I decided I wasn't in the mood for opera, and looked at him with Bob Scobey's Frisco Jazz Band playing between my ears, *SOS, SOS, Captain we are lost* . . .

'What do you mean by *look after*?'

'Westminster, we thought – a nice sort of lad goes to Westminster these days – then Cambridge.'

'Public school and university?' I couldn't see Dieter agreeing to that.

13

'Yes.'

'I'm a paid-up Socialist.'

'Yes, old chap, but are *they*?' He had me there.

'I've never asked them.' The implication was there, of course, so I asked him, 'What sort of thing could go wrong?'

'You could get hurt.' They never say, *You might get killed*: looking death in the face is terribly bad form in the place where his accent came from. 'I've already told you that you would be based in Cyprus for some of the time.'

'Cyprus was very peaceful the last time I passed through – beach parties, tombola, seafood and women with large black moustaches.'

He looked at me very levelly and said, 'Cyprus is not going to be very peaceful for much longer, Mr Bassett – in fact, British soldiers are already getting killed there. Practically a rebellion.'

'That sounds almost like Egypt in 1953. You can't deal with a few hotheads without my help again: is that it?'

He didn't do irony, so he smiled that smile again.

'If you put it like that.'

'If the locals don't want us there why don't we just leave?'

'Because we can't.'

'Why not?'

'If we left, we'd lose the Med. We could not control it.'

'It was never ours to control in the first place.'

He smiled again, and there might have been something genuine in there.

'Try explaining that to the Prime Minister, Mr Bassett . . . or his Cabinet or the heads of departments. Your argument has merit with me, but not with them. Apparently Britannia still rules the waves.'

'What will happen if I say no? You can't call me up again, can you? I'm no longer a reservist.'

He spread his hand on the buff-coloured file again, and said, 'No; I can't insist . . . but what I can do is cancel your passport, I'm afraid. Ground you.'

'And would you?'

'Definitely.' Then he smiled the smile I didn't like again. 'Why don't you toddle off and see Halton, and then come back here to see me tomorrow with your decision. I'm sure we can work something out.'

His name was Browne. It had said that in my letter. C. H. Browne. Charlie, like me? Then Harry? Henry?

'What does the C. H. stand for, Mr Browne . . . as in *C. H. Browne*?'

His face was back in my file again; an amused smile played around his lips. He answered almost absently.

'*Carlton* Browne.'

'And the H?'

He suddenly looked up at me. His eyes were as hard as playground marbles.

'Hannibal. Good at getting elephants over Alps.' And a camel through the eye of a needle perhaps. Bollocks.

My boss, Old Man Halton, owned Halton Air. I minded it for him. He had been gassed at Loos in the Great War, and consequently could cough for England; apart from that he'd weathered well.

Whenever I liked him I called him '*guv'nor*' to his face. He enjoyed that: it made him feel like one of the boys. If I was out of love with him I called him *sir*. Whenever you went into his office he rose, offered you his hand, and asked you to sit down; even if you were about to get a bollocking. This time I didn't give him a bloody chance. After he stopped coughing I demanded, 'Are you sacking me, sir?'

'Nice to see you, Charlie. Sit down . . .'

15

I ignored his outstretched hand, 'I said—'

'I heard what you said. Now bloody well sit down.'

I moved the chair around with several bangs before dropping into it.

Halton asked, 'There. Feeling better?' I was probably glaring at him. The older I get the better I get at glaring. He said, 'No. I'm not sacking you, and I'm not pressuring you to go off gallivanting with your peculiar pals in the War Office either. Someone just mentioned a little job they said they needed done, and I just happened to mention that you'd done something of the sort before, and might be free for a few months, that's all. I know you don't need the money, but things have been tame around here for a while, and I thought you might appreciate a change – suntanned girls, and warm beaches, that sort of thing.'

'What kind of a someone were you talking to?'

'The Air Minister kind of a someone – at a banquet at the Mansion House. He actually knew of you, I think, and seemed quite keen on the idea.'

I asked, 'Why are we moving from Lympne?' Our base in Kent.

'Because we have to. The owners have pulled the rug. They've had a better offer from Skyways, and we have to get out. A friend at the ministry pulled a few strings for me, and got us sole use of Panshanger out near Welwyn Garden City – pretty country.'

'So we're still flying?'

'Of course we are. We'll run a limited operation from our Berlin office with, say, two aircraft for a few months, whilst the rest of the fleet is being converted.'

'To what?'

'Troop carriers, Charlie, that's what I asked you down here to discuss. We have the new contract for troop ferrying out to the Med and the Middle East.'

I was still sulking. 'I thought Eagle Airways had that all sewn up?'

'They do, but someone, somewhere, has budgeted for a massive increase in the War Office's capacity to move soldiers around, and Eagle can't expand to meet it. I can.' Then he began coughing again. He always got me when he began coughing: he should have been dead years before. I poured him a glass of water from a carafe on a small side table, and took it round to him.

'So you want me to go back to Berlin, and run the operation from there for a time?' He was wiping his mouth with one of his monster white handkerchiefs – they became speckled with blood on his bad days.

'That's the point, Charlie. You *can't*, can you? The German authorities have placed you on their blacklist. That's why you'll have very little to do until just before the conversions are completed.'

Shafted, I thought; completely fucking shafted.

One of the things I failed to mention was that I'd passed June, the red-haired girl my two boys had taken a shine to, as I walked into Halton's office. The office was over at the Cargo Side at London's crass new airport at Heathrow. I was as relaxed with her as you can be with a girl with whom you've slept, and with whom you wished you still were. We were shy. I hated that. After getting a brief from the old man on what the next few months held for the air arm of our business, and collecting enough papers to fill a dustbin, I shot the breeze with her in the outer office. By which I mean that I had said *hello*, and she had totally ignored me.

I'm an *in for a penny* merchant; I can be really subtle if need be.

I told her, 'I still want to sleep with you, and I want you to smile when I walk in here; instead of that you turn your head away.'

'I know.' She still didn't look at me.

'I think of you a lot.'

'I know.'

'The boys ask about you all the time. They think it was my fault.'

She could have said, *It was.* Instead she said, 'I know.'

Len Hutton used to bat like that on his quiet days. Stone-waller.

I hadn't noticed that Halton had followed me from his office, and stood in the door earwigging.

He laughed, and said, 'She knows, you know!' His laughter turned to coughing again, and he lurched back to his room fumbling for his handkerchief.

I went to the outer door, but stopped there and turned to look at her again. In for a pound this time, Charlie.

'It's half past three, June. You finish in a couple of hours. When you do I'll be waiting outside in the car. I'll take you out to dinner – anywhere you like. Then I'm going to take you back to your digs, and lay you on your back.'

My chin probably lifted as defiant as a schoolboy's when I said that, and swung away. I expected a mouthful from her, because June had a temper if you pushed her too far. I took three steps away from the door, and then stopped and turned: what she said instead was, 'I know.'

She must have freshened up her lipstick before she left work, because as soon as she got into the car she kissed me, and left it all over my face. We drove straight to her place and made love. Afterwards she lay back in bed, sighed, and said, 'Thank God for that!'

'Thank God for what?'

18

'Thank God you still wanted me. I didn't know if you'd come back for me, or not.'

'You didn't give me any encouragement at all.'

'I wouldn't, would I?'

'Why not?'

She didn't reply at once. I wondered if she had heard me. Then she said, 'I'm twenty-five, Charlie. How old are you?'

'Why?'

'You don't know much about women, do you? Apart from how our bodies work.'

'Do I know enough about that?'

'Almost, but you don't know how we think, do you?'

'You could always teach me.'

She said, 'Not a chance,' and trained one of her breasts on me again. The nipple was still large. I think it spoke to me. It was telling me to shut up.

We ate at a new Indian restaurant in Hounslow. Occasionally I put my hands under the table, and ran them over her legs. She always stopped speaking in mid-sentence when I did that. We finished with a green tea which was new to me.

I asked her, 'Are you still going to marry . . . ?' I couldn't even remember his bloody name.

'Eric. Eric Tripp. Haven't made my mind up yet.'

She had been engaged to a soldier in 1951, until the poor bugger had been captured by the Chinese in North Korea. She had thought him dead, and was still grieving when I came on the scene a couple of years later. Then he came back, which spoiled things for a while. His experiences in a POW camp had made him as mad as a monkey anyway, and after he tried to kill a domesticated Chinaman somewhere in London, he was stuck in an asylum. It still might have worked out between us, but, just as I was getting the green light again, the government had sent me to Egypt for six months. Enter Eric Tripp: he had stepped in before I got back, and she had ended up engaged to marry again.

'Are you making me an offer?'

'I can't make up my mind either,' I told her, 'but I'm going to be based along at Panshanger from now on, so I could get up to see you more often.'

'Ask me again when you *have* made your mind up. Then I'll tell you.'

'But you'll still go out with him?'

'Of course I will.'

'And sleep with him?'

'None of your business, boss. Are we going back to my place tonight?'

Boss? I suppose that was technically right. The last thought I had before I slept, was that the boys would be pleased.

When I awoke in the morning she was staring at me, lying on her stomach, her chin propped up in her hands. It was a nice stare. Uncomplicated. Maybe even fond. She said, 'I'm going to say something rather bold.'

'OK.'

'I like you in my bed.'

'So do I.'

All the best relationships are based on having something fundamental to agree on.

Chapter Two

Hello, Pete

C. H. Browne of the FO sipped his coffee and asked, 'Well?'

'There was something I wanted to ask you, something we glossed over yesterday.'

'What was that?'

'Exactly what *were* the allegations these foreign countries have made about me? You said the file of letters you had was full of them.'

He still had both files on his desk. We were in a smaller office this time. He had a smaller desk, and the smaller chairs were comfortable. Maybe he no longer needed to impress. He read from the letters one by one.

'The Germans suspect you of racketeering, operating on the black market, and illegally owning bars, clubs and a brothel.'

'Is that all?'

'Communist Germany accuses you of illegal entry. Russia, according to a confidential source, has you meeting with persons since executed for treason. France complains of illegal entry and smuggling, and Egypt claims that you are co-owner of a nightclub in contravention of civil ordinances . . . and that you consorted with known terrorists. Turkey has reported you, again for illegal entry – have you a problem with passports and boundaries, Mr Bassett? – and for being involved in a murderous shoot-out in a singularly remote region. They *also* claim that you consort with terrorists – Kurdish Nationalists this time.'

'Any more?'

'The Shah of Persia would like us to extradite you to face charges of conspiring to bring down a legal government, and, as I indicated yesterday, the Americans aren't all that keen on you either.' He closed the file again. I thought the Commies' rejection of me a bit rich: I'd joined the CP in London, by accident, in 1947 – and as far as I knew no one had unjoined me yet. Again, that's another story.

'Can I still go to Scotland?'

'I think so, but I can't think why anyone should want to . . .'

CB's intelligence dossier on me was obviously a bit dodgy.

'My father lives there. Some people are funny that way.' I sat back in my chair. I desperately wanted to smoke my pipe but couldn't see an ashtray. So I asked, 'Where *can* I go, then?'

He stared at me and blinked slowly, just once. The old smile was back.

'You can always go to Cyprus, but we'll tell you when.'

Bugger it.

I've always had this problem. When someone tells me I can't do something, I find I simply have to do it.

So I drove down to Lympne and gave my secretary, Elaine, a nice dry peck on the cheek. It stopped there these days because her husband was around more often. Elaine was the first ex-lover I was still happy around. I liked to think that our comfortable and professional relationship was the result of us having put our wilder days behind us. I sometimes gave her a second glance, and she did me, but wasn't sure whether that derived from appetites or memories. You know how it is.

Then I explained what was happening to all the air crew and groundies kicking around. Some of them would move airfields with us, and some would probably sign up with Skyways. I was still a bit pissed off when I hopped onto Randall's old Airspeed Oxford. I didn't even bother to take my passport: if the Gestapo picked me up in Berlin with it in my pocket they'd still fling me in the pokey anyway.

Randall was a pilot who had been flying me places since 1945, and felt more like a brother. I couldn't imagine my life without him being part of it. I'd got him a job with Halton in 1947: he was one of those big Americans who know how to do bad things well, and good things badly. Bloody fine pilot too, unfussy in his flying – I liked that.

'I don't like Germany any more,' he told me. It was nice to be overflying the country without the Russians trying to knock us down, as they did during the Airlift.

'Why not, Randall?'

'They've mended it. It was better when it was busted.'

I liked Randall. Liked him a lot. The old Airspeed was beginning to show her age, but Randall loved her. I wasn't looking forward to the day when I would have to tell him that I was replacing her. He was also a mind-reader. He looked over at me, and grinned.

'When you retire this old cow I'll give you a Hershey bar for her.'

Randall did a gentle wingover, and she began to rattle a bit. He started the let-down for Berlin. It would be OK if the cops weren't around.

Tempelhof used to be the US-run airport at the German end of the Berlin Airlift. Now it was a main aviation hub just like any you could find all over the world. But, being German, it was cleaner. It had its military side, but Randall avoided that as well, and taxied us round to the small group of freight sheds used for internal traffic. I kept my eyes skinned as we bumped around the peri-track, but didn't spot any customs or police cars. Anyway, I was right about the Oxford: she seemed to bounce down to her wheel stops over every crack in the tarmac. It was time the poor old girl was put out to grass.

Bozey Borland was waiting for us in our nice little black Mercedes saloon. He had replaced the little flag posts which had once flown Nazi flags on the top of each wing. Now they carried small French tricolours, and the car had new registration plates since I'd last sat in it. It had been our first acquisition after we opened the Berlin office. Bozey had won it in a card game; he was my local station manager. We did the *Hello you*, and *Hello you back* thing, squeezed Randall into the back, and set off for a small side gate used by the domestic companies.

Bozey said, 'Turn your collar up, boss, and hunch down in the seat. Close your eyes. You're a bad-tempered French diplomat who's had a long and nasty flight.'

'OK. You're the boss.'

'I'm not, actually. You are.'

Before I could get in a riposte Randall said, 'This bloody dog has just pissed all over my trousers.'

Bozey never went anywhere without his incontinent three-legged dog, Spartacus – although I don't think the choice was his: the dog knew a soft touch when he saw one, and stuck to Bozey like glue. When we reached the gate, with a battered tin sentry box in which a copper was picking his nose, Bozey wound down his car door window, muttered, '*Diplomatique!*' and scowled.

The cop sprang to attention. His right arm twitched for the old *Jawohl Mein Fuehrer* salute, but somehow he managed to hold it down. Then he raised the single pole barrier for us . . . and we were in Berlin. Just like that.

A hundred yards down the road I sat up, and asked Borland, 'Is that a real word, that *diplomatique*?'

'Dunno, boss. It always seems to work. Welcome back to Berlin.'

'Thanks, Bozey. I'm glad to be here.' I was too; that was a first. 'Where did you get the diplomatic plates for the car?'

'Won 'em in a card game.' I don't know why I'd bothered to bleeding ask.

If home is truly where the heart is then my heart is still partly in Berlin – which is odd when you consider that I'd spent a decent chunk of my twentieth year bombing the shit out of it. More specifically, my heart was in a little bar called the Leihhaus – a cross between a nightclub and a brothel. It had been started by a couple of my old friends. For those of you who don't speak the language of oppression, *Leihhaus* means *pawnshop*. I owned a quarter of it now, so did Bozey. Halton Air owned another quarter – although the old man tried to overlook that – and I was never quite sure who owned the rest. I think Bozey had parcelled the remainder out in small packets for sleeping investors. Sleeping investors in a brothel: that's not bad.

I had a room on the first floor, and Bozey lived in a rather palatial flat round the corner, with his girl Irma. Irma owned a bar across town called the *Klapperschlange*, which she'd inherited from my mate Tommo after he got his in an air crash in 1949. Irma had been Tommo's last girlfriend – what goes around, comes around. In the forties we learned to pass men and women around like parcels at a party game, but I wouldn't let it worry you. I ate a bowl of the stew the Leihhaus was famous for, in the kitchen with Marthe and Otto who ran the place for us, then I went upstairs, and crashed.

*

When I woke up mid-evening Pete was sitting on the end of my bed, smoking a cheroot.

That was very difficult for me, because Pete was dead.

In fact he'd been dead a few times. The first time he died was when he was blown out of the rear turret of our Lancaster by our own dozy Anti-Aircraft gunners in 1944. Then he turned up in Holland in 1945 with a tale of a miracle escape. Then Tommo told me he had been killed in a shoot-out with a black-marketeer in a small town in Austria in 1947.

There had been others, but those are the two deaths which stick out in my mind.

Now he was sitting on the end of my bed, and he didn't smell like a corpse. I hadn't heard him come in but that wasn't surprising, because Pete always moved like a ghost anyway. I had seen dead people before, particularly when I was drunk – at big parties my brain often brings back the dead guys I've flown and fought with. My immediate task was to work out if Pete was one of my private spectres, or was back in the flesh so's to speak. I swallowed hard and said, 'You're dead.'

'No. I am Polish. You'll never understand the Poles, Charlie.'

'Go away, Pete. Tommo told me you were dead. We got drunk, and I cried.'

'I'm flattered, but don't do it again. Put your clothes on, and we'll go out and have a party for Tommo.' Pete was always wizard at drumming up a party.

'You know that he's gone, don't you?'

'Are you telling me, or am I telling you?'

'We don't actually know, do we? I climbed a bloody mountain to the place his aircraft crashed. They gave me his lighter and his watch, and showed me the rock his body had been buried under.'

'Did you lift it, and look?'

'No, I didn't; it was too big.'

'There you are then. Get a move on. I'll wait for you downstairs.' He stood up and walked to the door. The bed moved and creaked, relieved of his weight. He did not walk through the wall the way a ghost is supposed to: he opened the door, stepped into the corridor and closed the door behind him. After he had gone the smell of his cigar smoke hung in the air. That clinched it for the time being; old Pete was probably back.

We called Piotr Paluchowski the Pink Pole. Do you remember those words? They made the first sentence I wrote when I sat down a couple of years ago to tell you my story, and if you haven't read them already you've missed something, haven't you? Pete had been one of the best rear gunners in the squadron, although he had one serious failing – he was so keen on killing the bad guy, that he sometimes let the Jerry night fighter get too close to our Lancaster before he pressed the tit. He wanted to be sure of a good shot. I remember that our big Canadian pilot had to sort him out after he'd done that once too often, and scared the shit out of us. It's what I was remembering as I caught up with him at a table in the bar downstairs.

'The last time I saw you was near the end of the war, Pete. That was eleven bloody years ago. You were a service policeman in a new Polish Army which had materialized from nowhere.'

'And you were still chasing after that skinny bird – what was her name?'

'Grace.'

'Yes, Grace. Catch her?'

'Several times. She drops in and out of my life like a travelling salesman – I'm the legal guardian of her boy.'

'When was the last time you saw her?'

'Three years ago. She was running with an Israeli assassination team, and put a bullet in me.'

27

'You shoot back?'

'Yes.'

'Get her?'

'I think so. Leastways she hasn't reappeared.'

'Good.'

'I didn't mean to – I just shot back at her without thinking about it. Now I miss her more than I've ever missed anyone.'

'You always were a bloddy fool about women, Charlie.' *Bloddy*. I suddenly recalled how he always used to say *bloddy*, and smiled.

I leaned back in my chair. 'You were a colonel in the Polish Army, right?'

'Yes, Charlie, I was . . . but I gave it up. No future in being a colonel in Poland: the Russians came back and shot them all again, just like they did at Katyn.'

'Tommo once told me that he and the Cutter had seen you shot in some small place in Austria, and he'd had difficulty getting the right coffin for you – one made of lime wood.'

'It was a set-up, a Tommo special. I needed to convince the Reds I was already dead, so that they didn't send someone after me.'

'But you're in the clear now?'

'I never said that.'

'Where are you living?'

'Here, Charlie. I got the room next door to yours. Are we gonna talk all night, or start some drinking?'

I waved Otto over from the bar. He brought us a bowl of pickled peppers to peck at, bottles of beer, and a bottle of schnapps with a couple of shot glasses. Just like old times. Later in the evening, before we were crawling drunk, I asked him, 'Why didn't Bozey tell me you were here?'

'We didn't want to scare you, Charlie. It's what friends are for.'

Bozey and Spartacus joined us later. Then Randall turned up. I made the bridge between Pete and Randall without telling them what the connections were. Randall was as big as a bear, and Pete small and ratty, like me – although he was probably in his forties by then, and his black hair was thinning. He still had a straight pencil-thin moustache like the Thin Man. They shook hands across the table; Randall's big paw wrapped around Pete's small hand. Randall squinted through the tobacco smoke and asked him, 'Do I know you?'

'I don't believe so,' Pete told him. 'I would have remembered. Do I know *you*?'

'I don't believe so either. I would have remembered you too.' Randall was grinning. That settled it. They'd already met each other before – I just hoped they'd been on the same side when it happened.

'Can I stay here tonight?' Randall asked Bozey.

'If you can afford it. A bed and an A1 broad will cost you thirty DMs. We throw the breakfast in for free.'

I've seen Randall look resigned before, if he thought he was being ripped off.

'That's a lot of dough.'

Pete leaned over and smiled at him. 'I think you'll find that the woman is a lot of woman. Just pretend that you owe her to yourself, lie back and think of England.'

Randall was American, which made it kind of an odd thing to say.

I asked, 'Isn't that what the *girl* is supposed to do?'

Bozey shook his head, and poured me another drink. 'You been away too long, boss.'

The evening finished with the latest entertainment Bozey had come up with – a wheelbarrow race on which he ran a book. The difference was that the four wheelbarrows were all good-looking girls, and they appeared to have left their clothes somewhere else. The men wheeling the wheelbarrows were strapping fellows. It took a few minutes to get the couples connected up, but after that the race went off quite well. Irma had come in to sit on Bozey's lap. Spartacus, under the table, set up a jealous howl as she did so.

The wheelbarrow who finished last earned the largest round of applause. Irma regarded her seriously, sighed and muttered, 'She faked it.'

'But it's made me feel quite peckish,' Bozey told her. 'I think we'll have to go home.'

Irma leaned over, and touched my face.

'*Peckish*,' she said to me. 'You English use the oddest words. OK, Charlie?'

'Yes, love; top hole. I've just begun to get undrunk again. I hate it when that happens.'

'You want someone? That French girl you like is around somewhere. You want her later?'

'Maybe, Irma. Rather it was you.'

'All the men say that, but only my Bozey ever means it.'

She'd got us taped, hadn't she?

I was smoking the last pipe of the night when the French girl, Reimey, walked in. I put the pipe down, crossed the room and kissed her. She pushed my hair from my forehead, and asked, 'Tired, lover?' *Fatigué, amoureux?*

'Rather – and a bit drunk.'

'Am I working tonight, or getting a night off?'

'Tonight you're sleeping; so am I.'

We did what we always did. What I'd done since I'd first started spending Berlin nights with her: we slept the sleep of the chaste, cuddled into each other like an old married couple. It was a slick deal: she got a night's uninterrupted sleep out of it, and I went down to breakfast in the morning with my bad reputation intact. It was like being married without the squishy bits.

She slept before I did, and made little snorting noises, like a piglet. I thought about Pete's vanishing and reappearing tricks. Was it only a week or so earlier that I had lamented that Halton Air was running itself, and that my life was uneventful? Bloody Pete would soon put a stop to that, I guessed.

As usual Pete was down before me, and was shovelling his way through an enormous American-style breakfast. Most of the Leihhaus food stock came out of the back door of the PX. As usual I stuck to black coffee, black coffee and black coffee: no one in Germany can brew tea. Pete mopped the egg stains from his plate with a doorstop of greyish bread, and asked, 'She any good, the French girl?'

'A woman's as good as the man she's with. You taught me that, Pete.'

'Then I guess she weren't much good. Pity.'

'You're a bastard, Pete.'

'No, I'm a Pole. I already tol' you.'

'How long are you staying?'

'Few days. I have a business deal over in the East.'

'You'll be careful this time?'

'I always am, Charlie. You know that.' Lie. Not only lie, but big lie. Pete was one of the biggest risk takers I'd ever met.

'And stay in touch this time. The next time I hear that you're dead I want it to be true.' Those words didn't come out in exactly the order I expected them to, but Pete understood. He grinned his shark's grin.

'You gonna help that nice couple I took to Bozey for you?'

'What young couple?'

31

'The two Americans – looking for her brother, I think. They paid me a finder's fee to introduce them to Bozey, an' for him to hand them on to you.'

'I don't know what you're talking about.'

Pete paused to discharge his breakfast gases with a soft belch. I remembered that he'd always been unselfconscious about things like that.

'Bozey will tell you. They're good business – loaded with dosh, like Rockefeller.'

'How do they know me?'

'Maybe you been in the paper.'

'Nearly ten years ago now.'

'You never know, maybe they keep their old papers.' Then he switched tracks on me and said, 'This American couple – the woman's a real looker, Charlie. Small as you, long, dark brown hair halfway down her shoulders. Face of an angel, legs like the devil. I stretched out my hands as soon as I saw her, and got slapped down pretty damned quickly.'

I leaned forward in my chair. I was interested in spite of myself – I could not remember Pete getting a refusal before.

'Tell me about them.'

Afterwards – after he'd gone – I realized that although we hadn't seen each other for eleven years, we'd offered no explanations. He didn't tell me what he'd been doing; neither did I tell him . . . and that's exactly what doing a tour with a Lancaster crew in 1944 meant. Some soft bugger used the phrase on a film poster twenty-five years later. The truth is that having flown with men like Pete really *did* mean never having to say you were sorry.

Bozey suggested a walk in a park. A large statue of a large German in the Imperial Roman toga style dominated a circular gravelled area with a few seats. An old man in a tattered grey

Wehrmacht greatcoat sold miniature kites from a makeshift wooden tray. He had neither hair nor teeth. The statue was worse. It had lost its head in the forties – a lot of Jerries lost their heads in the thirties and forties. So did we. We sat on a bench in the pale sun. Spartacus circled the kite seller at a distance, growling.

'Some Americans were looking for you last week,' Bozey told me.

I pretended that I hadn't already heard. 'What for?'

'They want to employ you, apparently. I knew you'd have a quiet couple of months, and thought you might be interested.'

First the buggers at the Foreign Office; now Bozey. How come everyone was so keen to find me something to do all of a sudden?

'Pete mentioned them,' I admitted. 'Why didn't you just give them the bum's rush?'

'I couldn't get my mind off the woman for a couple of days, and wanted another reason to see her.'

'What did Irma think of that?'

'I didn't tell her. She'd kill me if I laid a paw on another woman . . . But when you see what this dame puts in the field, you sort of forget about what's in the stable at home.'

'What's her name?'

'Doris. Like one of the Waters sisters. She's married to the other one. He never lets her out of his sight, and I'm not surprised.'

'Any idea what they want?'

'They want you to take them to Scotland.'

'Can't they find it on their own? It's big enough.'

'You've climbed up a mountain to an American aircraft crash, they said – someone in the consulate in London told them that. They want you to climb up to another one, and take them with you.' There was just a chance this was on the level. I had climbed

33

up to the site of Tommo's air crash in the Scottish Highlands. Call it a personal pilgrimage if you like. One of the locals had given me Tommo's Swiss wristwatch, and like a sentimental fool I had handed it in at the US Consulate in London later, and asked them to pass it back to his parents. There had been a problem because the US Army didn't know for certain that he'd been on the plane anyway – but let's not go into that.

'Why? What do they want to go up there for?' I asked. 'All they'll see is an aircraft reduced to its component parts.'

'Her brother was flying the kite. They want to lay flowers where he died.'

'That's got to be crap, Bozey.'

'That's what I thought. I knew you'd be interested . . . and it pays well.'

Ten yards away the kite seller stood very still whilst Spartacus tried to piss on his feet – not easy for a three-legged dog which instinctively lifted his back leg. He fell over. Then he set up an angry yapping, chased his tail in circles and sprayed urine over anything within a yard of him. The kite seller got it over his feet. That's when I noticed his shoes: they were very expensive and highly polished.

'Is he one of yours, Bozey?' I asked.

'No. He must be one of theirs.'

'When do you want me to see them?'

'In a few minutes. They're waiting at that little bar alongside the bandstand.'

I looked fifty yards, and there, sure enough, was a pre-war bandstand and a small bar with several tables in the sun. One of them even had a couple at it.

I suppose it took us little more than a minute to stroll over. Don't ask me my first impressions of the bloke, because I can't remember. What I can remember is that he stood as we approached. The dame looked up, crossed her legs and smiled . . . and somewhere in my head the Mormon Tabernacle Choir began to sing 'The Hallelujah Chorus'. The guy stuck out his hand to me, smiled a wide smile, and said, 'Hi, I'm George Handel.' It could only happen to me.

The woman stood up, straightened her dress, and held her hand out in turn.

'Hello. I'm Doris. When I married George I wanted to change my first name to *Door*, but George has no latent sense of humour.'

George scowled as if to prove it. It was my turn to open my mouth.

'I'm Charlie Bassett.'

Doris said, 'We know. You're the fellow who's going to help us find my baby brother's aeroplane.'

'He hasn't agreed yet, Doris,' her husband warned.

'He will, though – won't ya, Charlie?'

Although my libido was screaming *Yes please* my tongue managed to get out, 'Maybe,' and, 'It all depends.'

Spartacus ran up. Then he wagged his arse all over the place – the dynamics of a dog that's short one of his rear legs wagging his tail, is that the whole back end wags. Doris said, 'Aw! A three-legged dawg, how sweet.'

I wanted to have her until the friction ignited us, and we burned to death still going at it. It was a very good reason to turn down the proposal and walk away. From the corner of my eye I could see Bozey smirk.

'OK,' I told them. 'I'll probably take the job.'

'Thanks, Mr Bassett,' George said. 'You won't regret it.'

I already bloody well was. I looked down at my trousers and thought, *Another fine mess you've got us into*. It was at that moment I decided to call my left nut Laurel, and the right, Hardy. When I looked up again I must have been smiling. So was Doris. George looked worried, and Bozey looked as if someone had just told him a very good joke. Spartacus sat on his balls, and gave out a mournful howl like a wolf. Doris lit one of those new long cigarettes, and turned her head to one side to blow the smoke away. Then she shook her head and said, 'Your dog needs to get a sex life.' And wondered why we all turned to look at her.

We had them over to the Leihhaus for the evening to show them a bit of gay old Berlin.

You noticed the small g. There weren't all that many bits left actually: we'd dropped bombs all over the best bits in the forties. The buildings we hadn't flattened in the big area-bombing raids had bowed to Russian artillery at the very end.

At my request Bozey had kept the big round wooden table we used in '49, but he'd tossed the rest of the interior out, and redecorated with Bakelite and chrome. A Russian copper I knew then used to sit with his boots up on my table. You could still see the grooves his spurs had cut. We made the table our own that night.

It gave me an opportunity to have a better look at Handel. He was a tallish, whippy individual in a grey lightweight suit and a discreet tie. His hair would have been lighter if it wasn't slicked back with so much brilliantine: he smelt like Friday night at a petrol dump. Every time he lit a cigarette I leaned back expecting him to go up in a fireball. He told me, 'I really appreciate you doing this for us, bud,' and gave Pete a hundred dollars. Pete solemnly peeled off fifty and handed them on to Bozey. I thought Brother George was giving the loot to the wrong people. Pete must have seen my look.

'Don't fret, Charlie. We done our bit when we delivered you. You'll get yours when you've delivered also.'

'I'll be almost a thousand miles away by then.'

'Everyone knows Scotland's a backward country, Charlie. Don't worry about it – your money will go further there.'

'You want an advance?' George asked me hurriedly.

'No, George, but thank you for offering. You're a gentleman. I'll tell you when I need money.' But he wasn't a gentleman; he was a thug. He had the long, coiled look of a knife man all over him.

'When can we start?'

'I'm flying back to Blighty tomorrow. There's room for you and Mrs Handel in the aircraft if it suits you. If you tell Bozey where you're staying we'll pick you up on the way to the airport – say ten-thirty.'

Mrs Handel wasn't at the table. She was in the room that girls disappear into for hours at a time, and then come out looking younger than when they went in. When she came back it felt as if she was walking across the floor directly to me. I think every other man in the joint felt the same. I sat back in my chair, and had a decent dekko at her this time.

She had a slinky black dress on, which clung to her curves like a racing car clings to the Brooklands' bankings: was about the same height as me, had dark hair that fell beyond her shoulders like wavelets, feline eyes, and flawless milky skin. Her shoulders were square, above a wasp's waist and wide flat hips. And front bumpers like weather balloons – I couldn't see how she held them up like that. We all stood up for her: she was that sort of broad. Her grin said she knew exactly what the score was.

We rearranged ourselves. Pete lit her cigarette – she used a small holder in the evenings – and snapped his fingers for some service. Spartacus took that as an invitation, and tried to climb on to his lap. Pete didn't even like four-legged dogs, so the way he jumped his chair away was no surprise to me. Doris had a confession to make.

'I got lost looking for the little girls' room, Charlie – and found my way upstairs. I opened a door, but a girl found me there, an' tol' me it was your room. You don't mind that I did that, do you?'

'No. We're gonna be partners for a week or two, so we'll get to know each other anyway.' Who was I kidding?

'I knew we were gonna get on, Charlie – right from the moment I first saw you.' That was what I was hoping too, but before I could say anything she asked, 'Can I get a Martini in this place? I feel like celebrating. This is the first progress we made in a month.' She crossed her legs, and leaned forward to open her fag packet again, having puffed her way through the first in a few minutes. The material of her dress stretched across her thighs, clearly outlining her stocking top and the button of her suspenders. In the fifties that was one of the things that could drive a man mad.

I said, 'I'll fetch you one,' because I wanted to get away to somewhere I could breathe again. She leaned over, and touched the back of my hand where it lay on the table. I'll swear I was scalded.

'No need. George's in the chair,' she said. 'Ain't you, honey? He'll get a round in.' George did as he was told: I suspect that most men did when she opened her mouth. There was something going on here. Part of me liked it, and the other part of me was telling me to run.

Before I went up, but after the Handels had left, I told Pete, 'I've a small pistol I like. I could always buy another on the black market, but I'm kind of used to it now.'

'I'm pleased to hear that, Charlie.'

'I need a box of older .32 rimfires for it.'

'How long have I got?'

'Until tomorrow morning.'

'No problem.'
Your local chief constable wouldn't like that at all these days.

When I got upstairs Reimey was in bed reading a Peter Cheney paperback. The guy on the cover wore a trench coat and a fedora, and held a pistol as big as a foot. The girl alongside him didn't have much on at all, and held a cigarette. That should have told me something. Its French title was meaningless – I wondered if they'd hired a cheap translator. Reimey was wearing a large pair of spectacles, and looked pleased to see me.

'Hard day?' I asked her.

'No day at all. I have Tuesdays off. I went to the market with Marthe and bought vegetables.'

'Are you wearing anything at all?'

'Just these.' She removed the specs and waved them gaily at me. She turned the light off as I slid in beside her. 'When I came upstairs earlier there was a very pretty woman in here. She yours?'

'No, she's my employer. She told me she got lost. What was she doing?'

'Turning you over. She looked quite professional.'

So; that was the way it was going to be.

I sensed there was more to come, so I asked, 'What else were you going to tell me?'

'Gonna fuck you tonight, Charlie – tired of waiting.'

Chapter Three

Love and Bullets

The man in the outer office chatting up Elaine, and sitting on the edge of her desk, could have come from the cover of that same Peter Cheney book. He had the trench coat and fedora, and used too much cologne. Why were men beginning to stink like French ballet dancers all of a sudden? He thought she'd fallen for whatever line he'd spun, but I'd seen that look in her eye before – she was about to run him through. My arrival on Randall's aircraft, with the Handels in tow, had saved him from a tongue worse than death: Elaine had the ability to cut a person in half with a dozen well-chosen words.

He stood up quickly, and stuck out his hand, trying for the usual bone-crusher. I did what I always did – locked my fingers, and watched his face turn white with effort. The women smiled at each other; they'd seen male mating displays before.

Elaine said, 'This is Mr Dory, Charlie. He's come all the way from London to see you.'

Dory pulled his hand back.

'My name is Harold.' His voice was high-pitched, the vowels oddly rounded, and he rolled his Rs. A working-class Geordie trying to sound as if he'd climbed the golden ladder. For a moment I couldn't place the sound in my memory. Then I realized that he sounded a bit like Pinocchio.

'He's been waiting an hour for you, Charlie,' Elaine continued.

'Mr Martenson sent me,' Harold explained.

I said, 'That doesn't help much, Harold. I don't think I know him.'

'One of your mates does though. Some Pole who was here in the war – Arnie owes 'im a few favours.' That figured. It was the way they did business in Pete's world. Dory added, 'I have to give you these.'

He pushed his hands into his coat pockets like Johnny Mack Brown going for his guns, and came out with a small cardboard box in each. When I took them their weight disagreed with their dimensions. Two boxes of bullets. Pete hadn't turned up before I left: I'd wondered if he'd forgotten.

'Thank you, Harold. Tell Mr Martenson I'm obliged. I'll settle up with Pete when I see him.' I had no doubt that I would. I gently ushered Hunky out of the building in front of me; bullets weren't something I wanted to discuss in front of the others.

He walked to his car – a smart two-tone Riley One and a Half with the mock-leather roof. I followed him. In maroon and black it looked even better close up.

'I like your car, Harold. What will it do?'

'More than a ton, Mr Bassett: I had twin SUs fitted to her, and lowered the suspension an inch. The coppers haven't a car in the kingdom that can catch me.'

'Not that they'd ever have to.'

'Nah. You're right.' And he laughed. He had a right nasty little laugh. I guessed he might even be a match for George Handel up a dark alley. 'I like you, Mr Bassett. You can call me Harry. Take this.' He'd pulled a visiting card from his top jacket pocket. All it had on it was a Plaistow telephone number. 'Call me if you think we can do business.'

'Thank you, Harry. I shall.' We shook hands again without breaking fingers this once. I watched him drive away. Nothing flashy. He gave me a wave, and I suppressed a shudder.

Randall walked out of the office door as I approached it. He growled, 'Those bastards!'

'What bastards?'

'Your fucking passengers! He tipped me thirty dollars like I was a goddamned taxi driver.'

'You keep it?'

He glanced down at his hand as if he didn't know. 'Yes. Yes, I did. I was too surprised to throw it back at them.' He had a bundle of notes crushed in his fist.

'Good. Save it for later. We'll have a few jars on them.' One of the nice things about the local pub was that they changed currency for us like a bank. I hoped we'd find somewhere as accommodating near Panshanger.

Inside the office Elaine was filing one of her nails. She always did that when she was feeling feisty. I asked her, 'Where are they?'

'Using the cloakroom. I phoned for a taxi to get them to the station. They say they're going to stay in a hotel up in town until you contact them. What are you up to, Charlie?'

'Never you mind. Fancy a quick one when you've finished up this afternoon?'

She pouted. 'I'd rather we went for a drink, if you didn't mind.'

'That's what I meant.'

'Oh.' Some you win, some you lose, and some you don't even bloody notice.

The Handels reappeared together. Americans take an inordinate amount of time to wash their hands, have you noticed that? Maybe it's a fetish. I wondered if Doris had searched our lavatories, while George had been polishing his knives, but

I didn't have to small-talk them because old Harris's taxi drew up outside – it was a big black Humber Hawk estate he'd bought from the undertaker. I always thought it smelt of formalin.

George did the handshake thing, and Doris gave me a kiss on the cheek. George had turned away from me as she did that. Her lips felt big and full, and I knew that she'd left her red brand on me. I had something to ask them.

'I'll phone you in a couple of days, but how will I know where you're staying?'

'We'll stay at the Savoy, won't we, Georgie? Your man in Berlin said they'll always make room for people like us.' *Which* man in Berlin, I wondered.

George nodded, and handed me an old pre-war Ordnance Survey map with cloth covers, saying, 'I marked the hills where the plane went in. The nearest houses are at a place named Shieldaig.'

'Never heard of it, George, but don't worry, I'll find a couple of native guides to get us up there and back.' He frowned momentarily; maybe he thought that I was about to take them up Kilimanjaro on my own. They turned away, and I showed them out, just the way I had Flash Harry. They even wanted to shake the cab driver's hand before they mounted up. Some people touch too much. Kids play pat-a-cake instead.

I stood in the doorway and watched the taxi float away on a cloud of blue exhaust smoke. Doris turned to look at me through the Humber's rear window. George didn't. Elaine came and stood behind me, and leaned her chin on my shoulder. Some people can touch me as often as they like. She said, 'Why don't you wipe that lipstick off your face, Charlie?' After I complied she asked, 'What have you got yourself into this time?'

'Don't know, love, but it's interesting. I don't believe a word they say.'

'Neither do I, but watch her – she's a man-eater.'

I telephoned the Heathrow office to speak to June, but the dialling felt more like a duty than a pleasure. That worried me. It needn't have; a different woman answered the telephone. She told me she was the new office junior, and sounded as if she laughed a lot. If ever I picked my own staff, I'd choose one just like her . . .

'June's having a week off. I think her boyfriend's just come out of hospital for a few days.'

'You mean the one from the loony bin?'

She laughed; I'd guessed she would. 'That's cruel.'

'I know it is. I'm sorry . . . but are we talking about the same man? A soldier just back from North Korea or China?'

'Yes. I think so. Who *are* you?'

'Charlie Bassett. I run Lympne for us, and in a couple of months' time I'll run Panshanger. I don't know what I'll be doing in between, so if you wanted a date I could probably fit you in.'

She laughed again. 'Not on your life – she's warned me about you.'

It was interesting. It meant that June had three men in her life at present: a nice reliable fellah she was engaged to marry, a nutty, homicidal soldier who she also had been engaged to marry once, and me. Being neither reliable, nor a nutcase, I was on the wrong end of that queue. It looked as if Dieter and Carlo had been backing the wrong horse; I'd better break that gently to them.

There was no reply when I called June's digs, so I phoned her parents' home. Her mother answered. After the preliminaries she asked, 'Where are you just back from, Charlie?'

'Berlin. It was cold and sunny. Berlin weather. How's June?'

'She's fine. She's out. Can I ask you something?'

'Of course.'

'Why don't you leave her alone, Charlie? You don't see her for months on end, but whenever she gets her life going again you come back . . . and if she sees you she mopes around for weeks afterwards. You make her unhappy. What are you trying to do?'

I ran the first two choruses of 'St James Infirmary Blues' in my head before I answered. It's always been one of my favourites.

'I don't know.' They sounded like strange lost words, even to me.

'Then why don't you leave her alone until you do?' And she put the phone down on me.

I was still holding the telephone when Elaine walked in. She took it from my hand, and replaced it on its cradle.

'Who's just had a surprise then?' It must have been in my face.

'Me, I suppose.'

'Good surprise or bad one?'

'I don't know.' Again they sounded like strange lost words, even to me, but Elaine knew how to handle it.

'Put your coat on then. Flying's finished for today, and the pub's open. Randall's up there waiting for us.'

'How do you know? Did he call?'

'No. I'm psychic.'

A few aircrew and some of the groundies were already there, so we made a party of it and the old thing happened.

I stepped outside after too many pints, wearing my old RAF blue battledress jacket – I don't know where that had come from. Some dead guys from my past were whooping it up in the car park without me. There was an American named Peter

Wynn dancing with Emily, a girl who had worked in the Red Cross Officers' Club, and the Toff — our mid-upper gunner — was with a pretty woman in WVS uniform. I felt I should know her, but couldn't retrieve her name. Marty, our bomb aimer, was dancing with a damned great empty bomb casing: he'd done that before. They waved to me as they jitterbugged past. The Russian I told you about was there, swigging from his usual bottle of expensive Tokay. I'd swear the music was the original Glenn Miller outfit.

I didn't realize that anything was wrong until I opened my eyes. I was still on my feet but my legs felt wobbly. Randall had hold of my arms and was gently shaking me, although *gentle* is a relative term if we're talking about Randall. Elaine looked on. Concerned, I'd guess.

It was Randall who said, 'You were out here shouting, boss. Out here on your own, shouting at nobody. As if you'd gone off your head.'

I muttered, 'I think I dropped my pipe somewhere.' Elaine stepped up, and handed it to me. It was still alight. Elaine looked a bit shocked. Randall wasn't going to let me off the hook that easily.

'You were shouting something like, *Go away and leave me alone!* What was that all about?'

'Drank too much,' I lied. 'Need to go and sleep it off.'

'I'll walk with you,' said Elaine.

She was taller than me and prettier . . . and when she linked her arm through mine it was well above my elbow. On the way down to the old dispersal hut I occasionally slept in I realized that this could be the last time I'd wake up in it. I asked Elaine, 'What about Terry, and that godson of mine?' Her hubby and son.

'Visiting his mum in Beaconsfield: they won't be back until Friday. What were you shouting about?'

It was chill. Elaine tucked in close alongside me. The narrow cement path to the Nissen hut was pale in the moonlight.

'Sometimes I see dead people, love. People I know.'

Elaine was smoking a long tipped fag. I wondered if Doris had subbed her a packet. She exhaled a lungful of smoke into the night air above us.

'Oh, that,' she said, and paused before saying, 'Yeah. It happens sometimes.'

'I thought it was only me.'

'No, darling. You're just like the rest of us . . . Join the club.'

Old Man Halton's club was tucked away behind a large walled garden off Regent's Park Road. I'd only been invited there twice before, and it was always when he was buttering me up for something. He knew that I knew that: I think it amused both of us. The fish dish was exquisite. We didn't really talk again until we were halfway through a rack of lamb.

He suddenly observed, 'When you were recalled as a reservist about three years ago we picked up three nice contracts from the War Office. Did you know that?'

'You scratched their backs, and they scratched yours.'

'Something like that.'

'I got shot at.'

'That was your own fault, wasn't it? Someone from your murky past.'

'My past was never meant to be murky, boss. It was meant to be serene. Nice house in the suburbs, friendly wife, three kids and a car. Golf on Saturdays.'

'*Do* you play golf?'

'No, of course not. It's infantile.'

He smiled and said, 'Good. That kind of life would have bored you to death. What do you make of the wine?' I've never understood the poncey language that wine buffs speak – I suspect that they don't either.

'I could drink buckets of it, if that's what you mean. Have you been offered another contract for Halton Air, provided I go out to play with your pals at the Foreign Office for a couple of months?'

He looked shifty, and began to cough. It was a bit of a grand opera once it got going, but they were used to him at his club, so nobody took any notice. I raised my hand to the waiter who came over with a large glass of water. Halton finished the opening salvoes, and had a couple of gulps of the water. He said, 'Thank you, Charlie.'

'Thank the waiter – he brought it. You were saying . . . ?' I prompted. He probably hoped I had forgotten.

'Yes. The government will give us a leg-up again.'

'Is it important, sir?'

'It would set us up for fully the next ten years.'

With Old Man Halton it was always best to cut to the chase. 'What would be in it for me?'

'I'll make you a co-director of the company, and give you a fifth share.'

For a moment I didn't know what to say. If you'd come from the labouring classes, like me, neither would you.

'There must be a snag – you don't mind my saying that, do you?'

'Of course not, Charlie, and yes, there is – the third director will be Frieda, and once I'm gone she'll fight you tooth and nail . . . over everything.' I digested that.

'Why?'

'Because she probably loved you a little once upon a time. Women never forgive you for that.' Frieda was his ward: the daughter of a German woman he had brought to the UK just before the war. She was going to marry me until she found someone taller, and jumped ship. I thought I'd behaved rather well at the time, but I could be mistaken. Halton added, 'I've no son, and the business will need a man who knows what he's doing. She would ruin it on her own, and sell what was left to the Americans.' Then he asked, 'Well?'

I did some thinking music in my head, Glenn's 'String of Pearls' – I've told you about that before as well. Then I grinned.

'Cyprus it is then, sir, although they indicated that it might not be for some weeks yet.' I always feel relieved when I've made a decision.

'Good. The family lawyer will contact you. There will be some papers to sign. I won't tell Frieda until afterwards.' No; nor should I. Frieda would play merry hell when she found out. What goes around comes around.

'Seen your boys recently?'

'I'm going down to them this afternoon. They're fine. Dieter wants to join the Merchant Navy.'

'Flying's not in his blood then?'

'Flying's not in my blood either, boss. My lot liked fighting their wars from trenches, or where there were plenty of things to hide behind.'

That set him off coughing again. This time when he pulled the handkerchief down there were those specks of blood on it. He saw me watching him, and demanded, 'What? What are you thinking?'

'That we'd better get those papers signed as quickly as possible. I don't know how long you've got.'

That set him off laughing and coughing again. The truth was that Old Man Halton could be a bit of a bully, and I was probably the only person around him who ever talked back. That was because we liked each other a lot, and of course, being men, it was something we never said.

'About my secretary . . .'

'Yes, boss?'

'I hoped that you and June were going to make a go of it this time. You light up every time you see her – did you know that?'

'I hoped so too. The boys adore her. Unfortunately I'm at the wrong end of a queue as far as she's concerned – there's the bloke she started dating when I was in Egypt, and now they've let her Glorious Gloucester out of the loony bin.' That was unworthy of me, and I immediately regretted it. We both frowned. 'Anyway, I telephoned her parents' house a couple of days ago, and her mother asked me to leave June alone. She said I made her unhappy . . . it made me think.'

'Well, don't think for too long. Women are like kettles.'

'Come again?'

'You can't do much with either once they've gone off the boil.'

The move to Panshanger was well under way and Elaine had told me to lose myself.

'You'll only get in the way, Charlie. Leave it to me, Randall and the ground staff, chiefy. We're moving everything up in the Yorks before they re-deploy to Berlin.'

'What do you mean I'll only get in the way? I'm the boss down here.'

'So?'

'I'm supposed to be giving the orders.'

'Whatever gave you that idea, dear?' And she roared off into peals of musical laughter. After a few seconds I was laughing myself. I'd wanted an excuse to drive up to London and fly formation with the Handels anyway.

It was cold and bright; a nice morning to stretch out my new car. I'd sold my old open Singer to Randall, so that I could buy the Sunbeam Alpine that Evelyn Valentine had tired of. I told you: what goes around comes around. It was a lovely pale blue thoroughbred with a column shift, a mile of bonnet in front of you, and a mile of tail behind you. I've told you about Eve; she with whom both James and I had taken a walk in the park. I'd skipped into the bar to find her and Maggs chatting away like old friends: I cannot understand women sometimes. When she said she wanted to get rid of the Sunbeam we did a deal there and then, and I'd paid her three hundred quid for it.

I folded the hood away, and howled down to Brighton before turning north: I wanted to open her up along the A23, then slip across and see what she'd do over the Hog's Back. The answer was damn near a ton, and that was good enough for me. Maybe I'd challenge Flash Harry to a race down to the Ace of Spades Café some day – the kids had started to do that on motorbikes.

I did something brave: I booked into Green's, the hotel that we always used to use in the war. By *we*, I mean the bomber crew I'd flown with – *Tuesday*'s children. I had been unable to set a foot over the doorstep for years after the war ended: it had been a 'bomber' hotel, one of several in the city. I'd only been back a half-dozen times since then, and when I did the ghosts never failed to come crowding round.

After I'd booked in I called the Handels in the Savoy. Doris answered the telephone.

'Where are you, Charlie?'

'Green's. We used to use it in the war – not too far from you.'

'Why don'cha book in here? George will pick up the tab.'

'No, thanks. Do you two want to meet up today, or are you busy?'

'We found a great pub called Ye Olde Cheshire Cheese.

That's *olde* with an *e*. See ya there in an hour.' I suddenly had the idea that there was something excessively Yankee about her pronunciation, and it made me uneasy.

'Fine.'

No one told me at first that there are two Cheshire Cheeses in that part of London, and I spent half an hour in the wrong bar before the barman asked me if I was waiting for someone.

'Happens all the time,' he told me. 'Sometimes we get one of their customers, an' sometimes they get ours. Even stevens.' I found Doris less than five minutes' walk away.

She didn't chide me for being late. She just demanded, 'An' where the hell have you been? Guys have hit on me three times since I sat down.'

I signalled the barman for a pint.

'Only three? I'd have thought you might have done better than that.' She opened her mouth for a riposte, but then paused . . . and smiled. 'Where's George?' I asked her.

'Stateside. He had to rush back for a business brief.'

I thought I'd take a chance.

'Tell me something, Doris, did you always sound like Calamity Jane, or is it something you caught?' Pause. When she smiled again it was almost sheepish.

'Too much, huh?'

'Too much,' I confirmed.

'I can do Olive Oyl instead if youse likes.' Her voice had suddenly slid into *Popeye* country.

'Grace Kelly?'

'Much easier.'

'Are you an actress, Doris?'

She pulled out a cigarette, and I lit it for her. She must have been a bit desperate because I guessed the purpose of the manoeuvre was to show me her chest moving, and stop my pendulum. After she blew out the first plume of smoke she replied, 'Tell me a woman who isn't, Charlie.'

'Stop trying,' I told her. 'I like you well enough just as it is. Can we get some food here? I'm starving.'

I suppose a plate of cheese sandwiches was all I could have hoped for. It wasn't even Cheshire cheese. She'd had a half-pint in front of her when I'd walked in, but as soon as I sat down began to match me in pints – I've met several women who did that, and liked them all. Eventually she asked me, 'Have you got a date for us, Charlie?'

'No, not yet. I've an old pal in the Ordnance Survey – they're the map makers – just outside of London. I want to go over your map with him, see if he can give me something in a larger scale.'

'Will he ask questions?'

'I wouldn't mind if he did. He was a navigator, and we did our basic training together – he won't let me down.'

'OK.'

'Then I'll make the bookings for us. There's a hotel in Shieldaig, just the other side of the hill your brother hit. If he had cleared it he would have ended up in their front garden.'

She sat back in her chair, and looked steadily at me.

'Hey, Charlie. Don't mind me. Don't mind my feelings.' Then she looked away.

I pulled out my old straight briar, and made a business of filling and lighting it.

'I'm sorry, Doris, but I didn't know him, and I don't know you. My generation doesn't grieve over strangers – we had enough grieving to do over folk we knew. OK?' She OK'd me back, but it was a bit on the grudging side. 'When I make the hotel booking I'll find out if they can hire someone to take us up the hill – a local stalker or gamekeeper, someone like that.'

'What will you tell them?'

'That you and George are related to someone killed in the crash, and are making a kind of pilgrimage to the site. That's the truth, isn't it? Is it a problem?'

'I'd rather people didn't know my business, that's all.'

'I think you'll find them very respectful. There isn't a community up there which hasn't given up sons to the war. They'll understand.' She nodded. I went on to ask, 'Whose idea was it for you to sound as if you'd just got off the Deadwood stage?'

'George. He says the British would expect us to sound like Americans – something to do with the war. Where I come from it's sometimes hard to tell.'

'Where do you come from?'

'Boston.'

'And George?'

'New York.' She switched tracks on me and asked, 'In a few days you'll be able to say when we fly up there?'

'Yes. Except we won't fly, we'll take the night train. You'll like it.'

She stretched her arms and sighed. Her body rippled as though a small earthquake was imminent. If you could measure sex appeal on the Richter scale it was about a Force Five. Every man in the bar stopped drinking to watch. Don't get me wrong; Doris loved it. She turned on the hokey-cokey voice again.

'What am I going to do in London, honey, while I'm stuck here waiting for you and George?'

'Go shopping for warm clothes. You're going to need them up there.'

She pouted and asked, 'At least you'll have supper with me tonight?'

'Yeah, I'll have supper with you tonight.' I was probably

leering: it's a sort of expression that comes over a man's face when he's not looking.

The Savoy Grill; and the best steak I'd ever tackled in my life. The waiter hovered. That wasn't my fault. Its was Mrs Handel's fault. Noël Coward was entertaining his pals at a big round table in the window: I didn't fancy his date – a washed-out specimen with a poet's flowing hair. Doris wore the low-front little black number again. Her shoulders were as white as the moon, and the streams of light from the chandelier caught in her hair. Every time she leaned forward her front bumpers surfaced like Moby Dick and his twin sister. If I had been the waiter I'd have hovered too.

As we worked our way down a bottle of claret she had selected from the wine list by simply going for the most expensive, my repartee probably veered towards the risqué. Not so much a case of *in vino veritas* as a hopeful *in vino coitus*. She dabbed her mouth with a napkin, and leaned forward to speak quietly to me.

'You really fancy your chances with me; don't you, honey?' she asked.

'Am I so obvious?'

'You and half the men in the room.'

'Only half?'

'The rest are fairies – you English are famous for it.'

'Should I apologize?'

'No. It's sometimes kinda fun, but it's better to tell you right now that you don't. Have a chance, that is. I'm faithful to Mr Handel – always will be. I don't see any reason to stray. I never did. I wouldn't want you two to fall out over me. So before you try . . . the answer's *no*. Big *N*, big *O*. This is the put-down.'

I dived into her eyes and began to swim for the shore.

'Hey, Doris,' I said. 'Don't mind me. Don't mind my feelings.' It was a joke I spoiled by finishing with a soft belch I had been unable to contain. I did apologize for that. What surprised me was that she smiled a quick smile before she paid attention to her plate again. She was saying, *Look but don't touch*: I'd have to settle for that.

I got the soft lips on my cheek again as we parted, and was conscious of the pressure of one of those wonderful bumpers against my arm. Consolation prize or just a twist of the knife?

When I walked outside and turned left onto the Strand I should have been conscious of a car pacing me from behind, but I wasn't. Black unmarked Rover. Eventually it pulled in front of me, and stopped at the kerb. The round-faced man with the pencil-thin moustache who rolled down the back window asked, 'Mr Bassett?'

'Yes, why?'

'Chief Inspector Fabian, sir. Metropolitan Police. Would you care to jump in? We'll give you a lift.'

'And if I said *no*?'

'I can arrest you here if you'd prefer it.' I believed him. He was a thoroughly unpleasant man being thoroughly agreeable. I was leaning in to his window by then. He could probably smell the wine and brandy on my breath.

'Do you have a warrant card, or a badge, or something like that?'

Another cat-like smile.

'My driver, Mr Webb, has a cosh in his pocket. Much more effective.'

I was drunk anyway. It was beginning to rain. Fabian of the fucking Yard: he used to be in the papers. I thought that he'd died or retired, but he hadn't. Just my luck. So I got in the car.

Chapter Four

Teamsters are Very Nice Men

There was just a small bar at Green's. The night manager, Ozzie Harrison, who'd once parachuted out of a blazing Halifax over Rouen, unlocked it for me and gave me the key.

'Settle up when you go, Charlie, OK?'

'OK, Oz. Thanks.'

He gave Fabian the up-and-down look, and asked me, 'You OK?'

'Yes, I'm fine. Just catching up with an old friend.'

'Didn't know you knew the London coppers. Just ring the bell if you need me.'

After he left us Fabian observed, 'They can always tell a copper, can't they?'

'I think it's the way you watch people . . . as if you're never going to forget.'

'You'd be surprised, Mr Bassett. Sometimes I forget to tie my shoelaces these days. Thanks for not making a fuss, by the way.'

'I do hope I don't live to regret it. Do you want a drink?'

We both settled for bottled beers. Ind Coope — light and yeasty. He said, 'Cheers,' and raised his glass.

'Cheers. I thought you'd retired years ago.'

'I did. I write a few articles for the papers. Murders. You'd

57

think people had had enough of sudden deaths, wouldn't you? I have.'

'Is that what you want to see me about?' I yawned. I wasn't kidding – I was ready for my pit.

'No. I freelance for a couple of the ministries from time to time. Delicate stuff . . . the princesses and gigolos, you know the sort of thing. Now somebody's interested in the woman you had supper with tonight, and the man who calls himself her husband.'

'Why?'

'Because Mr and Mrs George Frederick Handel is one thing they're not, Mr Bassett.'

'Who are they then? A couple of con artists?'

'Maybe, but I don't think so. Mind if I smoke?' He produced a pipe not unlike my own.

'No, I'll join you.' I asked him again, 'Who are they then?'

'I haven't got a clue. I was hoping you'd tell me.'

'I know as much as you then.'

'Where did you meet them?'

'Berlin. An old business contact introduced them to a current business contact, who passed them on to me.'

'What do they want?'

'To invest in an airfreight company. I'm supposed to intro-duce them to my employer.' I lied without even thinking about it – I've been doing that to coppers all my life.

'Halton? Are you going to?'

'I haven't decided yet. Your tobacco smells good – what is it?'

'Parson's Pleasure. Do they want anything else?'

I'd seen tins of Parson's Pleasure before, but had always shied away from it because its name reminded me of all those bishop-and-actress jokes.

'They didn't say. Why ask me? And why are you watching them anyway?'

He blinked before he answered. I once knew a rattlesnake. She always blinked before she struck.

'The hotel had a little word. With silly names like that, and a suitcase full of dollars they needed changing into pounds, they appeared to be a little unusual. There were exchange-control implications, don't you know . . . so we kept an eye.'

'How did you know my name?'

'You gave it at reception when you met madam this evening. Is she as clever as she is beautiful, by the way?'

'Probably more so. Way out of my class.'

Fabian blew out a thin stream of smoke, like a Blue Riband liner getting ready to sail.

'You'll stay in touch if you learn anything?' He pushed a card across the table to me. It had a Chelsea telephone number on it. 'My old nick,' he explained. 'They always know how to get hold of me.'

I didn't say *yes* and I didn't say *no*. I asked, 'What do you think's going on then?'

'Haven't got a clue.' It was the second time he'd used the phrase. Quite amusing, coming from a detective. 'But the next time you dine with them I'd take a very long spoon if I was you.'

'Official warning?'

'If you like, son.' At last. I had just had a brief glimpse of the steel in the man.

After he'd left I sat and smoked over a contemplative whisky. Then Ozzie came back and joined me.

'You in trouble, Charlie?'

'No, I don't think so, Oz. A little reveille, that's all.'

'What d'ye mean?'

'Wake-up call.'

*

I lay on my back and stared at the darkened ceiling before I slept. Halfway through that interview I had started to lie through my teeth. I asked myself why, and what I murmured out loud was Fabian's own catchphrase, 'I haven't a clue.' Then I rolled over and went to sleep.

I left Doris to stew for a day and then called her without giving my name at the switchboard. I just said, 'It's me,' and trusted that she had a reasonable memory for voices.

'Oh. What time is it?'

'Past ten. Why?'

'Still finishing my breakfast. They make the best scrambled eggs in the world.'

'You mean you're not up yet.'

'Something like that—'

I broke in before she could speak my name: I'd sensed it coming.

'Meet me down on the Embankment in half an hour. I have some news.'

'But it's raining, honey.'

'Then put a fucking raincoat on, *honey*.' And I hung up on her – always a good way to end a conversation.

She wore a raincoat and a man's flat tweed cap, and stared moodily out over the Thames, which was the colour of sewage. The clothes concealed her glamour. I took five minutes to check if someone was watching her before joining up. She didn't look round as I stood beside her; just said, 'I told a nice man that I was being followed by a creep, and he took me out through the kitchen. I guessed something was up.'

'Is George back?'

'No. Saturday lunchtime. He's on the BOAC flight from Idlewild.' She said *Boewack*, as if it was a word, not an acronym.

'That's cutting it fine – we're on the night sleeper from Euston.'

'George will be here, Charlie. I always wanted to travel on a sleeper – sounds so romantic.'

The rain was fine and filmy; blowing along the river like smoke.

'I know a pub we can hide in for a couple of hours. We have a card game to play.'

I could see from her face that that was a metaphor too far.

'What kind of card game, Charlie?'

'The kind where we take the cards we're holding too close to our chest, and lay them down one by one, *honey*.' I hadn't actually wanted to be reminded of her chest, but there you go.

I took her to the Printer's Devil up behind Fetter Lane. I loved the place because you could come to it via alleys and small lanes. After I had hung our coats on the pegs close to the fire I got us a couple of pints. Doris said, 'Kinda early in the day for me, Charlie, but I'll sip this to keep you company.'

I let a silence hang about for a minute, and watched the fire before telling her, 'I don't know what you're up to, honey, but the police are on to you. They've been watching you ever since clever old George tried to get the hotel to change a year's pay in small dollars. Something to do with exchange control.'

She made a fist, and her knuckles went white. 'Damn! I warned him about that.' Then she said, 'All that money is legal. We're just funding the trip, that's all.'

'Even if it is' – I wanted her to realize that I wouldn't necessarily give them the benefit of the doubt – 'if they know George is out of the country, the customs could well pick him up for questioning as soon as he touches down. Where's the money?'

'I still have it. The hotel arranged for a man from a bank to come round and change a grand for us – the rest is in a briefcase in the hotel safe.'

'We'll have to see what we can do about that.'

She took a deep pull at the beer, gave me the old eye bite and asked, 'How did you know the police were interested? Who told you?'

'*They* did, when they picked me up after our supper.'

'What did you tell them?'

'That you and George are Mr and Mrs Ordinary American looking to invest your hard-earned savings in a regular British airfreight company.'

'Did they buy it?'

'I haven't got a clue,' I told her. There; I was doing it again.

'I'll have to call George.'

'Yes, you do that. But not from the hotel.'

'I have an old school friend at the consulate. Maybe he'd let me call from there. When will you stop talking to me like you stepped on a snake?'

'When you tell me what you're up to.'

'I've already told you. I promised Mom I'd put some flowers on Petey's grave.'

'And George?'

'George is my husband; he'll do whatever I ask him.'

'And me?'

'My friend in the consulate said you'd experience of these high-ground wrecks, and had been in the RAF. He thought you were the man to facilitate the operation.'

'*Operation?*'

'That's the way to look at life's little difficulties, Charlie – as *operations*, just like in the war. You won't let me down now, will you?' She was wearing plain black trousers – not showy – and a thick cable-knit sweater which covered the rest of her.

When she covered up her body it was her hair which spoke to you, but for once I didn't listen: I pulled my hand back, and gave my brain a shaking. I knew that she was playing me the way an angler plays a fish: it was like being hypnotized against your will.

Later I showed her the map I'd smuggled out of the Ordnance Survey office at Chessington. The climb up to her brother's wreck looked absolutely bloody horrible. Why weren't Tenzing and Hillary ever around when you needed them?

The last thing I asked her before we split was, 'How much money is in that bloody case anyway?'

'Something above ten thousand dollars.'

'Strewth! . . . and it's clean?'

'Of course. My family came up with it to fund the trip, I told you.'

'What's the matter with you people? Haven't you heard of banks?'

'Nobody in my family's trusted a bank since the Wall Street Crash, Charlie. A banker will steal you blind if you'll let him, although no one will believe you if you tell them that.'

'What does your family do? Where does the money come from?'

'We own half a casino in Las Vegas. Uncle Joey runs it, and most of us work there in the summer.'

'Who owns the other half?'

'The Teamsters.'

I'd heard of them. They were a trade union. Some people had said they were also gangsters; my late mate Tommo among them. Great.

'What part of the line-up are you? The Grand Witch or someone as important?'

'Don't be silly, Charlie. Nothing like that. The Teamsters

are very nice men. Sometimes I dance for them at their convention – I used to be a cheerleader.'

'I'll bet you did.'

'So what's the problem with her?' I'd used Flash Harry's business card, and met him in the Castle on the Old Kent Road. It was just past noon – dinnertime in a shady pub with shady customers; now I was one of them.

'I can't believe that she's as dumb as she seems. Whenever you ask her a serious question she just breathes in and out, and sticks her tits in your face.'

'And you're complaining? You sound tetchy, Charlie. Are you sure this money's clean?'

'Of course it isn't clean, is it? It just walked into the country in a suitcase, and the exchange-control laws are supposed to prevent that. What gets my goat is that I helped them. But I see what you mean – apart from that, she says it comes from a family whip-round to pay for this trip to lay the ghost of little brother.'

'And you buy that?'

'No, I don't, but that's another matter. The question is, can your Mr Martenson change it for us without anyone asking questions?'

'He'll do it for about ten per cent. I'll want another one for placing the deal.'

'What will happen to it?'

'Go back across the Atlantic with all the other dirty little dollars that we collect in – on one of the *Queens* probably – and get reunited with the US economy back over there. It will cost us another two per cent, but we still get a decent return off it. Nobody loses.'

'Except the governments.'

'An' they're the biggest thieves of all, so why worry?'

'As soon as she grabs for the case the hotel will phone the police.'

'That's no problem. They're prob'ly waiting for her old man to get back anyway – so tommorer you get the lady to go down and pay her bill through 'til Sat'day or Sunday, an' while she's doing that you nip along to the station and change your train ticket to Friday. Come Friday you go up to their room, pack all the gear she'll need in one suitcase an' both go downstairs separately. You leave with her suitcase, she goes to reception and picks up the money-box. Joins you outside where I'll be waiting for the pair o' you. I'll run you to the station and we'll change your dosh on the way. OK?'

'What about the police? Will they fall for it?'

'You'll be a mile away in one of our cabs before the hotel puts the phone down.'

'Why do I get the feeling you've done this before, Harry?'

'Practice makes perfect, ain't that what they say? Want another drink?'

I had another question, and put it to him when he came back with the glasses.

'If I leave on Friday, what do I do about George? He'll be expecting to meet up with us on Saturday.'

'Let him find his own way – 'e's a grown-up, ain't he?' Then he said, 'That bird's terrible, ain't she. We should pay 'er to keep her clothes on.' A weary-looking stripper was working a small stage at the back of the bar, dancing to a Julie London LP played on a Pye Black Box. He must have seen something in my face because he asked, 'What happened? Someone walk over your grave?'

'Nope, for a moment I thought I knew her. I was mistaken, that's all.'

She'd reminded me of someone I'd met in 1947 when she was young and fresh. I hoped life had been kinder to her than the shell of a woman we looked away from.

The music finished, and one of the deadbeats shuffled over to set it going again. The girl didn't seem to notice. As we walked out there was that characteristic click from the music box, and Julie London began to sing 'Cry me a River'.

I told Doris a couple of hours before we were due to go.

She asked, 'Do I get any say in this?'

'Not until I get us away from here.'

'What about George?'

'Someone I know will explain to him. He knows where we're going, and the money will have disappeared – they'll have to let him go, because there won't be any evidence of an offence.'

'He won't like it.'

'Neither do I, but it's the best I could come up with at short notice.'

She sat on her hotel bed, and gave me a rueful grin.

'It's all our own fault, isn't it?'

'Yes, but there are worse crimes in the book. Don't worry about it, just pack a case of your warmest clothes.'

'What about the rest, and George's things?'

'He'll pick them up on Saturday when he gets in, and either come on with them or put them into left luggage.'

'If the police still want us, won't they follow George until they find us?'

'They could, but they probably won't. My friends think that because it's a relatively common offence, and the evidence will have disappeared anyway, they won't pursue it any further. Besides, George will recognize that risk, and take care anyway.'

'Do your friends know where we're heading?'

'No. Just you, me and George.'

'You've thought of everything, honey. You're quite good at this . . . In fact, you remind me of some of the guys in Vegas.'

She was taking the piss, of course, but she breathed in and out and pointed her guns at me, so I didn't mind too much.

I had a nervy few minutes sitting in the taxi with Harry and his money man, waiting for Doris to come away from reception. When she finally appeared around the corner she had a big happy smile on her face, and was swinging a small briefcase like a schoolgirl – and as soon as she was inside with us the cab moved off and into the evening traffic. Harry checked the back window from time to time, but always looked back at me with an unworried look on his face. The money man did what money men are best at – he took the briefcase and counted the dosh. The notes riffled through his fingers like sand running through an egg timer. He had a round face and thick glasses.

Harry said, 'I won't introduce you, but our friend here works in a bank in the day, and is one of our casino cashiers at night. He doesn't make mistakes with other people's money.'

'Good. How much is there?' I asked.

The little man had finished, and replied in a curiously deep voice, 'Twenty thousand two hundred and fifty dollars, in hundreds, fifties, fives, tens and twenties.' That was twice as much as she'd bloody told me. She didn't blush.

'That's more than I expected,' Doris told him, and crossed her legs. He went cross-eyed as he tried to prevent his eyes from following her.

'Don't worry, madam, I brought enough to cover that.' He fetched out an old leather messenger bag from under his seat, removed a couple of flat bundles of money from it – which he placed in Doris's briefcase – and then handed it to her.

Flash observed, 'It's better if we keep your bag, Charlie . . . You wouldn't want to be spotted with it.'

'OK. What are we worth in English money?'

' 'Bout three grand, I expect. Used nearly-new notes. Perfect. You gonna do all right out of this yourself?'

That was a thought. It was a question too many, but I told him the truth anyway.

'I don't know. We haven't talked about my fee yet.'

Harry laughed derisively at me; the other guy grinned.

'You can talk about it on the train tonight,' Harry said. 'You'll need to find something to pass the time.'

When we reached the station he stretched over to take my hand. His coat fell open, and I glimpsed the pistol stuck in his belt. A different league.

I hadn't told Doris that we were sharing a sleeper yet. It was all I'd been able to get at the last minute. Apparently the Friday night sleeper was always full of rich Jocks going home for the weekend. I hadn't any realistic hopes of her – she'd told me, after all, hadn't she? – but I anticipated she would pop on the upside-down smile when she found out. One way or another it was going to be an interesting night.

There was a neatly typed label on the door of our twin berth.

Doris was miffed because I hadn't carried her suitcase – but I wasn't their fucking native bearer.

She asked me, 'Mr and Mrs Miller?'

'Sentimental reasons, nothing to do with you. Trust me.'

'Where do you sleep, Charlie?'

'It's actually a case of where do you sleep, honeybunch. I'm sleeping in there. You can too, if you like . . . or if you'd be more comfortable curled up on a seat between a couple of drunken Scots on their way home it's up to you. This is all I could get.'

She was doing all she could to keep the lid on her temper. I liked that.

She hissed, 'I'm paying for this, you bastard.'

'And I'm truly grateful – but it doesn't alter anything.'

'George won't like it when he finds out.'

We hadn't discussed anything yet which George *would* like.

'Maybe George won't find out. It's your choice again. See, I'm a proper gentleman – one of my finer points. I'll always leave you options.'

'You're a bastard.'

'That's the second time you've said that. Actually I'm a hungry bastard, and I reserved a table for us at the first sitting for dinner.' I opened the door of the small compartment. 'Are you and your case coming in, or not? The bar's open.' I went in, and threw my small kitbag and the messenger bag on the bottom bunk. The door swung shut behind me. I started to whistle 'The Music Goes Round and Round', and got to the second chorus before the door banged open again, and Doris dragged her case in behind her.

'The steward asked me if everything was OK,' she said, 'and I didn't want to attract attention to us.'

I stepped forward until this was the closest we'd been. I placed my hands on either side of her perfect face, and told her, 'Don't worry about it, honey, you are so perfectly beautiful that you'll attract attention wherever you are. For the rest of your life probably. Get used to it.' Then I let her go.

Doris tried to slap me, but there wasn't enough room – and she was laughing at the same time anyway. When she finished there was still a smile on her face. Maybe it was a worried smile. Or a scheming one. We shimmied around each other, and agreed to meet in the bar. I took the messenger bag with me, wondering if I had become its custodian. I found myself with a decent Glenmorangie in my hand. As I settled into a velvet-covered Pullman chair there was a long, haunting whistle outside, and almost imperceptibly the train began to move. She was called the *Highland Queen*, and her take-off was as smooth as a bobsleigh on the Cresta Run.

We ate a four-course meal in the dining car. I enjoyed the men watching Doris. I enjoyed watching Doris as well. You can tell a lot about people if you watch them eating. She tucked into her grub like a professional – perhaps her brand of American fasted on Thursdays, and made up for it on Fridays. She didn't stop chewing in order to speak.

'Did you plan this, Charlie?'

'No. You and George have done all the planning so far. All I've done is mop up the little mess you made in London.'

'I mean – to get me alone on a train to Finian's Rainbow or somewhere romantic in your Scottish Highlands.'

'Point one, Finian's Rainbow was in Ireland – wrong country. You probably mean *Brigadoon*. Point two – ' I dropped my voice – 'we're here now because, thanks to you, we are running away from the bloody police. Point three, the Highlands are far from romantic – I've been there before, remember, and you haven't. It's not romantic at all – it's nothing like you've ever imagined – just a few people living in cattle sheds, and they'll hate us.'

'Why will they hate us? They haven't met us yet.'

'It's a point of principle. They'll hate us for not being Scottish.'

'You didn't answer my question, hon . . . the one about if you planned to get me on my own on this train.'

'No, Doris. I didn't plan to get you on your own, but now I have I'll just have to put up with you until George catches up with us. Listen . . . do you want to finish this wine, or shall I?'

We split it, and chased it down with another whisky. Doris asked me to give her time to climb into her bunk before I returned.

'How long?'

'Twenty minutes should do it, I have a face to scrape off.'

'If you thought of searching my sack, I wouldn't bother. It's just clothes, and not all of them are clean.'

'I wouldn't have dreamed of it, Charlie.'

'No, of course not.'

She took the loot bag with her. It did occur to me to wonder what George was going to do for money when he finally got here.

Doris was tucked up in the top bunk when I got back to the compartment. I undressed in the dark and climbed into my bunk, piling my clothes at one end.

After a few minutes Doris said, 'You lied.'

'What about?'

'There was a book in your bag as well as your clothes, a Raymond Chandler – good writer.'

'I think so too.' It was *The High Window*.

After another few minutes I asked, 'Doris?'

'Yes?' I heard her turn over above me.

'Did you ever see Robert Donat in *The Thirty-Nine Steps*?'

'No, why?'

'He got stuck on the night sleeper to Scotland with a beautiful stranger as well. We're not the first.'

'So?'

'She was a lot friendlier than you are.'

'He was probably better-looking than you, Charlie.' I heard her shift in her bunk again. Then she said, 'G'night.'

After a few minutes she chuckled briefly, and softly. I had no idea what she found so funny, but it was a sound you could learn to live with.

In my head I began to play through all the numbers I knew connected to railway journeys, one after the other, beginning with 'Chattanooga Choo Choo', and going on to 'Midnight special', and all the others. I fell asleep during the second chorus of 'The Little Red Caboose Behind the Train'. It never fails; even when you have Rita Hayworth's sister lying a couple feet above you.

We were awoken by the steward at about six in the morning with decent cups of coffee. The train was rattling slowly over Rannoch Moor heading for the station at Fort William.

Over the breakfast kippers she asked me, 'Tell me again . . .'

'We stay in Fort William for a night. There's bound to be a decent hotel – all the hunting and fishing types come up here in the season.'

'When's *the season*?'

'Not yet, I hope. I don't want a lot of trigger-happy idiots taking pot shots at us when we climb the hill.'

'Why can't we go straight on to the hotel you originally booked us into?'

'Because we aren't due to arrive until Sunday. Originally I expected a two-night stop in Fort William. If we stay there, and meet the train on Sunday morning, George might always catch up with us.'

'What then? We take a cab?'

'I doubt it. They probably wouldn't want to drive halfway across Scotland. No, we get a bus.' Her mouth turned down. I wondered what buses were like in the States.

'Buses are for poor folk, Charlie. I've got a better idea. We can buy a car this afternoon.'

'For only a few days? Then what will we do with it?'

'Sell it again, dummy. Trust me, I'll get more for it than we paid. You ain't seen me in action yet.'

I looked down over her Alps; one could but hope, I suppose. I'd thought that before.

*

A small, animated thimble of a woman booked us into the Royal Hotel under the names of Una and Samuel Anders. Doris's idea. We had become brother and sister: don't laugh. The Thimble didn't smile. The church the Thimble attended forbad smiling on Saturdays. Doris had come up with our new names on the spur of the moment, and thought she was being cute — you work it out.

'Cheque or cash, will it be?' we were asked.

'Cash. We don't have a bank in the UK yet.' That was Doris.

'Separate rooms?'

'If you have them.'

'But adjoining, of course?'

'Absolutely. I'd want Sammy to come running if he heard me having one of my panic attacks.'

The Thimble gave us an old-fashioned look. Maybe she'd met brothers and sisters like us before. Her dun-blue woollen dress reached to the soles of her shoes. It made her look as if she glided across the floor on casters. As Doris and I followed her into one of those old cage lifts that were all the rage in the thirties, I was aware of an odd tension in Doris: as if a storm was brewing.

I gave it a thought or two, and then pushed the idea away: she'd tell me whatever it was in her own good time — I knew her that well already.

We had old, dark wood-panelled rooms on the top floor. They smelt of polish, and each had a main door, and another which opened from one into the other. I didn't go anywhere near that one. I had a pygmy-sized four-poster. A clean but musty-smelling dressing gown was neatly folded on the end of it: the bedcovers were dark tartan blankets a foot thick.

Maybe the dressing gown was a hint, so I went along the corridor to the bathroom and had a shower in an Edwardian bath with lion's feet. The water was so hot my skin glowed when I stepped out of it. When I reached my room again I threw off the dressing gown, and enjoyed cool air on my skin.

Doris must have heard me, because that was when she barged in through the connecting door. She was wearing most of a dressing gown. A flowing silvery silk job about the size of a jacket, and at least two sizes too small for her. She must have brought it with her. It wasn't tied or buttoned down the front. That only took a glance.

When she crossed to sit alongside me I asked her, 'Is that your natural colour?' Her hair was dark; the colour of port wine.

'I hope so. Don't you feel randy, Charlie? This place makes me feel randy – it's so terribly old.'

'If old things make you randy, go downstairs and find a grandfather . . . and cover yourself up, woman. You're just playing with me.'

'I wasn't, honey, but I will now.' She reached out. One hand; long fingers. Carmine nail varnish. Your mind takes these pictures. Snap. Snap. Snap When she looked at me it wasn't at my face. What do you say to a girl at moments like that?

'I call them Laurel and Hardy,' I told her.

Doris bent her head, and murmured, 'Kiss me, Hardy.'

If you'd really been awake you would have seen that one coming.

I don't know why she'd changed her mind, but things were looking up, weren't they?

Some time later she asked me, 'When does our little soldier come to attention again?'

I've never been comfortable with grown women using baby talk, and I wasn't all that chuffed with the word *little*, so all I asked was, 'Come again?'

I suppose it was twenty minutes later before I told her, 'You have a perfect body.'

'I'll bet you say that to all the girls, hon.'

'No. I don't believe I've ever said it before.'

She stopped dressing for a moment and looked at me, her head cocked slightly on one side.

'That's nice, Charlie.'

'Maybe, but I don't suppose that George is going to like it, is he?'

'And I don't suppose he has to know. Isn't that what you said? It always comes up, and I thought if I couldn't avoid it, I'd get it out of the way before he gets here. That way you can save your strength for climbing a mountain.' She'd made it sound like my fault.

'You're really serious about that, aren't you?'

'Of course I am, Charlie. Wouldn't you be if your baby brother had died up there?'

She knew it was a lie. I knew it was a lie. She knew I knew it was a lie. I knew she knew I knew it was a lie. What *were* these bastards up to?

'Let's go find a car lot,' she told me, 'and buy us a limo.'

Chapter Five

Faster Than a Speeding Bullet

Some of you will remember the old Ford Popular, and some won't.

I have run this over in my mind quite a few times since then, but you simply can't describe a black upright Ford Pop as a *limo*. It's an unsprung rear-wheel-drive van, with a car's body shell. We bought one for a hundred and ten quid. It looked as if it had seen better days. There were pieces of straw in the cabin, and its spare tyre sat on the back seat. I recognized the smell of chickens inside it. I once lived six months on a chicken farm: there's not much I don't know about chickens. The owner of Loch Linnhe Autos was a tall spare man with thinning hair. His eyes were lost in worry lines. He threw in a full tank of petrol and a can of Castrol and insisted on shaking both our hands and giving us a printed Bible tract before we drove away.

I think he felt guilty at selling us such a clunker, but didn't want to say so. I parked it in the rear hotel car park – the Thimble had made me hide it around the back because it wasn't a good advertisement for the place. Doris dug her fingers into my left knee as we drew up, and laughed.

I asked her, 'What are you laughing at?'

'George won't like it,' she said, and chortled again. Bugger George. Then she asked me, 'Will he catch up today?'

'No. He can't get here until tomorrow at the earliest.'

'Good.' As we walked up the rather grand but tatty staircase she took my arm, and said, 'My appetite's come back. It must be all this Highland air.'

But she was the best. In every man's life there has to be one. Her bed was twice the size of mine: the covering on it was a deep crimson, and the scattering of cushions red. When I kissed her belly it was so flat and taut, it was as if my lips had touched the stretched skin of a drum. I could have beaten out a drum roll, or a tattoo, on it with my fingers.

If I thought fleetingly of Flaming June, it was only to wonder who she was with.

We paid off the hotel the next morning. The Thimble stood on the steps to watch us go: she wanted to be certain she had seen the back of us. I'm sure she was tut-tutting, and shaking her head as we drove away.

George, however, did not alight from the train. Doris shrugged, and said, 'We'd better get going then.'

'What about your husband?'

'Oh, hell, Charlie, *he*'s not my husband.'

'Your brother, right? Uncle? Third cousin?'

'How d'ye guess?'

'I didn't. I made it up, just like you.'

She did the cock-the-head-to-one-side trick again.

'You're cute, Charlie. D'ye know that?'

When the Yanks say *cute* they don't mean appealing; they mean something else.

Doris was in the mood to issue orders, 'C'mon, let's find the car.'

It rained. The drive took me two wrong turnings, and four

77

and a half hours. The Ford leaked, and leapt potholes in the road like a demented antelope. Doris slept on the back seat. Or tried to. When I suggested she read the map for me she just laughed, and shut her eyes again. You don't keep a dog and bark yourself.

I went back to that lodge hotel at Shieldaig a few years ago – I was doing a tour of the places I'd known before I sat down to write about them. It doesn't look any different now, although it's easier to get there. The roads are better, and so are the cars.

It's a red sandstone rectangular building. Edwardian maybe, or Victorian. It looks down a sea loch fenced with mountains. I'll swear the boats bobbing at anchor or tied up at its jetty are the same boats I first saw in 1956.

I pulled into its driveway and stopped the car with a lurch. That woke Doris up. She stretched. I turned back to watch her stretching. She liked that, smiled, and did it again. I liked that too. There was absolutely no sign of life from the place. Doris smiled again.

'What did you say the name was, Charlie? Brigadoon?'

'Don't worry, they probably all come to life again after the sun goes down . . . blood suckers just like the midges. It's why Bram Stoker wrote *Dracula* in Scotland – he got the idea for the vampire from the Scottish midge.'

'What's a midge?'

'In your case a very unpleasant surprise. A biting insect.'

'Can you do something about them?'

'I'll find some local jallop, and rub it all over your body.'

'Will that put them off?'

'No, but it will take our minds off them.'

'George wouldn't like that.' Sometimes she was like a record that had become stuck in one groove. She stretched again. Her whole body moved. So did the earth. Then she asked me, 'When do you think you'll be going off to Cyprus, Charlie?'

Now who in hell had told her that? Randall? Pete? Ah. The black widow she might be, but Charlie had no intention of falling into her web.

A cheerful young couple turned up in a civilized Jeep about twenty minutes later. Mr and Mrs Mine Host. He looked as if he'd either had a good war or none at all, but you can be wrong of course. The wait had given me time to let the tranquillity of the place sink deep into my bones. I sat on an old wooden bench, looked down the loch and smoked a pipe. Doris wandered off around the foreshore. From time to time I heard her shoes crunch on the stones – she couldn't have been far from me. I hadn't answered her question, and she hadn't pushed it. Maybe she regretted showing her hand.

I had booked two rooms – a double and a single – on the assumption that George and Doris would occupy one, and I the other. Her outburst at the station had put a doubt in my mind, so I asked her if I should get another single for her brother.

'What brother, Charlie?'

'Brother George. Or cousin George, or whoever he is.'

Pause.

'He *isn't* my brother.'

'I'd never have guessed.'

'Isn't that what you said last time?' Then she pouted and said, 'No. Don't change things. George will expect to be with me. He makes all the rules and carries a big stick.'

We were sitting in a nice little bar. There had been a few people outside waiting for it to open – God knows where they came from, the only nearby dwelling was a run-down farm a mile away. Doris had ordered a treble whisky, heavily watered it, and sipped it as a long drink.

She asked, 'I shouldn't ha' said anything about Cyprus, huh? You could have warned me.'

I looked away. I'd like to say my mind was working furiously the way it does for heroes in kids' stories, but my mind *never* works furiously. It sort of limps along way behind everyone else.

Doris gazed innocently at me and offered, 'Your Mr Borland let it slip. He said he thought you'd have time to help us out before you went to Cyprus. I didn't realize it was a secret.'

'It bloody isn't any more, is it?'

I ran Jelly Roll Morton's 'Blue Blood Blues' in my head. If I could work out who told Bozey I was off to Cyprus, maybe she was telling the truth. I'd told Elaine, hadn't I? She and Bozey burned up the telephone two or three times a day. My own fault then. Eventually I asked her, 'Does George know?'

'He didn't mention it, but he must have heard.'

'Don't mention it to him again.'

'All right, Charlie.'

I'd given a bloody hostage to fortune, and I didn't bloody like it. Life's like that. Most of the people you trust are people you *have* to trust, rather than people you *want* to trust. It's like throwing dice.

I leaned across the table and said, 'Did I ever tell you that you have amazingly perfect breasts?'

'Yesterday. But you can say it again if you want.'

'You have amazingly perfect breasts. Shall I tell George?'

'You can, but he wouldn't like it.'

'What *would* he like?'

'He would like to go up that hill behind us, come safely down again, pay you off and fly back Stateside as fast as he can.'

I decided to ask the question that had been interesting me since I'd met them.

'Why, exactly, do you need me?'

'George's afraid of heights.'

Ah.

The owner came to look for me. His name was Ean, yeah, spelled that way, and he favoured heavy Arran-knit sweaters with leather elbow patches, and suede shoes. His brush of hair stood up like one of the cartoon characters from the *Beano* comic.

'There's a telephone call for you – you can take it in the lobby. It's from the other gentleman. He's going to be late.'

George sounded bored. I asked him when he would get there.

'Tuesday lunchtime I guess, pardner. Monday-night flier. The cops and your customs wanted to know where you'd got to.'

'They're mad at us then?'

'Hard to tell. They might even be amused – they never expected you to take off like that.' The pips sounded, and George pushed some money into the telephone.

'How do the cops know your name, Charlie?'

'My fault. I gave it when I went to your hotel. Where are you phoning from?'

'Trafalgar Square. It looks pretty in the sunshine. You wouldn't lay a hand on Mrs Handel, would you, Charlie?'

'You wouldn't like that?'

'I'd cut your cock off.'

'How about me reassuring you that my relationship with your wife will be solely professional?'

'See you Tuesday, Charlie.' He hung up.

I went back to Doris. When I sat down at the table she asked me, 'Well?'

'If you have to have me again you're going to have to pay for it – I just promised George our relationship would remain entirely professional.' She smiled at me over her whisky, and gave a little shrug. The earth moved again. My legs trembled. Some girls can do that to me.

I called the Major's bar to check up on the boys. Maggs answered, and I asked her, 'Are you and the Major speaking?'

'Course we are, Charlie. I was surprised at meself.'

'Why don't you marry him?'

'Because we come from diff'rent sides of the beach. It would never work.'

'You've already lived together for ten years – some marriages don't even last that long these days.'

'If I say I'll think about it can we change the subject, Charlie? Dieter passed all his exams and wants to speak to you . . .'

He had, and bubbled about it for five minutes. I felt a very odd emotion coming over me, and took a while to work out that it was pride.

'You know I'm very proud of you, don't you?'

He paused before he said, 'Yes,' and then, 'You're a pretty good dad, you know.'

I hate it when things get mushy.

'How do you make that out? A few weeks ago you were telling me I didn't get home often enough, and couldn't keep hold of a girlfriend.'

'You don't make me do the things *you* would have liked to do. Most of the boys in my class are doing what their dads wanted to do.'

'OK, Dieter. I'll believe you. How's Carly?'

'Cubs tonight – he'll be in the Scouts soon.' Then he asked me, 'Do you have a *new* girlfriend, Dad?'

'Why do you ask?'

'You sound different when you have a new girlfriend. I can always tell.'

I swallowed. 'It isn't going to work out with June, son. I

know that will disappoint you and Carly, but she has a complicated arrangement with two other men. There's not much room left for me.'

'I knew a girl like that, Dad, so I understand. It's a bit of a pisser, isn't it?' When had my son begun to speak like that? I let it pass, but we'd need a chat about that some time. 'Where are you?'

'Scotland. But don't tell anyone. I'll be back at the end of the week.'

'Are you in trouble again?'

'No, nothing like that – I'm just being careful.'

He could always tell when I was lying as well – but he never complained about it.

When I went back to the bar Doris was flirting with the Arran-knit, so I walked outside to look down on the loch, and smoke a pipe. Dozens of those little black insects that live on Scotsmen followed me, but they didn't tuck into me. Probably the pipe smoke. Doris followed me immediately.

'You the jealous type, Charlie?'

'Truthfully, I don't know. I didn't mind you flirting with our host, if that's what you mean.'

She looked doubtful.

'I don't know what's come over me these last few days – I've been like a bitch in heat.'

'I do . . .'

'What?'

'Freedom. It does odd things to all of us. George isn't here to rattle your chain.'

Then something occurred to me. I don't know why I remembered our conversation on the station platform, waiting for George not to get down from the train. She'd said, '*He*'s not my husband, Charlie.' I said, 'Hang on a mo'. I've just realized. You *are* married, aren't you? Only not to George.'

She looked levelly at me, and just before she turned away she said, 'Yes, Charlie, I'm married. How about you?'

I tried to make light of it.

'No one will have me.' It didn't work.

A few seconds later the stones crunched under her feet, and all I had was her back. I hadn't thought I could move that fast – faster than a speeding bullet. Isn't that what they used to say in *Superman* films at Saturday Morning Pictures? I was behind her, and wrapped my arms around her waist, pinning her arms to her sides. She gasped.

My voice was muffled by her hair. 'I'm sorry, but I can't wait to get into your bed, and stay there all night.'

I hadn't realized that she had been holding her breath. She let it out in a long sigh, and we rocked gently from side to side. Then we began to laugh. I should have known better.

In the morning she broke the spell: gave me a ten-bob note to keep the relationship professional. They don't value sex as highly in the US as we do over here. To be honest most of them aren't as good at it either.

I'm remembering back fifty years here – but I think I could have had her to a band playing.

The next day was a corker, and immediately after breakfast I took my old briar pipe out to that seat looking down the loch. I'd eaten kippers, and sunk a couple of cups of coffee. Doris ate about eighteen bleeding courses, and then went back upstairs. Ean joined me outside, and produced a pipe and tobacco of his own.

He indicated the bench, and asked, 'May I join you?' It was his bloody hotel, and his bloody seat, wasn't it? Probably his bloody loch as well. But it was nice of him to ask.

His accent was soft. If I'd come across him whilst I was still in the service I would have taken him for an officer immediately.

'Help yourself. Have you kept this hotel for long?'

'I was born here. My mother and father turned it into a hotel – before that it was a shooting lodge.'

'Do you like being an innkeeper?'

He laughed and said, 'No, I loathe it. What do you do?'

'I manage a small airline, but it's on ice at the moment. There's not much work about.'

He'd got his pipe going. The tobacco was aromatic. I could smell the Latakia in it.

'So, you're taking a holiday?'

'No. I'm taking a job. A couple of rich Americans hired me to hold their hands while they climbed one of your hills.'

'You're a mountaineer then?'

'No, but I've done it once or twice before . . . and was in the mountains in Turkey a few years ago. I thought I'd try to recruit a local guide – it's best to have someone who knows the terrain. I was going to ask you about that today.'

He concentrated on his pipe until a new Pope was elected, then removed it from his mouth and said, 'I might do that for you myself. An extra few quid is always handy, and to tell the truth a change of company always does me good.' So, I'd hired a Sherpa. I held out my hand to shake his. He asked, 'Don't you want to know my price?'

'I'm not paying, am I? I'm Charlie, by the way.'

'Pleased to meet you, Charlie. Ean Galbraith. I was just going to take a dram before I went fishing. Would you care to join me?' Whisky at ten in the morning, I reflected, wasn't necessarily a good sign. I'd met officers like him before.

Upstairs, Doris was lying face down on her bed reading a Louis L'Amour Western story. I flipped up her skirt to expose the best bum in the West. She must have felt the sun from the window on her legs. She moved them a little apart, but didn't turn away from her book as she spoke.

'Help yourself if you like, hon – but you won't mind if I carry on reading, will ya?'

Probably a good book. She must have reached an exciting part of the narrative.

'I think I'll go out for a walk instead.'

She didn't even nod.

I recovered my temper on a walk around the loch. A nosy seal paced me for a mile, poking his whiskered head out of the water to track my progress. A crazy splashing as I approached a small burn slowed, and then stilled me. I didn't see my first otter: I saw my first two. They were playing about like kids. I sat on a rock and lit a pipe. They didn't seem to mind me.

Doris had finished her Western by the time I got back, and let me watch her demolish another eighteen-course lunch. Where did these bloody Yanks get their appetites from? As she pushed the empty fish plate away she asked me, 'Good walk?'

I replied something like 'Mmm.' I was trying to dig a trout bone from between my teeth.

'What are you thinking?'

'I was thinking that it would be nice to come and live up here one day.'

'Far too quiet for you.'

'You'd be surprised.'

She shrugged. I watched her shrugging. Her breasts made a Mexican wave. It would be nice to spend your time watching Doris shrug. We sat in a comfortable sitting room, and played backgammon and cards until it was time to start drinking and eating again.

She put away another huge meal in the evening. And then it was night.

I woke early. The light was cutting through the gap between the curtains. I stood naked at the window, and looked out at the sun dancing on the loch in a million tiny pieces. There was the ghost of a soldier from the Great War doing the same. He was down on the small pebble bay, smoking a big curved briar as if he enjoyed it. He had a big moustache, and still wore his soft peaked trench cap, but his jacket was off and draped over one shoulder – I could see his broad trouser braces over his washed-out khaki shirt. Even though I don't believe in ghosts I've seen something a lot like them ever since I started flying . . . so he didn't worry me too much. I slipped back into bed, and half-asleep Doris rolled over to face me.

When George turned up later it occurred to me that he no longer looked like George. He was dressed in a crisp olive-coloured fatigue suit secured with a wide webbing belt, wore US combat boots and had had a haircut. He looked like a soldier. And he was in a soldier's wagon – dark green Land Rover with civvy plates. The man who got out of the passenger seat was dressed identically. He did the handshake thing and said, 'Christopher. Chris.'

'Charlie. And this is—'

'Doris. I know . . . George has told me about you both.'

I turned to George and said, 'You suddenly look a mite military, George. Have you been holding out on me?' The amazing thing was that he seemed to have drawn on another personality with the clothes: he was relaxed – good-humoured even.

'No, Charlie. I was in the military once, but now I'm an owner driver. I have my own little company, and I freelance.'

'So if I'm working for you, who're you working for?'

'That's a commercial secret. It's legal, if that's what's worrying you.'

'What about Doris?'

'Doris is with me. Her brother *was* flying the aircraft. We told you . . .'

I was going to ask several telling questions one after the other; then I thought better of it.

'But there are interests here other than just the family's?'

'Bravo, Charlie.' People have been saying *Bravo, Charlie* to me all of my life: I think the words must sort of go together. 'Can you rustle us up some coffee? I'd kill for some.'

Yes, master. You never know, maybe he would – he certainly had that look about him now.

That night George and Doris retired early. I guess he must have missed her. I know I did. Chris drank with me down in the small bar until about ten, then he, too, made for the Land of Nod. He said he'd had a long day. He was a nice laid-back Somerset type who drank his whisky straight; like an Englishman. He was my age, although he'd worn better, and had been in the Engineers in the war.

I asked him, 'Building bridges and roads? That sort of thing?'

'Yeah, I did some of that.'

'What else did you do?'

'I played a lot of golf, I remember that.' It was the sort of thing I'd say to avoid the issue. 'But most of the time I just carried a frying pan.'

What the fuck George was taking a cook up a mountain with us for I had no idea. Maybe we were going to have a gourmet meal up among the clouds. Chris left me alone in the bar soon after that: perhaps I'd asked too many questions.

I smoked a pipe and chatted with Ean across the bar. He smoked his pipe too. I wasn't keen to get my head down: I told you, I was missing Doris already and her interesting demands even more. I could still feel her tongue in my mouth; urgent like a wren. After sampling several drams Ean pointed out to me that I seemed to favour what he called the Highland malts, whereas he preferred those from Speyside. I held up my empty glass to him. He poured me an Islay Ardbeg, and I fell in love with it.

Later I told him, 'These people I'm with?'

'Aye?'

'I'm not so sure of them.'

After a longish pause, during which Ean took a large sip of his whisky and rolled it around in his mouth, he asked, 'And why are you telling me?'

'Because you're coming up the hill with us tomorrow. I thought it fair that you should know I had my doubts.'

He nodded.

'OK. Fine. Thank you.'

Appearances can be deceptive, can't they? I asked him, 'What did you do in the war?'

'Lovat Scouts.'

'Pegasus Bridge?'

'Margaret doesn't like me to talk about it.'

So that was that, then. Another hard bastard. We were probably in good hands. We went back to teaching me the finer points of whisky appreciation.

Before I left him he asked, 'Can your people be ready to go by ten-thirty tomorrow morning?'

'Yeah. I warned them it could be even earlier.'

'Good. One last point . . .'

'OK. What?'

'If I say the weather's no good, we don't go . . . and no one argues.'

'I'll tell them, but George may not like it.'

'Yon Doris says that often, doesn't she?'

That was interesting. I wonder what Ean had been up to when she told him that?

It rained. It was bloody Scotland, after all; why should I have expected anything different?

Ean said we weren't going.

George's mouth turned down, but he spent the day in the small bar playing cards with me, Chris and a couple of shepherds. George didn't win at every game, and didn't seem to mind losing. You have to watch people like that. Ean watched a hand or two later on, and told us, 'The forecast is fine for tomorrow. You can reckon we'll be out on the hill.'

'Your call, captain,' George said without looking up from his cards. You'd think he didn't give a toss: he was a lot brighter than he pretended to be. Not for the first time I wondered what services George's company provided.

Doris didn't show at all that day. She kept to their room and Ean's Margaret took her food up to her.

Later I asked George, 'What's happened to Doris?' I thought it would be even more suspicious if I hadn't asked.

Again George didn't look up from his cards.

'Sore guts I guess, Charlie. It must have been someone she ate. We'll see her in the morning – she won't let us up on that mountain without her.'

Chapter Six

Lost John

We set out the next morning, walking back along the road we had arrived by, each carrying a small pack with our essentials. Chris was carrying something else, but I'll come to that later. Then we branched up along an old estate road past a farm, and up into the hills. Ean led the way. He wore a pair of cared-for army boots, and carried a nice old .243 rifle.

George asked, 'What's the gun for? I didn't expect guns.'

I had my small pistol in a pocket, but I didn't tell him that of course.

Ean said, 'I might spot a nice fat buck – cheap meat for the table.'

'Don't you need the landowner's permission to go shooting things?' George persisted.

'I gave myself permission this morning. Just before we set out.'

'You own all this land?'

'I think so. That's what my father told me.'

I may have been mistaken, but I thought that George's mouth might have turned down at that. He and Ean led us. Chris and Doris followed them, and I brought up the tail. Chris was carrying a golf bag. Yes, you read me right the first time: he was taking a golf bag up a mountain. Doris dropped back to walk with me for a while – it looked as if her sore stomach had given her a black eye. My enquiry was probably written all over my face. She told me, 'I hit my head on the basin while I was being sick.'

'It must have hurt.'

'Just my pride.'

George looked over his shoulder, and she moved up to walk alongside Chris again. I watched George's back – the small pack he carried between his shoulders – and wondered what I could do about him if he turned nasty. After an hour of zigzagging over the approaches to the hill my knees ached. Ean strode ahead with the ease of a feral goat. Twice Doris tripped in the scrubby heather, and twice I hauled her up. Each time she said, 'Thanks.'

I nodded at George and waved that she was OK, but I told her, 'I'm sorry, but I just can't stand the guy.'

She said, 'Snap!' Her mouth set in a determined little line. That was interesting.

At least the sun was shining. I decided to stop watching George until the train arrived at the station. I watched Doris's backside instead.

The last climb I did was in a dry summer, five or more years earlier and that had been easier. That approach had been along well established forestry tracks, and had been bad enough. This crumbly old mountain was wet, and it was falling to bits. You went from reasonably hard going into knee-deep boggy lichen without warning, and by the time we were making a serious attempt on the lower slopes my knees were aching badly from the boulders we stepped around. Ean called a halt. Breather. Doris disappeared around an outcrop for a spot of outdoor relief. Ean and Chris sat together, and being ex-army discussed the countries they had walked across during the war. George came and sat by me, handing me one of the small greaseproof-paper packets Ean had produced from his poacher's pockets. Two Abernethies and a hunk of cheddar in each: I knew that I had been right about that slimy bugger in the FO.

George said, 'I didn't expect the Scotch bastard to bring a gun.'

'Does it worry you?'

'Yeah, if you must know.'

'Why?'

He didn't reply immediately. He took alternate nibbles from the sweet biscuit and the cheese. Then he said, 'You saw I'd given Doris a black eye – I regret that now.'

'Good, George. You can tell her.'

'No, I can't, she won't come near me. I found one of the Scotch bastard's sweaters under the bed, so I lost my temper, and stuck my elbow in her eye.'

It was my turn to stay quiet. When I thought that I could conceal the relief I felt I said, 'I didn't know.'

'How could you? In a way I wish it had been you.'

Be careful what you wish for, George.

'Thanks.' It was an ironic *thanks*.

'No hard feelings, pal, just that you ain't exactly John Wayne, are you? She's hardly gonna lay by me an' think of you, is she?'

'I suppose not. So what's the problem with Ean?'

'It's obvious, ain't it? He might try to whack me "by accident" for giving her a smack. He has a stern and unforgiving look an' a rifle in his hand – I knew men like that in Oklahoma, and stepped wide around them. If I have to make a play I'll expect you to back me up – I'm paying you, after all.'

'What if I just try to keep the peace instead?'

'Even better. I like you Limeys – you're subtle. I appreciate that.'

'I'll just add it to your bill.' We left it at that.

Half an hour later I caught up with Ean as the others trailed behind.

'George thinks you might try to kill him because he slapped Doris.'

'Not a bad idea, but who would pay us if I didn't bring him off the hill safely again?'

'I'm just warning you to be careful. He's the type to get his retaliation in first.'

'Like the Japs at Pearl Harbor. You've got to hand it to them, haven't you?'

'Who?'

'The Yanks: fast learners. Why did he hit the lady?'

'He found one of your sweaters under their bed.'

Ean stopped to allow the others to come up. He sniffed the air like a gun dog.

He didn't speak for a ten-beat, and then said, 'He made a mistake. I lost that a month ago. I'd wondered where it had got to.'

As I dropped back I told George, 'You were mistaken. He lost that sweater weeks ago.'

I let the others draw ahead, and George fell back with me.

I asked him, 'Were you out in the war, George?'

'Sure, Charlie. Air force – jest like you.'

'Doing what?'

'Ordnance. I was out on the Marianas . . . Tinian Field.'

After the usual decent interval between two animals trying to size each other up, I asked him, 'Now I've come this far with you, George, would you mind cutting out the bullshit, and telling me what we expect to find up here?'

After another decent interval between two animals trying to size each other up, he told me, 'A bomb, Charlie.'

Bollocks. George had worked at Tinian Field in the Marianas. A very particular type of bomb had been delivered to Japan from Tinian. It's what you call being dealt a crap hand.

I had one more chance to square things with Doris. She sat on a boulder and told the others to climb on. George looked doubtful, but I waved him away. Ean looked impatient and Chris looked bored. He was carrying twice as much as the rest of us, but hadn't broken sweat yet.

'I'll stay with Doris,' I told them. 'I could do with a breather myself.'

Ean shrugged and said, 'Don't go off the track. You can get lost up here – too many little lochans that look all alike to an incomer.' The mountainside climbed away from us, and the track – which was barely discernible – led between two massive boulders. The men were out of sight within a couple of minutes. I grinned at Doris's shiner, and asked, 'How are you feeling?'

'My face hurts, Charlie. I think the bastard broke a bone.'

She winced as I ran a finger gently along her cheekbone.

'No, just bruised. You'll feel OK tomorrow.'

'It's not funny, Charlie. Did you just stay behind to gloat?' But at least her lips had turned up at the ends. I rather admired someone who could see the funny side of a slap in the puss – but I didn't tell her that of course.

'No, and we can't wait long. Do men always fight around you?'

'It's happened before.'

'Come here . . .' I reached down, and pulled her to her feet. As we began to follow the others I said, 'I waited with you because I need to know where you fit in. The true story this time . . . not the one about the little brother flattened up against a cliff face.'

She winced. I noticed that particularly.

'That's true, in fact. My brother was flying the plane, and it's why George needs me here.'

'I don't understand.'

'There was a law in the US banning US citizens from approaching within a mile of fatal aircraft wrecks . . . war graves. It was to discourage souvenir hunters and grave robbers, I think. Six months ago they relaxed it for relatives of the dead who wanted to visit the places their loved ones died. That's me. I am George's excuse for being here – his cover.'

'Does that law run outside the United States as well?'

'Not exactly, but there *is* one that states that any United States citizen doing anything abroad which would be a crime in the States is guilty of a felony. George is a coward at heart, and didn't take a chance . . . so he did his research, found me and hired me.'

'And he's not related to you at all? He's just some kind of hood?'

She nodded. 'Yep, he told me that he had to visit the wreck, offered me a thousand dollars to accompany him, a holiday in the Old Country – and a chance to say goodbye to Petey. I thought that sounded like the best deal I was likely to make.'

'Who does your box of money belong to then?'

'George, of course. I think the government gave it to him.'

'So you know he's up here looking for something else?'

'Oh, sure.'

For the first time since I'd met her in that park in Berlin her story was beginning to hold together – so why did I think she was still handing me a crock of old shit?

'Can I think about this?' I asked her. We were catching the others now – they were barely a hundred yards ahead. 'And talk to you again later?' Then I stuck in, 'You still haven't told me about the bomb.'

She stopped dead, and stared at me. I thought her black eye was less than black already.

'What bomb?' Ah. She looked levelly at me and explained, 'He's up here looking for a metal box of USAAF documents for a museum – the Smithsonian, I think.' After a gap in the conversation she asked me, 'What was that about a bomb?'

'Nothing, honey, forget it. I must have misheard someone.'

We plodded up to the crash site an hour later. Mysterious Chris opened his golf club bag, and produced a mine detector. It did indeed look like a frying pan with a very long handle. Broken down into handy transportable parts it fitted neatly into a golf bag. He assembled it, and went detecting. Presumably for George's bomb.

Ean sat on a rock pinnacle, and looked wary. George looked jumpy: he still spent most of the time watching Ean. For ten minutes Doris thought about the aluminium overcast we had strewn around us, and then burst into tears. *We few, we happy few*: I remembered the quotation, and opened the small pack I always carry and found a sandwich – freshly cut lean ham, and slices of apple between doorsteps of bread.

For those of you who haven't stood on a hillside with the bits of an aircraft spread around you, I'll try to explain. I've done it before.

What you have to imagine is a thirty-ton machine made of aluminium, steel, rubber and miles of electrical wire thumping into an unforgiving mountainside at two hundred and fifty. What is left, if she doesn't burn, is a lot of pieces – and I'm sorry to be blunt, but that is often all that's left of the poor sods who happened to be inside at the time. Got the picture? The Scottish highlands are full of them, and you can climb up to most – but if you do, read that Shelley poem 'Ozymandias' first, and expect your spirit to be humbled.

We were on a series of high ridges, crags and small flat plateaus. Just below us – and by that I mean about thirty feet below us – were four lochans: those small lakes. It was odd to find lochs up among the hilltops; as if God had popped them up there in some aberrant fit. The water in them was brown with peat or black . . . and they were full of bits of aeroplane. Everywhere I looked aluminium gleamed back at me from the shallows, under the water surface. On one small island a Wright Cyclone radial engine stood forlornly on its own.

In one of the small lochs a propeller stood upright among the shadows of the hills, one bent blade arching up like a tombstone.

Pieces of disassembled aeroplane glinted back at us from among the heather and coarse grass wherever I looked. It felt too much like a graveyard for me, and I wanted to get away as soon as I could. I still couldn't believe I hadn't set a price on this bloody job – can a woman really turn your head that quickly?

George suddenly lost his mind or his nerve. He shouted, 'Geronimo!' like the US Marines in cheesy war films, and ran at Ean. This was not a particularly sound strategy because he had to run steeply uphill to where Ean was perched, so by the time he reached him he was out of breath and going too slowly to be taken seriously, even though he was clutching a large American fighting knife in his hand. Ean simply moved out of the way. George couldn't stop himself. He plunged over the top, fell twenty-five or thirty feet, and rolled into the shallows of the largest lochan to lie among the pieces of aluminium.

Nobody immediately went down to see if he was OK. Doris and I climbed up to Ean, who asked, 'What the hell was that all about?'

'I told you. Your rifle gave him the willies. He convinced

himself that you're going to kill him for giving Doris a black eye.'

It was big, silent Chris who moved. He put his metal detector down, clambered through the tussocky heather, and dragged George out of the water.

Doris asked us, 'I suppose we can't just leave him there?'

'Not until he's paid us all, miss.' Ean smiled sympathetically. 'Then we can put him back if you like.'

The whole bloody thing had turned into a disaster, and I was half inclined just to walk off the hill and leave them to it. George had howled every time Chris moved him; either he was a big nance or he'd broken something.

Eventually Chris looked up at me and said, 'He fell on the knife. He's bloody stabbed himself as well as breaking a leg. How the hell do we get him off the hill?'

Doris stood up, and dusted herself down.

'Has he paid you yet?' she called down.

George groaned. I thought things weren't looking too good for him. We scrambled down to where he lay on his side in the heather.

'Did you find the bomb?' I asked Chris.

'What bomb? I'm looking for a container of a medical radioactive isotope. Something for X-ray machines. Nobody said anything about a bomb to me.'

'That isn't a mine detector you dragged up here then?'

'No, Charlie. It's a Geiger counter – can't you tell the difference?'

'He told me we were looking for a box of documents for some museum,' Doris complained.

Ean looked interested. Like an energetic working dog.

He asked, 'What did he tell *you*, Charlie?'

I quite liked talking about George as if he wasn't there. He groaned now and again to remind us he was. Maybe he was hoping to dissuade me from putting the words *Geiger counter* and *bomb* together in one sentence.

'That we were escorting the lady to the spot where her brother had died – he was the pilot. That turns out to be true, after a fashion.' I gave George a fraternal poke, and told him, 'George, it's time to come clean. Pay attention now, and tell me if we're looking for an atom bomb.'

He groaned and turned away from me, saying, 'That Scots maniac broke my leg.'

'No, he didn't, George. You broke it yourself because you are dumb. Let's try again – are we looking for an atom bomb?'

'*Yes*, fuck it.'

I was really pleased that everyone got it at once. However, nobody reacted quickly, until Doris said, 'What say we just roll him back into the water, and hold him under until he stops wriggling?' She had a point. If she had made the move I don't think anyone would have stopped her.

It was at this point that Ean played the Highland lairdy card, and decided to start telling us all what to do. But he wanted some information first. He, too, prodded George, but he was less forgiving than me because he prodded George's smashed leg.

'If the American government has really dropped an atom bomb on my rather spectacular mountain, old thing, would you mind telling us what you were supposed to do if you found it?'

'Mark it, go back down to the hotel and phone for some back-up.' He groaned again, and said, 'Shit, my leg hurts.'

'Breaks are meant to, George. Then what?'

'A US Army team would come and collect it. Discreetly. It would all depend on the condition the weapon is in.'

'And none would be any the wiser, was that the idea? Not even our curiously craven government?'

The real pain must have been hitting George by now, because all he did was bite his lip and nod his head.

'You Yankee bastards,' Chris said. Then he asked, 'What next?'

We all looked at Ean. We were on his patch, after all. He said, 'I'll go down and fetch a stretcher, some help to carry him down to the hotel – I'll travel fastest alone. You stay put, and babysit him . . . and if you find that bloody bomb, don't bloody touch it.'

Chris and I moved George further up the slope, and into the shadow of the low cliff face the aircraft had actually failed to clear. The pieces of airframe were noticeably smaller up against rocks. We moved sheets of ally around to give him some cover from the breeze. He moaned and groaned for America with every yard we moved him, even though we were as gentle as was practicable. I found his knife in the shallows, and put it in my pack. Doris took her revenge. She knelt down alongside George, smiled sweetly, and said, 'George, you are an absolute fucking louse. If I'd had my way we would have left you in the water.'

'Doesn't your country mean anything to you?' he groaned at her.

'What has our country to do with it?'

'I'm doing this for America, you bitch – saving face for Ike and the old country.'

'Balls, George, you're doing it for that suitcase of money that I've been carrying around for you for a month. I hope you die before we get you down off this mountain again.' And she stalked off to lend her captivating presence to Chris.

Some kind of instinct kicked in: something I must have picked up on. *You're acting, Doris,* I thought. *You're still bloody acting a part.*

Despite herself, I think she was interested in the bomb.

I asked George, 'Why didn't you just tell us Brits you'd lost a bomb that wasn't supposed to be here, apologize, ask Monty and the army to find it for you and give it back?'

'Go away, Charlie. I don't want to talk any more. I think I'm dying.'

I whistled one of those skiffle tunes they were beginning to play on the radio. I can't remember which one now. Maybe it was 'Lost John' – I was fond of that one at the time. Eventually George groaned again, and asked, 'Can I have a drink of water?'

I looked levelly at him, and asked it again.

'Why didn't you ask the British to find it for you, George?'

'Because it wasn't supposed to be here, stupid. The Prez had already decided to withhold the technology from you, so we couldn't tell you it was already sitting here in your back garden – all you had to do was find it. You got it later, after you paid for it.'

'So because you were frightened of us getting the Bomb before you wanted us to, an atom bomb has been lying out here in the rain and snow for ten years?'

'It's only a little one, Charlie, a model for the real thing – about a quarter-size.'

'Which makes me feel much better – if its casing has broken we're sitting on a radioactive fucking mountain, George! Doesn't uranium do something to your balls? How can you have been that foolish?'

'Not me, Charlie – the state department. I'm just a hired hand.'

'OK – then why not send the US Army to get it back – the *real* US Army?'

'They thought no one would notice a small outfit. When the army makes its own moves you find battalions of OD bastards wandering around. They can't think small, and they do tend to get noticed.'

'You can have that water now,' I told him, and gave him my water bottle.

'I think I stabbed myself in the guts, Charlie. I'm scared I'm gonna die.'

'Flesh wound, so stop bellyaching.' OK, so that was an unfortunate turn of phrase. 'If you turn on your side I'll dress it for you.'

'Doris could do that. She'd be gentler. She has soft hands.'

'Believe me, George, you're better off with me. Doris is not your friend today – you beat her up, and told her too many lies.'

George did say, 'Don't leave me here alone, buddy,' but I thought that it was time for him to learn one of life's hard lessons, and walked away to find the prospectors – they wouldn't be all that far away.

Chris's Geiger counter had stopped geigering: he was sitting in the heather taking it apart, and reassembling it. Doris sat on a rock a few yards away striking attitudes like Lady Hamilton. Chris wasn't buying them; he was in love with his instrument. I squatted between them playing the gooseberry.

I asked Chris, 'Assuming your box of tricks hasn't given up on you, how on earth did you expect to find this – what did you call it? – box of radioactive isotopes for X-ray machines?' I was glad I'd logged the word *isotopes* – you heard a lot of it in years to come. 'This aircraft is spread over a square mile – it will take you days to search it all.'

He grinned happily. I reckon he really liked his job.

'Don't worry, Charlie. If there was ever a large radioactive source in this wreck it will leave a spoor – just like big game. All I have to do is walk around the main impact area in a circle until the counter finds the radioactivity trail . . . then I follow the trail until I find the source. If it survived the wreck it's probably rolled a long way downhill.'

'But won't the radioactivity have been washed away in the rain and snow? It's supposed to have been up here for ages.'

'No, Charlie. If the hot stuff was ever here, I'll find it. It takes hundreds of years to decay.'

'Decay? You make it sound as if it was once *alive*.'

'Sometimes it seems that way. Out of the way now, there's a good fellow – let the dog see the rabbit.' He stood up and stretched; apparently he was ready to go geigering again. Doris gave me a po-faced smile, so I went to sit with her and watch the man at work. The breeze had veered, and changed direction. It was now a buffeting little cold wind – George was probably the only one out of it. Chris stumbled a circle of about a hundred yards around the main lochan, detouring for stubby tussocks of heather and juniper.

Doris told me, 'They said that Petey's body hadn't a mark on it – it's hard to see that that was possible. He was up in front of an airplane that smashed itself to pieces on that bloody rock face. Why do they lie to us?'

'The excuse they use is that it spares a family's feelings if you tell them that the dead person didn't feel a thing.'

'I think they tell us that to spare their *own* feelings, don't you?'

'Yes, but I've seen a few air crashes . . . and been in a couple myself. There's no sign of fire here, so I think it would have been over very quickly for him, practically instantaneous . . . Now you've been here, and seen it, you'll be able to tell your people that with a clear conscience.' She didn't reply; just leaned her head on my shoulder. I hoped I'd helped, and for once I'd been telling the truth.

Chris had a few false alarms – his frying pan showed a

marked affinity for the dials from smashed instrument panels, and his machine started to sing whenever it got within range of the luminous paint from the instruments. Suddenly he stopped hopping the bushes, and looked outwards from the circle and down the mountainside away from the way we had climbed in. He looked a bit like a dog that had got the scent. He raised his hand to signal to us, and moved off down the slope. We stumbled after him. Bollocks. I'd hoped the bloody thing had never been there in the first place. Half an hour later we found it in a fast-flowing burn; it had rolled nearly a quarter of a mile. It looked obscene. The Geiger counter went crazy anywhere near it, and the radioactive trail stretched away from us down the burn.

Chris went into man-in-charge drive, and angrily shouted, 'Shit.' Then he marked it with a small red flag on a whippy metal pole he had been carrying, and shooed us away uphill in front of him. We ran. Have you ever run up a mountain through hard stumpy heather, junipers and over a rockfall? That was my first atom bomb. Unless one of the radioactive governments gets even flakier than they usually are, it will also be my last.

We stopped when we reached George.

'You bloody bastard,' Chris shouted at him. 'Why didn't you tell me?'

George opened his eyes, and asked, 'What?' as if we had disturbed a reverie.

I told him. '*What*, George, is a battered bomb lying in a small stream bed a quarter of a mile away . . . and it's corroding and leaking. There are going to be a lot of people very annoyed with you.'

'It wasn't my fault.'

'You could have told someone. We could have brought someone up here who knew what he was doing.'

'You're not going to leave me here alone, are you?'

'We should,' Doris snorted, 'but we won't. Mad Angus is slogging his way up to us with a rescue party – not that you deserve it.'

'What happens after that?' he asked me, as if Doris hadn't spoken to him.

'Wait and see, but whatever it is you won't like it.'

Nor will I, I thought. *If Fabian of the bloody Yard gets hold of me after this, he'll bloody strangle me.* I heard some shouts drifting up from low down on our original path, and hollered back. All of a sudden Cyprus was not so bad a prospect after all. Provided I could get there before I was picked up.

Carrying a man on a stretcher down a mountainside is one of the few situations where a small man like me comes into his own. It always helps to have a couple of small guys at the back – you work it out. The other small guy was a shepherd who'd come in for a drink and had been shanghied onto a rescue party. I knew he was a shepherd without asking, because he smelt like a wet sheep and was sure-footed. George groaned all the way, and I was tempted to drop him. The laird was still doing the lairdy thing and leading the party, but he dropped back from time to time to keep my morale up.

'Doing OK, Charlie?'

'Yeah. How long before we're back down on the flat stuff?'

The light was beginning to draw in. I didn't fancy stumbling around in the dark.

'About twenty minutes. Then a couple of the bigger guys can finish the job. You've done very well under the circumstances.'

'And you're a patronizing bugger.'

'It's Lord of the Isles syndrome – I slip back into it as soon as the need arises. I'm supposed to be Galbraith of Shieldaig up here. Sorry.'

He was right though. Twenty minutes it was. He was

probably quite good at this sort of thing – his family had probably been directing hill rescues for generations. As soon as the paths began to flatten out, two hulking great brutes took over from me and the shepherd, and matched up with the two hulking great brutes on the front of the stretcher. Oddly, I found that when I handed it over my right arm and curled fingers had locked shoulder height in the stretcher-bearer position, and for a few minutes I had to march along with a raised clenched fist like an Italian Boy Fascist. That made Doris laugh. I didn't mind – we all needed a little something to laugh at. It dropped suddenly as the blood flooded back into it, and was temporarily too heavy to lift. All my strength had been expended carrying George. Doris had been behind me with Chris. Now she moved up, and took my arm. The track was wider, but even so we swayed like a couple of boozers.

She asked me, 'What happens to George?'

'Arrested, I hope . . . along with all the silly beggars who put him up to this.'

'He won't like that.' They seemed like words I had heard before. I laughed, and eventually Doris laughed with me – the others must have thought we were touched.

'And what about me?'

'How good are your good friends at the consulate?'

'*Very* good. I knew one of them very well.'

I could imagine Doris's *very wells*.

'Then I should imagine you'd be all right.'

'And George's bomb?'

'I think I'll leave that to our bold new leader. He seems to be properly in charge, and I suspect he knows what he's doing. Did you deserve that black eye George gave you?'

'Only with you. *Ut victor praemium.*'

'What does that mean?'

'To the victor the spoils, I think. George lost this time. We won. I flunked Latin.'

'I learned some Latin phrases from a girl in Egypt a few years ago.'

'What were they?'

'Tell you tonight if we're not in a cell somewhere.'

After a pause she squeezed my good arm, and said, 'Maybe if we're good they'll put us in the same one.' Doris was a girlful of transferable allegiances. George was suddenly not a good bet.

When we stumbled into the hotel it was full dark, and I was reacting to the physical effort I'd just put in. I was shaking. Doris was so close alongside you'd think she was welded. There was a new Scottish Ambulance Service Daimler outside, a police Land Rover and a police car. And a policeman at the door who said, 'You'll be Mr Bassett, of course.'

I couldn't stop shivering. I hoped he didn't think I was in a funk. Doris pushed us past him, and on into the small bar. She said, 'Yes, sheriff, he is, but he needs a fire, and his hand around a whisky glass before I let you at him.' She must have thought I was worth looking after: that was nice.

The copper smiled. That was nice too. I suppose you can afford to smile if you are about eight feet square and built like the proverbial brick privy. He said, 'As you say, ma'am, there's nothing that can't wait.' His smile had turned into a big grin as if someone had told him a decent joke. He followed us through to the small bar where the fire was burning. He even went behind the counter to pour me the drink himself. That wasn't a first as it turned out. When he couldn't hold it in any longer he kind of smirked, and said, 'Hello, Charlie. Long time no see.'

'Hello, Alex. What are you doing here, and why do you sound like a Scottie?'

The last time I had seen him he had been an RAF policeman quick-marching poor bloody National Service recruits into their farcical medicals in 1953: our paths had crossed several times since the 1940s. I looked on him as proof positive that it was indeed a small world.

'I *am* a Scot, didn't you know? I made my bid for freedom after doing twelve – I wasn't going any higher in the RAF – and joined the civvy police. Better pay and nobody shoots at you . . . well, not so many, anyway. They made me a sergeant.'

'And I suppose you're here by accident?'

'Not entirely. I'm at the police office at Fort William. Your name came up on a general request from London yesterday. I didn't think there were that many "Bassett C"s in the country, so when Shieldaig himsel' phoned Fort William for an ambulance and a bomb-disposal squad, mentioning a small fellah named Charlie who might just know what the devil was going on, I put three and three together, and got in the car. The Scotland Yard signal didn't say much – who have you upset now?'

'Have you heard of a long-nosed fellow called Inspector Fabian? He caught murderers, writes for the papers, and is supposed to be retired.' I'd knocked back my Scotch. Doris was watching the conversation go from me to Alex and back like a spectator at Wimbledon.

Alex said, 'Hard luck. He's a tough bastard, isn't he? You'd better have another.' What he meant was that we'd both better have another. My body gave a final tremor, and then began functioning again.

'Pour three. One for Doris. Doris, this is Alex. He used to be a friend of mine but he's wearing a funny dark blue uniform, so I'm no longer sure. Alex, this is Doris. She's an American and plays by American rules. I wouldn't believe a word she says if I was you.'

Doris gave him her Marilyn smile. She held out her hand for the ritual. He shook it, and then placed a hefty Scotch in it.

She said, 'That's right. I'm Doris. I probably have diplomatic immunity.'

Alex smiled again. He liked jokers.

'What does *probably* mean? Don't you know?'

'It means that I probably don't have it right this moment, but will have as soon as you let me speak to the embassy.'

Alex lifted his glass in a silent toast, and asked, 'Would it help if I suggested putting off any more talk until you two had soaked in a bath for an hour, and put some warmth back into your bones?'

The bathroom was at the end of the corridor on which our rooms were situated. Doris ran the bath half full of steaming hot water — that seemed to be something that none of these Scottish hotels were short of — stripped me off like a baby, and helped me into it. I thought she'd underfilled it until she stripped off herself, and joined me. I hoped she'd turned the key in the door lock. With both of us semi-submerged the water came up to within three inches of the top of the tub: maybe she'd done this sort of thing before.

We took the hour Alex had given us, but when we came down he had gone. So had George and the ambulance. So had mine host and our brave bomb detector. Ean's wife beamed at us and said, 'The sergeant will be back in the morning — he has to meet some people from the army. He said to feed you well — you've had a trying day. He'll see you tomorrow.'

'What's the time, Mrs Galbraith?' I'd left my watch upstairs.

'Just past seven, sir. Dinner's in an hour, but the bar's open.'

'Maybe we'll just go upstairs and rest,' Doris told her. The glorious Freemasonry of women exchanged sly smiles. They'd be speaking in tongues next.

Upstairs I flopped on the bed. Beat, but not too beat. Doris looked relaxed.

'Don't worry, Charlie. The state department is very good at

papering over the cracks, and your government will muzzle the natives with some sort of *Hide the Secrets* Act, and lots of money – no one will want any of this to get out. They'll probably be very pleased that there was someone as diplomatic as you along to hold our hands. I wonder if someone may even have steered us to you for that very reason in the first place.'

'I doubt it. Apparently the FBI has already complained about me to our Foreign Office.'

'Posturing – you know what these civil servants are like. They'll probably give you a Purple Heart on the quiet – to keep you quiet.'

'Don't want one.'

'What do you want?'

'I want you again.'

After enough of a pause Doris sighed, and whispered, 'I wish you wouldn't talk so crude,' as she clambered over me. I don't understand it. I've met them from time to time, and so have you: these wonderful and terrible women who – periodically – can't get enough of you, but don't like saying it with real words. So I kissed that superb triangular hollow in her shoulder blade, and whispered, 'I want to take you on a trip to the moon on gossamer wings.'

'That sounds much too corny – as if it's from a song.'

'If it isn't, then it soon will be.'

Alex came in and plonked himself down at our breakfast table the next morning. He didn't say no to an enormous free breakfast: that's cops the world over for you. What goes around comes around. Egg yolk was dribbling delicately down his chin as he said, 'I hope that you two have said your goodbyes. I'm to see you packed this morning and carry you into Fort William at lunchtime, where you'll be split.'

'Where am I going?' Doris asked him.

'Edinburgh. There's an American consul there. If he bats for you you'll be on your way – free as a bird. If not they'll lock you up in the castle, and fling the key away.'

'George?'

'Mr Handel? He's handcuffed to a bed in the cottage hospital. Important people coming down from Glasgow to see him – my chief constable won't like that.' He probably wondered why the words made us smile.

'Chris whatever's-his-name? If that was his name.'

'Crawling all over Sheildaig's hill with a bomb disposal squad and some scientists from AWRE, happy as the day is long – he'll probably get a reward.'

'And Charlie?'

'I've to put him on a train, with an escort to keep him straight . . . all the way to London. Somebody wants to talk to him.'

'Fabian of the bleeding Yard,' I muttered gloomily.

'No,' Alex said. 'Not as it happens. Mr Fabian has been outbid. An English twit from the Foreign Office has exercised some obscure privilege, and has first shout on you.' Then he asked, 'Where's the money, by the way? I spoke to Mr Fabian and he was very keen on the money.'

I opened my mouth, but Doris got there first.

'We don't know. George must have it. He took it away from me when he came here.'

Alex pushed his chair away from the table. He gave her the old eye lock.

'Last night Charlie told me not to believe a word you said.'

She held her room key up to him, and let it swing from side to side.

'You can search my things if you like.'

He shook his head, but took it. Then he held out his hand

for mine. After he left us I leaned over the table to Doris and hissed, 'Where is it?'

'In one of the boats on the shingle, under a thwart, under a cover. Don't worry, honey, he won't find it. I took enough out to pay off the Galbraiths and you. I'll smuggle the rest back into my stuff before we leave. They won't search me twice.' Where had I found a girl who could suddenly use words like *thwart*?

'What else haven't you told me, Doris?'

'Anything actually, honey – not even my name.'

There didn't seem to be anything to say to that, so I stood up.

'I think I'll just go for a short walk, and smoke a pipe or two.'

'OK, hon, but stay away from the boats until I tell you . . . or I'll drop ya.'

You need a short walk and a couple of pipes to accustom yourself to the idea that you've been had over. I'd been guarding against entirely the wrong person for the last week. I had been so concerned about George the maniac, that I'd failed to notice Doris the mobster in my arms. My father would like this story, and laugh at it. I'll rephrase that: he'd laugh at *me*.

We took the back seats in the Land Rover. Alex sat alongside his driver up front. Doris shivered and thrust a hand into my flying jacket pocket to keep it warm. She said, 'They didn't build these buggies for comfort, did they, hon?'

'They built them because we were giving too much of our money to America in exchange for Jeeps.'

'I'm going to lean against you and close my eyes, is that all right? It's the only way I don't get carsick.'

'Sure.' I smelt her hair. If smells have colour her hair smelt a chocolatey brown. Rich and very sweet. I wondered if I'd ever smell it up close again. When she withdrew her hand from my pocket I knew I wouldn't. She'd left a flat lumpish packet in there – I'd been paid off. Doris was cute. Yeah: the way the Yanks use the word. She gave me a kiss on the police station steps when we said goodbye. She kissed me on the lips, but it wasn't a soul sucker. Alex looked away embarrassed.

As I went to get back into the Land Rover for the trip to the railway station Alex pulled me aside and said, 'You've got a pistol in your pocket, Charlie, and a box of bullets in your kit. I found them when I searched your room. Have you got a licence for them?'

'You know I haven't.'

'Then bloody well get rid of them as soon as you can. I don't want to arrest you for something as silly as that!'

Yeah. Alex was my pal again, and I supposed that one good turn deserved another. I shook his hand.

'I don't suppose you've got a great hairy policewoman hiding in your police station by any chance, have you?'

'We call them police offices up here, Charlie, and *yes*, we have. How did you guess? Her knuckles drag along the ground as she walks, and we try not to let her out without her trainer. Why?'

'You're being very unkind. I could report you to the animal protection squad.' I waited for a nine-beat intro – Jelly Roll Morton's 'Ballin' the Jack' – gave him the innocent wide-eyed look, and asked, 'I suppose you still want all that money back?'

'Yes. Do you know where it is?'

'I'd find an excuse for your feral colleague to body-search Little Annie Oakley, and turn over her bags again . . . before you let her get away. You never know, you might get lucky.'

Alex nodded at me. Slowly. He got the message. Doris was at the top of the steps to rather an impressive old building behind us. My voice was low, so she was more or less out of earshot. She smiled and waved. She was a touch of the exotic in this austere town. I smiled and waved back, and climbed into the wagon. I felt a lot better after that.

The young detective who accompanied me to London was named Angus. Actually it wasn't. It was something like Aonghas. He said it was the Gaelic for Angus. We had seats in an otherwise empty First Class smoker – coppers don't sit with the plebs unless they're sitting on top, knocking the shit out of them. As soon as we had crossed the border into England he produced copies of an American magazine with nearly naked girls on the cover, and a packet of Vantage cigarettes. He offered me one, which I declined.

'Thanks, I'll stick with my pipe if you don't mind. I like fags, but I smoke too many once I get going. Where did you find those things?'

'There's a specialist tobacconist in Glasgow, just off George Square. He sends them to me. I think I first bought them because of the advertisements in this sinful magazine.'

He showed me one: a miniature naked Vargas girl with tanning marks sat on the side of a cigarette packet, with another between her legs. It wasn't exactly a subtle message.

I asked, 'Do you genuinely believe in sin?'

'It's what I do, isn't it, Mr Bassett? People commit sins we call crimes, and I detect the sinners and lock them up. Nothing like a bit of friendly sin to sell a few newspapers.'

'I couldn't help noticing you waited until we were in England before you opened your comics.'

He gave me a very straight look, and lifted his nose in disdain. Hundreds of years ago John Knox taught the Scots how to do that, and then they patented it.

'It's smut, Mr Bassett, dirty smut. We don't approve of

smut in Scotland. Would you care for a dram?' He'd produced a half-bottle of Red Label from another of his capacious raincoat pockets.

'Why not? Don't mind if I do. You can call me Charlie, by the way.'

He magicked into existence two shot glasses to go with the whisky: he must once have been a Boy Scout. We drank the bottle inside half an hour, and I fell asleep. I don't know what Angus did; probably went looking for more girlie magazines. I awoke when we were an hour from London. Angus was still giving me the look. He observed, 'You talk in your sleep. Did you know that?'

'What was I saying?'

'Something about AWRE. People aren't supposed to talk about that, it's secret. The Atomic Weapons Research Establishment at Aldermaston, right? I should report what you said.'

'And I should report your pockets full of dirty mags, and that you drink on duty. Don't be such a twit, Angus. Lighten up a bit. We're nearly at London. Sin City Central – you'll love it. I can give you the name of a wonderful pub on the Old Kent Road that has striptease dancing at lunchtime.'

There was a long pause. A tune started to bounce around between my ears. Hoagy Carmichael was doing 'My Resistance is Low'. Anyway, old Angus perked up.

'Lunchtime, you said? That's very decadent.' Ah, well; he smiled in anticipation the rest of the way to Euston. A man, I thought, at peace with his right hand. I couldn't wait to get rid of him.

Chapter Seven

Where the Hell is Loughborough?

'Nice temperature at this time of year,' CB told me. 'Tight little island. Drink's cheap, women and whisky galore.'

'It's on, then?'

'Of course it's on. Always was. Abernethy?'

We were in a small British Railways office looking down over the platforms, talking about Cyprus. He'd met me from the train, and signed for me as if I was a parcel. Commuters were forming orderly queues at the barriers. Why do we do that? Most of the trains were late.

'Can you just do this?' I asked him. 'Take over someone else's office? What do you do, wave a wand?'

'Ask my brother usually. He's the station superintendent. They don't have stationmasters any more. Pity.' He dipped his biscuit in his tea, lifting it out just before it disintegrated. It was something to do with the way he'd lifted his elbow; I'd seen that before. I said, 'I *know* you.'

'Of course you do. We chatted a couple of times a couple of weeks ago. Can't you remember?'

'No. I mean I've met you before that. Germany 1948.'

He gave me his cheesy smile.

'Possibly, old boy. I got caught for National Service just like the rest of them. I spent eighteen months in Germany.'

'You were an intelligence officer in the RAF.'

'No, I was a cook. Army Catering Corps. Came out a stone heavier than when I went in.'

'You had a pencil moustache, and wore tweeds.'

'Hardly, old boy. You must be mistaking me for someone else. Not surprising – there were a lot of us about out there. I have enough cousins and brothers to form two cricket teams. We do, actually, most summers. Sure you don't want a biscuit?'

I shook my head. He thought that meant *no*. It also meant that I didn't believe him. I had stumbled into the hall of mirrors his kind inhabited years ago, and had never managed to completely find my way out.

I asked him, 'Do you know what I've been doing for the last week?'

'A little birdie told me, yes.'

'Do you know more about the Americans I was with than I do?'

'Probably.'

'Who were they working for?'

'Handel was working for himself. Civilian contractor – just like you will be when you get to Cyprus. Didn't he tell you that?'

'Yes. I didn't believe him.'

'There you go, Charlie. Appearances can be deceptive. We'll hold him until he's hopping about a bit more handily, and providing he cooperates we'll deport him.'

'And the woman?' I hoped my face wouldn't give anything away.

'State Department. She's a Hoover.'

'She's in the FBI?' J. Edgar Hoover. Even I had heard of him.

'No, *a* Hoover. She is a state department vacuum cleaner –

she vacuums up diplomatic messes before they embarrass anyone. Very intelligent girl by all accounts, although she messed it up this time. She was running George. He didn't know that, and was very offended when we told him.'

'So, she's in the clear. She said she probably had diplomatic immunity.'

'She may have, but not yet. She's sitting in a cell at Fort William in nothing but a prison gown – because her own clothes are material evidence – just about to be charged with money smuggling by the local PF. Wonderful to-do. There's already all hell to pay – the transatlantic telephone lines are red hot.'

'Will she be tried?'

'Of course not, old boy. We'll give her back in a month or so, and promise to keep the story quiet . . . after they've done us a considerable favour or two.'

'And me?'

He leaned back, and tried to balance his teaspoon on the surface of his tea. It gave the impression of deep thought. Or psychological detachment to the point of idiocy.

'You know our American cousins were never all that keen on you, don't you? Well, they'll positively dislike you now, won't they, old boy? What makes it even worse is that within a couple of months they'll hate the rest of us as well. You won't even be able to trade on "the special relationship" to keep you out of trouble.' I disliked the relish with which he pronounced that. It was the first I'd heard of any growing international tension: usually all we argued with the Yanks about was the price of oil, and the taxes they placed on our exports – that was after the bloody accountants had taken over in the Land of the Free, where nothing would ever be free again.

'What's about to happen to upset the apple cart?'

'Wouldn't know, old boy – they never tell me. I've probably said too much already.' He looked momentarily annoyed.

'You haven't said anything.'

'There you are then, old boy – nothing to report. Weren't we talking about the American girl who ended up in clink in the Highlands somewhere? Apparently she blames you for her predicament, and doesn't use your name without attaching several colourful and imaginative expletives. She thinks you took advantage of her, and says you done her wrong.' He was quoting from either 'Frankie and Johnny' or 'Miss Otis Regrets'. They were popular songs – you could hear them on the radio all the time. 'I wouldn't be surprised if the Yanks even sent some people over to teach you a lesson. They're a simple but unforgiving race.'

'Will you protect me?'

'Why should we? We didn't ask you to go carousing around the glens looking for an illegal and inefficient weapon.'

'So what *do* you suggest I do?'

'I suggest that there are very few Americans on Cyprus at this time of year . . . and those that are, are squarely in our sights. So how about it, old boy?'

His *old boys* were beginning to get on my nerves. Before we got down to business I asked him, 'I don't suppose she *was* related to the pilot of that crashed plane?'

His smile could have meant anything.

'I don't suppose she was, either. More tea?'

I went back to Green's Hotel and booked in. It was Ozzie's night off, and he agreed to come out on the skite. His wife said he didn't get out enough, so it would do him good. They don't make wives like that any more. We ended up three sheets to the wind in a small club off Soho Square. The dancing girls were uniformly beautiful – young actresses looking for the first step up the ladder. Three fat guys from the film business sat at the next table, and discussed them as if they were meat. Ozzie wanted to thrash them, but I held him down. It was the way of the world these days. It made me think of the Americans again, and the American way of life – how long would it take for the Yanks to realize that it wouldn't necessarily suit the rest of us?

I treated Fabian to lunch in the Savoy Grill. I was rather taken with the place. It was pricey of course, but not *that* pricey. They could do you a decent lunch for seven quid, and a bottle of house red for thirty bob. We were greeted by a black jacket who took the inspector's raincoat, and asked him, 'Your usual table, sir? It hasn't been booked today.'

Fabian nodded, and smiled.

'Thank you, Michel.' After we had been seated – a small table overlooking the area of Savoy Yard in which the taxis turned – he told me, 'He's not French, of course. He came into the world as *Michael* . . . in Camberley.'

We took the *menu à choix*, and Fabian chose the wine. He didn't make a pig of himself. When he asked, bluntly, 'What is it you wanted?' I was taken a little by surprise and replied too loudly.

'To make sure I wasn't still in the shit before I go abroad again.' Then I realized where I was, and looked round hurriedly, hoping no one had overheard. The woman at the next table had. She smiled at my discomfort, but it was a big sort of smile that suited her big hair, which fell below her shoulders in glorious auburn waves. It was a film star's smile that forgave and included you at the same time. She was very beautiful; I'm sure you've seen some of her movies. I'd have to tell Dieter about her as soon as I met him. Fabian smiled too.

'I understand you're in the clear. You seem to specialize in that, don't you? Not that I know anything, of course, I'm retired these days.'

'Of course you are, Inspector. Can you recommend the fish?'

'Not as good as the fish in Cyprus.' Then he winked.

Bollocks.

I had phoned Dieter before I boarded the rattler down to the south coast. He asked if he could meet me at the station.

When we met the first thing he said, smiling, was, 'You've lost your new girlfriend, haven't you, Dad? It's written all over your face.' I hate smart-arses.

The first thing I said to him was, 'When you said you wanted to meet me, I didn't expect you to be doing the driving.'

He'd driven into the station forecourt at Chichester in a green pre-war Hillman Tourer. He'd parked it too far away for me to see who was in the front passenger seat. He hadn't L-plates up, but that wasn't surprising – he wasn't seventeen yet, and he couldn't legally drive. He said, 'I wanted to surprise you. I bought it from a man in the yacht club for twenty-five pounds. Mrs Valentine is teaching me to drive.'

What else is she teaching you? I thought, but all I said was, 'Hmm.' He knew that I wouldn't have him lose face by delivering a bollocking in front of his passenger, even though he deserved one.

'Where did you get the cash?'

'Working in the bar, washing glasses for the Major.' He wasn't officially old enough to do that either.

I obviously had a few more fences to jump before I left.

Eve said, 'Hello, Charlie,' and didn't look embarrassed. Neither did Dieter. So I suppose that was all right then.

He asked me, 'Do you want to drive, Dad?'

'You drove her here, you might as well drive back.' Yeah; his bloody face lit up. I scrambled in behind them, and wondered where I'd hide if the local traffic cops stopped us. He whistled as he drove. Eve leaned back to me, and brought me up to date on the Bosham scandals: if things carried on at this rate the *News of the World* would appoint a special correspondent for our little port. Maybe there was something in the water.

Dieter's driving abilities? You guessed it: better than mine already. He was a bloody natural. I'd have to watch the little bugger. And not so much of the little, either: when we tumbled out of the car alongside our prefab I realized for the first time that he was already taller than me. Ten minutes later Carly sat me down at the kitchen table and produced a cardboard box containing six roughly shaped pieces of solid balsa wood, a tube of glue, a piece of sandpaper and a plan drawing of a Lysander aircraft. We'd called them *Lizzies* in my day, and some of the guys I knew had flown them out of Tempsford. What with helping Carly with his new hobby of modelling aircraft, and Dieter's driving lessons, I could see that I'd have my work cut out for the next few days. Carly was eleven going on twelve. He worked on shaping the oddly angled wing leading edges while I concentrated on the fuselage. We soon had balsa dust all over the kitchen table, and smiles on our faces. He asked me, 'Are you still in the RAF, Dad?' They both called me *Dad* now; Carly had copied Dieter.

'No. Too many people to boss me about.'

'Would you mind if I was? When I was old enough, I mean?'

'No, son. I'd probably be very proud. Why don't you come back to my company with me as soon as I get another few days off, and have a closer look at *our* aircraft?'

'I'd like that.' So would I, I realized. Times change. You get older. It looked as if both my boys were being drawn to proper men's jobs: I could live with that.

After the boys had turned in I wandered across to the bar to give James a hand. Eve was propping up the customer side. Before I asked she told me, 'I'm not a cradle snatcher, Charlie. Give me some credit.'

'I do,' I said. 'That's why I'm worried.' She smiled and raised her glass to me.

'Where are you going this time?'

'Cyprus, they tell me. How did you guess?'

'You're down here for a week, and making a fuss of the boys. That usually means you're going away.'

'For the last time.'

'Famous last words.'

'Trust me.'

'Why?'

I didn't have an answer for that one.

When I looked at the bundle that Doris had pushed in my pocket I was ashamed I'd turned her in. I gave five hundred to Maggs for safekeeping. She was safer than the Bank of England. Safer than the Bank of Scotland as well. But it was one of the things I still liked about Britain: nothing would ever go wrong with the banks.

I phoned the Foreign Office and told my new boss, 'OK. I settled my affairs as best I could. The police didn't arrest me, and I'm ready to go when you are.'

'Good. I'll cut the arrangements for you. Give me your telephone number . . . And for Christ's sake remember to take a warm coat – it can be bloody chilly up there at this time of year, old boy.'

'In Cyprus?'

'In Loughborough, old boy, *Loughborough*. Recovery training – you won't have seen the kit you're working with before. New stuff, I understand.'

'Better range?'

'How the hell would I know, old son? I'm just the office boy.' He could have fooled me. In fact, come to think about it, he did.

Where the hell is Loughborough? *It happens every bleeding time*, I thought. Three years earlier the RAF had signed me up for Egypt, but as soon as I'd broken out my tropical kit they sent me to Dungeness for training instead. Dungeness is one of life's great disappointments: even Egypt was a relief after that. I decided to spend a few days in London before I took off.

Loughborough is in Leicestershire, a county that has nothing going for it except the death of Richard III at Bosworth Field. Even that is debatable – the historians can never seem to make up their minds whether that was a good or a bad thing. It was never a problem for me; he was a *king*, wasn't he? The country's had far too many of those, and none of them much good. The weary, skinny man behind the St Pancras ticket office counter shrugged when I told him I wanted to go to a village named Woodhouse, near Loughborough.

'Where's the nearest railway station?'

He consulted a gigantic and ancient book, took off his specs and told me, 'Loughborough itself is not much further than the nearest station – Barrow upon Soar – and to get *there* you'll have to go to Loughborough and change trains anyway.'

'What would you do?'

'I wouldn't go to either. Loughborough's a terrible place – I was there in the war.'

I bought a ticket for Loughborough, and made a note of the cost in my diary. I was a civvy this time, and had been told to note my expenses and keep the bills. If I was lucky I would be able to claim them back.

I stood on the platform, and waited for the 10.10 to Loughborough. The platform was empty of people, and empty of trains. It was empty of everything except me. Even the pigeons had deserted it. A cold wind blew in under the glass.

Half an hour later the man from the ticket office walked up to me, and asked, 'What you doing still here then?'

'Waiting for a train. You sold me the ticket.'

'You'll be lucky!'

'Why?'

'The guards are on strike – didn't you know? No trains until tomorrow.'

'Why didn't you tell me that?'

'You never asked.'

I nearly clouted him. 'Can I travel on the same ticket tomorrow?'

'Providing the train's not full, but I expect it will be.'

'You're a helpful bastard, you know that?'

'And using language like that on the railways is an offence, so hop it, Shorty, before I call a copper.'

I had a kitbag with my tropicals and a large suitcase of winter weights for bloody Loughborough. There was no porter in sight, and no barrow. My nemesis stalked slightly behind me all the way back to the station steps, not offering a hand. As I dragged myself towards a taxi he observed cheerfully, 'Did you hear we just invaded Egypt this morning? Won't take long to teach the ruddy Gyppoes a lesson!' *In your dreams!* I thought.

I'd been there, and I guessed he hadn't. It wasn't the Egyptian military we had to worry about, but the rest of the world – when the canal closed, and the oil began to dry up, that's when the pressure would come on. You'd have thought we could have at least waited until the Hungarian revolution had petered out. I wondered what effect it would all have on my Cyprus jaunt: maybe they wouldn't want me after all.

I went down to Loughborough the next day. The train had few passengers. Its heating didn't work, and there was no buffet. It was like being on an empty troopship. I pulled on an extra pullover, and wore my old flying jacket over that for the entire journey, and the train arrived at Loughborough twenty minutes late.

I'd intended to get a cab from the station, but there was a three-tonner in the station yard leaning against a grizzled signals sergeant. He wore one of those old sleeveless leather tank jackets over his battledress, and looked as if he'd seen as much service as it had. His beret was perched on a hedge of greying hair, and he was smoking a fag.

I asked him, 'You're not going to Garats Hay, by any chance, Sarge? I have to report there today, and wouldn't mind a lift.' *Yesterday* actually; but we'll cross that bridge when we come to it. He grinned.

'You look a bit long in the tooth for the call-up, mate. What happened – couldn't you keep away?'

'No, I'm still a civvy – I used to be in the RAF, and apparently you want some civvy radio operators to go on holiday to Cyprus. That's me.'

'Lucky you. What they paying you, if you don't mind me asking?'

'Thirty quid a week, all found. What does a National Serviceman get these days?'

'Three bob a day, seven if he signs on. They'll *love* you when they find out.'

'Then they'd better not. What about that lift?'

'Sling your bags in the back, and then hop up in front with me. I'm picking up a draft of seven lads off the York train. Another ten minutes.'

Oddly enough, it felt comforting to be back among the guys in uniform, and their green-painted lorries. I knew where I was with them. Do your job, stay out of trouble and you were OK. Welcome back, Charlie.

Woodhouse is a small village built in the middle of a large army camp. It tries to ignore the army camp, but rarely succeeds. No. 10 Wireless Training Squadron of the Royal Signals ran the set-up in my time. Quite an impressive bunch, even if it always hurts to say anything nice about the Brown Jobs. The rail strike had been on for three days: so there were Services returns and boys from the call-up arriving up to three days late, knocking on the guardhouse door, expecting a bollocking and to be up on a charge. What they were given instead was a mug of tea for their effort – while their papers were sorted – and a ticket for the messes.

'What's the point with punishing a kid because the bleedin' railway let him down?' a corporal signaller explained to me. 'How much classroom attention would we get from a lad who's doing eight days' CB?'

'If the army's come over all *live and let live*, Corp,' I told him, 'then I've died and gone to heaven.'

'Not heaven, exactly, Mr Bassett, just a technical training school. Men come here to learn how best to use our latest radio equipment, not how to salute and stamp their feet all the time. We leave that sort of thing to Catterick.' He sounded like an educated man to me, and he smiled a lot. I wondered if the RAF had grown up too. No, probably not.

It was the sergeant who eventually appeared on the other side of the counter to sign me in. He referred to the camp as both Garats Hay, and Beaumanor, which confused me at first: the two names seemed to be interchangeable. It was a hutted camp: hutted accommodation and training on one side of the road through the village, with an old manor house, Beaumanor, where the colonel and all the nabobs lived on the other. The admin section and officers' mess lived over there as well.

'As a civilian trainee, sir, you'll be allocated accommodation in one of the huts, but you're entitled to use the officers' mess. I'll see you're issued a mess number, and get someone to take you up.' I noticed that; I'm sure you did too. Out in the land of the free I'd been *mate*; now I was a civilian trainee, and *sir*. I wasn't sure I liked that. I leaned across the counter to him.

'In the RAF I was a sergeant, Sergeant. I'd be more at home if you could wangle me into the sergeants' mess instead.'

He paused.

'I'm sure that your papers said you had been a pilot officer, sir.' He sounded doubtful.

'I was, for a short while, but it was a bad mistake. Nobody asked me.'

He sighed. Life is full of difficult decisions, isn't it? 'OK. But don't tell anyone.' That was the second time we had said something like that: the armed forces were becoming curiously secretive.

I was given a dirty-green boiler suit, like the four other civvies I shared a big hut with, and we were expected to walk from training session to session. As far as I can recall I never saw anyone doubling anywhere the whole time I was there. On the first morning our course leader – a smart young corporal – read us the list of courses we would complete in our time with the Signals. We were all down for W/T Test and Selection, and W/T (Special Communications), and something extra. Each of the something extras was different – to make us feel like individuals, I supposed. Mine was firefighting. Fucking fire-fighting! Someone somewhere had blundered. I knew exactly what the NCOs and troopers of the Light Brigade felt like when they looked down the valley towards those bloody Russian guns. I also knew well enough not to argue. I asked the corp, 'How do they teach us firefighting?'

'Not my subject, Charlie' – it was a nice informal sort of course and we were quickly on first-name terms – 'but I understand that they fill an old airframe up with aviation spirit and set it on fire. You have to put it out on your own. If you succeed, you've passed. If you die you haven't.'

'I did parachute training a few years ago – same principle.'

'It's always good when our students already know the ropes.'

He tested my Morse receiving and sending. I wasn't as fast as I used to be, but even so could outperform everyone in the classroom except a talkative little Welsh geezer from the call-up: in Civvy Street he'd been a fully qualified radio officer on a merchant ship. I reckoned he'd have a stripe up before the end of his training. The RX 108 radios they sat us at came as a bit of a shock – larger than the sets I was used to, and with a better range if you had the right aerial array. Providing it was doing so with a signal, I could have heard a fly fart in Shanghai with that kit.

After a week it was obvious that they weren't interested in my sending speed – I was going to be a listener again. In '47 I'd listened to the Reds and the Poles before they demobbed me. In '53 it was the Wogs and the Israelis. Who was I to be eavesdropping on this year? I remembered what CB had said, and just wondered if it was the Yanks.

I learned the Yorkshire Two-Kick Game in the sergeants' mess at Garats Hay – there was nothing much there to do except congregate in the bar, and it could get a bit boisterous. There was a liberty bus to and from Loughborough every night, but if you've ever been to Loughborough you'll know why we declined the offer.

On the night I learned the Two-Kick Game someone spotted a ten-bob note which had been dropped on the floor of the bar. A burly sergeant and a small Yorkshire civvy went for it at the same moment, and each managed to get half a foot on it. Stalemate. The civvy just about came up the Brown Job's shoulder. A discreet circle gathered around them.

I offered five bob on the civvy – not because I thought he'd win, but because he looked clever. He produced a tanner from his pocket and spun it in the air. He didn't withdraw his foot. Everyone's eyes were taken by the small silver disc, spinning and catching the light.

He told the sergeant, 'We settle this sort of thing with the Two-Kick Game where I come from, Sergeant.'

'What would that be, Tiny?' The sergeant. He grinned around.

'One of us stands still, while the other takes two kicks at him. Then we swap round. It goes on until one of us gives up.'

'How do we choose who goes first?'

'Toss for it – I'll toss, and you call.' The tanner was lofted skywards again.

'Heads.'

The small fellow caught it – 'Tails. Me first.' He opened his hand to show us fair was fair. I enjoyed the first signs of uncertainty in the sergeant's eyes, but he squared his shoulders and said, 'OK. Your shot.'

The small man immediately kicked him hard on the knee, and the soldier fell; we all stepped out of the way, and let him go. It was like a great tree coming down. He took the second kick in the balls. He rolled onto his side groaning, and holding himself. He had staying power and courage though; he dragged himself first to his knees, and then to his feet. The room was roaring him on. When he managed to get upright his eyes were red with rage, and the smile on his face was not a thing of beauty.

'My turn,' he snarled, and pulled his boot back for strike one.

'No,' the Tyke told him. 'I give up. The ten bob's yours –

you keep it.' He turned away, and broke the silence that enveloped the room by telling another civvy alongside him, 'That'll be a quid, Artie.' Then he looked across the ring at me, and said, 'I bet Artie a quid I'd get one of these dumb buggers to stand there and let me kick him in the goolies.' His tanner piece was weighted, of course.

After that we civvies sat together at a separate table: it was the only way we felt safe. I didn't know it, but our bold kicker's course was finished. He left later that night; away on the last train. When he wasn't kicking folk in the balls he seemed like a mild-mannered little guy. But you never can tell.

His pal Artie told me, ' 'E only came out six months ago. These Brown Jobs think they know it all, but they never learn.'

'Came out?'

'Fra' Armley Gaol – Leeds Prison. He was in for bashing a copper, an' breaking his jaw.'

I had another week to do; at least it broke the monotony.

Before the week was up the Yanks were telling the Brits and the French to fuck off out of Egypt again, and not to come back. I'd met Nasser once – by accident, mind you – and I think he was canny enough to have provoked us into it, knowing the Yanks would ride to his rescue, and that we wouldn't have the stomach to deny them. There would be no second chance. It was just too much of a coincidence, wasn't it?

Suez in 1956 was the shortest-lived, least-effective, successful invasion the British Army has ever carried out. The Americans and the UN had taken a tough line with Russia over what it was doing in Hungary; so they could hardly turn a blind eye to us doing exactly the same in Egypt. Within five days of our successful invasion of Suez they were threatening to sell up all of the UK loan stock they had acquired (which would have bankrupted us), and in the shadow of Big Ben people were shouting for the Prime Minister's head. If Eden had waited until after the Hungarian affair was over before we went in we would probably have got away with it. I wonder why he didn't. Anyway, the poor old sod was gone by January – ill health, they said – but he was visited by the American ambassador just before the announcement was made, so you can draw your own conclusions.

The army, meanwhile – that November – didn't give me much time to think about it: they did exactly what the corporal had told me they would do with me. They set fire to an old airframe and made me put it out. It had once been a Sikorsky helicopter belonging to the Army Air Corps. It stood alongside another, with about ten yards separating them, but when you're splashing it about, a few gallons of aviation spirit go a long way.

A lance jack with a fancy badge underneath his Signal Corps flash drove me up to it in one of those new Austin Champ heavy jeeps. We parked up about thirty yards from the aircraft corpses, but I could smell the fuel in the air as soon as I got out. There was a foam bowser parked up much closer. The lance jack's name was Ryan. He said he'd show me the ropes. He fired up a generator motor on the bowser, unhooked a wide flexible hose, and pulled an asbestos hood with a clear screen over his head. It covered his shoulders. Then he fired a flare pistol into one wreck, but I think that was for effect: a box of Swan would have done the job as well. The fuel ignited with a soft 'whoo-o-of', and I felt the wall of heat immediately.

I may have told you already, or I may not, but I have a pathological fear of fire. It's what happens to your brain when you survive being in an aircraft which decides to sacrifice itself to the Fire God. It happened to me in 1944, and the explosion that followed threw me into a nearby cemetery, and burned my shoulders and face. The face was only lightly grilled and came back to me – but my shoulders still carry the scars.

Ryan advanced on the heli frame carrying the foam hose, spraying great gouts of fire suppressant foam ahead of him. It seemed to be over in seconds.

'We suppress the fire, guv'nor,' he explained to me after he'd dragged his hood off. 'We deprive it of air. You aim at the base of the fire, and advance on it as you suppress it. It will seem to move away from you. All you've got to do is follow up, and smother it until it's dead.'

He showed me the simple on/off lever for the hose, and then turned to light my wreck up.

I said, 'Aren't you forgetting something? Can I have the hood, please?'

'You won't need it, sir; you're going to extinguish the fire, aren't you?' Then the airframe went up with another gentle whoo-o-ooshing noise, and the flames reached towards us. What I can remember now is that nasty little bastard of a lance driving and pushing me towards the fire with phrases like, 'Get in *CLOSER* – the trouble with you, Mr Bassett, is that you have no fucking *guts*, sir – closer, sir – get your *fucking* act together, sir, there's men dyin' in there!' and so on. He called me every name I knew, and a few I didn't, and was right behind me every step of the way. The barrier of heat was stunning; it stopped my brain from working.

If you'd asked me, I would have said that it took me ten times longer to extinguish my fire, than he did his. When I finally dropped the hose on the ground I was alongside the smouldering wreck, had no eyebrows and the curl which fell over my brow was frizzled. I could smell my own burned hair. My cheeks were glowing. To tell the truth if my bladder had been more than empty I would have wet myself. Maybe that would have done a better job on the flames than the foam. Back at the Champ Ryan spread some paste on my cheeks and forehead.

'You may lose a layer of skin,' he told me, 'but it's nice to know you can do it, isn't it?'

I took a gulp of water from a water bottle he handed me before I replied.

'I suppose so. Did I pass?'

'We're still here, aren't we?'

'I was in an aircraft crash once – the bastard thing burned like that.' I was still pulling in air in great gulps; I must have been holding my breath as I fought the fire, so it can't have taken all that long, can it?

'Why didn't you say?'

'What difference would it have made?'

'I would have made it harder for you, guv'nor – to compensate for the lack of surprise. You knew what was coming, didn't you?'

In the mess that night the sergeant on the end of the Two-Kick trick came up to me with a beer for each of us. Like most sergeants he rolled with every punch, and kept grudges. He lightly touched the paste on my forehead: it had set like plaster.

'Got too close to the matches, did you?'

'The bastard teaching me drove me into the fire until my eyebrows disappeared.'

'My baby brother. He must have heard about that trick you lot played on me – I must tell him *thank you*. Honours even?' He held out his hand, and we did the shake-it-up-and-down ritual. I got drunk with his people after that – they seemed like a decent bunch.

At about 2300 hours, after I knew I'd drunk enough to land myself with a hang-over the next day, he leaned across the table and said, 'Pack yer gear tonight, Mr Bassett. You're off tomorrow.'

Chapter Eight

Hello, Pat

I stood on the tarmac in the rain apart from the group of National Servicemen and reservists who were flying out with me. It seemed unfair that on the very day that my craven government had agreed to comply with international demands to uninvade Egypt again, they were bunging me on a plane to fly in that general direction. Two people had come to see me off. That was nice. Both were men, and that was disappointing. There's nothing like a bit of skirt standing at the edge of the runway, waving her knickers as you lift off to fight another day.

Old Man Halton had greeted Carlton B by saying, 'Hello, Hannibal. How are things in the Madhouse, these days?' I took it that the Madhouse was the FO.

'Mad,' CB said, 'quite mad.'

'You two know each other?' I asked.

'From years ago,' Halton beamed. 'Our families were close, and Hannibal once asked me for a job.'

'And he said not bally likely,' the Mandarin told me, 'so I joined the Home Civil Service instead. Thus I have your employer to blame for everything that's happened to me ever since.' The smiles they were banging off, and the way their handshake went on for ever, said that they liked each other as well. 'I drove down to see Charlie off,' he added, 'and to warn him to try to stay out of trouble.'

'So did I. It's going to keep raining . . .' Halton looked at the cloud base, and sniffed. Then he treated us to one of his wondrous rolls of coughing. It was like standing alongside a thunderstorm. 'Do you think we have time for a drink? The transport hasn't turned up yet.'

We were hanging around on a Royal Canadian Air Force Base, RCAF Langar, waiting for an aircraft to turn up, and we hadn't even got as far as Canada yet – just bloody Nottingham-shire. I'd been trucked over in a one-tonner before respectable people were awake.

Langar was a bloody great piece of old England surrounded by unfriendly Canadian conscripts with unprincipled dogs and big guns: the main Canadian base in Europe. Our Egyptian folly had used up so much of our own runway space that we had to borrow some back from friendly allies . . . and there were fewer of those by the day. As you can imagine, we hadn't asked the Yanks for help, because none would be forthcoming. I've liked almost every American I've ever met, but politically they still haven't got over the Boston Tea Party.

Eagle Airways, a civilian mob whose trooping contracts Old Man Halton had his eyes on, was doing the needful, but because the government wanted to hide the number of troops we were moving around the globe most movements had to occur from military airfields.

Browne asked me, 'What kind of aircraft will you use?'

'I went to Cyprus three years ago on a converted Wellington Bomber – it scared me half to death. I think Eagle uses real aeroplanes – DC-6s or Hastings. Things like that.'

Halton began to cough again; we'd have to get him out of the rain, so we let him lead us to a small square chunk of a building alongside the watch office.

At least the Canadians had the ability to surprise: we found ourselves in a rather plush little lounge with a small bar, and a white-jacketed steward. I was a VIP for a day, and I might have known that Halton would have known it was here. I quietly sipped a pint of Ruggles beer, whilst they threw back Rusty Nails like nobody's business. I hoped the old man hadn't flown himself here in his Auster, or that if he had then he had the sense to stay overnight.

He toasted me, and I said, 'It's nice of you to see me off, sir, but you didn't do it last time, so you have me a little worried.'

He had a twinkly little smile which was always hard to resist.

'You weren't my co-director then, now you are – everything was written up in Companies House last week. I decided it was my duty to make sure you leave the kingdom safely—'

'And to lock the door behind you, I should think. I shouldn't trust him an inch if I was you, old boy – look what he did to me!' That was CB; he must have thought life was pretty dandy. They both found this uproariously funny, which was brought to a close with one of Halton's coughing fits, of course. I just had this feeling that I was being had, as the actress said to the bishop.

'Did you hear what happened to my quiet Americans?' I asked him.

CB shrugged.

'Gone, but not my department, so I don't know what it cost them.'

The old man touched my shoulder and said, 'Make the most of this, Charlie, take care and safe return. There's so much work coming in you won't get another holiday for years.' Then he gave me a bottle of Scotch as a going-away present. He hadn't done that before either; maybe he was going soft.

An RCAF corporal chose that moment to intrude. He shook the rain from his khaki cape, and asked, 'A Mr Bassett here?'

'That's me,' I told him.

'Your carriage awaits, sir. I was sent to find you – everyone else has boarded, and they're waiting for you.'

'Good show,' Browne said. Then, 'Toodle-oo.'

Old Man Halton nodded. He was holding a handkerchief to his mouth, and I could see it was speckled with blood. Whenever I left him I wondered if I would see him alive again. I nodded back: I liked the tough old stick really. The last thing that Halton said was, 'June sends her love . . . says she'll write.' I nodded, but in my heart I doubted that. Then I turned away to follow my conductor: off into the wide blue yonder.

Only it was grey, and still bloody raining. The oddest thing about the English, I thought as I climbed the steps into one of Eagle's shagged-out old DCs, is that despite the weather and our damn awful governments, most of us still choose to live in England. It momentarily brought Bosham to mind again.

It may have looked sky weary on the outside, but the DC-6 was the plushest transport the government had yet provided for me, and because it was a contracted privateer, Eagle Airways had thoughtfully provided in-flight refreshments – excluding alcohol – and a couple of pretty stewardesses. There was a smattering of banter, but it was quickly blanketed by the two NCOs conducting the draft to the land of sunshine.

One of the pilots walked through the cabin before we moved out onto the taxiway. He had the word *Pilot* on the front of his cap, in place of a house badge or crest. I wasn't so sure of flying with an outfit that needed to give its people hat badges so they knew what job to do. What if he'd picked up the wrong cap?

I was the only civvy on the flight, and was given a row to myself at the back – I felt good about that. I don't know if you've noticed, but in most news photographs of air smashes, the few recognizable parts of what was once an aircraft tend to be the rear fuselage and the tail. About half an hour into the flight a young woman in an Eagle Airways uniform slid into the seat alongside me, crossed her legs with a whisper of nylon that gave me goose pimples, and lit a Rothmans. She exhaled its fine blue smoke, and said, 'Hello, Charlie. I love these troop flights – we're not leaping up and down after the pax all the time, and the company doesn't mind if we sit down, and get to know the boys.'

Alison. When I had last seen her in 1947 she had been sixteen, and I had been all of about twenty-three, I think. She had been the daughter of my landlady, on a chicken farm just outside Cheltenham. I had danced with her once at a jazz club down by the river, and my last clear memory of her was leaning against my bedroom door frame in a Jane Russell pose, asking me to marry her. When I'd laughed and turned her down, she had told me, *You don't know what you're missing.*

I said, 'Alison.'

'Yes. Good memory.'

'I do now.'

She screwed up her nose a little as her brain processed my words and couldn't work out where they fitted. 'Do what?'

'Know what I was missing. You were right, and I was wrong – I should have married you.' I thought I'd surrender completely: 'You look like a film star, simply wonderful.' She laughed. It was a nice gurgling sound. A couple of the squaddies turned to look back at us. I hoped that they were jealous.

'You remember that? I'm embarrassed. What must you have thought?'

'I'm embarrassed *now* – I must have been blind as well as stupid. I thought you were going to go to university to shame the lot of us?'

'I did. I did that for Mum – she didn't want me to end up on the farm. The week after I graduated I signed up for the BOAC trainee scheme. I'd wanted to be an air hostess for ages. What about you?'

'Was I just about to be demobbed to join a private outfit as a radio operator?'

'Yes. I was jealous.'

'I'm still with the same people, but I became their route manager at Lympne, and now by some fluke I've been asked to be a director. I still haven't got a clue what that means, but it will pay well.'

'Maybe I'll phone you up one day, and ask for a job.' She leaned over to stub out her cigarette, and gave me a peck on the cheek. Wide mouth. Soft lips. 'That's my first break. I'll have to give the others a hand now. I'll come back later.' As she moved I caught a discreet whiff of her perfume, and for a moment a picture of flowers all the colours of the rainbow exploded in my head. I leaned out to watch her walk away from me, along the narrow gangway between the seats, and for a microsecond saw her as she might be naked: I'd never really thought of her that way previously. Men do that sort of thing, and women never stop complaining about it. One of the squaddies also followed her with his eyes, then looked back at me and gave me the thumbs-up. I probably grinned back at him.

I went back to Cyprus for a late holiday a few years back. It was a reward for growing up. The sun was shining, and on the Greek side the houses gleamed white or faded pink under new coats of wash. A UN truck with a couple of bored-looking French Legionnaires on loan patrolled the Green Line keeping the Greeks and the Turks apart.

To outsiders like me the Greeks and the Turks appear to be two sides of the same coin, and I like both races a lot. I just can't understand why they have to keep on inventing new reasons to kill each other. The Israelis and the Arabs are the same, I suppose – more similarities than differences. The problem with the lot of them is that the radicals can't let go of the characteristics which make them radical: maybe they would have no purpose to their lives without the hate.

Anyway, when I had last returned it was like any old holiday island in the Med, apart from the swirling knots of drunken squaddies who took over the bars after midnight.

It wasn't like that when we slid down the runway in 1956. The first thing I saw out of the aircraft window as we taxied in was a recently burned-out airframe. Smoke was still rising from it: I wondered which poor sod had had the job of putting the fire out. Still, it was nice to know I'd had some practice: welcome to Cyprus, Charlie. The second thing I saw was a lioness lying in the scrubby grass alongside the runway, as we taxied past her. She looked like the Sphinx. I'm sure we made eye contact, but she didn't budge. I had seen a lioness several times in Egypt, but the doctors told me she wasn't really there: something to do with stress and alcohol. It was good to know she was back.

There was only one woman passenger on the flight. A starchy-looking army lieutenant. She gave me three looks while we were standing on the tarmac waiting for our bags to be sorted out. I counted them. The third time she smiled. It was an *I know you're there and stay out of my way* smile. She was my sort of size, and had severely cut fine blonde hair. Wide eyes; deep forehead; wide mouth. The distance between us meant that I couldn't read her flashes. She had the look of someone who was going places and didn't mind who she knocked over on the way.

Alison must have seen where my attention was. She stalked over and said, 'I wondered when you would notice her. She asked me to point out a passenger to her.'

'Which one?'

'This one,' and she poked me in the chest. 'Charles Bassett RAF (retired). I've never thought of you as a *Charles* before, or retired – makes you sound stuffy.'

'What is she?'

'A military policeman – are you in trouble already?'

'Not as far as I know. Name?'

'It says Ann Thirdlow on the passenger manifest, but you can't trust the MPs with names. She could be anybody.'

Then I paid attention to Alison. I held both her hands, and looked at her. 'You outgrew me – you grew up to be taller. That's not fair.'

'We have a three-day stopover. Maybe I could take you swimming, and make up for it. Some of the beaches are still safe.'

'That,' I told her, 'I would love.' I didn't tell her that I could only swim six feet before I began to drown. 'But it depends on Her Majesty. I don't know what her minions have planned for me. How do I contact you?'

'Tony's Hotel in Famagusta. I'll be there until Monday – but don't worry, I'll be back again the week after.'

'Is that its real name?'

'No. It has a Turkish word with about three hundred syllables and the odd squeal, but everyone knows it as Tony's. Inside the old walled city – the safest place for Brits is alongside the Turks. The Greeks are scared of them.' She spotted her bag in the heap coming out of the hold, and gave me another peck on the cheek before she went to collect it. I had that *hairs on the back of your neck* feeling, which told me I was being watched. A staff car had come out for Lieutenant Thirdlow, and she had paused before climbing into the front passenger seat, to look my way again. This time she didn't smile. Maybe one a day was all you got. Short rations. I knew immediately that she was one of those people who were unable to laugh at themselves. That was always trouble, wasn't it?

I watched her car disappear towards the watch office, picked up my bag and wandered over to a sandy-coloured bus that would take us to a row of long huts where I reckoned the customs would be lurking. A plump corporal barred my way when I tried to board. He must have been a moonlighting cook: normal soldiers aren't fed enough to get fat.

'Mr Bassett, is it?'

'Yes. That's right.'

'I've been asked to tell you to wait for your transport, sir. It's a little late. There was a pipe bomb on the road – it backed up the traffic.'

'Any idea how long it will be?'

'Any minute now, I should expect, sir.'

He ushered his charges onto the bus, and I watched that disappear as well. I was left alone with an aircraft that the terrorists probably wanted to blow up. I felt lonely there under its wing – which was the only proper shade I could find. The military, of course, runs on military time, which isn't the same as yours and mine. My transport didn't appear for another half-hour, and then I saw an Austin Champ barrelling towards me from the far side of the airfield in a cloud of dust. The driver either spun it sideways with a flourish as he stopped, or had lost it completely on a patch of oil-soaked tarmac and didn't want me to notice. His face and visible hair were dusty, and under his black beret he wore goggles. He pulled them up, and grinned. Patrick Tobin. Pat. Our jack-of-all-trades and black-market king from Egypt three years ago.

'Hello, Pat.'

'Wotcha, Mr Bassett. Sorry I'm late.'

'Bugger off, Pat. I'm not going to work with you lot again.'

'Mr Watson's compliments, sir. You remember the wing

commander?' Yes, I remembered the drink-sodden bastard. Only too well.

The last time I'd worked for Watson he'd fooled me into thinking I'd been called up – recalled to the colours as a reservist. He must have known he couldn't work that trick again, so he'd lured me in as a civvy. I might have guessed. I said, 'Bugger the lot of you!'

'Hop in, sir. I know a nice safe little bar on the way. Time to introduce you to Keo.'

'Keo?'

'K-E-O. The local beer. Smashing stuff and so cheap they're almost giving it away. Much better than that make-believe Stella they served in the Zone.'

Suez was the last time our paths had crossed.

'I passed through Cyprus on the way there in '53,' I told him. 'The Stella I drank here was pretty good if my memory is still OK.'

'Just wait until you've a couple of glasses of Keo inside you, sir – life will look much better then.'

I slung my kitbag into the back, and dropped my old flying jacket on top of it. In for a penny. I asked, 'Where are we going, Pat?'

'Out on the plain, just this side o' Famagusta.'

'And the natives don't like us?' I asked that because a reminder of my time in Egypt was right in front of us – a narrow vertical steel girder rising six feet from the jeep's front fender: high enough to break any wire strung across the roads to decapitate the unwary.

'Some does and some doesn't, but soon we'll have enough troops here to deal with anything the Greeks can chuck at us. Had you heard we was pulling all our people out of Egypt, and the UN is going in?'

'Yes. I always thought the Gyppoes would win eventually.'

'Cyprus is almost full to bursting with squaddies on their way back home already.'

'Then what do they need me for?'

I didn't need to be sensitive to recognize that he ignored my question completely.

We'd reached a side gate at the airport. It was guarded by two Royal Engineers, two Cyprus Police officers, and two other policemen in faded KDs. They were Brits.

'From the Met,' Pat explained. 'They're training the Cypriot police how to be policemen, and how to look after our boys.'

'Isn't that where we went wrong in Suez? We trained their policemen to take over, and they bloody did. They showed us the fucking door.'

He didn't answer that – that was twice. He just gunned the Champ down a narrow road not much better than a dirt track. It ran parallel to the airport chain-link and barbed-wire fence. From time to time we passed the burned-out shells of cars. Two, I noticed, were riddled with bullet holes. I asked him, 'Ours or theirs?'

'Theirs probably. If they're challenged on this road at night, and fail to stop, we make the assumption they are terrorists, sir, let fly at them. Better safe than sorry . . . And to answer your question about why they need you back – I would hazard a guess that you have some sort of special skill, sir.'

'We want you to listen to people, of course, Charlie. Eight hours on, sixteen off. Five-day weeks, but back to back – then four days off. Piece of piss.' *Piece of piss* was Wing Commander Watson's favourite phrase. Whenever he used it anyone who worked for him became very afraid.

'Every time you sit me down in front of a radio, Mr Watson, I end up out on my own somewhere with people shooting at me. It's not fair.'

'And very good you are at it as well. Being shot at is your special skill.'

I had called him *Mr Watson* deliberately to remind myself that I was a civvy. The expression on his face said he hadn't liked it. Three years earlier I would have called him *sir*, or *boss*. He added, 'I forgot that you bellyached all the time.'

'I don't.'

'And argued. You can call me *sir*, by the way – nothing's changed that much.'

'I shan't. I'm a civvy.'

Watson looked up at Pat Tobin who was standing at ease just inside the door. He was wearing a side arm. Why hadn't I noticed that before?

'Toss him in the cooler, Pat. Maybe I'll see him again in the morning.'

I followed Pat out onto the veranda because I knew Watson was joking: he had a dry sense of humour. Five minutes later I was sitting in a small wooden box made from railway sleepers, closed by a stout wooden door with a barred window. I had a bed with two old army blankets, a small saucepan full of tepid water, and a po. That was it. I doubt that hell will be as hot as it was in there. Tobin apologized for locking me up.

I said, 'Then bloody *don't* – you know he's mad. Since when did you start siding with the boss class?'

'Since he gave me my second stripe, sir.'

'You don't have to call me *sir*, either, Pat. I'm a civvy now, and I'm going to stay one.'

'I understand, sir.'

Then he turned the key, and I was alone in the shadow. It was stifling. The last time I'd worked for Watson he'd welcomed me with a glass of Scotch; this time he'd locked me up in a wooden box. He was definitely getting worse. Maybe power had sent him off his head: it happens to most people with authority over you sooner or later. I removed my shirt and trousers, folded them to provide a pillow, and lay on the bed. A narrow band of light from the barred window in the door fell across the cell's dirt floor. I watched a small grey scorpion shimmy across it. I was going to fucking love Cyprus, wasn't I?

Watson's office looked for all the world like an old-fashioned wooden cricket pavilion. It was painted dark green, and was rather smart. To my knowledge it had followed him from Cheltenham and to an RAF camp on the Suez Canal so far. He was like a tortoise: he carried his shell wherever he went. The cell was a comparatively recent addition, I'd guess – hidden around the back of the pavilion, like a dog kennel.

They brought me a plate of Spam and boiled potatoes, and another small saucepan of water at nightfall. By then I'd put my shirt and pants back on, and had wrapped the blankets around me. The potatoes were cold, and the flies in my cell became very excited at the smell of meat. Pat was accompanied by a small aircraftman who looked like Abbott of Abbott and Costello, and also looked a bit of a Greek – dark and swarthy. He leaked a lot, and I watched a drop of sweat from his brow fall on my food. He brought my provisions into the cell on a tin tray, while Pat waited outside. Holding the tray out to me he whispered, 'Don't worry, comrade, we'll see you all right,' and as my hand brushed his, he pushed something into it. A bar of wilting chocolate. He'd probably risked a slap in the chops for passing it to me. *Comrade*. They get everywhere, don't they? I was being welcomed back to the Party.

The next morning Pat let me out, and took me to the wooden hut I was supposed to live in. It had beds for four, but no sign that any were slept in.

'This is one of the civilian blocks,' he told me. 'We used to have four civvy operators, but we lost them. I think that's when Mr Watson thought it was time to get you back, sir.'

'*Charlie*, not sir. I won't talk to you if you can't manage the word *Charlie*.'

'OK, Charlie.' That was better.

'What do you mean you *lost* your civvies?'

'*Lost* them. Just like that. They went out one night and never came back.'

'Bodies?'

'No, nothing. The general opinion is that EOKA got them, but . . .' He looked away from me and out of one of the windows.

'But what . . . ?'

'Between you and me, I think they just decided to jack it in, and pissed off.'

'Seriously?'

'Seriously, sir. The boredom drives you crazy after a while. There's nothing to do out here.'

'I'll remember that, Pat. I suppose that Lord-God-Almighty wants to see me now?'

'No, Charlie. You had your induction interview yesterday, on yer own in the can. Now I've got to show you the ropes.' I glanced around as we left. My kitbag and jacket had been dumped on one bed – I'd be lucky if they hadn't been robbed out – and I noted a half-decent washroom and latrine by the door. There was a hook in the ceiling above each bed for the mosquito net, and one big flat paddled fan revolved slowly with a monotonous click. That noise could get to you. Tobin locked the cabin behind us, and handed me the key. 'Welcome to Camp Careless,' he told me. *Careless* didn't sound like a WD name to me.

'*Careless*?'

'We made that up ourselves – if we get careless we get killed.' It was enough for me: I'm not that brave.

'When can I go home?'

'God knows, Charlie. After *me*, with a bit of luck.' It's one of those phrases that you remember afterwards.

The Nicosia road from Famagusta hit a roundabout with four exits after about ten miles. The dirt road to the south led to our RAF camp, and the dirt road to the north to a couple of large army camps – including the comms HQ block – and the blockhouse they wanted me to work in. Continuing westward took you to Nic. In normal times I could have walked from where I slept to where I was to work in less than fifteen minutes. In normal times no one would have shot at me for doing so. These, everyone I met in the next few weeks assured me, were not normal times. In fact there was a street in Nicosia – Ledra Street – everyone called 'Murder Mile'. If we had stopped going down it, I thought, no Brits would be murdered there . . . then we could have called it something else. I suppose they'd only have started killing us somewhere else though.

We didn't carry straight over towards the camps: we stopped at the roundabout to let a bunch of cyclists past. They were heading towards Famagusta – about ten of them, equal numbers men and women. Most of them were blonds, and their skins were tanned a nice healthy brown. I knew that because they weren't wearing any clothes. My mouth had probably dropped open: it does that when I'm not looking. I said, 'Pat . . . ?'

'That's a Danish UN contingent – must be off duty. They cycle everywhere.'

'In the buff?'

'Frequently. Funny thing is . . .'

'What?'

'EOKA never seems to target them.'

'Maybe we should stop, and take our clothes off.'

Pat didn't take me straight to work: he took me back towards Nicosia and a big base camp called Wayne's Keep. The road appeared almost white and glared back at me in the sun. I'd have to get some shades.

If you go to Wayne's Keep today all you will find is a big cemetery. It's where the British men, women and children murdered in the Cyprus emergencies were buried. There was a cemetery there in my day as well, a base camp, and a military prison. As we were passed in I pointed out to Pat, 'Didn't you introduce me to Egypt by taking me to a British cemetery in Ismailia and marking my card, Pat?'

'I did, as it 'appens, but that's not why you're here. I reckoned you learned that lesson first time round. You're here to see Captain Collins. Captain Collins is a military policeman, and if you're a clever man, Charlie, you'll make him your friend.'

In Egypt Pat had been in the black market up to his pointy ears; he'd even run his own bank. I couldn't see him knocking about with a copper . . . but you never know, do you?

'Why would I want him to be my friend?'

'Because you wouldn't want him to be your enemy – geddit?'

I nodded. I got it.

Captain Collins had a black moustache as big as a broom head. Military policemen seemed to go in for them; it wasn't the first I'd seen. Maybe he was trying to look like a Cypriot. It didn't quite go with his big bald head. He looked like a Potato Man. He waved me to a chair and said, 'Happy birthday, as of yesterday.'

'I beg your pardon?'

'This came for you.' He tossed an envelope across his desk to me. It had been opened. 'I opened it. We censor mail in and out on a random basis. It's a birthday card.' It was from Dieter and Carly. They hadn't my Cyprus address, so they had sent it to the administrative HQ. It was a decent drawing of a DC-6, the front of which had been replaced with a smiling face that looked like me: Dieter's work. I put it back in the envelope for later. I wondered what the boys would say when I told them I'd spent my birthday in a cell. He waved an African fly whisk ineffectually at a dozen flies in orbit just above us.

'Welcome to Cyprus.'

'Thank you. You wished to see me, Captain. My driver brought me here.'

'No, you need to see *me*, as it happens . . . although I admit I was curious – every bit of paper we have on you indicates that you're a pain in the proverbial.'

'I'll try not to be.'

'Gratified. At least you're saying what I wanted to hear. How much do you know about the situation on the ground in Cyprus?'

'Not much. I had a bit of a briefing from a bod at the Foreign Office, but it was all *old boys*, and *old things*. Made it sound like Mandalay in the 1860s. When I was through here three years ago, it was more or less peaceful, and we were using it for a staging post to Suez.'

'We're using it as a staging post *from* Suez this week. The UN has made us abandon the canal, but I suppose you knew that?'

'Yes.'

'So the island is temporarily chock-a-block with squaddies on their way home, and the tensions we already had have ratcheted up ten clicks. The Greek government has claimed that the invasion of Suez was only a feint to justify us trebling the size of the garrison here.'

'Are they wrong?'

'Not wholly, I suspect. I'm sure the powers that be will use the opportunity to keep our numbers out here up to scratch.

More work for my people of course, so I can't say I'm over-joyed.'

I made my mind up then. I rather liked this big bastard, and I suspected that most of his crew liked him as well. I reached him a hand, and said, 'My name's Charlie, and I'm pleased to meet you. I'll try my best to stay out of trouble.' Then I asked, 'What exactly is going on out here, and what do I do to make sure I get home again in one piece?'

'What you do, Charlie, is follow Army rules. You may have been in the RAF – and worked with the Navy and the Funny Folk in the past – but the Army is the only mob which really understands what's what out here.'

'What *is* what?'

He paused before he replied, and made a steeple of his hands.

'The Greek Cypriot has conceived of an unnatural need to be politically reunited with his brother in Greece. He calls the movement for union with Greece *Enosis*. It has a legitimate political wing, and an illegitimate armed terrorist wing, just like the Irish did in the 1920s. Unfortunately, or fortunately – I haven't worked out which – a third of the Cypriots are still Turkish, not Greek . . . and they don't want anything to do with it. We happy Brits sit between the two, guaranteeing the rights of both factions.'

'There must be more to it than that?'

'Of course there is. Cyprus is strategically placed to dominate the eastern Med – that's why we're here. Hence Turkey doesn't want the Greeks to get it, and the Greeks don't want the Turks to get it. We, of course, don't want *anyone* to get it. If Cyprus becomes Greek the first thing that will happen is that we will get booted out, and the Greek government will give the Soviets our bases here . . . the last thing we want. Am I losing you?'

'No, Captain, not so far. Surely America and Israel would have something to say about that?'

'A Third World War, probably. Cup of char?'

A young soldier with dull police flashes on his uniform had arrived with two enormous mugs of tea. I've told you before that the MPs make the best tea in the world. I sipped mine – it was as sweet as girls' kisses. Then I asked him, 'Tell me about the troubles. Who's killing whom most frequently, and in what order?'

'The Greek terrorists are killing us, and then we kill them back. We are killing more of them than they are of us, but sometimes it's touch and go . . . then, they *are* killing our women and children as well.'

'Then why don't you send the civvies home, and reduce the number of targets? This is exactly what happened in Suez when I was out there – haven't we learned anything from that?'

'It so happens that I agree with you – which is why my family is still in Aldershot – but there are several reasons for not evacuating the non-coms, both political and cynical. The government is determined not to press the panic button, and declare what's happening in Cyprus a civil insurrection – although it is. They argue that that would encourage the terrorist, the agitator and the bolshie Hellenic government. It would also bring us under pressure from home to crack down even harder here, and that, in turn, could bring the UN down on our heads again.'

'So we encourage serving soldiers, civil servants and police-men to bring their families out here, and watch them get killed in the streets?'

'Some are, yes, despite our best efforts. Good summing-up of the situation.'

'What a cock-up!'

I looked around the room properly for the first time. It was a long, low, air-conditioned brick-and-concrete box. A soldier outside was washing the wired-glass windows. At the far end, with her back to me, was the woman from my flight, murmuring into a telephone. Collins followed my glance and said, 'Liaison officer between the military and civil police powers. She came in on your flight, didn't she?'

'Yes. I noticed her.' I don't know why, but even with her back to us and maybe forty feet away, I'm sure she knew we were talking about her.

'What can I do to skew the odds in my favour?' I asked him.

'Exactly what I said. Obey the army's rules, and stay alive. From now on never go out without a side arm. You have one?'

'I might have,' I said cautiously.

'In that case it will be a dinky little private piece with the stopping power of a blancmange – am I right?' I nodded. 'Get Tobin to issue you with a proper weapon. A Colt or a Browning, I'll sign the paperwork. And never go out without it, OK?' I nodded again. 'He'll also get you military uniform without flashes. Wear that too.'

'Won't that just invite someone to have a pop at me?'

'If you were a terrorist who would you be most likely to shoot at – an apparently unarmed civilian, who can't fire back, or what could be a British soldier, carrying a gun?'

I took a deep breath. At the other end of the room someone had turned on a radio and tuned it to *Forces Favourites*. Tex Ritter was singing that there was blood on the saddle and blood on the ground, and a great big puddle of blood all around. Just one of God's little messages. I nodded again – slowly – and said, 'OK. I understand.' I took another couple of gulps of the strong tea, and asked, 'Tell me again, who are these people who will be trying to kill me?'

'They call themselves the EOKA organization. The *Ethniki Organosis Kyprion Agoniston*. They are not your usual Brighton

Pier glee club. They believe that it will be necessary to get us out, before turning on the Turks and joining up with Greece. Their preferred method of negotiation is walking up behind Brits in the street and shooting us in the back. How good's your hearing?'

'Not too bad.'

'When you hear a click assume that someone's cocking a gun, and dive for cover. If you hear a shot – even half a mile off – get off the street. Don't expect a Greek to help you if you get into trouble. If you need help and there are no Brits around, find a Turk.'

'How do I know which ones are Turks?'

He smiled at last, and stroked the cat on his upper lip.

'They have much better moustaches.'

There was another half an hour of this sort of advice. The dos and don'ts of Cyprus. How to stay alive in a country where the Brits were at the top of the Hit Parade, and it was nothing to do with music. Some streets were already off limits between 1700 and 0700. That Ledra Street in Nicosia I'd been told about was one of them. In fact whole chunks of Nicosia were closed to British soldiers after dark. It reminded me of Ismailia in 1953 – one half of the population, it seemed, was after your money, and the other half after your blood. I asked him about the outlying areas.

'Cyprus is an exceedingly beautiful island, Charlie – particularly up in the mountains. Very tempting. Some think it was the Land of the Lotus Eaters . . . and the Cypriots claim the goddess Aphrodite as their own. The temperature can be cool, and the cypresses and pines scent the air. Very romantic and peaceful. Unfortunately, the further you get from civilization, the higher the density of terrorist per head of population is . . . and the higher and more isolated the village the less chance you have of walking away from it. The Troodos mountain range, north of here, is desperately full of the opposition: if you wander off the beaten track on your own, no one will want to go and get you back. We're combing it with armed patrols all of the time, and gunfights are a daily occurrence. It can be like the OK Corral up there. Just try to remember that wherever you are on this damned island, there will be someone watching you who wants you dead.' He must have seen the wry smile on my face, because he asked, 'What?'

'I was in Lancasters in the war. Night after night over Germany with people trying to kill me. I was just thinking . . . *nothing changes.*'

He gave me his grin again.

'You're right. I believe the French have a phrase for it.'

'Bugger the French. Haven't they run away from Suez even quicker than we have?'

'No, they were just slower at getting in, that's all. I believe it was their lunchtime.'

I asked him a question that had been on my mind for a couple of days. It was just one of those boxes I had to tick.

'I don't suppose there are any lions loose on Cyprus, are there?'

He was already looking for his papers; I had been dismissed.

'No, I don't suppose there are. Why?' But he wasn't interested in my reply, so I didn't give him one.

Pat took me to an equipment warehouse, and I came away with light KDs. Shirts, a jacket, shorts and regulation-length trousers. And a decent pair of lightweight boots. Don't forget that bloody webbing belt which always dug into your guts, and a webbing holster. They refused to give me a cap, but that was all right – I still had my old faded RAF cap pushed down at the bottom of my kitbag. I looked up at myself in a mirror and grinned.

Then I realized that I'd been wrong about something all my

DAVID FIDDIMORE

life – I'd always said that Mrs Bassett hadn't had any stupid sons. I was wrong. One was grinning right back at me, and looking curiously pleased with himself back in a semblance of uniform again. What had I asked Collins half an hour before? *Haven't we learned anything?* Pat was grinning as well. I snarled, 'What's so funny?'

'You are, Charlie. Look at yersel' again. Pleased as punch to be back in the colours.'

'I must be mad.'

'We all are. Ain't you worked that out yet?'

'Collins wants me to carry a gun.'

'I'll sort that out when we get back. Colt or Browning?'

'How the hell would I know?'

'Colt then. Easier to strip and clean, and it jams less.'

'I want one that won't jam at all.'

'Bow and arrow then. Quit worrying – it'll all work out in the end. It always does.'

I had this thing about having the last word when I was in my thirties.

'That's what worries me.'

He took me back along the Nicosia–Famagusta Road. My head was dancing on my neck like nobody's business. There was a terrorist behind every white-painted cottage, olive grove or goat pen. I remember a small boy in ragged clothes slowing us down with a flock of scabby goats he'd spread across the road. Pat reached for his waist, and unclipped the cover on his pistol holster as we slowed, but the boy gave us a cheeky grin and played a tune on his home-made flute as the animals parted. Relieved, I smiled back.

'I know that tune,' I told Pat. 'I've heard it before, but I don't know where.'

'The Olympics,' he told me. 'It's the Greek national bloody

anthem!' and put his foot down. We only slowed once more, and that was when we saw the cyclists coming back towards us. They cycled slowly in orderly pairs. Two of the men were smoking pipes, and left a trail of aromatic tobacco smoke. I watched a couple of the girls. One waved gaily to me.

'You ever heard of a painter named Picasso?' I asked Tobin.

'Sure. I even got a couple of his small drawings – an investment, see? Probably never be worth nothin'. Why?'

'I met him once. I thought about him just then. I think he'd understand what was going on here. This whole island has gone mad – it's a living example of surrealism.'

'We all are. Fancy a Keo in a safe bar in Famagusta? Too late for you to go to work today.'

Later he took me to the armoury, and had me fixed up with a .45. It hung on my belt like a diver's lead weights: wearing it, I felt as if my body was inclined permanently to the right. The armourer would only issue me with twenty-five rounds, but Pat gave me another couple of boxes from a locker he had in the motor pool, 'Just to be on the safe side.' As he turned them over to me he said, 'Silly to ask, I know . . . but I suppose you do know how to use that thing?'

'I had a short course at Lydd a few years ago.' I wasn't about to tell him that *short* meant less than an hour.

'I'll take you over the range tomorrow evening. You can put some time in. You never know when it'll come in useful.' Sometimes you have to wonder where the human race is going: we shouldn't be living in a world where pistol practice is considered *useful*.

I felt more or less secure inside the wire. Walking back to my billet I came across Watson marching his gawky march in the opposite direction. He stopped and smiled.

'Afternoon, Charlie. Sleep well, did you?'

'You know I didn't, sir. I was in your bloody cell all night.'

His cheeks and nose were red. If it wasn't sunburn he was back on the juice. He said, 'Worked though, didn't it, old son?'

'What do you mean?'

'You just called me *sir*, and didn't even notice it. You're a quick learner, Charlie – always knew you were.' He had an old leather-covered swagger stick which he touched to his cap peak before he moved on. 'Bye for now.'

And he was off again: *just li' that*, as the great man would have said. I hated the bastard, but I just couldn't seem to get away from him.

We had to drive up to the army den for supper – it was the closest I'd come yet to my working office. Spam fritters and chips: I still look on that sort of thing as *men's food*. Lashings of good old HP sauce. That's one company and brand they can't sell off to Johnny Foreigner, can they? We wouldn't stand for Houses of Parliament brand brown sauce being made abroad, and imported.

'Spam again?' I asked Pat.

'Every meal. Get used to it, Charlie, you're gonna eat Spam in every guise God can think of, and then some more.'

'Spaghetti Spamalese?'

'Thursdays.'

'Is there anything that's good about this goddamned island?'

'It's very cheap. The only thing to spend your money on is beer – and that's very cheap. You'll get by on a fiver a week and still save money while you're 'ere.'

'Girls?'

He shook his head. 'Probably not. The nice ones are gen'rally spoken for.'

I pushed my plate away, leaving half a fritter for the cook's dog.

'Your Captain Collins told me about these EOKA people
. . . *Ethniki* something . . .'

'Yeah.'

'What do the words mean?'

'National Organization of Cypriot Fighters . . . although they
don't do all that much fighting. Their idea of fighting is stabbing
British women while they're out for the Saturday shop.'

'He told me that. How many terrorists are there?'

'Someone told me about eight hundred and fifty – maybe a
thousand.'

'And us?'

'I never thought about it.' So he took a thoughtful swig of
his beer. 'Ten thousand at least. Maybe twenty.'

'So EOKA's way of fighting us has a certain logic.'

'Christ, Charlie – you only been here a day! You going native
already?'

'No, Pat. I just want to know what I'm up against, that's all.
This feels like Suez all over again, doesn't it?'

He looked across the canteen. The thousand-mile stare that
goes back years.

'I liked Suez, you know that? Plenty of opportunity. A lotta
grift goin' on. The coppers have got this place sewn up tight –
I have to be careful.'

'Do you still run your own bank?'

'Nah, I sold it to David Yassine – remember him?' I nodded.
'The Wogs bought him out: made it legit. They call it the
Ismailia Banking Group these days, an' all their government
ministers go there for preferential rates. I was pleased when
I heard that – he'd never become a proper banker. It was
bound to end in tears.' I smiled. I had good memories of
Yassine, and his club – the Blue Kettle – and his dancing girls.
I hid there once, dressed up as a woman, to avoid the MPs, but
that's another story.

'Am I going to work tomorrow, Pat?'

'Yeah. I'll pick you up at your hut at 0700, OK?' I nodded again. 'Breakfast, then you goes on duty at 0800.'

'OK. Look, I met an old pal on the plane over, and agreed to look them up in their hotel in Famagusta.'

'Tony's place?'

'That's what they said.'

'You like nice surprises, Charlie?'

'Sometimes.'

'We'll take a run in after five, when we've finished. Should be OK.'

Chapter Nine

Spontaneous Reproduction

Don't even bloody ask.

Fried Spam, but at least they made their own bread and fried it, and the army was always pretty damned good at training bakers. In the middle of breakfast there was a pistol shot inside the canteen, and we all hit the floor. Some silly bastard had swaggered in with his gun still around his waist: not only that, he'd left the safety on the pistol *off*, and had then clouted it with the chair back as he turned to argue with a neighbour. The bullet went through his thigh and calf without touching a bone. It took ten minutes to restore order, and another five to find a medic.

'I love the smell of gun smoke,' Pat told me.

'Even at breakfast?'

'Particularly at breakfast. At least the silly bastards aren't shooting at each other yet – that happened last month.'

I'd said it before: I was going to *love* Cyprus, wasn't I?

As Pat dropped me off he asked, 'This *them* you're gonna meet at Tony's: a he or a she?'

'Just a *them*, Pat.'

'Girl then. Hope she's pretty. See you later, alligator.'

*

In the 1950s the British military had a thing about building large square buildings with very small windows. These evolved into even larger square buildings with no windows at all. Then someone cottoned on to the idea that if you were in a building that had no windows you might as well bury it beneath the ground. The excuse they gave at the time was to make them impervious to nuclear attack, but it was really just an inability to deviate from an evolving design pathway: another way of saying *lack of imagination*.

They hadn't buried all of the communications block. Yet. Maybe they should have done. It was the ugliest thing I'd seen in years: windowless reinforced concrete, with a skin of local brick – a sort of architecture to make your average dead pharaoh feel at home.

What I hadn't expected once I was through the blast-proof door, and past the small security and admin office on one side – and the aerial room on the other – was that I would emerge into a single open space. A blessedly *cool* air-conditioned open space. No clicking fans. The area was broken up into smaller open rooms around the wall, like chapels in a cathedral. Each had a couple of radios, and one or two operators. A couple of the operators waved to me. I waved back. No harm in being friendly.

The young man who let me in and conducted my initiation was an untidy-looking Signals lieutenant with a spotty face, and an engaging grin. Handshake.

'Andrew de Whitt. Andy.'

'Charlie Bassett.'

'We were expecting you yesterday, weren't we, lads?'

There was a series of grunts – not all of them enthusiastic, I thought. As we walked into the centre of the space he continued, 'The room's broken up into churches and chapels.' At least I'd got that right from the word go. 'And each chapel is a listening post, manned by one, two or three bodies depending on the level of traffic.'

'Who's listening to whom, Andy – and where do you want me to sit?'

'I'll come to that. The two guys here are monitoring the Communist Bloc – we call them the Russian Orthodoxies. Those three over there are doing the Israelis . . . their spot is known as the synagogue, and the guy in the small cell has the Greeks . . . and Makarios and Grivas. To his right Tom, Dick and Harry over there have all the Arab states except one. The big empty space is for eavesdropping on our allies – some goons come in from time to time, but we don't know who they work for, and they never speak to us anyway.' That left one small cell containing what looked like two new RX 108s. It was backed onto the aerial room.

'Tom, Dick and Harry?'

'Sheer coincidence, but I placed them together myself – couldn't resist it.'

'And you said they listen to all the Arab countries except one?'

'Yes. Saudi Arabia – that's where you come in, Charlie. The Saudis have bang up-to-date comms, and they're leading us a merry dance. We asked HQ to come up with more experienced operators who could chase their signal, and not lose it. You're the latest.'

'I haven't met any others yet.'

It was the first time he hadn't met my eye.

'I know. Some went for a walk, and didn't come back . . . and your immediate predecessor shot himself.' He had seen me check my weapon at the door. 'I'm surprised they let you have a gun.'

At least he hadn't ducked the issue.

'What happened to the ones who didn't come back?'

'Probably EOKA – they were a sloppy bunch – but there's a rumour they stole a fishing boat, and got clear across to Turkey in it. Can I check you out on your sets? It's going to be a busy morning.'

I will be honest, and tell you that I've had more demanding jobs than that. I had a comfortable chair, as much iced water as I could drink, and sat in an air-conditioned room, whilst the PBI outside were sweating their bollocks off in the sun, chasing teenaged terrorists around the island. At midday an orderly brought round lunches for us.

Prince or King – I wasn't sure which – Ibn Saud had three radio stations, and we listened into every bloody word. Not many people know that. The call sign for his Jedda office was HZJ, Riyadh HZN, and the tricky one, which is why I was there, was on his personal train which criss-crossed the country like a taxi driver on double time – HZAC. It was the one they were having particular difficulty keeping up with.

In the RAF in 1944 I monitored individual aircraft that could move at 250 knots, and change height and elevation at the same time. If I couldn't hang on to a signal from a bloody train it was time I got out the pipe and slippers. But the train was also why they'd stuck me next to the aerial room. The aerial array for our radios was in a big guarded aerial field out on the plain miles away, and the knack was, as soon as the Saudi signals began to fade or break up, to nip next door to the aerial room – which looked like a sophisticated telephone switchboard – and get the operators to switch my sets from aerial to aerial until I had him again. Cat-and-mouse stuff. His people were very good, but from my memory the Jerry night-fighter operators were better. At the end of the shift I was tired and stiff; good chair or no good chair. As I stretched, yawned and handed my first record flimsies to de Whitt I asked him, 'Where are they read?'

'Downstairs, I think – maybe some are sent through to the intelligence team at Wayne's Keep. Ours not to reason why. You can't decode them, I suppose? Sight-read them, or something freakish like that?'

'Of course not. Gobbledegook. They'll eventually break it down to strategic Arabic. I don't even know which are the coughs, and which are the spits. Why?'

'If you could, I'd probably have to lock you up at night.' He was grinning, but I think he meant it. One of the spots on his face had come to a livid yellow head during the day, and was ready to erupt. It hypnotized me.

Pat was waiting for me outside. I told him, 'Little Lord Fauntleroy in there mentioned something about "downstairs".'

'HQ Comms. Twice the size of your place. Two floors down an' cut into solid rock round the back. People like you and me don't get invited.' Maybe that was where the obsession with burying offices began. 'OK, was it?' he demanded. 'The boss is bound to ask me.'

'Fine. No problems so far. Why doesn't he ask me himself?'

'I don't think 'e wants to see you – not in a literal sense, that is.'

'Has he come over all enigmatic again?'

' 'E has a new secretary bird, an' the guys in the car pool think he's trying to impress her by keeping his distance from the rest of us.'

'I suppose it will get him off our backs. I'm thirsty, Pat, so get a bloody move on if you don't mind.'

Pat sniffed, and said, 'You're beginning to sound like a bleedin' officer again. It didn't take long, did it?' Maybe he was right.

Ten minutes later, when we were halfway to Famagusta he asked me, 'Lunch?'

'Spam sandwiches, lashings of mustard. NAAFI tea.'

'Told you.'

Famagusta is an old walled city – so's Nicosia come to that.
That's two of the things the army doesn't tell you about Cyprus.
You drive through the usual suburban sprawl until you come up
against enormous walls and defensive gateways. It's as if the
crusaders or the Templars are still only a breath away. I looked
up at the walls and expected to see a soldier in steel armour on
top. Once the Champ was through the gateway we plunged
into a medieval city, but Pat seemed to know where he was
going. From time to time a local would raise a hand to him,
and give a quick smile of recognition. I guessed that we were
moving inside Pat's personal fiefdom.

And another thing, Collins had been right: the men had a
much better class of moustache. If my face had still done hair –
and it never did once it had been burned in that air crash – I
would have grown one myself. Tobin threaded us down a
narrow old lane, and made a sharp right turn into a walled,
flagged courtyard which fronted a big old residentia. The sign
on the wall outside was a Turkish word about four feet long,
but someone had painted the word 'Tony's' untidily in black
paint across the end of it.

Steep, wide stone steps climbed to a porticoed door large
enough to have occasioned envy in Whitehall. The man who
stood at the top of them was grossly overweight, and wore a
gleaming white dishdash and a red fez. He was smiling a smile
which cut his face in half, and holding his arms open; Pat was
grinning like a dervish.

When I reached the top of the steps I was hugged. I hate
being hugged, but it's something that happens all the time when
you are as small as me.

He said, 'Charlie.'

And I said, 'David. Pat told me you'd become a banker.'

David Yassine.

'Only when I was in Egypt.' In Beirut, where he had been born, he was a club owner, with premises along the Corniche. He had a spice business in Istanbul, and in Germany . . . well, he was my partner in the Leihhaus, and the Klapperschlange club with Bozey, but I've said it before – that's another story.

'You are well then?'

'Very. I have two more children, both boys.'

'Is this your place?'

'Of course.'

'What about that dancing girl I liked? Mariam?'

'Pouff! She married a German weightlifter, and went to America. Hollywood. Los Angeles. She wants to be in the pictures. I hope she ends up sweeping floors in a brothel.' But he was smiling, and I knew he had a soft spot for her. Mariam had had some nice soft spots if I came to think about it. 'Come in, Charlie. Come in. I need someone to manage this place when I am away – maybe I sell you a share.'

'Who's Tony?'

'I am. Me. Anthony. My middle name is for the saint. Didn't I tell you?'

'No.'

'We can always call it Charlie's Place.'

Yassine did business at breakneck speed, as if his world was going to end tomorrow. It never failed to seduce me.

An hour later I remembered why we were there. Sitting in a private walled garden, beneath a fig tree, with three empty beer bottles in front of each of us I told him, 'I came here to meet a woman. An air stewardess with Eagle.'

Yassine's face always telegraphed his emotions. He suddenly looked as if his favourite wife had died in childbirth. Desolation invaded him.

'Alas, she has gone. They checked out this morning.' Then he smiled. 'But she left you this.'

He had picked up an envelope as we passed the reception desk, and had been fingering it ever since. I didn't mind his sweat marks: he had once given me a name and address that had saved my life. Inside the envelope was a cheap postcard of the ruins at Salamis. I turned it over. The card bore my name, and the imprint of a pair of lips. Nothing else. When I bent over it I could just smell the lipstick. It smelt its colour – a deep pastel pink. That was interesting: I had received a similar card when I had been in Egypt three years earlier, but had never identified the correspondent. I still had it, and would compare them when I got home.

I pulled a sad face, and showed the card to Yassine and Pat. David leaned across the small table between us, and placed his hand over mine. 'She trusted me with a message for you. Verbal. Do you wish to hear it?'

Pat rolled his eyes to the sky, but I said, 'Yes, please.'

'She wants me to tell you that she never makes the same mistake twice, and she thinks that you shouldn't either. Do you know what she means?'

'I think so, David,'

'Good. She will be back in a week, maybe less. You will be a little more familiar with our beautiful island by then.' Then he switched tracks on us. 'Will you be staying tonight? I have a fine cook, and new girls.'

Yassine left us to talk and drink as the food was being prepared. It became cooler in the garden, even a little chill. I asked Pat, 'Why didn't you tell me that Yassine was in town?'

'I didn't want to worry you.'

I left it for a minute, and finished another beer before I told him, 'The next time I get a business enterprise going I think I'll offer you part of it.'

'Why, Charlie?'

'I like your style. I like the way you anticipate me.'

He smiled, and shook his head.

'Thank you, Charlie, and when the time comes I'll think about it . . . but don't be offended if I turn you down. I might have bigger plans.'

Soon after that we went in and joined Yassine at the bar. There were two belly dancers. David always knew where to get the best dancers.

It was three days before Watson had me in. His little mind games didn't bother me because, in truth, he had rather a little mind . . . it was like playing chess with an ungifted child. He telegraphed his moves miles ahead, but the trouble was that he always had the big battalions on his side, so he usually won.

'Settling in, Charles?' *Charles*?

'Yes, sir. No problem, sir.'

'Sit down.'

'Yessir. At attention or at ease, sir?'

'Stop being a prat, Charlie.'

'Then don't treat me like one, sir.'

'Are you going to tag *sir* onto every damned thing you say?'

'It's what you wanted, sir. If I don't, you'll sling me in the cooler again, sir.'

'Then damned well stop it. It's unnatural – coming from you, that is.'

'That's what I think too.'

I pulled out a chair, and slouched opposite him across the desk. I knew that would get to him. He had two small piles of message flimsies in front of him. I was reminded of my interviews in the FO, and sensed a rocket coming on. He asked me, 'You know what these are, but do you know why they're sitting on my desk?'

'Spontaneous reproduction? I have no way of knowing.'

'Why are you always a smart-arse when I am preparing to be nice to you? You always have to spoil it.'

'I know. Bad breeding. Sorry, what *are* they for?'

'To show you, that's what. The big heap on the left is your intercepts for the last three days. The small one, on the right, is what your predecessors, between them, achieved in three weeks. Every time the Saudis flipped the signal they lost it and peed their shorts. You didn't – you followed them, and picked them up again. For all the radio users out there, you are, in some ways, a very worrying little man. Her Majesty will be very pleased you're on our side.'

'I still don't see your point . . .' I sulked.

'The point is, Charlie, that whenever you bellyache and ask me what you're doing out here, I'm going to wave these two piles of sheets under your nose, and tell you that you're doing rather well, and that the Boss Class is very pleased with you.'

'I got away from you in order to get away from the Boss Class. I hate it.'

'I know. That's why I'm really enjoying having you back under my command.'

'You're a sadist.'

'Stop moaning, and get us a couple of drinks from the cupboard. I'm sure you remember which one.'

There was an unlabelled quart bottle of greasy-looking clear stuff in his drinks cupboard. He had me pour two half-tumblers' full, and had me sip one. It was like paint stripper; I probably pulled a face. Then he topped up each glass with cold water, and the mixed fluids went cloudy. I tried it again, and fell in love. Liquid aniseed balls. Probably the most refreshing pick-me-up I'd ever come across.

'Ouzo,' he told me. 'Greek stuff. Bloody marvellous, isn't it? We'll have to sort out this bloody island without getting rid of all the Greeks – it would be a tragedy if I lost my source of this.'

I had to get him back on track. He hadn't called me in to say *thank you*, and give me a drink.

'What else did you have in mind for me, boss? There's always a something else, and your last one almost killed me.'

'Nothin' much.' He sniffed, and squinted at me through his drink. 'I don't know why you're bothered. Remember the Canal Zone? Piece of piss.'

Of course I remembered the bleeding Canal Zone. As well as getting shot on an unscheduled trip to Turkey, I had nearly been killed by a yellow fever jab in Port Said, and stalked by a lion . . . and he'd sent me on several desert patrols with the Brown Jobs, earwigging radio traffic from both the Israelis and the Egyptians. It had been uncomfortable and dangerous. Not at all like being in the Boy Scouts. And I didn't even get a proficiency badge for it.

'Yes.' A cautious *yes*. 'Of course.' A cautious *of course*.

'How about some of the same? A bit of this and a bit of that?'

'With the Brown Jobs?'

'Yes, if they ask.'

'Do they ask?'

'Sometimes. In your case they're bound to – word has already got about.'

'What kind of word?'

'They're saying we have a wizard W/Op on the books. *Wizard W/Op* – that's not bad. Is it?'

'Do you really expect me to go chasing all over the island with the army, listening in for something that helps them deal with their terrorists?'

After a long pause he said, 'Not often, and not officially . . . but yes.' Bollocks. 'Anything else on your mind?'

'I heard you had a new girl. I rather liked the old one, but we'll let that pass – what's the new one like?'

He looked over my shoulder at the door in his shed which concealed his assistant's office. It was ajar. I'd always suspected that it was where the real work was done. Watson called out, 'I know that you're listening, cow. Come out and meet Charlie. He wants to see you,' and an Amazon walked into the room.

Pat blagged his way past the lieutenant at lunchtime, and flopped into the seat alongside me. I held up my hand to silence him because I was into a signal from Riyadh, and didn't want to miss a digit. They signed off about three minutes later.

By the way the sending speed went up I guessed they'd switched from doing strategic positions in the Middle East, to running a book on the *Miss World* contest. A tall blonde Swede was odds on to win.

I'd met guys like Pat before. I'd met Pat before, come to that, but he had reinvented himself since then, and had come out with more influence – what they call *wasta* in the Arab-speaking countries. He was still only a corporal, but a corporal who seemed to be able to go anywhere, and no one actually knew what he did, except run the motor pool. He almost certainly didn't have the clearance for the radio room, but no one was going to challenge him; probably half the guys around me owed him money. I wondered how much de Whitt was into him for – he looked suddenly nervous when Pat strolled in.

I was dry. I got us both a half-pint of water from the cooler, and when I sat down asked him, 'Why didn't you warn me about Watson's new monster?'

'I wanted to surprise you. Neat, ain't she?'

'Neat? She looks as if Aveling Barford thought her up during a slack period.' I was being cruel again. Aveling Barford was a company which made road rollers and caterpillar tractors – like Blaw-Knox or Massey Ferguson.

'I think she's kinda neat. Gonna take her out at the weekend.'

'Don't go near the zoo – they'll never let her out again.'

'There used to be a zoo,' he said wistfully, 'but all the animals were Greek, so I think the Turks let them out and shot them.'

'Where will you take her?'

'A few places in Famagusta still safe, if you know whose palm to grease – then back to my place and knickers off.'

'You got to be joking!'

'I told you, I think she's kinda neat. I called her Tarzan the first time I met her, an' she smiled. I knew she liked me for not duckin' the issue.'

'She smiled at me too. I think she thought I was a snack.' But I was interested in spite of myself. 'You said *my place*. Where *do* you billet, Pat?'

'I got a room to myself in the motor pool – used to be the orderly room – but I meant my flat. I got a nice flat in Famagusta, round the corner from Tony's place.'

I reminded myself to remember that.

'What did you want, anyway? Carrying another message from our master?'

'Nothin' like that. Jest wanted half an hour under the AC, and a glass of cool water. You got it easy in here.'

'And?'

'I was thinking of going over to Yassine's place again tonight. Wanna come?'

'Yes, please. When?'

'Stay put an' I'll pick you up.'

As he got up to leave I asked him a question that had been hovering since he'd shown up.

'Is there anyone out here who doesn't owe you money?'

He gave me his sunny smile.

'You, Charlie, but I'm working on it.'

Halfway through the evening David Yassine put a large plate of stuffed vine leaves on the table. It wasn't the first time I'd come across the dish, but I've always loved it. I can take you to a small seafront café in Kuwait City where they serve it for breakfast with a Lebanese platter: you'll never forget it.

David's dancing girls were never hired for possessing the Middle Eastern standard dancing figure. They were young, hungry and slim. He picked them for their dancing ability, not their rolling figures. Spend an hour watching them at work, and your brain is lost for a fortnight. One of them reminded me of Mariam, and after too many beers and Yassine's best bootleg brandy, that made me feel unbearably sad. OK, so I'm just making an excuse: it was why I woke up in the small hours alongside her. I couldn't remember having had much conversation with her before we went skin diving.

She asked, 'What's your name, sailor?'

'Charlie. What's yours?'

'Stephanie – Steve.' She left my side, went to the window and drew back the blinds. It was still dark outside. I lay on my side, and counted the stars I could see. Eleven. I thought one of them was Sirius: it was low down in the South and very bright. Twinkle, twinkle, little star. Stephanie came back to bed, cuddled in to me, and said, 'Go on. Why don't you ask me?'

'Ask you what?' I bent and kissed her brow. I sensed one of my tender moments coming on; this is where I usually fucked up.

'What's a nice American girl like me doing in a joint like this?'

'No.'

She paused. I had captured her attention. That was interesting. I cupped one of her breasts in my hand and stroked it with the ball of my thumb. That was interesting too.

'What do you mean by *no*, Charlie?'

'No, I'm not going to ask you that. I don't want to know. I'll make up a reason for myself.'

'Such as?'

'Maybe you ran away from a circus.' I already felt like having her again, but couldn't remember having agreed a rate. Sometimes it pays to be direct. 'How much shall I leave you in the morning?'

'As much as you like – it will be my tip. David told me to take care of you, so he'll do the paying. He's a honey, isn't he?' Someone else had used the word *honey* about men recently, but the thought eluded me.

As the sky began to clear we fell to talking again. I asked, 'Can I take you for breakfast somewhere, when we get up?'

'What?' She sounded sleepy; like a diver ascending from a deep dive. I feel like that myself from time to time.

'Is there anywhere safe nearby, where I can take you to breakfast later?'

'Why?'

'Because I'd like to see what you look like in daylight. Nothing special.'

She kept me hanging on a string for at least thirty seconds. I started Humphrey Lyttleton in my head, doing 'Bad Penny Blues'. Then she said, 'OK, Charlie. I'd like that. We gonna grab a couple of hours first?'

I rolled on my back and slid an arm under her neck. It seemed to me that in a very few seconds she was snoring softly. I was probably smiling. I wondered where Tobin was – in a room somewhere near me, or in his flat. I hoped that he was smiling too.

I don't know why it occurred to me then, but I realized that not only did I not owe him any money, but that he had a sizeable amount of mine from three years past. So at least I had some spending money, and didn't have to rely on Watson. That probably made me smile even more. I slept.

When Pat picked me up I was sitting on the steps in the courtyard of Tony's place smoking a pipe. A lot of my best memories are tagged by pipe smoke – you may have noticed that. After I've had a good time I sit down with a pipe, and seal it into my memory. He must have asked me what time I was due on duty, or checked independently, because I only had a half-shift commencing at 1300, and he delivered me on the nose.

As I checked into the office the female policeman who'd been on my flight was leaving. She was munching a Spam sandwich, and gave me a quick guilty look.

'I know,' I said. 'I've been eating Spam for ten years too, and still can't get enough. It's crazy.' She paused, as if undecided whether to reply, then gave me a cheeky little smile.

'It's the salt in it, I think . . . your body just demands it all the time.' Then she was past me and gone. She had a nice low-pitched voice; I wondered who she'd dropped in to see.

De Whitt looked up and grimaced as I flapped my security pass at the goon on the door, and walked into our cool blue world.

'We were looking for you earlier, Charlie. The Orthodoxies got into someone difficult and we thought you could help.'

'Sorry, morning off.'

'Granted, but if you know you're going to be off base it would help if you could let us know. We panic these days when we can't find someone.' What I thought was going to be a bollocking had turned into a hint and a gentle reproof. He had been genuinely worried.

'I was with Pat Tobin,' I told him. 'He was showing me the ropes.'

'Try not to worry us too often. Leave a note on your desk, OK?'

'OK, boss. Sorry.' That time I meant it. I had been away from the action too long, and had forgotten some of the rules. If Watson found out I'd never hear the end of it. A small light started to flash above my booth – it meant that a scheduled listening watch had started: it wouldn't be long before the Ibn Saud express was back on the rails. I smiled at de Whitt, and nodded to the light; it would go off as I switched my sets on. I told him, 'They're playing my tune.'

He nodded. Maybe both of us had learned something.

It was as I tuned the 108s that I remembered Stephanie. I probably grinned again. Then I remembered that Alison bunked at the same hotel between flights. There was no doubt about it: I was going to have some explaining to do. To somebody.

A few days later I sat at a table in David Yassine's shaded garden with Alison. Playing mothers and fathers didn't really suit us. We had his fine coffee in a tall brass pot. Alison played Ma, and poured it into exquisite porcelain cups – as fine as glass. Another stewardess in mufti sat on the raised edge of an ornamental fountain, trailing her fingers in the water. This water baby wore a silky thing like a sari, and the fabric flowed over the contours of her body. Her skin was as pale as milk, and her short hair as black as a shoe brush. A couple of bulbul birds piped musically in the small trees, although at the time I didn't know what they were.

'That's Laika,' Alison told me. 'The men go mad for her. A

179

man at every airport – literally. Blood will be spilt over her one day.'

'*Laika*? What's it mean?'

'Her mother was Russian, so is her name. Ronnie – he's the second pilot – says it would be a good name for a dog as long as it was a female. Only he doesn't use that word.'

'That's rather unkind.'

'Plain people can be rather unkind about beautiful ones – haven't you noticed?' At least she smiled. But there had been a tremor in her voice: something was up.

She looked away, stirred a heaped spoonful of coarse white sugar into her coffee, and had a sip. Then she gave a little secret smile, but I think that was for the coffee, not me. Out of the blue she said, 'I was just turned sixteen when I first saw you, and from that moment I wanted to make love with you. It was the first thing I thought of when I saw your pinched, underfed little face.'

'And I was twenty-three, and not long back from Europe.' Then I lied. 'If it helps, that was what came into my mind too. I wanted your clothes off.'

'You told me there were rules about that sort of thing.'

'There were, when you were sixteen. Now you're old enough to make up your own rules.'

She shook her head and smiled ruefully.

I looked around the garden, taking my time. Anything other than look at the beautiful woman across the table from me. I had a very empty feeling in the pit of my stomach; the sort of feeling you have when a distinct possibility becomes a definite impossibility. Alison had been unfinished business for nine years. Now she was finished business; two ships that just failed to pass in the night . . . and it had made her as sad as me.

I smiled at her, hoping that it didn't look like too much of a death's head grimace.

'I'll look you up again in another nine years. You'll only be thirty-four.'

She pursed her lips. Shook her head. She didn't want to meet my eye either. She never made the same mistake twice, did she? I indicated Laika, and tried to lighten the air of doom that suddenly seemed to have enveloped us.

'Think she's more my type?'

All Alison did was stand up, shake her head again and walk inside. Laika turned on cue and smiled at me, but I was distracted by another woman sliding into Alison's seat whilst it was still warm.

'Hi,' she said. 'My name's Stephanie. You can call me Steve.'

'I had a friend called that, not so long ago.'

'Still have. Did I just miss something?'

'No. I did. Twice, with nine years in between. Would you be surprised to learn I've been very stupid?'

'Why don't you tell old Stevie about it?'

I felt all the tension flowing out of me. Laika was playing with the water again. I said, 'Can I tell you upstairs? I have a pocket full of money, and nothing to do with it except give it to you.'

'David was right.'

She stood again, and stretched. Her jeans and shirt stuck to her like a second skin.

'What about?'

'He said you were my kind.'

'What kind is that?'

'The complicated and uncommonly generous kind.'

By then we were climbing the stairs to her room. Yassine passed us halfway up, gave us a beaming smile and observed, 'This time you pay, OK, Charlie? The other night was just a welcome-back present.'

'Of course, David.'

'Unless you wanna come in with me on the business? Twenny per cent. Then the girls come for free – just like the Blue Kettle?'

'I'll think about it, OK?'

Steve hooked her arm through mine, and whispered, '*Wrong* actually. A girl from America never comes for free.'

I liked the pun, and told her, 'I know. I learned that a couple of months ago. I'll tell you about it one day.'

Chapter Ten

On His Blindness

The next time I woke up in my hut Pete was standing near one of the windows smoking a narrow cheroot. His old pack was on one of the beds, and he looked immaculate, as usual, in a tropical civvy suit.

'I wish you wouldn't do that,' I told him. 'I thought I'd locked the door.'

'You had. I picked it. Can I stay for a couple of days?'

'I don't see why not, if it's OK with the RAF.'

'Is OK. They see me as an *old boy*. You English are big on the *old boy* thing, aren't you?' He hadn't expected an answer.

'What are you doing over here?'

'Some deals. Since the Greeks started to have a go at you half the wide boys in Europe turned up to make their deals here.'

'Why here?'

'Police got their hands full of terrorists, haven't they? No time to bother the rest.'

It made sense. Of a kind. I yawned, and asked him, 'What time is it?'

'Past six. You better get up. There's something going on. Jeeps dashing around.'

*

Pat clattered up the step half an hour later. He and Pete gave each other the eye.

'Pat, Pete,' I told them, and, 'Pete, Pat.'

'We met,' Tobin said. 'About a year ago. I think it was in Dresden.'

'Yes. Nice to see you again.' Pete.

'You gonna be around long?'

'Few days.'

'Maybe we can catch a drink?'

They had been talking as if I wasn't there. All I was wondering was how they had both managed to meet up in the Soviet Zone last year. Pat turned back to me anyway. He said, 'We got a little job on. How long before you can be ready to move?'

'I'm ready now.'

'Good, let's go.'

There was a Land Rover outside the door. Captain Collins was in the passenger seat. The back seats had been modified so that one turned in to face the vehicle within arm's reach of an old 1155/4 aircraft radio rig, which appeared to have had an aircraft compass and a D/F loop bracketed on top. Pat sent me back for my side arm and old flying jacket. He had a sheepskin-lined jerkin that must have once graced a shepherd, and Collins had a duffle coat. Between us we looked like refugees from Popski's Private Army. If you don't know what that was you'd better ask one of the old guys.

From behind the wheel Pat told me, 'It's gonna be chilly when we get high. Get the radio fired up, will ya? We're goin' to need it.'

'We lost an AOP a couple of hours ago,' Collins said. 'It was over the Troodos at first light.'

An AOP was a little Auster Army Observation plane – flown by the Army Air Corps. The RAF tended to be a bit snotty about the AAC, but generally speaking they were fine pilots. The Auster had a high wing, and a single engine in front of the pilot. The pilot and his observer/radio operator had glass all around them, giving them a fine view of the surrounding land, and what was on or in it. The army used them as artillery spotters, and to deliver essentials to patrols out in the field. Old Man Halton had a civilian version of his very own. They also flew around with loudspeakers telling the insurgents not to be such naughty little boys: I don't know who thought that one up. I had nothing against the type yet. Nothing I could put my finger on.

My radios came in quickly. They had their own power source – two big glass accumulator batteries, which looked as if they took a charge from the car's engine. I was curious as to where the compass fitted in. I didn't have to ask. It fitted in as soon as I made a sweep. As the circular aerial above the radios moved round, the compass needle swung with it: a makeshift radio repeating compass.

'Kinda neat, isn't it? Remember your pal Nansen back in Egypt?' Yes, I did. Oliver was an RAF photographer who was killed when a Gloster Meteor went in somewhere over the Sinai Desert. I'd shared a tent with him for a while.

'Yes.'

'He built it. We kept it because the wing commander always knew it would come in handy. We've used it a few times in the last coupla months.'

We were rolling now – out to the roundabout, and turn left: heading for Nicosia. No traffic on the road. One of the good things about the Land Rover was its high windscreen – the Indians were unlikely to catch us with the wire-across-the-road-at-neck-height trick. We had to shout to make ourselves heard by each other. When I asked, 'Tell me what happened to the Auster,' Collins leaned back and shouted.

'Nobody's sure. They were reccying some of the tracks that go in and out of the trees on the mountainsides. The goons move their stores around at last and first light, on the backs of mules. The mules get spooked by the sound of a low-flying aircraft, and sometimes break cover. It tells us which paths are active.'

'So, what happened?'

'They went off the air.'

'Any last messages?'

Collins consulted one of those small policeman's notebooks held shut by a piece of elastic. Then he shouted back at me, 'The observer broke into a routine check-in with, quote, *Christ, they're shooting at us*, unquote.'

'And?'

'The pilot's voice about thirty seconds later: *Stall, stall!*' After that there was nothing . . . just the automatic positioning signal, until the control room lost that too.'

'If the observer knew they were being fired on, it must have been because they were being struck by bullets – it would be too noisy up there to hear small-arms fire from the ground.'

'Worked that out for ourselves, Charlie,' Pat butted in. 'Hang on.'

The road was empty. Miles of dusty tarmac. We hit a chicken outside an isolated farmhouse west beyond the northern out-skirts of Nicosia, and for a moment we drove through a feather storm. The sun was out, and low behind us. The feathers danced in clouds of reds and browns. One settled by the radio. I picked it up before it blew away, and placed it in my pocket. Don't know why: just one of those irrational things. We slowed down when we overtook a small purposeful convoy head and tailed by a couple of Dingo armoured cars sporting Brens, and nervous-looking gunners. There was another Land Rover of MPs, and a one-tonner with a canvas-skinned wagon bed. You could get half a dozen squaddies and their kit in there. Pat slotted us in to head the convoy. I'd driven in convoy in Egypt three years ago, so I knew the form – if it was going to be attacked the enemy always went for the first or last vehicle. I was now in the first, and didn't like it. Bollocks.

We stopped in an olive grove in the foothills of the Troodos mountains an hour and a half later. We had been delayed by a puncture to the other Land Rover, and the need to change its wheel. Stopping in olive groves for a brew-up is something that the British Army has become very good at over the years. The sun was up, and it was getting hot. I left my jacket in the wagon, reflecting that in Britain people were beginning to pay good money for winter holidays in places as warm as this. Maybe Cyprus had a future when we all packed up and fucked off home . . . Billy Butlin could buy it.

I split a tin of cold baked beans with Pat. Collins went into conclave with his military policemen and a lieutenant who had climbed stiffly over the tailboard of the covered lorry. Tobin said, 'Don't let the sun fool you – it's goin' to be bleedin' cold if we have to go up into the bleedin' mountains.'

'I'm familiar with mountains, Pat. Watson sent me into Kurdistan a few years ago, didn't he? It was freezing cold at nights there too. Do you know if the positioner from the aircraft just faded, or was it cut off suddenly?'

'No. Is that important?'

'Could be. Can you find out?' He finished the beans, and threw the can away. We Brits travel around the world leaving our rubbish behind us; no wonder we aren't all that popular. He asked, 'Weren't you shot in Turkey?'

'You know I was.'

'Still hurt?'

187

'Only in the cold.' He could take that how he liked. Sometimes I limped quite badly, but it wasn't something I discussed freely.

We split. Pat wandered over to the back of the lorry, and chatted to the guys inside. He was probably trying to sell them something. He must have drifted past Collins at some point, because the big man pulled me aside before we mounted up and asked, 'Why did you want to know if the signal faded, or was cut short?'

'If it only faded it means they could still be alive – drained batteries. If it was cut off it's more likely that the set was smashed up, and them with it.'

'It faded,' he told me. 'That's why you're here. Don't worry. I'll hurry things along now.' If it faded there was a chance the radio was still pumping out a weakening signal. If they could get me near enough, I might be able to pick it up . . . and if Nansen's compass worked we had a chance of finding them. Not much of one, but one of the good things about the Brown Jobs is that they're the world's last great graspers at straws.

The AOP – or rather, its weary radio – spoke to me a couple of hours later, halfway up a mountain in the Troodos the army called Mount Menelaus on account it was shaped like a king's head; crown and all. The signal was weak – but that was obviously a battery problem, wasn't it? I read the compass bearing off against the strongest signal to Collins as we came to a point where a forest track split. He drew a line on his chart. All I could see was a mixture of pine trees. Some short, with a thick canopy. Some high and lofty, like cypresses or cedars of Lebanon, climbing in lines underneath steep ridges. Even though I was cold and my leg ached from its old bullet wound, the sky was a brilliant blue and the low sun hurt my eyes. I needed sunshades – something to ask Pat about when we got away.

After that, it was my job to hold on to the signal as the track climbed and twisted. The whole thing reminded me of Shangri-La, without beautiful people playing the extras. The air was thinner: I hadn't expected that. Pat was breathing through his nose. Even the vehicles didn't like it, crawling from rise to rise in first. The moment I heard a genuine dip in the signal I shouted, 'Stop. Stop here.'

Pat stopped the Land Rover, and Collins rose in his seat to wave down those following: they were spread out over a couple of hundred yards, and took minutes to get up with us. Collins asked me, 'Here?' He stared around. Like me he could see nothing that had once been an aircraft.

'Near enough, Captain. This is as firm as your signal gets.'

'How far?'

'Can't tell you. Not far. Their batteries are going flat.' He looked at me as if hoping for a suggestion. Didn't get one, and made up his own mind. I could get along with officers like him. He had a dozen men excluding me and Pat, and the gunners on the Dingoes. He left the four of us with the wagon train, and deployed the others in a circle around us – then he had them walk away, into the scrub and the trees. The rock underfoot was grey and crumbly; I reckoned we'd be lucky to get away without a busted ankle or two. We soon lost sight of them, but could hear them from time to time, moving away from us in a widening circle. And the occasional curse as someone went down over a hidden obstacle. Pat pointed out to the captain that he and I could provide another two pairs of eyes, but Collins smiled back, and said, 'No, thank you, lads. You've done what you were brought up here for. Just stay here, and mind your box of tricks for the next time.' He must have seen the doubt in our eyes, because he swung back and added, 'You've done what you're good at, now let us do what *we're* good at – army business.' Then he sat on the lorry's running board, and waited for contact.

It took about twenty minutes, and then a yellow flare popped low into the sky down the slope from where we'd parked up. Collins got to his feet, dropped the cigarette he had been smoking and said, 'Come on,' to me. When Pat made to move he was waved back.

'I know the radios,' I told Pat. 'He'll need me for the diagnosis.'

It took less than ten minutes for Collins to lead me to the wreck. Neither of us bust an ankle. The Auster was tipped up on its nose at the edge of a steeply inclined clearing, making it appear to stand almost upright to the sky – its tail like a signpost to nowhere. There was a strong smell of aviation spirit, but it hadn't burned. The Dingo driver who had found it was just about to light a fag he had dangling in his mouth, when I yelled at him. The Auster's fuel had soaked into the very ground he was standing on. I think I scared him. Collins dragged him away, and delivered a tasty few words out of my earshot. The poor guy, having found what we were all looking for, had expected to be hailed a hero: instead Collins's tirade left him white and shaking. The captain crossed to me again, and we went over to the aircraft to look in through the opened cabin door.

The Auster didn't look too bad except for a dozen bullet holes: two through the engine cowling had done the damage. The observer curled up behind the seats didn't look too bad either. Not bad for a dead man, that is. His head was at a very odd angle to his fuselage, and a small trickle of blood had fallen from one ear, and dried in a thread. Collins sniffed.

'What do you think?'

'Broke his neck in the crash — what a pity. It was a very survivable impact in every other way. After all, the pilot seems to have got away.' I wasn't exactly sure of that: the front windscreen panels had caved in, and some recent dark smears on the cowling could have also been his blood. I was half inclined to think we might find him in the woods some yards ahead. While I was talking I leaned in to switch off the observer's radios. It seemed an oddly religious thing to do — completing his last duty for him. The radio man's final prayer.

Collins had obviously been only half listening to me, because he asked, 'What was that again?'

'I said the pilot might still be around here somewhere . . .'

'Yes. I wonder what happened to the woman.'

Bollocks. What woman? They hadn't told me about her yet.

Then some bastard took a shot at us. The bullet kicked up the ground a yard away. I quickly whipped around the plane, putting it between me and where I presumed the shooter was. Another shot. That flat crack from a British Lee Enfield .303. It hit the airframe somewhere. The rudder swung aimlessly as the aircraft swayed. Then another. At Collins that time, I guessed. He still hadn't moved. I looked around the Auster. The big captain had drawn his .45, and was facing the great tree under which the Dingo driver was crouching. He crooked his left arm up, and balanced the big pistol in its angle, aiming up into the tree's canopy. Bat Masterson or Wyatt Earp. I was impressed that he seemed to have all the time in the world — great gun-fighters do, I'm told. He fired once, and a small man tumbled immediately from the tree, preceded by his rifle.

Unfortunately the Dingo driver had been sheltering underneath, and it hit him. It obviously wasn't his day.

Collins beckoned me out.

'It's OK. I got him. They left someone staking out the plane.'

I followed him across the clearing. Shouts in English closed in on us.

The man who had shot at us wasn't a man. He was a boy, and he was already dead. Collins's bullet had taken him through the chest. It was a small chest, and there were bits missing. A hole big enough to put my fist in. His eyes were open. He looked surprised.

'How old, do you think?' Collins asked me.

'Maybe fourteen.'

'Poor little sod.' Then he sighed, and said, 'They don't give me nightmares any more, you know. They used to.'

Just as the other soldiers filed into the clearing the driver struggled to his feet. They'd done this before: they fanned out, and kept to the edges.

The driver was cradling one arm with his other hand. Collins seemed to notice that immediately.

'What happened to you?'

'Rifle fell on me, sir. Don't think it's broken, sir.'

Collins sighed again. He was good at it. Then he used his *big* voice.

'You just stood in a puddle of petrol, and fired off a flare; then you tried to light a fag in the same place. Then you stood under a tree with a terrorist in it, who, for his own reasons, chose to shoot at me instead of you. Finally he drops a rifle on you, and still you get away with it. You know what you are, don't you, son?'

A few knowing faces of the other squaddies were wearing smirks by now. The driver looked properly crestfallen, and went for it.

'A bleeding idiot, sir?'

'That too . . . but *no*, son. What you are is bloody *lucky*, and I like having lucky men around me. Consider asking for a temporary transfer to my troop when we get back.'

'Seriously, sir?'

'Very seriously. I could use a lucky driver.'

'Yessir.'

'What were you saying before we were interrupted, Mr Collins?' I asked.

'Something about wondering where the bint had got to. The girl.'

'Which girl? I think I missed something.'

'The one they were giving a ride to – the observer's girlfriend. I think they were trying to impress her.'

I considered my options. I didn't have any.

'We're stuck up here for a bit then, aren't we?'

'I'm afraid we are. Better make the best of it.'

'Any idea how long for?'

'Until they organize a couple of patrols. The rest of the day at least, OK?'

'It has to be, doesn't it?'

What I was thinking was, *I hope this isn't the day that the Saudis invade a friendly neighbour without me.* When I ran that scene in my head I decided it was very unlikely: I'd heard nothing but good of them before I arrived in Cyprus.

We pulled back to the vehicles – Collins had them reversed under the cover of the trees – taking the two bodies with us. They were laid side by side in the bed of the lorry, and covered by ground sheets. I shared a cigarette with the young lieutenant, and asked him, 'Is it always like this?'

'Not all of the time. Periods of absolute normality, sometimes for weeks at a time. Then all hell breaks loose for a couple of days. It's an odd way to live.'

'I was in bombers during the war. It could be the same – bombing Dresden one night, and dining at the Troc the next. Sometimes it was like dreaming.'

'Working out which is the dream, and which isn't. That's the way to get through it. I'm Warboys, by the way, Tony.' The same as Yassine's hotel, and why had I thought of Dresden, not the twenty other places in Germany I'd flown over by night? Bloody Pete, of course.

'I'm Charlie Bassett.'

'I know. You're supposed to be hot stuff with a radio.' I let that pass. We all have reputations we didn't earn. Most of them are bad; so be thankful for small mercies.

When Collins called him over I followed. My nose always got the better of me.

Warboys asked, 'Sir?'

'Fancy a scout around, Tony? See if you can pick up which way they went, and if the pilot and passenger were with them?'

'Didn't know about the passenger, sir.'

'Well, you do now.' Collins sounded moody. 'Some girl they were trying to impress. Daughter of a navy commander, I'm told, and a bit of a troublemaker.'

'Shall I go with him?' I offered. Warboys seemed an all right type to me. I didn't like the idea of him trailing a terrorist gang on his own. But Collins only grinned at me.

'No, I need you to ride the radios. Stop bloody volunteering for things – you're old enough to know better. You've nothing to prove. Let the youngsters get on with the bad stuff – it's what they're here for.'

Warboys explained, 'My old man has an estate in the Borders, and I've been stalking since I was a kiddy. So thanks for the offer, but you'd probably only get in the way. No offence.'

'None taken. I just get bored quickly – short attention span.'

Lying of course. The truth was that sitting about waiting for some gunman to fire on me was certain to give me the willies.

I'd fought my wars from moving platforms. I hated the idea of stooging around until some Greek thought I was a tasty target.

'*They also serve who only stand and wait,*' Collins said portentously. 'Today that means the rest of us.' John Milton, 'On His Blindness', if you didn't know it. The soldiers and the MPs seemed to melt into the tree belt around us, and settle down. Warboys tossed me his cap as he left. He had tied a light khaki cloth around his head Arab fashion: it fell over his shoulders. I know I've said it before, but Lawrence of sodding Arabia has a lot to answer for. Collins sat down, and leaned against a tree adjacent to our radio vehicle. I sat alongside him.

I was suddenly cold, drew my jacket around me, and filled a pipe.

'Permission to smoke?' I asked.

'Sure. I couldn't stop these blighters smoking to save their lives.'

'Not worried about the terrorists coming back, and smelling us out?'

'No. If they were going to make a scrap of it they would have left more than that boy behind.' Despite what he had said I could sense that it had troubled him.

I said, 'It wasn't your fault. You couldn't have known.'

'Is that what I have to tell the priest on Sunday?'

'Are you a Catholic?'

'I am, as it happens.' That wasn't going to make it any easier.

'OK, Captain. Let's pass the time by you telling me about being a Catholic, while I sit and worry silently about Mr Warboys.'

That brought a smile to his lips I hadn't looked for. He gave me a very old-fashioned look.

'I shouldn't bother. Tony's murdered his way from one end of this island to the other. He's a homicidal maniac. The Cyps

– particularly the GCs – are terrified of him. They think he has the supernatural power of invisibility. Some even think he can change his shape into that of a big cat, and pass unseen.' I worked out that *GCs* meant Greek Cypriots. The Turks, I presumed, would be the TCs.

'So I don't have to worry about him?'

'Only if you see him crawling towards you with his knife in his teeth.'

There didn't seem to be anything else to say. Even though I was cold the sun was shining through the trees casting a dappled shade on us. The leaves of the brittle oaks were rustled by a choppy little breeze that periodically silenced the insects. This was a deceptively beautiful place; hell probably will be as well. I wondered where Pat had got to – maybe he was fleecing a couple of MPs with a pack of playing cards.

Warboys came in dirty and thirsty mid-afternoon. He was carrying a woman's cotton dress which had been torn, but there was no blood or dirt on it. He'd identified two hill farms, a monastery and a hamlet in the general direction a small group of people had appeared to travel, and marked them precisely on Collins's map. I examined the dress myself, and for a moment held it up to my face. The scent it still carried spoke of jasmine. A gentle purple.

I said the obvious – my speciality.

'No blood, and it's still clean.'

'Looks like they tore it off her to see what they'd got. No sign of the pilot. Maybe they didn't get him.'

'What do you know about the girl?' I asked Collins.

'Flirted with the enlisted men. Had a Greek boyfriend, but threw him over for a Turk. Trouble on legs, my people told me.'

'She's bitten off more than we can chew this time,' Warboys

observed. Then he asked, 'Drink for a thirsty soldier, or have you lot swigged it?'

Twenty minutes later we heard the 7th Cavalry grinding up the slope in small lorries and armoured cars. Collins stood up and stretched, and his men began to come out of the trees. In the Land Rover, as we drove down through the foothills looking for the road to Nic, Collins repeated, 'Flirted with the enlisted men . . . Christ, she's sixteen years old. What did they expect – bringing her out here?' It was then I realized he was on her side after all.

We left them at Wayne's Keep, and on the road back it was warm enough for me to shuck my jacket. I retuned the radio and we got that intermittent signal from Radio Luxembourg. We listened to Dan Dare fighting the Treens, and then Eartha Kitt was singing that her heart belonged to Daddy. It quietened us for a few minutes.

Chapter Eleven

Murder Mile

As I went off duty for my first long weekend I asked de Whitt, 'Who covers my targets when I'm not here?'

'Someone comes in. They're not as good as you, but we've scheduled your watches against the previous frequency of the Saudi exchanges, and again, they don't do much at night or on holy days. Between the two of you, you get most of it. If you knew how much an improvement this is on before, you'd know why we were so pleased to see you.' He was so open and sincere it was hard not to like him, but I did try.

'Who is it? Anyone I know?'

'No, and you don't need to. What are you going to do with your days off?'

'I thought I'd drive over to Nicosia if I could find some transport. Then maybe Famagusta again. There are some ruins just north of the city – someone told me they were quite spectacular.' The someone had been Alison. She had been going to take me there, but somehow that had got lost in the storm.

'Salamis, yes – well worth a gander . . . and if you fancy a swim we have three bathing beaches with a guard with a Sten at the ends of each, just to be on the safe side.'

'Probably the best beaches on the island?'

'Yes, just about – now I come to think about it.'

'And the Cypriots aren't allowed to use them, I assume?'

'That's right. Why d'ye ask?'

'Because it was that sort of thing that got us tossed out of Egypt. We never learn.'

'You'd rather be getting shot at, I suppose?'

'No, I'd rather be back in Blighty, sitting outside a pub in the sunshine sipping a decent pint of bitter looking down the dress of a farmer's daughter.' I asked him, 'Do you want me to wait for my relief?'

'No, neither the twain shall meet – master's orders. Anyway, your man's outside with your carriage – been waiting ten minutes already. Have a good weekend.' He beamed his sunny smile, and turned his attention to the papers on his desk. He smiled at them as well. I knew it then – another halfwit.

Pat Tobin ferried me back to my hut, where I had a quick shave and shower and changed into a clean, pressed set of KDs care of the invisible laundry service. Pete's things were still neatly stacked at the end of his bunk – we'd met for supper once. He hadn't told me what sort of deal he was doing over here, and I hadn't asked. He'd tell me if the time came. Pat came back for me half an hour later, similarly spruced. The bastards didn't actually think I was going to lock myself up in Fort Watson for four days, did they? We headed for Famagusta.

We left his transport in Yassine's yard, and headed for a café bar a block away. Pat stopped half a dozen times on the way to glad-hand, or exchange jokes with, locals he knew. All men.

'These are Turks, I take it?' I asked him.

'Sure. TCs. Friendlies . . . well, most of 'em, anyway.'

'How do you tell the difference between them and the Greeks?'

'They talk Turkish, of course.'

'So a Greek Cyp talking Turkish could fool you?'

'Yeah, I suppose. But he wouldn't fool these guys.'

In the café we got into a heavy argument about *Miss World* with a group of hard-looking middle-aged men, all of whom were going for the moustache of the year award. Money changed hands. I managed to get an each-way bet on the girl from Cuba. Pat said it was a fix, and was taking money against Miss Venezuela.

These guys were drinking an aniseed drink identical in all respects to the Greek juice Watson had served me in his office. It had been invented in Turkey, they told me, and stolen by the Greeks. Their heavily accented English was more than adequate for the usual men's conversation about dames, football teams, or for whom Fangio and Hawthorn were going to drive next year, and by the time they blew I had added a few Turkish words to my vocabulary as well. Later Tobin warned me, 'Watch yourself when you're around these guys – they're heavies. They support the Turkish resistance to EOKA, and they'll try to get you into a fight with some Greeks. Then they'll accidentally slit a few Greek throats as they rescue you, and a riot will break out.'

'How much did you take against the Venezuelan girl not winning?'

'Too much. I gotta lay some off.'

'How will you get anyone to do that? She's not fancied.'

'Go into a bar on Murder Mile, and tell them the Turks are all betting against her. I'll get buried in her instant supporters putting money on her to win. You ever ate kebabs?'

'No. What are they?'

'Meat pieces on skewers. You put them in a flat bread envelope. Tonight's your night to discover Turkish meat cooking.'

When we got back to Tony's, Collins was up at the bar on a high bar stool with Steve. There was a vacant seat between them, and I slid onto it. Steve said, 'Where have you been, sailor? I been waiting an hour . . . don't expect me to do that again.'

'Sorry, love, I didn't know you cared.' I supposed she'd recognized Pat's wagon in the forecourt.

'I don't,' she told me, 'but a customer's a customer, in both my language and yours. I don't let go of you *that* easily.' Then she began to laugh. So did Collins. So did I. The bottles of Keo began to do the rounds – Pat found David, and asked him when the dancing girls were coming on. Two musicians in traditional dress emerged from a corner and struck up a tune. It was going to be a decent night.

I awoke in her room again at about three. She yawned, and woke up at the same time. I lit one of her American cigarettes, Luckies I think, and we shared it. We still hadn't exchanged a word. Then I broke the spell.

'We're getting on all right together, you and I, aren't we?'

Nothing. A stream of tobacco smoke climbing away.

Then, 'Don't know what you're getting at, Charlie.'

'I'm telling you that I feel comfortable with you and trying to say *thank you*.'

'Nothing sloppy?'

'Nothing sloppy, Steve. I'll warn you in advance before I say anything sloppy.'

'You do that.'

I leaned on one elbow, looked down at her and ran a couple of verses of 'Careless Love Blues' in my head. I couldn't work out whose version I liked best, Bessie Smith's or Neva Raphaello's. I think the Dutchwoman just had the edge.

'I love this time in the morning,' Stephanie said. And then, 'You don't want to go back to sleep just yet, do you?' She reached up suddenly, looped an arm around my neck and kissed the bottom of my ear. Then she whispered, 'Don't think because I'm in this line of business that I don't need sleep, just like regular people.' And made a small sound that was halfway between a smile and a laugh.

Right at that moment something happened. I don't know what it was, but something happened. And whatever it was she knew it too.

We slept deeply and late, and when we walked downstairs looking for breakfast she slipped her hand into mine.

Does luck come into it, or does God just sometimes deal you some very nice cards?

'Nicosia is a shitehole,' Tobin told me. 'You've driven through part of it once, and round it once. That should be enough for anyone.'

'I still want to see it. When I get home everyone's going to ask me what Nicosia's like. They won't ask about the sea and the mountains. They won't even ask me about Famagusta. They'll ask about Nicosia.'

'That's because of the Brits getting killed there. It's in all the papers. Why indulge them? The papers should be encouraged to report uplifting and interesting things instead.'

'Such as?'

'Such as cricket matches, or golf.'

'Golf?'

'What's the matter with golf?'

'It's infantile, a game for living corpses. Someone hits a ball towards a minute hole in something like somebody's lawn . . . and then fifteen minutes later they take a hike and do the same thing all over again.'

'You got something against golf, Charlie?'

'Yeah, I got something serious against golf.'

'Good, 'cos I got somethin' against Nicosia. Understand now?'

Stephanie had been smiling good-humouredly at both of us.

'I'll take you into Nic, Charlie. I know an old Maltese banker there. He's always pleased to see me.'

I put my hand over hers on the table; couldn't stop myself. Her fingers curled around mine. I asked, 'Is there a downside to that offer?'

'You might have to wait outside until I finish work.'

Pat's laughter always erupted in small bursts. I laughed too. Then I looked away across the garden. Birds were sitting on the rim of the fountain where Laika had tried to weave a spell. Dipping their heads, and drinking delicately. Tipping their heads back. Whistling more like caged songbirds. She squeezed my fingers again.

'I'll take you tomorrow morning, Charlie, before EOKA is properly awake. Pat will lend us his jeep.'

'Will you?' I asked him.

'Why not? As long as you wash the blood off before you bring it back. I'll still be in bed, so if anyone asks I'll say you stole it.'

One of the other dancers walked up behind him; a blonde with a fresh citronade in her hand. She put her arms around him, and bent to kiss the nape of his neck. She had been rehearsing, and was dressed for dancing. Very beautiful. Filmy blue silks. Where her flesh met the air I could see the faint sheen of perspiration on her arms and her legs. The curious thing was that in this old-fashioned garden it was the rest of us who looked out of place, not her. Pat hooked out the fourth chair at the table for her with his foot, and nodded her into it.

'This is Inga. She's from Uppsala in Sweden.'

'Are there any genuinely Middle Eastern belly dancers left anywhere?' I demanded.

'Only in Vegas,' Steve said. 'They still like the big ones there. Would you like to come for a walk around the walls? There are some stupendous views towards Turkey, and you'll meet some nice people.'

Collins walked from the hotel deep in conversation with his officer Thirdlow. The garden was beginning to feel crowded. I glanced at Pat – he was still my mentor here, the guy who knew how things worked. He nodded. A walk with Steve would probably be OK. I could have made all manner of a witty acceptance speech, but I simply smiled at her and said, 'Love to.'

Ledra Street in Nicosia wasn't crowded at that time in the morning, but I'd heard too much about it, so I rode with the flap of my holster loose. It was a long, dirty shopping street, and the hundreds of telephone and electricity cables close overhead made a net that would have defeated any but the smallest bird. No one had cleared away the day before's litter – it was like Borough Market the day after market day. Steve nosed along it quietly. Occasionally locals would have to move aside for us – mostly women out buying early-morning treats for the breakfast table. A few of them smiled as we inched past. Most of the men scowled, or refused to meet our eye. For a few minutes we crept along behind an Orthodox priest who strode lord-like along the centre of the road, deliberately keeping us in our place behind him. That raised a few smiles.

Steve looked a bit rattled for the first time, and whispered, 'If anything happens I'm going to cream him,' and hooted the horn twice before he deigned to move over. That just served to draw even more attention to the stand he was making, and he was wearing a smug smile as we passed. A small boy suddenly grabbed an apple from his mother's wicker basket, and hurled it furiously at us. I fielded it instinctively – a nice high left-hand slip catch, half standing – bowed to him and shouted *thanks* before I bit into it. That didn't go down at all well: a young man stepped into the street behind us, and shook his fist. Another joined him. They began to run. Steve put her foot down, and shot us out of the lower road towards Eleftheria Square.

'Touchy lot, aren't they?' I asked her.

'You weren't supposed to catch the apple – you were supposed to be hit by it.'

'Pat was right.'

'About Nic?'

She was wrenching the car from corner to corner, out through one of the Old Wall gates, heading west.

'No, about cricket. If that little bastard had been exposed to the game at an impressionable age he might have been able to hit me.'

'You're a silly bugger, Charlie!'

She slowed the vehicle, and we moved through a wealthy suburb at a more sedate pace, not saying much. A small estate of bungalows which wouldn't have looked out of place in Eastbourne. A Champ with a couple of policemen sitting in its access road. Who lived there? I wondered. Politicos or service personnel? Still dropping away to the west, and away from the city. We'd both just sailed close to the edge.

I asked her, 'Where are you taking me now?'

'The Keep. They have a decent NAAFI, and you've probably got enough pull to get us in. We might still be in time for breakfast. Give me a bite of your apple – I'm starving.'

'What about your Maltese banker?'

'I decided to give myself the weekend off, like you. Besides, it's Sunday – he spends Sunday with his family, and goes to church.'

A maid, in her Sunday best and wearing a headscarf, was

pushing a couple of kids in a big Tan-Sad. She gave us a broad smile, and waved. I could feel the sun warm on my forearms: it was as if we had passed into a different world. Normality.

'Serves you right,' Tobin said, 'and I hope you've learned a lesson – that could have been a Mills bomb instead of an apple. Where would that have left you?'

'Needing an upper plate?'

'Funny man.'

'I get it, Pat. Safety first from now on. Sorry.'

He nodded. I'd recounted my Ledra Street adventure to him. He thought for a minute before responding.

'And it's not as straightforward as you think. There are some Turks living around North Ledra Street as well, but in Nicosia they are well outnumbered by the Greeks, which is what makes Nic such a dangerous place – especially for you, because you wear no tabs or insignia: they'll think you're I Corps or an MP. EOKA's sworn to kill every I Corps man on the island.'

'Thanks. I thought wearing KDs was supposed to be safer than wearing civvies.'

'It is, but not as safe as a proper uniform – as long as it's not I Corps.'

'Then give me some unit markings to sew on, for Christ's sake!'

'Can't.' He shook his head. 'You're not entitled.'

I went to get up. Afternoon in the shady bar. I wanted to sit in the small garden and smoke. Pat waved me down.

'I 'aven't finished yet. I was saying that the security situation in the cities was more complicated than meets the eye.'

'You were.'

'Here in Famagusta there are more Turks than Greeks, so it's generally safer . . . but there *are* some Greeks and they bear you ill will. Also, an EOKA murder squad can waltz in here as easy as you an' I, do its business an' waltz out again. Savvy?'

'You mean I'm not safe anywhere?'

'You're safe behind the wire – most of the time, but don't forget we have Cyp laundrymen, cooks, waiters . . . and many of the officers have local maids and cleaners, and more than half of them are Greeks. They're the only jobs they can get, an' they pay well.'

'So . . .' I let out a long breath. 'Recommendations?'

'Always keep yer wits about you, an' don't believe a word anyone says.' He drained the Keo he had been drinking, and stood up. 'I'm going out for a while. Business to do. Will you be OK?'

'I thought I'd sit in the garden, have a smoke and enjoy the view.' There were girls in the garden.

'Good idea. See you later.'

Captain Collins was at a table in the garden. He had a tall glass of cloudy liquid in front of him on the table, and an unbroken pack of cards. Ten yards away the girl Inga – looking different in slacks, a modest pink shirt and a ponytail – was playing chess on a stone bench with one of the Lebanese maids. The Thirdlow woman sat on the lip of the fountain where the birds had drunk the day before, and where Alison's friend Laika had been before that. When you looked closely at her you realized just how striking but unapproachable she was. I looked. A classic bone structure: breath-taking, in some lights. She must have been off duty, but she wore a plain KD shirt and skirt; the skirt was longer than knee length but had a small slit on each side so it swung free around her legs. Sensible shoes. Small feet.

When I slumped into the chair opposite Collins I noticed a well-thumbed paperback. It was a Scott Fitzgerald: *Tender is the Night*.

'Any good?' I asked him.

'Hers.' He nodded at the woman by the fountain. Then he sighed. The birds were in a tree now, still whistling noisily – they even whistled as they quarrelled. It was I who nodded in the direction of the woman this time, and I used the same question.

'Any good?'

I meant her work, but that's not what he answered.

'I have no idea . . . I doubt it, actually. She has a terrible inner coldness, hasn't she? An ego as big as an elephant. Quite the psychologist, ain't I? Don't get me wrong – actually I quite like her. She reminds me of someone.' I sensed he was laughing at himself.

'Yourself, maybe.'

He looked oddly vulnerable – something you didn't expect of him – then he said, 'In that case, although she doesn't know it, she's going to be lonely for the rest of her life, God help her . . . and God help any man who ends up with her.'

'Not you then?'

'Sleep with staff? No, Charlie, that way madness lies.' He nodded in her direction again. 'You shouldn't either, unless you have a death wish.'

'Thanks. I'll remember.' He could have been warning me off just to keep his own way clear, but as it happened I agreed with him. 'Do you know what those birds are?' No one had told me.

'White-eared bulbuls. I don't know whether they're residents, or only like us.'

'Like us?'

'Just passing through.'

'Do you know a lot about birds?'

'A bit.' It was odd seeing a domestic side of a tough policeman. I thought I'd rather like him for a neighbour. I don't know why, but my mind glanced back to the woman again.

Would I like her for a neighbour as well? No, I definitely wouldn't. In fact, the very thought made me shiver. Collins noticed.

'What's up? Someone walked over your grave?'

'No, it was just something I thought on.'

He read my mind. 'I know, she can do that to you, can't she? Two hundred years ago they would have burned her. When's your next shift?'

'Tuesday. Late. Another day yet. Do you always stay here when you're off duty?'

'No, just occasionally. Some of my people are working at this end this weekend, so I decided to be around. It's an excuse to get away from the office, but they know where to get me.'

'A change from Spam with everything?'

'You said it, son. Have you tried the bean salad Yassine serves here?'

'Yes. He had a place in Ismailia. I first had it there. He used to call it Beirut Sunshine then.'

'It's Salamis Sunshine now. That scans better, but it's probably the same.' He'd answered my questions but there was still something missing.

Collins left. Pat Tobin replaced him about half an hour later, and Pete slithered in half an hour after that. The woman recovered her book, smiled a mysterious smile and went to find a bench at the other end of the garden.

Pete was dressed like me now, in anonymous KD thins, although he undermined them with his hallmark highly polished black shoes. I stuck with a pair of comfortable old suede desert boots. They were a bit smelly by now, but I could wear them all day without sweating up. Pat asked me, 'Anything planned for tomorrow, squire?'

'No, why?'

'We have, an' someone asked me to invite you.'

'Who?'

'Mr Warboys.'

'I suspect Warboys is bad news, Pat. He has a fanatical gleam in his eyes.'

'That's why the GCs don't fancy him. He out-fanatics the fanatics – most of those SAS guys do.' At least we'd reached the stage of calling a spade a shovel. I'd worked with a couple of Australian Special Service guys a few years ago, and recognized the type. I respected their stubborn professionalism.

'What does he want?'

'To take another drive.'

'Purpose?'

Pete leaned forward; his small dark eyes were positively glittering. 'Get that girl back. Maybe even the pilot. He says he knows where she is.'

'Why us?' I asked Tobin.

'Me,' he told me, 'because I can lay my hands on the equipment we need, no questions asked. You and Pete because you're not constrained by Queen's Regs any more, the way we are . . . an' all three of us because we got a day off tomorrer, an' no one will miss us. Good enough?'

'And you?' I asked Pete.

'They paid me.' And he shrugged. I believed him too. Pete would do anything for money, except, I thought, shave off his silly little Douglas Fairbanks moustache. The trouble with bastards you'd served with was that old ties died hard: ask any serviceman. They only asked a favour in the first place because of what you had been through together, and they didn't ask it unless they guessed you'd play along. I knew that they wouldn't have told me the worst yet. I asked, 'What's the rest of it?'

'Maybe a hundred armed GCs up there who'll guess we're coming. Whether they decide to do anything about us will depend on whether Grivas wants to cause trouble this week — he likes to keep us on the hop.'

'And?'

'We leave from your hut before light tomorrer, so we're getting out of here in a couple of hours. Check the kit, and a good night's sleep.'

Pete gave a dry little chuckle. 'Just like operations, Charlie. *Berlin next stop.*' I hoped not. Two of the guys who'd flown in *Tuesday's Child* with us had never made it through the war. Pat coughed. He had something more to say.

'An' don't tell your bird what we're up to. Stay schtum.'

'She thinks I'm going to be around until tomorrow.'

'So surprise her!' he said nastily. 'She's only a whore.'

That's when the second thing happened, because I realized immediately that she was no longer an *only* anything: she was rather special. I felt my chin lift, and something must have shown on my face because Pat immediately dropped his gaze and looked away.

I had a brief, involuntary mental glimpse of all the girls I'd dated since I first met Grace in 1944 — and there weren't as many as you'd think. What I realized was that although I'd kidded myself from time to time, I hadn't had anyone really special since Grace had gone. Steve was out shopping and hadn't returned before we split, so the practical problem solved itself. We crept away like thieves, and I felt like one.

Chapter Twelve

Let's Hear It for the Dead Men

Pete and I slept with our small packs made up, and our clothes laid out – both placed on adjacent bunks ready to go. He hadn't been wrong: it was like old times. Sleep was a long time coming, and I remembered the sounds we used to share in the airfield Nissen hut we called the Grease Pit in 1944. I listened for Marty's snores, but Marty was dead. When he was drunk he would sleep under his bed, with his arms around an empty bomb casing. The Toff, our mid-upper gunner, would sometimes whistle quietly between his teeth until sleep claimed him: I always knew that, like me, he would have been looking at the ceiling. The Toff was dead as well. Eventually I heard Pete say, 'G'night, Charlie,' and roll in his bed to face away from me.

'G'night, Pete.'

Let's hear it for the dead men.

Pat woke us with a muffled tap on the wooden door. That's not quite true. Both of us had been awake and waiting for it, and had heard the vehicle arrive a minute before. We had a nondescript four-wheel drive Humber one-tonner, with a canvas tilt over the back: the windscreen had a makeshift wire-mesh grille. She was probably originally army green, but was filthy dirty with that Cyprus dull dust, which had softened its lines. It had once had UN markings and a serial number, but they had been daubed over with a dirty green wash. The steel cab had a round metal port, like a dustbin lid, over the passenger seat, and there were thin mattresses in the wagon bed under the tattered canvas.

Pete and I climbed over the tailboard, and lay in the back beneath the tops of the metal side panels, a .5 cal heavy machine gun between us. It was set up, and ready to go – all we had to do was lift it onto its mount. When I looked up I could see that the inside of the canvas tilt had been lined with chicken wire – with a bit of luck any hand grenade would bounce back to its thrower, and give him a surprise.

'I jus' realized something,' Pete said as he closed his eyes, and prepared to doze.

'What's that?'

'Ain't gonna be a comfortable drive, is it?'

I grinned in the half-light. It was good to be back with him.

Warboys drove. In the SAS they do a lot of things back to front – the officers do a lot of the driving, and carry loads as heavy as their men's. It seems to work for them. Pat Tobin sat alongside him. Under his sheepskin jerkin his unit flashes had disappeared, so he looked like me, and as I glanced into the cab before I mounted up I saw a Bren propped up behind his seat. Part of me felt the old adrenalin rush, the other part asked me what the fuck I thought I was doing.

Two hours later we were back in the lower Troodos, and it was beginning to get colder. Warboys pulled up under a tree which spread a wide low canopy over a sharp climbing bend in the mountain road. Pete and I got out and stretched. We both pulled on our flying jackets, and mounted the machine gun so it had a field of fire over the tailgate.

Pat Tobin stood on his seat and mounted the Bren on the port above him, and handed me and Pete a Sten gun apiece each with two spare mags. When he got back in his seat he cradled his own Sten in his lap.

'I don't know if I could get to the Bren in time,' he told me, 'but it discourages the natives to see it up there.'

We got back in the wagon bed and hunched down, and Warboys put it into gear.

I don't know how far we got into the Troodos on that trip, but at noon we were still climbing along roads that were barely more than goat tracks. It was bright and chilly.

He pulled off the road again just as we crested a saddle; there was a small village spread out immediately beneath us, white houses, freshly painted, clustered around a village square with a small church on the far side. We all dismounted again. I asked, 'Do they know we're here?'

Warboys muttered, 'For certain. Mechanical noises travel for miles in the mountains.'

As if to confirm his observation a black-robed priest, wearing one of those tall boxy hats, came out of the church and looked up at us. My previous idea of priests had them swinging smoking censers, and wearing strings of black juju beads and crucifixes. It's hard not to conclude that there is something seriously wrong with people who face the world with an image of a horribly executed man around their necks.

This one was different: instead of a crucifix he had a pair of binoculars around his neck. He looked at us through them long enough to be doing a head count, and then walked back up the two steps into his church. He didn't seem to be in any hurry. A minute later the church's single, tinny bell began to toll. I've heard cow bells which sound like that in the Pyrenees.

Still Warboys held us back.

We watched the houses disgorging their inhabitants – play

people, dolls. Some were larger than others, and some were faster. Warboys waited until they had all gone into the church. One boy was late, raced across the square, and had to hammer on the door for admission.

'OK, chaps,' Warboys told us. 'Now we go.'

We tore down the track into the village so fast that I was sure we'd break a spring over some of the embedded boulders we jumped over. Warboys raced the truck in a tight circle around the square, and came to a halt with me and the .5 which Pete squatted behind, facing the church door. Pete had been the rear gunner of *Tuesday's Child* – I know, I've told you that already. He was always very serious about heavy machine guns, so putting him on the trigger had been an obvious choice. The bloody scientists would probably call it natural selection, and use the fact to prove that the apes we descended from were basically homicidal. I knelt beside him with a Sten.

Time stopped.

Not only were Pete and I facing the church, it left us facing the four guys and a girl ranged across the square in front of it. I don't know where they came from. The men stood like the sheriff and his three deputies facing the bad guys in a bad Western film. I also knew that Pete would drop them if they so much as twitched without permission. It was in his nature.

They were in full EOKA dress uniform: filthy dirty sheepskins, sweat-saturated woollen shirts, and baggy trousers which hadn't seen a tub in ten years. Ammunition belts worn across their bodies. One beard, one moustache with four days' stubble, and one spotty teenager with a twitch – I'd have to keep an eye on Pete. The girl was about six years old, and had a grubby face. She carried a dirty white scrap of a flag on a short stick. The beard had an old German machine pistol dangling from one hand, the moustache had a rifle, and the spotty kid with a twitch had a small pistol. The priest, remarkably, had simply a smile. He wore a full-length priestly black number. Coco Chanel would have loved his sense of style.

I heard and felt Warboys leave the wagon. He left his door open; a little cover against a back shooter, I'd guess. He moved up alongside us, but not into the machine gun's field of fire. I noticed that the boy had a black eye, and there was a recent red blow mark high on the moustache's cheekbone. Warboys spoke first; so cool you'd have thought he was announcing the guests at a mess dinner. English.

'Hello, Adonis. Everything OK? No problems?'

Eventually, after a lifetime, the priest replied, 'Hello, Tony. Yes, everything is fine. As we agreed. Everyone is pleased to see you.' That was a turn-up for the book. If Makarios had been telling the truth all this time, the villagers must have been the first GCs to be pleased to see an Englishman in about ten years. Warboys failed to respond, so the priest added, 'If there was an ambush it would have been sprung already. My friends here,' he indicated the three fighters, 'are here to save face, nothing more.'

'S . . . o . . . o.' Warboys drew the sound out. 'You have something which belongs to us, and we agreed a price for her return.'

'We did.' The priest looked a bit shifty. 'But we have to talk about the money again. My friends here, and my villagers, have been unable to agree the sum.' So, we were here to do a hostage exchange, and the first EOKA men I had seen in the flesh were going to shake us down.

'Then keep her,' Warboys said tersely.

The priest looked agonized. He spread his hands, and said, '*Please*, Tony.'

Warboys sounded doubtful.

'We agreed one hundred pounds sterling, Adonis, and you shook hands on it.'

'I did. But these are poor people, Tony. Farmers and peasants. They could only raise thirty-five.'

That was interesting. Something was slightly arse about face here.

Pete leaned over and whispered, 'This is curious. I think they are paying us to take the woman away. Do you understand it?'

'No more than you do.'

Warboys hadn't said anything, so the priest continued. 'This is so important to them, Tony, that Leonidas has led two of his captains down here to meet you. You can select one as hostage to ensure your safe passage out of the hills. You must take this girl away – she is disturbing the village. She will not choose. Men fight over her.'

Leonidas was a famous EOKA killer and leader. Like many of the successful EOKA men he had taken a field name from the ranks of the Greek heroes. What ill could befall the leader of three hundred Spartans? If he had come to supervise the exchange in person something very serious was going on here.

'I'm surprised you didn't kill her, and have done with it,' Warboys observed. His voice was low-key. Disinterested.

The moustache spoke for the first time. Good English, but a gravelly voice born of a love of tobacco.

'And start a civil war, Englishman? There are men who think they are in love with her already. Read the classics – do you think Greeks learned nothing in Troy?'

Warboys let the ensuing silence drag on a bit. Negotiation was obviously one of his strong points. Then he sighed and said, 'OK, Adonis. Just this once, in memory of our past friendship – for thirty-five pounds I will take Leonidas's hand on it, and take the girl.'

The priest momentarily looked as if he was about to cry, but he was made of good stuff. He said, 'Thank you, Tony. I will not forget this.' Then he looked at his feet, almost as if he was ashamed.

Warboys moved towards the three armed men, his right hand extended for the ritual handshake. He wasn't taking any chances though: his left arm rested on his Sten, which he wore over his left shoulder on a sling. Moustache stepped forward, and held out his hand, but Warboys ignored it. He moved to stand in front of the boy, offered his hand and said, 'Hello, Leonidas.'

'Hello, Lion.'

I suppose that there wasn't all that much difference in their names. The boy seemed to change almost as we watched him. He stopped twitching immediately, and straightened up from the slouch. Even his spare frame seemed to fill out. Not a boy: a man then. Maybe he was in his mid-twenties. He smiled a spiteful smile, handed his pistol to the priest and took Warboys's outstretched hand. Two enemies; eye to eye. I had seen this sort of thing before – and it always ended in tears. I suppose everyone on the square knew then that Leonidas was going to take the long ride down the mountain with us. His two older captains looked anguished, but they didn't protest – he had them completely under control, which impressed me.

Warboys asked ironically, 'Where is she, this demon?'

'She is besieging a farm.' Leonidas shrugged. 'Fifteen minutes. No more.'

'You will accompany us?'

'Of course. I gave the priest my word.'

Pat and Warboys handcuffed Leonidas's hands behind his back before they helped him into the back of the wagon with us. It was a tense moment. Anger and devastation crossed the faces of his men and the priest, but words got us through – they often do.

'I wouldn't want you free to get your hands on the machine gun,' Warboys explained loudly to Leonidas. 'This is just a precaution.'

'Not necessary.' The terrorist sounded scornful. 'I promised. I gave my word.'

'I often give my word, but I have found that there are promises . . . and *promises*. I'm sure that you understand. I have also promised.'

'To do what?'

'To release you unharmed when we are finished . . . now, get in.'

Pete pushed him down on one of the mattresses, and had him lie there. I wished the wagon had been larger because he smelt terrible. As we pulled away through the village onto a track which descended into a shallow upland valley I turned to look at him.

He must have read my face, because he said, 'Your soldiers chase me from cave to cave, and tree to tree for a year. I stink because I have nowhere to wash. What did you expect, an old-fashioned brigand chieftain in silks?'

He did not need to direct us, for the track led to only one farmstead – a low house with a Roman-tiled roof, a muddy yard and a couple of long, low barns. Warboys repeated the trick with the Humber. He drove it into the yard, made a circle and came to a halt with us facing our exit, and the machine gun facing the farm. I don't know how the others felt, but I was ready to fill my trousers. I felt naked, and exposed to any madman with a gun. Leonidas told me, 'Tell him to switch off the engine.'

I relayed that to Warboys through the small open window between me and the cab.

'Why?'

Leonidas heard him, and replied, 'I will call to them. They will come out for me. They are too scared to come out for you – British soldiers have been this way before.'

Warboys let the engine run for about three minutes before he turned it off. I ran another of Julie's songs in my head: 'Why Can't We Just Be Friends?' It seemed appropriate. I could hear Pete breathing deeply through his nose. He always did that if he thought he'd have to pull the trigger. Into the silence, and it *was* a silence – even the birds and the beasts had shut down – Leonidas spat out a few loud sentences in fast colloquial Greek. Even if I had known anything of the language he would have spoken too quickly for me.

I tried Julie London again: 'Calendar Girl' this time. Then the door of the farmhouse creaked open, and another small girl in a dirty, shapeless dress came out to face us. Bravery is a characteristic that manifests itself early in Greek Cypriot women. Like her predecessor she was carrying a large stick which had a grubby piece of white cloth tied to the top . . . someone had obviously rehearsed them. Then an old woman in formal black weeds followed her out into the open. She had reached that ageless stage for Mediterranean working women when she could have been anything from eighty to four hundred and forty years old. Her voice sounded strong. Commanding and harsh. I asked Leonidas what she had said. He struggled to sit up, with his hands still cuffed behind him.

'She asked if you have come to take away the she-devil.'

'Tell her *yes*.'

The old woman gave him a couple of sentences. An even older man – in his six hundreds maybe – came out and stood behind her. He walked with a stick, and his face showed pain with every step. I asked our tamed terrorist, 'What did the woman say?'

'She asked if I was Leonidas, and then went on to complain that my father still owed them a debt from two years ago. How could I be a famous bandit if my family cannot pay its debts?'

I heard Warboys snort, 'How much?'

'A few hundred mils, probably, Lion – maybe two pounds sterling, no more.'

Then the old man began to shout and wave his stick, so I asked, 'What's all this about? Where's the girl?'

'They are bringing her. The old man says she has ruined them. His sons have fallen out, and refuse to work. His daughter has run away to another farm.'

The old man hobbled closer. Pete tensed and cocked the .5 with a loud mechanical click. Leonidas said, 'You are in no danger. Not if I am here.'

When he had approached close enough for his purpose, the old fellow pulled up his trouser leg to show a livid red and purple bruise on his shin. I noticed that he had marks on his face, and maybe the makings of another bruise. He looked as if he had been in a barney.

'Some of my people sold the girl to this family,' Leonidas explained. 'She is young and strong, and spirited. Once she was broken they thought she would make a good wife for their youngest son. Instead she hurt the old man – you can see. She marked anyone who went near her uninvited. He wants his money back.'

'How much money?' I asked him.

Leonidas shrugged. 'Not much.'

Now one of the barn doors swung open, and Pete moved the machine gun to cover it. Leonidas said impatiently, 'I told you that you wouldn't need that!'

'And I'm the Queen of Siam.' That was Pete. He spoke pleasantly. Pete was always at his most dangerous when he was being nice.

Two younger men emerged. A young woman dressed in the respectable married woman's black shroud walked between them. Even though she kept her head down I could see that she was pretty – and blonde. Maybe that had been the trouble; natural blondes have often been highly prized in Greece. One of the young men had deep and recent parallel scratches on his cheek, and the other what looked like part of his scalp missing. They were both good-looking, presentable young men but with the girl between them they looked a bit sheepish.

They came to a halt alongside the older folk, and the girl looked up at us. Pete let out a low whistle. She was definitely pretty in a conventional sense, but her eyes were black and venomous; even when she was smiling. I had once known a diamondback rattlesnake named Alice, who lived in a Plexiglas case and had travelled around Europe with the American forces. She had a hit list that the Compton brothers would have been proud of, and this girl had Alice's black eyes. I wouldn't have wanted her in my family either.

I beckoned her over. Her smile broadened and she said, 'Hello. You're English, aren't you? Have you come to rescue me?' What was the accent? Not uneducated, but maybe north-east somewhere – Gateshead, I thought. Somewhere like that.

'Yes. You're going home now.' Was I wrong or was there a small grimace flitting across that heart-shaped face? 'I'm sorry if you've been mistreated.'

She said, 'It was no worse than my boarding school. I think I've been a bit of a bother to them.' That sounded like a candidate for the understatement-of-the-year award.

Warboys entered my line of vision from stage left. He said, 'I'd like you to ride up front with us, if you don't mind, miss – it's getting crowded in the back.' Then he passed a grubby handful of notes to the old man. I think it was some of the money he had had from the priest. The old man looked at me, and shrugged. Then he smiled. He was still smiling as we drove away. The hand he waved in farewell was full of money.

Leonidas scowled. 'You paid my family debt, you bloody bastard.'

Warboys must have heard him, because he laughed back at him through the small cab window. 'Yes, and by the end of the week every village in the Troodos will know about it, won't they?' Then I heard him tell Pat, 'Terrible gossips, these GCs.' Pat laughed, and I heard the girl giggle.

Pete pushed Leonidas back behind us again, and on his side.

'Reminds you of Alice, doesn't she?' he said to me – he'd obviously noticed it as well. I probably made a face and nodded. He made the machine gun safe, but stayed behind it all the way down to the first made-up road.

Occasionally, on the roads back through the mountains, and down onto the lower terraces, we would pass a shepherd or goatherd with a few animals. Invariably it would slow our progress slightly, and invariably the shepherd or goatherd would be sitting on a bank alongside a bundle covered by sacking or an old coat. Invariably the shepherd or goatherd's hand would be resting on the bundle. Pete would traverse the MG to cover them, and they would smile toothless smiles, and wave the hand that had been on the bundle. I was in no doubt that under each bundle was a gun, or grenades. Leonidas's men were doing what they could to cover him.

Warboys let him off a mile up the proper road to Nicosia. After we had stopped, and Warboys and Pat had walked round to let the tailboard down, Pete and I manhandled Leonidas down onto the road. He immediately sat cross-legged in the dust with his head bowed. He looked exactly like men in photographs I had seen from the war, of prisoners or Jews about to be executed by German soldiers. His head was bowed for the neck shot. I wonder if he expected it. Warboys squatted alongside him.

'You think I'm going to shoot you? Is that it?'

'Why not?' Leonidas's voice was strained and low.

'Is that what you would do?'

'I would probably have to, wouldn't I? Get on with it.'

'No, Leonidas, not today. I'm going to do something much worse.' He hung a key on a string around his captive's neck. Handcuffs. 'I'm going to give you two days to get off the island. Will that be enough?'

There was no reply. I asked Pat, 'What's going on? I thought we were supposed to let him go.'

'We will, Charlie. That's the point – nobody really expected it. Standing instructions say you catch a terrorist, under any circumstances, you bring him in. We know it and the GCs know it . . . and this pig's wanted for several murders. If we let him go every Greek on the island will know within twenty-four hours that Mr Warboys had the notorious EOKA killer Leonidas in irons, but then paid his debts and let him go. What would *you* think?'

'That we turned him, of course. What will happen?'

'If he's still on the island in forty-eight hours the GCs will kill him themselves – no one likes a turncoat. Athens is his only hope now. Mr Warboys is offering to hold back the news of his release for two days to enable him to get clear.'

'Won't we get into trouble then as well?'

Pat shook his head.

'It won't be that kind of news broadcast, Charlie. It will be a word here and there, in the markets and the bazaars. There will be nothing on paper, an' if yer asked we'll just deny it, won't we?'

'What about the girl?' It's in my nature, I suppose. I like

the i's dotted and the t's crossed. Warboys looked up from Leonidas.

'She'll be out of here on a plane tonight – after a brief but telling reunion with her family. I hope they find a stout cage to keep her in.'

It was at that point that the girl wandered back. She looked down at the Greek and said, 'He had me, you know, but I made him pay for it. Are you going to kill him?'

Warboys said, 'No, we're going to let him go, and he'll probably come after you. That's why you have to leave tonight.'

'Why not just kill him then?'

Warboys turned away. Pat said to her, rather harshly I thought, 'Get back in, love. Your father's waitin' for yer,' and pushed her back to the cab in front of him. Pete and I clambered into the back, and he dismounted the MG. When we were rolling he said, 'I told you. Just like that bloody rattlesnake.'

I watched Leonidas from my place at the tailgate until he was out of sight: he didn't move, and didn't raise his head to look at us. I suspect that Pete did as well. After a few minutes the distance and the dusk consumed him. Up in front I could hear a cheerful and animated conversation, and a lot of giggles. She was looking for allies before we dropped her off.

Collins was waiting for us at the main gate at Wayne's Keep. We all got down – probably they felt as stiff as me. Pat walked the girl over to Collins like a postman delivering an awkward-shaped parcel. Collins asked her, 'How are you, miss?'

She just nodded for the minute, and didn't reply. He stood her by the gatehouse door, and came over to us. Fags all round. I told you I could get on with his sort of officer. He said, 'Thank you, Tony,' to Warboys, and, 'Thank you, gentlemen,' to the rest of us. And, 'Any trouble?'

'Apart from her?' Warboys asked him. 'No. They were glad to get rid of her. I think half of the men in the parish were fighting over her. It looks like a first-aid station after a trench raid up there.'

'What shall I tell her father?'

'Just tell him she's been mistreated, and that she'll need medical support after she's been evacuated. She could well be pregnant, but let him find that out for himself.'

'*Was* she mistreated?'

'No idea, sir. She was laughing, flirting and joking all the way back, but that could be nerves. Time will tell, I expect.'

Pete gave me the look, but neither of us said anything. Pat shook his head.

Collins asked, 'What about the pilot?'

Warboys said, 'Nothing, sir. Nobody said a dicky bird, and I rather think that if they had him, or had killed him, they would have told me. It's not their way to hide their atrocities, is it? They want us to hear all about them, so our politicians will make a quick decision to bugger off.'

'But you'll let me know?'

'Of course. The first.'

'I'll get her back to her family after the doc's certified her for travel.' He turned away. He'd already said *thank you* once. It wouldn't have been his way to repeat himself. As he reached the step leading inside the girl burst into tears and threw herself at him. He had no choice but to hug her. Pat Tobin grinned wickedly at him as we climbed back into the wagon. Once we were rolling Warboys asked, 'What was all that about, Pat – the sudden cloudburst?'

'She'd noticed something,'

'What?'

'That he was a captain, while you're only a lieutenant, Mr Warboys. She was renewing her insurance policy, that's all.'

Pete snorted alongside me. Pat turned to look back through the small rear cab window at us. I thought he suddenly looked tired; older.

'My place, OK? It's bigger than yours, and more comfortable. I feel like doing a crate o' beer in.'

I don't know where the others came from, but there must have been a dozen folk there eventually. Pat had a big quarter he had converted from an office and workshop. It was far roomier than Watson's – I wonder why the old man never complained. I ended up on a posh leather settee with Collins's woman Thirdlow; she had tucked her knees up between us, and smiled at me over a gin and it. I was half a dozen beers ahead of her already, and in the hazy zone.

'You recovered that girl lost in the mountains. Well done. Cheers.' She raised her glass.

'Collected her, you mean. Warboys did all the work. She'd been found by some GCs who didn't know what to do with her.'

'That's not quite what I heard.'

'Are you really a policeman?'

She said, 'Mmm.' Then, 'What do you think?'

'I think nobody's who they say they are any more. We're like all those old Venetians, wearing masks in bed so they don't know who they're sleeping with.'

'Dominoes – I think you'll find they called them dominoes.'

'And when you pull off someone's mask—'

'You find another one underneath. Yes, I know. Who are *you*? I ask myself.'

'I'm a radio operator, you know that. You've seen where I work.'

'But I've just pulled off your radio operator's mask, and found someone else altogether underneath. One of Mr Watson's *funnies*.' She smiled, but I noticed her shoulders shaking, so the smile was probably a laugh as well.

'Is that what you think?'

'No, Charlie, it's what I *know* now. Maybe we should be friends.'

'Why not . . . what was your name again?'

'Ann.'

'Why not, Ann? Wannanother drink?'

'Why not?' Almost my favourite words.

I lost track of her after that. She went off after different game. I made a mental note to remember that she held her drink well. Pete chatted up a WAAF stores sergeant, and I didn't see him again for days. Pat danced with that bruiser of a woman a foot taller who gazed out over his head with a glazed, dreamy look in her eyes – Watson's new aide-de-camp. Watson himself came over for a word, but I was halfway to Berlin in my head by then. My stomach was churning with memories I hadn't asked for. I don't know when he turned up. He said, 'Well done, Charlie. I knew you'd come in handy.'

I made room for him on the settee, but he didn't sit down.

'I don't know when I last drank this much beer,' I told him. The *sir* got lost in the alcohol.

'On the squadron probably, old son. We didn't drink all that much in Egypt, did we?'

'No, although I got drunk with Oliver Nansen a couple of times. Do you ever think about him?'

I managed to play a long Jack Teagarden trombone solo in my head before he replied.

'Often, Charlie. As often as you, I should think.' He looked away.

'Did they ever find the bodies?'

'Not as far as I know.'

'I saw him not long after he bought it, did you know that?

Sitting on his camp bed as large as death, but charred a bit around the edges. He asked me to find all the photos of the girls he'd made, and to make sure their husbands never saw them.'

'I wondered why you'd got mixed up in that. The MPs probably still have an open file on it.'

'There you go, sir. You can call them up in the morning, and tell 'em it was me all the time.'

'And lose my radio operator? Perish the thought! You look a bit shagged out, Charlie. Why don't you go home, and sleep it off?'

I stood up. It wasn't as easy as it looked.

'Good idea. I think I'm getting too old for this sort of lark.' I meant partying, but I think his reply was about something else altogether.

'Aren't we all? Goodnight, Charlie, and thank you.'

When I thought about that in the morning those last few words worried me: I might have been wrong, but I couldn't remember him having thanked me for anything before.

You will have noted that he didn't query my having said that I met up with Nancy, some hours after he'd bought it in an aircraft crash. I think that was because all of us who survived the war still carried our ghosts around with us for a long time. He had his own somewhere, and maybe he'd mention them one day. Or maybe not.

My little wooden house on the prairie was less than five hundred yards away, across the parade ground. I was halfway there when my lioness stood up from where she was lying down in the gloom, stretched, yawned and paralleled me from maybe thirty feet away. I didn't mind her. We'd met in Egypt during my Canal Zone jaunt. She wasn't a ghost. She was just something loose inside my head; I understood that now.

Warboys's voice suddenly sounded from close by: I thought it was word association. Lion: lioness.

He said, 'Heading off early, Charlie?' He was alongside me. I've known them all my life: these bastards who move as silently as an owl flies.

'Yes, Tony. Early shift tomorrow – I thought I'd get some kip. Why?'

'You're walking in the wrong direction. Come on, I'll walk you home.'

How had that happened?

The last thing he said was, 'Thank you.'

'What for?'

'Coming up into the mountains. You didn't have to do that, and I appreciated it.'

'I worked with some Aussies like you once.'

'I know, they told me.' I was at the door of my hut now; I was so pissed that I'd walked straight past it.

'Goodnight, Charlie.'

'Goodnight.'

The last person I thought of before I slept was Stephanie: Steve. I wished I was in her bed instead. Then it was dark.

Chapter Thirteen

The Chanctonbury Ring

Pat picked me up again in the morning. Obviously I wasn't old enough to walk to school on my own yet. I had a sore head, and Pete's bed hadn't been slept in.

'Watson's running the show, isn't he?' I asked him. 'I worked it out when I was shaving. It's not Collins, or Warboys, or de Whitt in the radio room. It's bloody Watson again.'

Tobin winced. Maybe his head was giving him the gyp as well, or maybe he simply didn't want to talk about it.

'He just doesn't like to make a song and dance about it.'

'Where does the budget come from? Who pays?'

'Fuck knows . . . but there's plenty of it. I think the boss has friends in low places.' Then he threw the points on me, and put us on another track. We were coming to the gate of our compound. 'Make sure you have your pass handy – they're running checks this morning.'

We turned left and on to the dusty road. It was going to be another bloody lovely day, and I would miss most of it cooped up in their communications box. After the roundabout, on the track up to the operational block, Pat suddenly said, 'I came from Sussex. Did I ever tell you that?'

'No.'

'The first girl I went with wasn't that different to the one we picked up yesterday. I was fifteen, so was she. Mary Walters.'

'I don't usually talk dirty at this time in the morning, Pat. In fact, I don't often talk dirty at all. Is this conversation going anywhere?'

'I haven't come to the point yet. We used to call her the Chanctonbury Ring. It was where we came from, see, a place called Chanctonbury. She was like me – an early starter. Her old man had a market garden there.'

'I thought there was a stone circle or a burial mound called that?'

'No, a hill fort. It was where she went a lot – we took our girls there when we wanted to get laid. That was the joke about her nickname. We're cruel little beggars when we're young, aren't we?'

We were approaching the gate to the ops block compound.

I asked him, 'What about it?'

'I've been thinking about her since yesterday. I've been thinking about all sorts of things, that I wished I'd done differently.' This was a new rueful Pat.

The guard waved, opened a small wired picket gate for me, and Pat began to turn the Land Rover.

'It sounds to me,' I told him – I was probably grinning – 'as if you need a few days' hard work, to get both the booze and the women out of your system.'

Pat smiled weakly back, but didn't respond. He said, 'See you at around four, OK?'

Maybe I should have listened more closely.

I'm sure that I'd heard that story before, but I couldn't place it. It banged around in my head all that shift without finding a home.

*

Saudi Arabia was on a self-imposed radio silence, or the lazy so-and-sos hadn't bothered to get out of their tents that morning. All my radios gave me back was a reassuring hiss of static. I switched from aerial to aerial now and again, but was unable to tempt them – so I grabbed a couple of year-old *Picturegoer* magazines from a heap on a small table in the empty Allied suite. Brigitte Bardot was all at sea with Dirk Bogarde – when was he going to make a picture about what was going on in Cyprus? On the cover of the other one Jayne Mansfield was posing again: I knew she was a film star, but couldn't for the life of me name a film she'd been in.

Just before the Spamwiches came round the telephone alongside my radios rang. It hadn't done that before, so I probably looked stupidly at it for a few seconds before I lifted the receiver.

'Yes?'

'Mr Bassett?'

'Yes.'

'Gate here, sir. You have a visitor.'

I wasn't expecting one.

'Who?'

'A young lady in blue, sir. Very fetching.'

'I'll be right over.'

Wouldn't you have done the same? It had been a pretty slow day so far.

Stephanie. Steve. As pretty as a Gainsborough. Royal blue summer dress which flared from the waist. No stockings. Flat sensible shoes. A small blue car which almost matched the dress was parked a few yards from the picket gate. The corporal talking to her moved away as I reached them. We spoke through the wire. I said, 'Nice dress. Very nice, in fact. It looks expensive.'

She smiled and pouted at the same time.

'Not very. It's from Gor-Ray. I bought it in New Bond Street the last time I was over.'

'I could pretend that I know what you're talking about, but I won't. All I can say is that it's very nice.'

'And that will do nicely. Will they let you out to play? I have a picnic for us in the car.'

'No, I'm stuck here until Pat picks me up at four – one of the rules.' I beckoned the guard over, and asked him, 'Can my friend come in? She's brought me a surprise lunch – it would be a pity to waste it.'

He looked doubtful, but made a friendly decision. His face cleared.

'Civvies aren't allowed in, sir, but just this once I'll let you use the seat under that tree over there. By the MT workshop. I can see you from there, so if anyone asks I can say that she was never out of sight.'

The tree was a low twisted thing with a wonderful dark canopy of flat leaves which rustled against each other in the breeze. The seat beneath had been constructed around it: you sometimes see things like that in the gardens of stately homes, or parks, don't you? We made our way to it after she had retrieved a picnic basket from the car, and had been let into the compound. I asked her about the car.

'I knew a French colonel. He left it for me when he went home – something to remember him by. Why do these stupid men always want me to remember them?'

'Do you miss him?'

'Don't be silly, Charlie. I'll miss the car when I have to leave it behind. It's famous.'

I squinted at it. It didn't look famous to me – one of those little four-seat Renault 4 CV saloons, with the sloping back.

'Famous for what?'

'She was in the Le Mans sports car race in 1950, and finished twenty-fifth. I sometimes imagine my little car chasing all those big racing cars for twenty-four hours, until they all drop out one by one . . . and Antoinette is still going strong at the finish.'

'Antoinette?'

'She's a small car with ideas above her station.'

She had been unpacking the lunch. That tasty Turkish flat bread, two cheeses – one of which was white and gluey – leaves which looked like lettuce, but weren't. Two bananas and a couple of bottles of Keo. I wasn't supposed to drink on duty either, but what the hell; it had been quiet. Steve read my mind as I hefted one of the bottles in one hand, and made a decision.

'I've never had a girlfriend with a man's name before.'

'And I've never liked a proper Charlie as much as I like you. Why do you think I'm here?' Then she added, 'Call me Stephanie if you like – my family did.'

'No. I like Steve. It will do for me.'

'And I like Charlie. I could never call you Charles.'

Our sentences were merging into one another. I looked at her. She had a smear of soft cheese at the edge of her mouth. I made a mental mark; one of those events to remember. Memories which warm you when you are an old man. You see, I wanted the meal to go on for ever.

I didn't know when I would see her again. I promised to make it as soon as I could, and that satisfied her. No protests; no upside-down smile. Unless you counted the one on my face as I fingered the wire on the picket gate as I watched her drive away. The blue of her car was picked up in the dust. I watched until it disappeared, and trudged back to the ops block suddenly browned off. De Whitt looked up from his desk.

'Not a peep from your lot, Charlie, but the Orthodoxies

found, and then lost, a Red sub in the Black Sea. Can you give them a hand to chase it?'

Better than doing nothing, I supposed. As I walked over to the army operators I messed the words around in my head, and wondered if there were any black subs in the Red Sea. That brought a tune, and a song with it. Irving Berlin's 'How Deep is the Ocean'. I liked Frank's version. It ached with love.

I did four days on the trot, and then Watson called me into his shed at the end of a shift. He was in another of those unnerving grateful moods, and said, 'Thank you, Charlie, well done,' before I'd even closed the door on the veranda behind me. Second *thank you* in a week. Maybe he was going soft on me.

'Thank you for what, sir?'

'The last signal you intercepted – thirty-five seconds' worth, if I remember. The intelligence people have come back to say that it told them a tank division was moving up to the border. Fancy a snifter?'

'Which border? Haven't they got several?'

'Nobody knows, apparently. I sometimes wonder if intelligence is as intelligent as we give it credit for, but they're pleased with us anyway. Cheers.'

Two hefty straight-sided glasses of ouzo, topped off with water and ice. Just what the butler ordered. He flapped one hand vertically up and down. It was a signal to me to sit. Watson speared me with a glance across the top of his glass.

'Want to go flying again?'

'No, sir. Too dangerous.'

'Good-oh, knew you'd be up for it. Cheers.' We cheered again.

I asked him, 'What is it this time?'

'One of the army's funny little Austers, like that one you found in the Troodos a couple of weeks ago. Pretty aircraft.'

'Doing what? I'm not going treasure hunting again. People shoot at you when you're treasure hunting.' Three years earlier he'd sent me into the mountains of Kurdistan looking for a military aircraft full of money. It's not a bad story, but it has a sad ending – I should try it some time if I was you. Watson wagged a long finger: I was forgetting the *sirs* again, and that made him unreasonably touchy.

'Officially you'll be flying an RX 108 up a few thousand feet to see if the extra height gives you better range with a trailing aerial. We're not sure that when our Middle Eastern neighbours go quiet that they're *actually* quiet. Maybe it's atmospherics – one of the bods at Cambridge thinks that sandstorms out over the desert shut down our long-range listening capacity.'

Why didn't these buggers ever listen to what they were told? I sighed, and shook my head.

'They just stop broadcasting, sir, believe me. I can recognize the difference between bad signals and reception, and a complete absence of them. Sometimes they just don't talk . . . usually on Fridays and Saturdays, when they're mostly talking to their God instead. Or maybe they simply get into a huff with each other.'

'You know that, Charlie, and *I* know that. Unfortunately the dumb scientific class that now runs our world doesn't . . . so they want it proved to them. That's where you come in.'

'You said, '*Officially* . . . that *officially* we were flying one of the radios higher than the aerial array. I take it there's an unofficial angle to this jaunt as well.'

'Yes. You'll fly a Cook's Tour around the island afterwards, sweeping for EOKA signals – can you believe that they still don't know how many sets the opposition has out there, or where they are?'

'Will they shoot at us?'

'I shouldn't be surprised – especially if you get too close.'

'Bugger.' I held my glass out for a refill. It was always best to take advantage of the wing commander when he was in a drinking mood. 'What's in it for me?'

'Hidden glory, and the satisfaction of knowing you've served your country.' Then he belched. I didn't respond, but I expect my face said it all. Watson grinned a foxy grin and continued, 'What if I gave you another couple of days off first? That do?'

I raised my newly charged glass to him.

'That's more like it . . . *sir*.'

If you think about it we'd probably both got to more or less where we wanted to be. I asked him, 'I take it somebody *does* monitor my targets when I'm not there.'

'Course they do. Didn't we tell you?'

'Yes, but I wasn't sure I believed it. Who?'

'That's for me to know, and you to speculate. Don't ask awkward questions, Charlie. Weren't you told that as well?'

I had been, of course, but my nose was bothering me. Watson knew that, and smiled like an angel on a thunder box. He wasn't going to bloody tell me.

'What the fuck do you call that?'

Pat was showing me some transport. After all, what else do you do when you've been given an unexpected day off, and everyone you know is working? He said I could go off for a stooge as long as I kept my wits about me, and a pistol within reach, and offered me a vehicle to get around in. When we got down to the MT section he showed me an old one-and-a-half-tonner which looked as if it had been in more battles than Field Marshal Montgomery. It just so happened I'd driven it before; in Egypt. It was Watson's favourite transport, and I'm sure he dragged it around the world with him.

'Mr Watson's little Bedford. Nice old bus.' He gave it a hefty thump on its front wing to prove its worth, and I tried to ignore the heavy flakes of rust which fell out of the wheel wells and onto the concrete floor.

'I expected a car.'

'I've only got one – a Humber Hawk, an' that's out. Mr Watson's gone visiting.'

'What about the Land Rover, and your Austin Champ?'

'Sorry, Charlie. We need the Land Rover, and the bloody Champ's in the workshop again. It's gotta Rolls-Royce engine which is exac'ly no bleedin' good. I bet Rolls is ashamed of what Austin done to it.'

'So I get to ponce around in a 1940s land crab?'

'You could always stay in an' read. Wotcha gonna do, anyway?'

'I thought I'd slip in to David's place for a late breakfast and then maybe drive up to those ruins at Salamis de Whitt is always going on about.'

He gave the suggestion some genuine thought.

'That should be all right for the first time we let you out alone. The knack is not to let the GC get close to you. They like to be near enough to knife you in the back, or shoot from so close you get muzzle burns. OK? And *seriously* – take someone wiv you if you gets the chance. Better safe . . . an' all that.'

'Don't worry, Pat. I've got the message. I won't do anything stupid.'

I ran over all the rules he'd been laying on me, on the road to Famagusta – every time I rode with him he gave me a different tip, and they accumulated with a drip-drip consistency. Even someone like me eventually understood that this was becoming a dangerous little island for those who flew the Union flag. I can remember some of his lessons even now: *Always tell someone where you're going*, and *Don't go into a Cyp shop on your own, even if you know the people in it*. I expect there's some old sweat in Basra or Afghanistan telling our boys the same things today.

Parking a square canvas-covered truck in Yassine's small courtyard was a manoeuvre fraught with difficulty. David himself came out onto his steps to supervise. He watched me scraping his gate columns.

'Next time bring something different, Charlie.'

'It's all I could get. Don't you like the British Army in your car park?'

'British Army, no problem. Fucking great truck, big problem. Who else can get in here now?' It was actually a small truck; he was just making a point. He also made me smile, and of course he smiled back. 'Next time come in a jeep.'

'We don't have any.'

'No problem – I sell you one.' He would too.

He offered me breakfast, but I put him off at first.

'I'll go up and see Stephanie. Will that be OK?'

'I don't know, Charlie, I'm not her keeper. Knock on the door – it's always best.'

When I knocked on the door of her room there was no immediate response. I did it again, and heard someone mumble and begin to move.

'It's Charlie,' I said.

'I didn't expect you.'

'I didn't expect me myself. I've been given a day off.'

She yawned. After a longish pause – enough time for the usual Glenn Miller intro, and a few bars – she said, 'Why don't you go down and have some breakfast? I'll clean up, and see you in fifteen minutes or so.'

'OK.'

She didn't say anything, but I knew there was a guy in there with her.

I ate poached eggs with Yassine in an alcove off the bar. Figs.

Coffee. Yassine travelled the Middle East with the best coffee makers in the world accompanying him.

'All right?' he asked me.

'I don't know. I think I may have embarrassed her.'

'You will find out – she will tell you.'

A tall, thin guy in light khaki drills – KDs – came down the stairs, and walked out through the front lobby. He was carrying a blue UN beret scrunched up in one hand. He didn't look at us. Steve appeared five minutes later. Her hair was tied back in a short ponytail, and she hadn't any make-up. It took years off her. The first thing she did was kiss me. Yassine smiled to himself, and looked away. The second thing she did was say, 'Next time, phone up to my room from here. OK?'

'OK. You're not mad?'

'No. I think I'm pleased. I just need to get used to the idea of having a boyfriend, that's all. You *are* my boyfriend, aren't you?'

'Of course I am. Want some breakfast before we go out?'

I smoked a pipe, and David smoked a long, thin cheroot. We both watched her eat. I don't think I had been happier. But I was confused. The fact that I hadn't told Watson that I hated flying in small aircraft moved to the forefront of my mind. I was confused about that as well.

We took her racy little saloon – its engine revved like one of those new petrol-driven lawnmowers. Yassine asked if I would mind if he had the Bedford moved to a closed garage that he kept around the side of the hotel. Steve drove north out of Famagusta through a gap punched in the Old Wall. One of the Byzantine emperors had needed an inappropriately large gate.

It's the sort of structure tourists are photographed alongside to prove to their neighbours they've been abroad – it's a bloody horrible-looking thing, if you ask me. As we curled through the old streets her small car attracted more than an occasional wave: she was obviously as well known as Pat Tobin.

'I take my passing clientele to their shops,' she told me. 'They buy me expensive souvenirs by which I am supposed to remember them for ever. After they ship out, I take the gift back to the shop, and collect half the profit. Then the shop sells it again. I have received one allegedly Byzantine candelabra three times from three different men – it's back in the shop right now.' She swerved to avoid a lazy dog, and swore. We were still new enough for me to find her directness endearing.

'What will we do in Salamis?'

'Explore the ruins, paddle in the sea. Make love in the undergrowth if you like – *undergrowth* is a lovely word, isn't it? Just made for lovers. First we must stop at Ekrem's shop.' When she was excited Steve spoke at top speed, as if each conversation was a race.

'What for?'

'Picnic. We'll get hungry and thirsty out there.'

Ekrem's shop was in the shadow of the gate, but just outside the Old City. The UN had a station alongside it with two French Hotchkiss jeeps parked up outside. Nothing much seemed to be happening. There was a chain and a lock on the UN's front door.

The man Steve greeted was a tall, heavy fellow in his forties, I'd guess. He had a moustache big enough to swing on, and, if his face was in a cup, black enough to hide where it ended and the coffee began. His hair was thick and black, but thinning on top. She went on tiptoes to kiss him; one cheek after the other.

'Ekrem, this is Charlie. He is dear to me.'

'Like a brother?' The man had a deep, sonorous voice. I could smell the morning coffee on his breath. It was like confronting a grizzly bear.

'No, not like a brother — nor like the other men I have brought to you.' He wrinkled his forehead. He might have been expressing surprise: I wasn't sure whether that was good or bad. 'So don't cheat him.'

'What do you want today, Perihan?' he asked.

'Lunch. Something we can eat and drink in the fields.'

Then he turned to me, and held out his hand. 'I am Ekrem.'

'I am Charlie.'

'You like Cypriot bread, Charlie? New bake.'

'Very much.'

'Cold meats? Cheeses?'

'Yes, of course.'

'Then come into my cave.'

I don't know how thick the walls of Ekrem's shop were. It was dark in there, and cool — almost damp. The scents of a hundred different foods competed for space. It wasn't a process you could hurry. When Steve pointed to something that was past its best Ekrem would shake his shaggy head. If she persisted — as she did with some pickled artichoke heads — he would look sad. As if his best friend had died. But it was all a performance — as were his ecstatic sighs when she chose right. She bought as much food as my mother would have done in a week in the 1940s, and then stood back for me to pay for it.

'Where are the spices?' I asked him. 'I can smell spices.'

He beckoned me to follow him through the shop, through its heavy walls to an attached room that was little more than a wooden shed. It was also dark, but dry and musty. The spices were on slatted wooden shelves just above the floor. Sack after sack with their tops rolled back to show their contents. Dried peppers; sandalwood and willow; cumin and turmeric. Reds and browns and yellows. The very air in there was like snuff. I told him, 'I was in Istanbul — three years ago. They have a spice market.'

'My uncle Arslan. He also has a shop. Maybe you saw him there?' I had said the right thing; the giant was beaming.

'Maybe I did. But I cannot remember the names.'

He nodded, and we walked back to where Steve was guarding his still-open cash drawer. He fixed me with an eye lock, and I knew exactly what he wasn't saying: *I trust this woman with my money. Look after her.* I nodded: there are some things you don't need words for.

In the street outside the sun was momentarily dazzling. Steve was putting the food on the back seat of the car.

Ekrem held me back. 'She said your name is Charlie.'

'That's right?'

'The same Comrade Charlie who was locked up in the English stockade the first night he was in Cyprus? Failing to salute an officer, isn't that right?' OK; so he had the story more or less right.

'I rather think that's me, Ekrem. Is it a problem?'

He shook his head and smiled.

'No. I am a comrade too. We are strong in Northern Cyprus – we have to be. EOKA is a gang of fascists, you see. Someone will have to stop them if you British leave, or Belsen will happen again.' He shook my hand a second time. It was a comradely shake this time.

'*Will* we leave?'

'You've left everywhere else, comrade.' He smiled again to soften it. 'But remember to come to me if you are in trouble again. OK?'

'OK, Ekrem, and thank you. I appreciate that.' They were the words that Warboys had used to me. I've said it before; what goes around comes around. The last thing I asked him was, 'You called her something else when we met.'

'Perihan, yes.'

'What does it mean?'

'Fairy queen. You will see. When you walk with her it is as if she glides above the ground. Just like a fairy. Perihan is what my children call her.'

In the car again Steve asked me, 'And what was that all about?' as she slipped it into gear, and revved the engine for take-off.

'Nothing. We found we had something in common, that's all.' I looked out of the window away from her.

'Both Freemasons?'

'Something like that.'

It was something I wasn't prepared to explain yet. I joined the CP by accident in 1947. I had been squatting in a large North London house with a number of war homeless families, and gave the organizer some cash to contribute towards what I was eating and drinking: it had only seemed fair. A few days later he handed me a Communist Party membership card in the name I was using at the time, told me I'd joined an international brotherhood, and that he was very proud of me. It was too late to back out by then; besides, he was far bigger than me.

Steve didn't push it. That was nice.

Famagusta didn't end. It thinned out. The houses − some quite substantial, some not much bigger than sheds − began to have more and more ground between them. Large gardens with vegetables and unfamiliar flowers . . . and eventually a sea of thick, high scrub, with the Mediterranean looking over its shoulder. A million sparkling lights on the surface of the sea.

When she stopped the car under a stunted tree at a crossing of two dusty tracks the first thing I heard was . . . nothing. Silence. Like an English country churchyard early on a Sunday morning. Then I began to hear birds; dozens of different kinds of birdsong. Call and counter-call.

I don't know what I'd expected, but I asked Steve, 'When do we get to Salamis?'

She replied, 'It's all around you. You're inside an old Roman city right now, swallowed up like the castle in *Sleeping Beauty*.'

A couple of hours later we sat alone in an ancient, stone-tiered theatre, ate cheese and apples and washed them down with that thin Cypriot white wine drunk from the bottle. We hadn't seen another soul all morning. I took her back to an earlier conversation, and asked, '*Do* you remember the men you go with?'

Steve took a bite of a sweet, green apple, and thought before replying.

'Does a jockey remember every horse he rides?'

It may have sounded abrupt, but was an oddly reassuring answer. I leaned back and watched gulls thermalling in the blue sky. A necklace of cumulous clouds stretched low along the northern horizon.

I asked, 'Where do we start, Steve?' I knew what I meant, but also that the words I'd used hadn't expressed it all that well. She took her time anyway. Waited until we were looking at each other. She was smiling, and I wondered if my smile was as wary as hers. She leaned forward, and kissed me quickly full on the lips.

'We start by telling each other the worst thing that we've ever done in our lives – the very worst. Then there's no turning back. We start with the bad and work our way forwards towards the good.'

It made me uncomfortable, but I'd asked for it.

'OK. You first. It was your idea.'

She leaned over, and kissed me briefly again. There was a lightness about her that caught you up with her somehow.

'Not here, Charlie. Even after two thousand years the acoustics are so good that if I whispered my secrets to you, someone could hear them up in the gods. Let's walk over to

246

the gymnasium – it still has columns and walls. I'll tell you there.'

'You think I'm an American, don't you? Most men do.'

I said, 'Yes.'

'I'm not. I'm from South Africa. We have a family farm about fifty miles from Durban.'

'Then why——?'

'Hush . . . I'm going to tell you . . .'

We had counted the columns down one side of the gymnasium, and Steve was leaning against one of the stunted walls, one foot raised and braced against the stonework behind her. The area inside the square of columns was mown rough grass, the sun was almost directly overhead and the shadows were short. She had looped the basket containing the remains of our food over one shoulder, but put it down now while we talked. She said, 'The worst thing I did was seduce a native houseboy named Saul when I was about twelve. He and I had been brought up together – I'd known him all my life. I was always a precocious child – I had tits soon after I was ten, and boredom was the enemy all my childhood. By the time I decided it wasn't what I wanted, it was too late – we were doing it.'

'What happened?'

'You guessed it. I ran to my father, and told him Saul had raped me. So my father beat him with a bull whip, and nearly killed him. He crippled him before turning him off the farm. The whip cut so deep you could see the white of his ribs.'

'What happened to him?'

'I have no idea. He didn't come back. What happens to a cripple with no money and no prospects? In SA most of them die.' I thought it best to say nothing, but she hadn't finished anyway. 'That wasn't the end of it. I did it again with a

neighbour – early access to booze and the boredom again, I
suppose. But my father saw through me. He watched me go to
work on the guy at a family party, and walked into my bedroom
while we were at it. I think he must have realized immediately
that what had happened the first time was my fault. After that I
think he never stopped hating himself for what he'd done to
Saul.'

I used almost the same formula I'd spoken before.

'What happened?'

'A few weeks later they sent me away to a church school in
the States – fresh start. I was thirteen. I never went home again.
I could never forgive them for sending me away. It was like
banishment.'

I took her hand, and we walked. We walked around the
columns of the gymnasium again. When the silence between us
was easier again she said, 'Your turn. What was the worst thing
you did?'

I did some Duke Ellington in my head for a couple of
minutes, because I didn't want to hear the words aloud.

'I shot the woman I loved,' I told her. 'I think I killed her.'

Steve stopped walking immediately. I felt her fingers tighten
around mine.

'Christ, Charlie!' That was the second time she'd said that.
We took a couple more paces. Then, 'Any mitigating circumstances?'

I could have said that she'd shot at me first, and hit me, but
I didn't. I shook my head. I still had Steve's hand. We started
walking again. I felt the sun on my neck.

What had she said? Explore the ruins, paddle in the sea and
make love in the undergrowth? We walked for a couple of
hours in the ruins, paddled when our feet were hot, and finished
the food and the wine. We didn't get round to the other thing:

instead we sat on a tumbled column for an hour, and didn't say much. She sat with her back to me, and I sat with my arms wrapped around her. I supposed that it was all up to her now. When we stood up by unspoken consent we began to walk back towards the car.

A couple of teenage boys came out of the bushes a hundred yards away, and began to move towards us. Their eyes swung this way and that; the height of innocence. It was as if they were trying to reassure us that they weren't really closing on us at all. They looked as if they had just left their classrooms. I turned half away, so that they could clearly see my pistol. When I turned my face back to them my hand was near it, and I made eye contact. Both pulled up sharp, and turned away from us – almost hurried along a path towards the sea. Good decision. One, I noticed, wore a gutting knife tucked into his belt in the small of his back.

When we got back to the car one of the tyres had been slashed. Steve kept cavey while I sweated over changing the wheel: it took me half an hour. After we were rolling again she sighed, and said, 'This used to be a nice little island, you know that?'

I tried to see it through her eyes, and those of others who had lived here before Makarios and Grivas began to stir the pot. Suddenly their little slice of heaven must have seemed full of snakes.

Talking of snakes, before we got back on to the metalled road a large one crossed the track in front of the car. Steve slowed to let it go. She was right; we had nothing against each other. I was surprised at its size though – maybe three feet long and as thick as my arm.

'Blunt-nosed viper,' she told me. 'That was an old one, wasn't it?'

Silence.

Later she said, 'I'll need to think about you, Charlie. OK? I didn't expect you to be a killer.'

'I didn't expect to be one . . . but I understand. Can we still see each other while you're thinking?'

Another long pause.

Then, 'No, probably not.'

It took another half-hour to get back to the hotel. We didn't say much. Neither of us had much left. As she was nosing the Renault up the narrow lane to Yassine's place she suddenly asked me, 'What are you thinking, Charlie? I'm uneasy when I don't know what you're thinking.'

'I was thinking that the next time a woman asks me to tell her the worst thing I've ever done, I'm going to lie.' At least that raised a wan smile. We got out of the car in the small courtyard in front of the hotel, and faced each other across its blue roof. The sunlight on her pulled-back hair made it look glossy, like a helmet. She was going to say something else; I was sure of it.

'You're a murderer, right? That *is* what you said?'

'Maybe.'

She looked at my face for maybe a thousand years. Then she said, 'I'll call you,' and ran up the steps. Somehow I didn't think she would.

I had a beer with Yassine, and then another with Pat when he came in. I saw Pete sitting in the garden with a woman but didn't go out to speak to him.

Yassine asked me, 'Staying tonight?'

'No. Early start tomorrow. They want me to go flying again.' We had all been together in the Canal Zone; it wasn't worth the effort of hiding things from them.

Pat asked, 'Have you told your bird?'

'No. Didn't you once warn me about that anyway?'

He looked uncomfortable.

'The way I said it was way out of line. I didn't know things were serious between you two.'

'Don't worry about it, Pat. I think I just found out they aren't. Let's have another beer all round.'

Chapter Fourteen

Returned to Sender

Kermia used to be a small airstrip north of Nicosia. Flights 1910 and 1915 of the Brown Jobs' private air force, if my memory serves me right. The Turkish Air Force has Kermia now, and probably calls it something else. In my time it had a hard tarmac runway, crossed by a packed earth one for days when the wind was playing silly buggers. One of the problems with flying out of Cyprus is that the prevailing winds change direction in the middle of the year, so if you leave yourself with only one runway you're bound to be disappointed for six months. The first time I saw it the tarmac runway was new, and they were gearing up to make the cross runway metalled as well. Flying control was a large tent, which set the tone of the whole place really – because everyone lived in them as well. You might be forgiven for wondering if you had wandered into a tented encampment from the Boer War.

Watson had played a wicked joke on me – he had his ADC drive me up to Kermia. She was the only person I ever met who made an Austin Champ look small. We had about sixty miles to cover together in the dawn. She had a flying jacket like mine, but about ten sizes larger. And we needed them. Anyone who tells you that Cyprus is forever a land of swimming shorts and cold beers is having you on. Before sun-up, and high in the mountains at the unfashionable times of year, the tight little island can be quite nippy. At least she raised the canvas hood, but there were no side screens. I had my small pack containing a blank pad of signal flimsies, several pencils, and a flask of coffee – I threw it in the back behind the front seats. I thanked her for getting up to drive me.

'Don't mention it – our master's voice. I don't think he trusts you not to get lost on your own.' Over the years I had developed this reputation with Watson – of being unable to find my way about. It was totally unjustified. 'My name's Fiona, by the way.'

'Charlie – but you already know that.'

Fiona had a bit of a lisp, but I suppose that God had to handicap her after all the height advantage he'd given her.

'How did you get tied up with this unit?'

'I was at Cardington, and Mr Watson saw me. He asked my boss to transfer me – I think she was rather keen on him at the time.'

I shuddered. I couldn't imagine anyone being keen on Watson.

'You didn't get a say in it?'

'Do we ever?'

'Do you get on with him?'

'He tried it on early on, but I thumped him for it, and knocked him over. I thought he'd get rid of me after that, but he didn't.'

I think I chuckled.

'You and I are going to be friends, Fiona.'

'I hope so.'

I wasn't so sure I liked the sound of that. About half an hour into the journey and the sun beginning to show behind us, Fiona said, 'Your pal Pat can be a bit fast, can't he?'

'In what way?'

'*Come out for a drink, and take your clothes off while I'm up at the bar* – that sort of way.'

'I don't know. He's never asked me. I think he goes for blondes like you.' She had short-cut blonde hair. I thought that was her best point.

We slowed for a small flock of goats. The sheepskin-clad thing driving them raised his hand in greeting as we passed.

She grunted and said, 'Probably one of the friendlies, not a churchgoer.'

'What d'ye mean?'

'The churchgoers are the real bastards. The Orthodox priests encourage them to discourage us. It's not unusual for an EOKA man to get a blessing from a priest before he stabs a civilian in the market, or tosses a grenade into a bus.'

'How's this all going to end?' I asked her.

'With us leaving. That's how it always ends. We don't have the stomach for wars any more. Eventually all the colonial Brits will be forced back to our crowded little island and the colonies will take their revenge.'

'How?'

'They'll all come and live with us. Probably until we've nothing left to eat, no room to move, nowhere to live and no jobs.'

'In the 1940s we bombed the hell out of the Germans for thinking like that,' I told her. 'They said they needed *Lebensraum*.' If I thought that would shut her up I was wrong.

After a thinking break she said, 'I wonder who'll bomb the hell out of us?' Then she started whistling the 'Star-Spangled Banner' just to make sure I got the point.

She skirted north of Nicosia onto the roads across the plain which led up to Kyrenia, and we could see the tented airfield long before we reached it. The trip had taken nearly two hours, and the sun was full up. Fiona knew the form – waved through by the RAF regiment guys in charge of security, and driving me right on to the flight line.

I asked her, 'Do you go back, now?'

'No, I'll drive down to Wayne's Keep. I didn't mind driving you, to get a few hours with my boyfriend. He's a medical orderly at the stockade.' I thought that for an overlarge, unfriendly-looking woman she had a very successful social life. I guess that my face must be easy to read, because people have done it all my life.

Before I had a chance to get out, she said, 'Give us a kiss,' and grabbed me.

It was like being seized by a python. It took me minutes to break free, though to be honest by the end I wasn't trying all that hard. She actually pushed me out, saying, 'Good luck, Charlie. Get you later.'

I found myself standing alongside an Auster AOP bearing the fuselage code letter *L*, watching Fiona's departure. A sergeant my size in KD lights walked around it.

'Hello, squire. Is she your bird?' he asked me. Stiff fair hair and a smooth face. His face, arms and knees were browned by overenthusiastic exposure to the sun. His flying jacket was draped over one of the long bracing struts which supported the high wing.

'No, she works for my boss.' I stuck out my paw. 'Charlie Bassett.' Then I nodded at the green and brown aircraft. 'I'm looking for a driver.'

He had a decent handshake. A lot of pilots have good hands, have you noticed that? He sported a set of wings of course: a sergeant pilot. Always get an NCO if you can.

'You've got one, squire. Wilf Pickles, but without the Mabel.' Wilfred Pickles and Mabel were a couple of comedians on the radio. Who remembers them now? 'A chappie named de Whitt was here yesterday, and wired your radio into the back – bit of a big heavy bastard, isn't it?'

'It's supposed to have a long reach, just like Freddie Mills. Do we get a briefing for this mission?' The word *mission* slipped out by mistake. That's what we called the trips we made over Germany in 1944.

'Yeah, and the CO wants to see you before we go. He'll brief you for the army's end of this jaunt.' He picked up his jacket, pointed out a big open-faced tent to me, and casually asked, 'Weren't you in Lancasters in the war?'

'Yes, I was.'

'Like it? The Lanc, I mean.'

'Yes, why?'

He kicked one of the Auster's small main wheels, saying, 'You *won't* like this.'

At least he was upfront about it. I shrugged, and said, 'Take me to your leader.'

There is less room in an Auster than in a Morris Minor, even for men my size. I want you to get that into your head right away. I was used to aircraft you could get up and walk around in, and not at all keen on tiddlers. I looked aft, from my rear-facing seat – I have a natural prejudice for facing the direction of travel, but nobody had asked me – the fuselage dimensions behind my newly rigged receiver were barely sufficient to slot a coffin into. Maybe that's a bad simile. I sat back-to-back with Pickles, and we both wore earphones, mics and seat harnesses. We needed the earphones because the damned thing was so damned noisy.

He clicked over the intercom, and said, 'Sorry about all the racket, squire. The nice little Bombardier engine she was born with didn't like the heat and dust out here, so we swapped it for a power pack robbed out of an old Chipmunk – much more reliable.'

I didn't care what was under the bonnet as long as it got me up in the air, and down again – but I didn't want to disappoint him.

'OK. Let me know when you're about to go.'

I had stood outside the aircraft to watch them fire it up. They thought I was showing a professional interest in the starting procedures: actually I was delaying getting into the dusty glass-and-metal box as long as I could.

A glaikit-looking mechanic swung the propeller slowly four times through the priming sequence and Pickles, grinning from the cockpit, gave it three full strokes on the priming pump, and a thumbs-up. Then the mechanic gave the prop one more decent pull, through the compression stroke, and stepped smartly back. The nasty little bugger – the Auster, not the fitter; it wasn't *his* fault – coughed, and sprang to life. The arc of the spinning prop shimmered in the hard light, and grey-blue smoke from the exhaust quickly became invisible. That said it was time for me to mount up, through the back door on the starboard side. As I strapped in I reflected that the army was still using a start-up sequence that the RAF had ditched not long after the First World War. What had happened to cartridge starters, or mobile electrical sources, while I had been away?

Sitting in the Auster was like sitting inside a closely tailored greenhouse which vibrated at the rate a modern electric tooth-brush would work up to today. I hated it, and so would you. You have to trust me in this, although I can't say that Pickles hadn't warned me.

He did his checks, and ran the engine at various rev settings. Then he ran it up against the chocks for a couple of minutes. I could feel the beast straining to fly. Pickles clicked, and said, 'Luna One. Taxiing.'

The guy in flying control was having a fit of the giggles when he came back with, 'Permission to taxi, Luna One,' and then, 'Permission to take off.' I looked at the rudder in front of me as he checked its travel, and privately doubted that this little kite would be able to get us over the top of Box Hill.

Pickles taxied the beast fast. It was light on its feet when it was on the ground. That was good, because it was as slow as a pregnant pachyderm in the air. In 1943 the clapped-out Wellington bombers I did my primary training in were quicker than this thing. I know that some people love them, but the Auster is actually the technological equivalent of a grasshopper.

A nippy little cross wind told us to use the cross runway. Against the Auster's small main wheels it felt a bit lumpy, but Pickles gave it the gun, and it seemed to me that we were flying almost immediately. Maybe *grasshopper* wasn't too bad a description of it. It didn't need much room; either on the ground or to get airborne. On the other hand one of the bad points was that the rear-facing observer – yours truly – was left looking almost vertically down at an airfield receding slowly beneath him: a steep rate of climb but not a good one.

A few years ago another old army pilot told me I should have picked up on the fact that we were going to climb steeply when I heard Pickles's voice crackle, 'Fifty knots,' in my ear. Apparently there was a tree not all that far away that took a bit of hurdling, and fifty knots gave you the best engine setting for a steep rate of climb. I looked down at the tents getting smaller, and felt sick.

He climbed us in lazy circles, calling out high points from time to time, and other prominent features below. After twenty minutes he got us to eight thousand feet. That's a mile and a half in your language: far enough for anyone to fall in mine. Every time he turned up sun the cabin warmed noticeably.

'High enough for you, Radios?' I think he momentarily

forgot my name. Not bad, actually: it reminded me what I was there to do, and to stop feeling sorry for myself.

'Fine, Wilf. Where's the aerial spool?'

'In the roof. Look over your left shoulder, and up.'

It looked a proper Heath Robinson lash-up to me, but it worked. Wilf slowed our IAS so much before we deployed the aerial, that it was almost as if we hung motionless in the air: aircraft aren't supposed to do that. Ten minutes later, when we were out over Famagusta Bay, I fired up the radio, and the signals came in from everywhere, like a pack of hungry foxhounds disappearing underneath your bed.

My first thought was to tear off my phones to prevent my eardrums bursting. Then I settled down to it, cranked it back to comfortable, and swept and wrote whilst Pickles flew us slowly eastwards in reciprocal parallels – like a farmer ploughing his best field. He was probably bored, but we gave it a good hour.

There was no doubt about it. The 108 enjoyed its trip to the roof of the world: a bit of height, and a hundred and fifty feet of trailing aerial, made a ridiculous difference. The only signals I could identify for certain, of course, were the Saudis and their damned train . . . because I knew their call signs. But I had the wavelength and the frequencies of everything else, and de Whitt could compare them with what he was getting on the ground. The interesting thing, of course, was that the Saudi signals were just as easy to intercept as any of the others. I thought this probably finally proved that *no signal* meant that no one was signalling. The trouble was that I knew in my heart the boffins wouldn't buy it: it was too simple an answer, and no one would win a Nobel Prize for it.

'You got enough yet?' Pickles clicked.

'Fine. Ready to go when you are.'

He slowed us to about sixty knots again as we recovered the

trailing aerial. Again I had that odd feeling of hanging motionless above the island. Then he put us into a gentle side-slip – but only for half a minute or so – and we dropped down, and round towards the West. The sun was overhead, and those bloody mountains were somewhere in front of us. I had the feeling it was going to be a long day.

'The trouble is the fuel tanks,' Wilf clicked. 'They're in the wings – close to the roots.' Just up above my head, he meant. 'They're self-sealing of course, but if the GCs have a crack at us, it's what they're aiming for.'

'Do they catch fire?'

Click. 'Sometimes, Charlie.'

'What then?'

'I'm supposed to side-slip to keep the flames from the cockpit.'

Click. 'Does that work?'

'Not always.'

'What then?'

Click. 'We ditch the doors, and jump for it.'

'We have parachutes?'

'Nah, they're fer cissies. You're in the army now.'

Where did they find these people?

Over a small village in the Cedar valley an hour later I began to understand what the army was up against. From above it looked like the village that Warboys had taken us into. That wasn't all that surprising. After an hour of flying over them, I realized that most of them looked the same. I guessed that anyone who lived in the Troodos spent most of his income supporting a bleeding great local church.

Wilf had handed me a map marked with areas from which the EOKA radios had previously been thought to be active. The army intercept vans – all four of them – had been deployed around the foothills of the Troodos for me. The idea was that they would triangulate on anything I picked up from the plane, so that we could plot a map of exact locations, and send patrols in to switch them off.

The village was called Agios something – they were all called Agios something – and Wilf spiralled us gently out of the clear blue sky above the church.

Unexpectedly, the church fought back.

Well, the half-dozen guys on its roof did. Luckily for us they had no automatic weapons, but the rifle and pistol fire were bad enough. They didn't start until we were about five hundred feet above them, and at that height it was like flying into light flak. Two bullets went through the cabin. One careered off the bracing spar above my head, and exited out of the side window with a *snap*. Showers of Plexiglas shards. I probably screamed. I know that Pickles did.

He skidded us sideways in the air. I still don't know if it was a brilliant bit of flying or pure funk. Our horrible little aircraft staggered away, clawing for height like a cat trapped in a cage. By then, of course, I was looking down at the church, over the tail . . . and was surprised by the grenade. I put it down to the errant ambition of an oversexed teenager: teenagers are the same the world over.

I suppose that it is theoretically possible to bring down an aircraft with a hand-thrown grenade. But it would take a hefty throw, and for the fates to be well and truly on your side. His fates had deserted him that day. Maybe Godfrey Evans could have managed a throw like that, but my little grenadier didn't stand a chance. It's a horrible bloody feeling to see blokes shooting at you, and to be unable to do anything except duck. It's even worse when they start to chuck bombs at you.

I saw the little matchstick man throw something up at us. At first I thought it was a stone, hurled in frustration. Then within microseconds I knew it was a Mills bomb. He simply forgot to wait long enough before he threw the damned thing: he just chucked it, and threw himself flat on the walkway around the church roof. Ten seconds later the grenade returned to sender – it fell back alongside him, of course. I saw one of the gunmen give it a quick look, then take a header over the side. Under the circumstances it's a decision I would have agreed with.

Then the grenade exploded. And the church roof fell in. I lost sight of the building immediately because we were on our side, and hanging from our straps. That was because of the updraft, or because Pickles had an idle moment, and was trying to see what the airframe would put up with before it fell to bits. When I had my bearings again we were up at a thousand feet, the church roof had caved in completely, and there were small fires inside the building: God was having a very bad day. A dust cloud hung in the air above it like the demon in a Dennis Wheatley story. There were two bodies spreadeagled in the square – and people were running from their houses with buckets. I put the earphones back on, and did a quick sweep.

'Their radio's gone very quiet,' I told Wilf.

He laughed: quietly at first, and then like the Laughing Policeman. Eventually he clicked and said, '*Balls*. You know who's going to get the blame for this, don't you? The papers will say we bombed a church.'

'They threw a grenade at us,' I told him, 'and then caught the fucking thing again before it went off. It was self-inflicted idiocy.'

I thought the engine sounded a bit clattery, and maybe we were leaving a visible blue exhaust trail in the sky. Pickles sighed. 'I think our ride's a mite weary. Let's fuck off, shall we?'

We did a slow circuit low around Kermia, and a man with a trailing mic, outside the control tent, examined us through binoculars. It wasn't because he didn't know who we were; it was to examine the airframe to see if he could spot any damage we hadn't logged yet. I heard his considered reply to the pilot: it was, 'OK to land, Luna One, but *my*, haven't we a dirty arse!'

There had only been one jangly moment on the return, and that was when the engine pop-popped, threw out a trail of black smoke, and cut completely. Pickles had managed to restart it after we had lost a thou, and before he did reassured me.

'Don't worry, Charlie. I can glide her in from here.'

In the event I was glad he didn't have to.

A Land Rover crash tender followed us down the runway. When I stepped down on to the good earth again I thought its crew looked disappointed that their skills hadn't been called for. When we walked around our little mechanical insect it was impossible to miss the fact that most of her engine oil was spread along the bottom of the nose, and the fuselage. In the army the technical description of that was *a dirty arse*.

'What kind of engine did you say it was?' I asked Pickles.

'From a Chipmunk. Why?'

'Apparently it runs without oil. It's wearing it all on the outside.'

He grinned back.

'She doesn't know when she's beaten.'

I could feel the heat coming from the engine bay from a couple of feet away, and hoped that my firefighting training wasn't about to come into question. Even so, Wilf stretched out his right hand, and gave her an affectionate pat.

'Shall we go and find a beer?' he asked. I wonder what my life would have been like without alcohol.

In their mess tent we swallowed a couple of quick Keos before Wilf's major, Brede, found us. He signalled up another round, and sat at a long table with us.

'What did you get, Wilf?'

'About ten decent signatures, sir. Charlie will give you the details.' I'd already been introduced to the guy at briefing, of course. I think he didn't quite know how to relate to a civvy working for the military: I was neither fish nor fowl.

'I'll write my report up later, if that's OK,' I said.

Then Wilf said, 'Suddenly I don't feel very well,' in a distant voice, and surprised both of us by collapsing, sprawled across the table.

I think I'd noticed that since we'd climbed down from the crate he'd kept a handkerchief balled up in his left hand. He let go of it as he passed out, and we saw that it was heavily stained with blood . . . and his hand, open and slack on the table, told its own story. There was a bloodstained hole through the palm. It began to bleed again as we watched. Brede called the mess servant back with, 'Run for the MO, there's a good chap. Tell him to *jildi*: Mr Pickles has a bit of bullet trouble.'

A nice khaki-green Austin ambulance came for Wilf a little later. It had *MBH Famagusta* stencilled on the door, big red crosses and a pretty nurse from Queen Alex's: a fully paid-up member of the Grey Mafia. Before Wilf was whisked away the mechanic who'd seen us off came in with a buggered-up bullet wrapped in a piece of muslin. He'd found it on the cockpit floor, and now he put it in Pickles's good hand for luck.

'I knew a fitter who lost a finger in '44,' I told him. 'A pig bit it off. We buried the finger with full military honours, and ate the pig.'

The engineer looked at me for a few seconds before he replied. He was trying to work out if I was pulling his plonker. Then he said, 'Changed times, sir. They'd try to sew it back on again today. Ain't science wonderful?'

I walked out to the ambulance with Wilf. He was on a

stretcher because the MO had banged him full of morphine, and if we'd left him on his feet he would have walked in circles.

'Why didn't you tell me you'd been hit?' I asked him as they lifted him into the back of the meat wagon. He gave me back that ghastly drugged grin.

'Didn't want to worry you, squire.' Then his brain kicked in again, and he asked, 'Was my flying up to scratch? RAF piloting standards?'

'Better than that. Much,' I told him. 'Look, I run a small civvy airline in my spare time. Why don't you come and ask me for a job when you demob?'

I could see from his eyes that I was losing him to the drug, and the nurse looked impatient anyway. I had to bend to hear what he said next.

'Knew it . . .'

'Knew what, Wilf?'

'Knew I hadn't seen the last of you.' Then he closed his eyes.

The next voice I heard was from slightly above me, and behind my right shoulder.

'Have I missed something?' Fiona: she hadn't forgotten me.

I had Pickles's bloody handkerchief in my hand. She nodded at it. I dropped it in a waste bucket, where it lay among the beer-bottle caps.

'Not all that much.' I probably grimaced. 'I'll need to wash before we can get going. Thanks for coming.' *Coming back for me*, I meant, but I didn't get to finish the sentence.

I already told you that after all of the wars we fought around the Middle East the British Army became rather good at finding things to do in olive groves. Well, the RAF wasn't that bad either, and Fiona was not to be denied her chance to demonstrate it. She found an isolated olive grove not far past Angastina on the Famagusta road, and we sat on the ground, drank a bottle of warm beer each, and nibbled some biscuits she'd brought up from the Keep. I don't know if she had anything else in mind, but if she did she didn't say so.

Neither did I. Maybe I was learning that sometimes it's nice just to be friends. I remembered the little bugger and his knife at Salamis, and couldn't settle . . . I jumped at every noise. Even so, we got to know each other and smoked and talked, and left as soon as the sun began to dip.

Rolling back down the road to camp I was relaxed. None of the tension I had carried to Kermia with me. When Fiona stopped the Champ outside my quarter in the twilight she left the engine running, so the evening was ending there anyway. I turned in the passenger seat and said, 'Fiona?'

'What?'

I reached up, and kissed her cheek. It was dusty.

'Thanks for coming.'

I liked her laugh.

Pete was sitting on his bed playing patience. He asked, 'How did it go?' These bastards always seemed to know my business.

'Fine. Someone got shot in the hand by one of the local monkeys, but apart from that it was pretty routine. Watson's new woman drove me there and back.' I couldn't remember if Pete had been at the services burial of the finger in '44, or had missed it during one of his unofficial absences. His game came out. Nearly all the games Pete played did.

'Wanna find a bar?'

'No thanks, Pete. I fancy an evening in. Good book, roaring fire and smoke a couple of pipes. Thanks for asking though.'

'You OK?'

'Yeah. I told you . . . I just feel tired.'

'Woman tired?'

'No. Not woman tired. Just tired.'

He gave me the look, but for once he was wrong.

'OK,' I told him. 'You win. Give me half an hour to clean up and we'll find somewhere to drink.'

Be careful what you wish for. Isn't that what they say?

The roaring fire I'd longed for broke out in the cookhouse a little later. It was blamed on a waiter who'd been sacked for stealing sugar, and decided to become a hero of the revolution instead . . . We were all turned out to fight it. Not a bloody chance. The kitchen block was full of cans of fat and cooking oils, which exploded like bombs. The wooden building burned better than a Guy Fawkes bonfire. By the time I was trudging back to the billet between Pat Tobin and Pete we each had soot stains on our arms and faces and clothes, and nowhere to have breakfast.

'I have a proper bottle of whisky – my boss gave it to me as an embarkation present,' I told them. 'What say we arsehole it?'

Pete grinned, but it didn't seem to lift Pat's spirits. Something was biting him.

Chapter Fifteen

The Lone Rider of Santa Fe

Warboys. I was sitting on the step of my billet reading *Moby-Dick* – a copy from the camp library. The step was in a nice slab of shade, and there was a bit of a breeze from somewhere. Warboys drove past alone in his little lorry, heading for Watson's cricket pavilion. He waved as he went past. His truck stirred up the dust.

He returned an hour later, stopped and switched the engine off. It sounded as if it was a much better power plant than that in Pickles's Auster. Maybe they should have started bunging Humber engines in their aircraft. The engine block ticked as it cooled. He didn't get down from the cab. I took my pipe from my mouth.

Warboys said, 'Your boss said you had a couple of days off. What are you going to do?'

I didn't want to tell him that I didn't particularly want to go into Famagusta. It wasn't that I didn't want to go to Tony's – I couldn't think of anything better than lazing under one of Yassine's fans with a glass of Keo in front of me. The problem was that if I didn't run into Steve, I'd run into Alison, and I didn't want to be responsible for an atmosphere of spectral doom.

'Nothing planned. I'm enjoying my book, and not having to work.' I waved my pipe at him.

'Fancy seeing a couple of castles?'

'Come again?'

'I've a few days off myself, as it happens. I've been sketching the castles on the island in my spare time. I wanted to go back to Kyrenia and St Hilarion. I wouldn't mind the company, if you were interested.'

He made the offer the way men always do; as if a rejection wouldn't matter.

'Can I get some pipe tobacco in Kyrenia?' I asked.

'I know a place where you can get anything.'

'Then I can pack in five minutes.'

We headed back towards Nicosia on the road that I had driven with Fiona the day before. On Cyprus, Nic is like Rome: all roads lead to it. I asked him about sketching castles.

'Not only sketches,' he told me. 'I'm making architectural drawings and schemes. I plan to do a book on the Cypriot castles one day. I met a mad novelist in a bar, and he encouraged me.'

'Bully for him. Wasn't that what T. E. Lawrence was doing when he joined the army and got into trouble?'

'Yes, he was drawing Crusader castles in the Holy Land. One of my heroes.'

'I feared that.'

'Meaning?'

'He was an idiot.'

He smiled. He didn't take his eyes off the road when he drove. I liked that in a driver. He asked me, 'How do you make that out?'

'He promised Arabia to the Arabs, and then helped give it to the French – they'll never forgive us for that. Then he fell off his motorbike and killed himself. The man was an idiot.'

'He wrote a wonderful book by all accounts.'

'He wrote an *unreadable* book. I know – I tried it. All of the *would be's if they could be's* were reading it in the Canal Zone. Anyone who tells you it was a good book is just trying to show you how terribly intellectual they are. Lawrence couldn't spell, and his editor didn't even bloody try.' Warboys seemed amused by the way the conversation was going; I thought I ought to finish by keeping him on side. 'Don't worry about it. You probably wouldn't like the books I read either.'

'What *do* you read?'

'The Americans mainly. The language is dead and buried in Britain or the colonies – the Americans are the only ones keeping it alive. Hemingway and Steinbeck, Spillane and Chandler – people like that.'

'Weren't *they* a colony once?'

'Yeah, but they got out because they didn't like the books we were writing.'

Warboys laughed again. I was sure that he had gone to school at one of the places where they have fags, instead of smoking them.

'Who would be a good American writer to start on, in your opinion?'

'Zane Grey or Holly Martins.'

'Never heard of them – interesting names though. Ready for a coffee stop? I know a tidy little Turkish café in North Nicosia.'

'That's a very good idea, Tony. Perhaps a decent coffee will stop me sounding so much like a berk.' It was a word we used in the fifties; it meant fool.

'No,' he said. 'Keep going. I like being challenged.'

The coffee was as good as he promised, and he was able to park the wagon where he could keep his eye on it. The café – Café Truva – was on a big, sun-splashed cobbled square, looked down on by old three-storeyed buildings. Washing strung across the streets like flags. Five roads led into the square, or more importantly *out* of it. I suspected that this fact figured in Warboys's choices. We stood up at a high aluminium bar, swallowed a coffee each, and pushed our cups back for a refill. It was like drinking an electric shock.

'I don't quite know why I was beginning to sound so angry, Tony. I think it was something to do with your speaking voice.'

'How *do* I sound?'

'Like an upper-class berk: I'm a lower-class berk. Where *did* you go to school?'

'Guess.'

'Somewhere very expensive.'

'Wrong. Round the corner. This is my home patch, old son. The English School in Nicosia . . . T-E-S, as it's known over here. My old man was in the Foreign Office, and was out here ten years or more.'

'I don't suppose he knew someone called Carlton Browne?'

'Old CB? Course we did. Everyone knows him.'

Ah. I knew there was something. There's always a little bloody something.

'So you knew I was coming out here?'

He didn't reply. He just smiled his best smile, and hoped to get away with it.

He said, 'You needed tobacco, you said? Why don't you pop through there, and see if my friend Alev here can help you?' Alev was a tall, bony Turk with an outrageously naked upper lip: he probably wanted to stand out from the crowd.

There was a bead curtain shielding an arched doorway. I elbowed my way through it and found myself in a large room like a warehouse, full of life's little necessities. I hadn't seen anything like it before, not even a country Co-op . . . and I couldn't believe in the three two-ounce tins of Sweet Chestnut Flake I shortly found in my hands – it was difficult enough to get it in Blighty! McVitie's Digestives, Callard & Bowser

Creamline Toffees, Liquorice Allsorts and Wine Gums . . . and those new-fangled drip-dry shirts you never had to iron. An Aladdin's fucking cave. There was even a pile of dog-eared English paperbacked novels.

I walked back to Warboys having done a deal for the tobacco, two shirts and a case of Watney's beer.

'Where the hell does he get this stuff?' I asked him. 'There's a king's fortune in there.'

'I steer him in the right direction. Your pal Pat mostly – he won't mind me telling you.'

'What about the police?'

'The civvies raid us now and again, but we always get a warning, and send them away with a few cartons of fags to keep them happy. Old Collins leaves us alone – he knows I work out of here.'

'And Alev here,' I indicated the tall, calm man who seemed to run the place and who had followed me out, 'is peculiarly discreet, I suppose?'

That bloody smile for all the world again. Warboys said, 'It's this way, Charlie. My mother died when we were still here. I was about four. My father sought consolation in the arms of others – a surprising number, if the truth be told – so Alev is actually my kid brother.' I should have spotted the resemblance: it was there if you looked for it. The two brothers then gave each other the hug they'd been holding back. 'Alev is a comrade,' Warboys continued. 'He wants a free Turkish republican state in Northern Cyprus after the British leave.'

'And I suppose you've *promised* it to them?'

'Yes, and with all my heart. They will be free of these bloody Greeks, or I'll die trying.'

There was just that moment. That gleam of the fanatic in his eyes. *Bloody* Lawrence again; why couldn't he have stayed at home, and written learned monographs about Templar castles? Fuck it!

Alev gave me a hug as well before we drove away. In the cab of the truck I recalled something that Warboys had said.

'Tony?'

'Yes?'

'When you were telling me who Alev was, you used the word *comrade*.'

'That's right, old son. Alev is a comrade . . . just like you and me.' Bollocks. A Turkish freedom fighter, a throwback to the days of empire, and reluctant Red Charlie. We'll keep the Red flag flying here. My dad would have liked this. What I really thought was, *What have you got yourself into now, you fool?* And, then, after I had worked it out – *Bollocks!* Again.

We passed Kermia: the road wound past it. Another ambulance stood beside the flying control tent. A sadly misused Auster was sitting on its side at one end of the tarmac – a wing had been ripped off but it hadn't burned. They must have been having a run of bad luck. Just before we started to climb up into the Kyrenia range Warboys pulled over so that we could have a drink. He fished a couple of warm bottles of Keo from under his seat.

'Don't worry, old son. We're off duty, ain't we?' I gave him the second-hand book I'd bought for him from Alev's library. It was Holly Martins's *The Lone Rider of Santa Fe*. I think he was genuinely touched by the gesture. He riffled the pages before he put it in his small pack. 'Very nice of you, old son. I shall enjoy it.'

'My pleasure.'

'I'll give it back when I've finished it.'

'Don't bother: I've read it – pass it on.'

'Right you are. Ready to go? We're only half an hour from St Hilarion now.'

St Hilarion sits at the top of a mountain pinnacle commanding the plain to the south, and the road which runs north to south between Kyrenia and Nicosia. The people who built it were probably very nice people, although a lot of them were Venetian, so you never know. Only three good things ever came out of Venice: proper drinking chocolate, the *ombra*, and girls in dominoes lifting their skirts in dark alleys during a Festival of Fools. I met a Venetian a few years ago who boasted that Venice was the true father of international banking: I suppose that says it all, really. Anyway, the Venetians had a lot to do with how St Hilarion looks today: crouched narrow on a mountain top, like the petrified skeleton of a constipated vulture. It's made of stone all right, and kind of droopy . . . but you can't mistake the air of tension in the architecture.

The castle is supposed to have been an inspiration for Walt Disney when he was making *Snow White*, so remind me never to visit Orlando. The road up to the damned place is narrow, cutting past precipice and pass, and narrowing to widths that even a naked cyclist would shrink from. Warboys sprinted us up it as if he was driving in the Monte Carlo Rally.

Maybe that was something to do with getting away from what looked like a lorryload of armed Afghan tribesmen, who were trying desperately to keep up with us. I looked nervously over my shoulder and told him, 'Don't look now, but I think we're being followed.' I think I'd borrowed the line from *Dick Barton*.

'Don't worry, they can't get past.'

'But don't we have to get back down past *them*?'

'Good point. Should have thought about it.' I think he was about to laugh.

'And what happens when they get within rifle range?'

'They already are. You worry too much, Charlie. If they were going to bang off at us they would have started before now.'

It was good to be in the hands of a professional, as the gardener said to . . . OK, so you've heard that one before.

There was another truckload of shaggy armed tribesmen barring the gatehouse to the castle when we reached it, but they didn't look quite the same. There was a qualitative difference between the ones chasing us, and the ones in our way, but I couldn't put my finger on it. They let us through, and into the castle, but moved to block the lorry following us. It stopped, and the two groups did the head-to-head thing. They blew the horns of their vehicles in protest against each other, and then fired their rifles in the air.

'It's like dealing with children,' Warboys told me. 'How on earth are they going to run the show when they have independence, and have to manage their own affairs?'

'Wait a couple of mins until my heart has slowed down, Tony. Then you can explain in simple words what's going on.'

He pulled us to a halt in the shadow of a crumbling wall just inside the main castle court. It was narrow, like the fortress, and followed the line of the rock it sat on. Looking down into the plain I could clearly see two birds of prey circling high over the tents at Kermia: the lads had better watch out for their dinners.

Warboys whistled a tune. The first bars of 'The Red Flag'. He was probably only doing it to annoy the Greeks, who had taken a political position somewhat to the Right of Oswald Moseley. What's modern Greek for 'Hurrah for the Blackshirts'?

'The lorry behind us is full of TC resistance men, Charlie – the TMT. They are resisting the Greeks, and they are here to look after us. The ones who let us through into the castle are EOKA GCs. They're the enemy – they're resisting *us*.'

'Then aren't we on the wrong side of this fight?'

'Who said it was a fight, old son? We're just coming to lunch.'

There was a table in the sun in the middle of the court. It had a white tablecloth, and was set with three places. The chairs looked rustic and solid. A mixture of breads, fruits, meats and cheeses climbed around bottles of white wine which still bore the beads of the water they had been cooled in. The man waiting for us, a priest, stood, smiled, and opened his arms. Tony Warboys accepted the invitation, and they hugged each other. I wasn't as surprised as I had been the first time, although all the men hugging each other on this bloody island would eventually get me down. Warboys said, 'Hello, Adonis.'

'Hello, Tony,' from the priest. 'Are you hungry?'

'Starving. Did you bring your mother's olives?'

'She insisted – and gave me a bottle for you to take away. She sends her love.'

'My father would have sent his greetings if he knew we were about to meet again.'

Too bloody much.

'Another one of your brothers?' I asked Warboys.

They both laughed. I suppose that was better than one of them throwing a pink canary.

'No.' It was the priest who spoke as he smiled. 'My mother is much too sensible for that. Tony and I were at school together – TES. We studied in each other's houses. He helped me with Latin, and my father taught him Greek.' Then he gave me a shrewd sort of look and said, 'You must be Charles Bassett, the radio man.'

Betrayal is a very odd thing. Although it creeps up on you slowly and unnoticed, when it happens, it happens very fast.

Bastard. We were sitting down by then. The priest was offering me a glass of wine. I half stood, and swung on Warboys demanding, 'Why did you bring me here, you bastard?' Might as well use the word.

The shrewd look was from Tony this time. He said, 'Because they asked me to. Sit down again, and eat your lunch. They'll be offended if you don't.'

We ate. On my part it was a sullen affair. Warboys and the priest talked as if I wasn't there. EOKA was the enemy: they had murdered British servicemen, policemen, civilians, women and children . . . and we were sitting down to scoff with them. The food was probably very good, but it tasted bitter in my mouth – like lemons. They talked about school, and mutual acquaintances. Families. Tony had a sister.

'I was in love with her once,' the priest laughed. He told me, 'My parents were horrified.'

Warboys grinned at the recollection.

'What about *your* sister? Half the boys in the town were crazy about her.'

'And she was in love with you, but you never noticed.'

There was an odd moment of silence. Warboys looked away over the plain.

'No,' he said. 'I never knew that.'

The priest looked at me. The expression on his face said he wanted to explain something.

'We are all mixed up, you see, Mr Bassett. Those boys outside the gate, Tony, me . . . we went to school together. Lived in each other's houses, seduced each other's sisters – or tried to – shared meals. Cribbed each other's exam papers. *Loved* each other . . . there is no other word for it. Now we are killing each other over a few conflicting ideas. It is quite mad. Have you read Dante?'

'No. Why?'

'Get a good translation of *Inferno* – Tony will get one for you – read about Hell, and recognize it as Cyprus.'

I perked up at that. I had been trying to work out how to get away on my own, and save my skin, but at least he was speaking of me in the future tense.

'Just *stop*,' I said. 'Tell the politicians and the lawyers and the accountants to fuck off and leave you in peace. Stop fighting.'

'Come off it, Charlie.' That was Warboys. 'You've seen this sort of thing before. You know it's gone too far for that. The politicians had a chance to avoid bloodshed three or four years ago, and they fluffed it. I think they do it on purpose. They're so mentally impoverished the only thing that gives a politician a stiffy is his own cute little war. It's the only logical conclusion – politicians take us into wars so often because they *want* to. They need to be able to cause the deaths of a few hundred people, and get away with it . . . to legitimize themselves, I suppose. I hate the bastards.'

'I hate the bastards too,' Adonis said, and raised his glass, 'even though I'm not supposed to swear, and I'm not English.' I wondered if he was supposed to drink either.

'And so do I,' I told them, and held out my glass for a refill. The wine was thin and vinegary, and exceptionally refreshing. 'Pour me another drink, one of you.'

The priest obliged. 'Retsina – the sharp flavour is pine. From the mainland. Not all of their ideas are bad.'

I knew that they'd get round to telling me what I was there for eventually, but I decided to shorten the odds. I asked Warboys, 'Why did you tell them my name?'

'I didn't. Adonis sent me a message asking me to bring a Mr Charles Bassett, RAF, retired, to see him. I was rather intrigued, and came through to ask your gaffer this morning. He OK'd it as long as I guaranteed to return you in one piece.'

'Why didn't you just ask me?'

278

'Because you're not stupid. You would have said *no.*'

Not a betrayal then. Something else. I sipped my wine and studied the priest. His move.

'Well?' I asked him.

'I needed to see you face to face – *again*, as it turned out – to help me help some others to make a decision.' It was one of those moments when you know you should keep your mouth shut. I was never any good at them.

'Tell me about it.'

'We have to decide whether it will be in my friends' interests to have you killed, or kept alive.'

Bugger. Still not out of the woods then.

'If you killed me I wouldn't be able to read that book about Hell you recommended.'

'You would find out personally. You wouldn't need a book.' Bloody priests and parsons. Have you noticed it? They have an answer for everything. 'Please understand that your death will not be a tactical decision – it's nothing to do with the civil war.'

I think he was the first person I heard use the words aloud. I put my glass on the table, and filled a pipe, reflecting that I wanted to stay alive at least long enough to smoke those precious six ounces of Sweet Chestnut. I said, 'One of you will have to explain that to me.'

'EOKA is like any other nationalist army,' Adonis said. 'It's poor. Most of the time we're broke. Athens gives Grivas just enough to keep him on their leash.' I'd heard of this Colonel Grivas. He ran EOKA like an old-fashioned warlord.

'So?'

'We need money. We always need money.'

'To buy arms to kill innocent civilians with?'

'Innocent civilians? Sometimes. And not so innocent soldiers, and policemen. You are occupying my island, Charles. I want you to go home.'

'And your Turkish Cypriot neighbours?'

After a pause he said, 'Yes, they will have to go home too.'

'This *is* their home,' Tony told him. 'They belong here as much as you do.'

The priest shook his head, and looked at the ruins of lunch on the table as if they had some meaning for him. He sounded genuinely sad when he said, 'Not any more.'

I realized then that I had just been given a better explanation of the Cyprus Crisis in three minutes, than any politician or academic could have managed in a fortnight.

'I still don't understand what this has got to do with me,' I said.

'Simple. Someone has offered EOKA money to kill you,' the priest said. 'An English person.'

'You can say it now,' Warboys told me.

So I said, 'Fuck it.' For once my brain worked fast enough, and the logic chains ran in the right direction. I dispensed with *who* and *why*, and even *where* and *when*: they could wait until later. I asked the priest, 'How much?'

It was Tony who said, 'What?'

'How much? How much have you been offered?' I wasn't short of a quid or two myself.

The priest wrinkled his brow. He probably couldn't see why it should matter. He said, 'Two and a half thousand pounds sterling, as I understand it . . . but if I know the brave colonel he will stick out for more. It seems to be a seller's market.'

'I'll give you four not to kill me, but kill the person who made the offer instead.'

A long long pause, then Tony said it again. He took a sip of his retsina, and asked, 'What?'

'You heard me. I'll outbid whoever asked them, and turn the tables . . . but on one condition.'

'And that is?' the priest asked.

'That mine is a once-and-for-all offer. You don't go back to the originator, and bid him up again.'

'How could you guarantee that?' Warboys demanded.

'By placing a side bet on the priest. You're not the only one with friends in low places. If *I* get it, *he* gets it . . . and a relation . . . say, his mother you're both so fond of. Easy to arrange.'

There was a moment of absolute silence. I could hear the birds of prey keening out on the plain below us. For the first time the priest looked startled. He went as deathly pale as his namesake was supposed to have been. That lovely boy.

He stared, and asked, 'You would do that?'

'Yes, of course. Why not?'

'And you *can* do that?'

'Of course. Do you think you're the only person who can command a killing? Ask Tony.'

The priest glanced at Warboys, who sat back in his chair, stroked his chin as if caressing a long-lost beard, nodded and said almost absently, 'I'm afraid Charlie *does* have a certain reputation.'

The priest stood. There were crumbs of bread on his clothes. As he began to walk away he told me, 'I have to consult with our people. They will make the decision, not me.'

Tony and I stood up as well. I wasn't prepared to let the priest go without another word.

'Make sure I'm informed, won't you?'

He paused, and spat back, 'You will know of the decision when the bullet comes for you.'

'No, Adonis. You will tell me of your decision, and if necessary you will give me a chance to run.'

'Or?'

'If anything happens to me, your mother will die. It is easily within my reach, and I promise it . . . and maybe your sister as well.'

He had been moving away from us. Now he stopped, turned and put the eye bite on Warboys. Tony said, hastily I thought, 'Adonis's sister is dead. She died while I was in England.'

The priest suddenly looked very tall. Ascetic. Distanced.

'She hanged herself,' he said, then turned and stalked away.

Although the sun was shining from a cloudless sky I was suddenly cold.

Warboys said, 'I didn't know that.'

I didn't know if he was talking to me or Adonis.

Warboys went back to sit at the table. I joined him. We picked over the food and finished the wine. He seemed pensive. After the noise of both vehicles departing down the mountain road had died he asked me, 'Do you have as much money as you said?'

'Yes. I had a very good war eventually.'

'Uh huh . . . and *would* you? Would you call down a killing on an old lady, just to prove a point?'

'I don't know. If it was the only way to stay alive myself. Let's hope we never have to find out.'

'You know that if you did that, I'd have to come after you myself, old son?' The old silky voice of the assassin had come back.

'I can always put you on the list as well, Tony. I wouldn't want to, but would if I had to. Anything happens to me, happens to you – maybe to somebody close to you as well. You'd do very well to keep me in one piece – just like you promised the wing commander.'

He suddenly began to laugh. It was a very odd, hollow sound in that empty castle bailey.

'What?' I demanded.

'I was thinking about old CB. He said that you were a *thoroughly nasty piece of work wrapped in blarney.*'

'So?'

'Next time I'll listen more closely. You OK by yourself for a couple of hours?'

'I expect so. Why?'

'I want to take some measurements, and make a few drawings.'

Some of it had been true after all. But after that I wasn't going to turn my back on him in a hurry.

I dragged a chair into the shade, out of the breezes, and opened *Moby-Dick* again. Soon my mind was filled by a sailor's church, and a pulpit shaped like a whaler . . . and a man scared by the sea and his own shadow. From time to time Warboys would come into sight on a tower, or in a window, with a notebook and a surveyor's tape measure in his hand. If he looked my way he would wave. When he came down to me his forehead was glowing with the sun it had been exposed to, and his shirt was sweat stained.

'Can you imagine labouring to build this damned place? First they had to get the stone up here to build it – none of it was local – and then they had to assemble it.'

'If they'd had trades unions then they would never have got it built.'

'That, Charlie, is an interesting observation . . . I'm not sure I like the implications.'

'Want a beer?'

'Yes, please. Then we can kick off for Kyrenia, and be there before nightfall.'

'Who have you got lined up for me there?'

'No one. After this lunchtime it's exactly what I said – castles and sketchpads.'

I fetched a couple of bottles of Watney's from the back of the truck. They were warm, but some British beers are better like that. We clinked bottles and toasted each other.

'About your pal Adonis——?'

Warboys shook his head.

'Shall we leave it for an hour or two, Charlie? It will give us both time to mull it over. Talk after supper. That OK?'

I nodded.

'Where are we going to stay?'

'Surprise.'

I don't like surprises. I've probably told you that before.

He took it easier down the narrow road from the castle. We passed no one going in the other direction.

I asked him, 'What happened to all the hairies that were around?'

'Gone home for their teas. They were just the insurance policies.'

'Come again?'

'The lorryload behind us was there to make sure nothing happened to you and me. The ones up at the castle were there to make sure we didn't grab Adonis. If anything untoward had happened today there would have been a bloodbath, but neither side wanted that.'

'The priest is an EOKA man then?'

'Good Lord, no! That would be against his principles. He doesn't take many vows, your Greek, but those he does, he keeps. Adonis is a liaison officer – a go-between and a fixer. A peacemaker when he gets the opportunity. He wouldn't hurt a fly. He was like that at school – I had to stop the other boys bullying him.'

'He's a fixer and liaison officer like you?'

He paused before replying. I could sense him weighing up how much to tell me. We had just reached the place where we joined the road over the Kyrenia range. As we pulled away he said, 'That's only one of the things I do. You know sometimes I play a more practical part.'

'Would you be offended if I showed no curiosity about that at all?'

He laughed before he said anything. Short and puffy sounds.

'No, Charlie. I might be rather chuffed. Fancy a fish supper tonight? There's a safe café down at the harbour.' I might have been wrong, but I'd say his voice was tinged with relief.

'Fish and chips?'

'Not quite.'

'OK.'

'I was in France just after it fell in early '45,' I told him. 'My driver was an old hand, and had been around the block a few times. Although I was travelling with a major, and by then they'd made me an officer, this private soldier was actually in charge to all practical purposes – he was the only one of us three who knew how to keep us all alive.'

'I've met men like that. Is he still around?'

'Yes, Les is one of my best friends.'

We were sitting at the rear of a small diner with our backs against the wall. There were tables outside under the stars, but Tony had chosen cover.

'I sense this conversation is going somewhere . . .' he said.

'We ate at cafés and restaurants as we moved through France and Belgium. Things were just getting going again. The point is that although the places were meant to be safe, they weren't – all sorts of gangsters were settling scores with each other – and Les always made us sit just like this. At the back, with our backs to the wall. He watched everyone who came in.'

'That's why you're still here?'

'I think so. I once asked him who'd taught him that, and he

285

replied *William Butler Hickok*. The only time he sat with his back to the door someone put a bullet in it.'

'I know that story as well. Wild Bill's killer was a gambler named Jack McCall, I think – wonderful the things you remember. What was your point?'

'Only that you seem to know what you're doing – and I'm rather pleased about that.'

'Charming compliment. Thanks, old son.' We raised glasses, and toasted each other in a rather curious thin red wine. 'Now what was it you wanted to ask me?'

'Your pal Adonis claimed that EOKA was asked to bury me. Is he likely to be correct?'

'Yes. He's usually well-informed.'

'It would still be useful to know who asked them.'

'Mm . . .' He raised the wine glass to the light, and squinted at it. 'Anyone wanted to kill you before?'

'Hundreds of Jerries in '44, I suppose, but that was different . . . I was dropping bombs on them then.'

'And since?'

'More than my fair share. I had a run-in with some Israelis in 1953, and I annoyed a couple of Americans some months ago. A woman shot me in Turkey a few years ago. Your man CB warned me that the Yanks could come after me. He convinced me that I would be far safer in Cyprus for a few months than anywhere else in Europe.'

'He's a tremendous liar, you know, so I wouldn't take that as gospel . . . These people you offended – are they the kind to harbour grudges?'

'They all worked for their respective governments, I think, so they're probably bad types.'

He swilled the wine around moodily, and then swallowed it in a oner. I signalled the owner behind his bar for another bottle.

'Governments *do* bear grudges,' he said, 'so I see what you're getting at. It would be handy to know who's got it in for you. Do you want me to see what I can do?'

'I'd be obliged.'

'And in return you'd make sure your pals, whoever they are, lay off Adonis and his mother? Just between you and me, of course – no reason for Adonis to know.'

That seemed like an agreeable compromise to me. So I said, 'Thank you.' Then, 'I should also thank you for bringing me here in the first place, shouldn't I? You could always have said *no*, and let them knife me in the dark.'

He grinned like a boy.

'I wondered when you'd work that out. As it happens I didn't want the apple cart being upset at the minute – not until we find out what happened to that army pilot – so preserving you suits me. Good job all round.'

A waitress with a nice figure, spoiled by a light moustache and a cast in one eye, propped a great bowl of fish pieces on the table between us: it was like a spicy fish stew. There was a side plate of sliced potatoes fried in olive oil, and I was suddenly hungry.

Halfway through the meal I asked him, 'Where are we going to sleep?'

'Out there, unless you buy Konstantin's girl for the night. She's not all that expensive.' He was talking about the waitress, but pointed out into the harbour with his spoon. 'Pater's boat – an old Greek caique with a bloody great Mercedes engine. You'll love her.' I was sure that I wouldn't, but it wasn't the right occasion to indicate just how quickly I became seasick. Steve had called me *sailor* the first time we woke up together; maybe she was a clairvoyant.

He'd parked his small lorry up in the UN compound, so all we had to do was walk down to the quay and find a boat. He rowed me out into the harbour to the large, odd-shaped sailing vessel which sat sedately at anchor. Big thing. Maybe sixty feet of greasy woodwork and two masts. We secured the skiff to a tired-looking Jacob's ladder dangling from the well of the craft. Warboys went up first, with a pistol in his hand – he didn't make a sound. The first thing he did was search the vessel. It didn't take long; there wasn't all that much to search. There was a small cabin above the stern and an even smaller engine bay beneath it. A single cargo space and a small forecastle. Another small skiff – aluminium this time – was lashed down in the well of the vessel.

'They love my father in this town,' he told me. 'I don't think they could bring themselves to blow up his son, but it's always better to be safe than sorry, don't you think?'

I did; but it's not one of the questions you answer. I slept under a few damp blankets on a wooden bunk in the cabin; Warboys slept out on deck under the open stars. I think that he'd been exposed to too many copies of *Boy's Own* when he was a lad.

When I awoke we were at sea. The pitching of the vessel had thrown me from the bunk.

Chapter Sixteen

Aphrodite

A caique does not cut the water like another ship. Neither does it ride it. Caiques attack the ocean as if they hate it: that should probably tell us something about the men who first built them. The design has been around in its current form for at least four hundred years, so for the deceptively turbulent waters of the Eastern Med it is probably a perfectly evolved design. My stomach didn't think so. The only reason I didn't vomit over the side was that I had nothing left to vomit, so I contented myself with dry retching for ten minutes before clawing my way back to the raised poop deck, where Warboys clung to the wheel. He was so wet that his clothes were stuck to him, and the grin on his face said it all. The pitch of the boat threatened to explode my head as it rode up the waves coming for us . . . then crashed down. The sky was a brilliant blue. Within a minute I was as wet as he was.

'I didn't know two of us could handle a thing this size,' I shouted.

'We can't.' He had had to shout back against the wind. It came back as 'We ca . . . n . . . t!' He took a deep breath and shouted once more, 'We could never handle her under ca . . . nnn . . . vas!'

I clung to the compass binnacle. It and the wheel were between us.

'I'm no good as a sailor.'

'Don't worry, neither am I.'

'I get seasick.'

'Don't worry, so do I. Isn't it smashing though? You feel so alive.'

You feel so alive, I thought, because we are shortly going to be dead. When the ship wasn't trying to bury its head in the sea, it was trying to stand on its tail. He gestured violently to a box built onto the deck to my left. I staggered to it between the leaps of the deck, and threw back the lid. There were half a dozen filthy-looking USAF-style Mae Wests. I braced myself against the bulwark, and pulled one on. Then I lurched across to Warboys with another. He had me hang on to the great kicking wheel as he struggled into his. When he got back we shared the wheel between us. It wasn't until I had my hands on it that I felt the trembling of the engine beneath us, and realized how powerful it was.

'The Jerries converted her in the war and used her at Crete,' he shouted at me. 'Dad bought her as a wreck, and brought her back from the dead.'

Why? I wanted to ask, but contented myself with, 'Where are we going?' instead.

'Morphou Bay.'

This time I did use the word.

'Why?'

'I want to show you something. Don't worry, we'll be out of the wind once we've rounded Kormakiti Point. Plain sailing after that.' Something told me that his definition of plain sailing might not be the same as mine. Still, after another ten minutes of assaulting the waves we did round a sort of point, and as soon as he turned south into a wide bay the water flattened into a long slow swell. My diaphragm muscles actually ached from the effort of holding myself upright. In the calmer water of the wide bay the thudding of the engine sounded as loud as Thor's hammer. *Wrong ocean*, I thought – *wrong period*. The sky was still an eggshell blue, and the sea flashed like blue sapphires in the sun. Seabirds glided in our wake. Warboys, I decided, had gone over the top far too often, and needed a rest: he was as mad as a monkey.

The deeper into the bay he took us, the smoother the swell became. He had me take the wheel, and follow his directions as he sighted on two landmarks using a makeshift triangle of three small pieces of wood, just as the Dam Busters' bomb aimers did: a row of three high trees, skinny affairs with dense flat canopies, and a distant brick-built church tower. When he was satisfied that they aligned correctly he abruptly cut the engine, and dropped the stern anchor, and as we swung round it to face the making tide, scampered along the deck to drop the bow anchor as well. Then we had a cup of water each, as he told me he was going to turn me into a skin diver.

We sat on the deck with our backs against the bulwark, our clothes drying on our bodies. As soon as I took a sip of water I realized how salty my lips tasted: it wasn't altogether an unpleasant sensation.

'Does it matter that I can't swim?'

'At all?'

'About six feet in any one direction, but I'm better at *down* than any other. After about six feet I roll over on one side and begin to sink, usually head first. The woman who tried to teach me thought that unusual – she always sank feet first.'

'Mm. You know what they say about women with big feet.'

'We were talking of swimming – and I can't.'

'You won't have to. I've done this with several people – that's what the stones are for.' I had noticed a couple of open boxes of large stones on either side of the well deck – each stone more or less the same size, a foot or so across, and weighing a good few pounds. 'I've invented what I call *unscientific plunge diving*. Most people who try it, love it, and get better at it each time they dive.'

'Tell me how you get better at it.'

'You hold your breath, longer and longer each time. Look, it's easy – you put on one of the Mae Wests, flippers and a face mask. Then you drop over the side holding one of the stones against your belly. The stone overcomes the buoyancy of the life jacket and pulls you slowly down to the bottom. When you run out of breath you let go of the stone, and the jacket bungs you back up to the surface – like a cork out of a champagne bottle. Smashing feeling. Then I fish you out.'

'Don't divers get the bends or something, if they surface too fast?'

'Yes, but you're only in twenty-five feet of water out here – safe as houses.'

'Is your idea of *as safe as houses* the same as mine?'

It was hard to resist Warboys when he grinned: he looked about sixteen years old and unsullied.

'Probably not. But someone told me you make a habit of throwing yourself out of high-flying aircraft, and I'm buggered if I'd do that for fun – no head for heights. I only bring the people I like out here, and show them my private treasures – we're moored halfway between two of them right now. One is about twenty-five yards in that direction.' He pointed over the stern, at the shoreline: a narrow beach and scrub dunes. 'The other one is the same distance to starboard.' I glanced involuntarily to our right. Why is it that when someone says *right* or *left* you tend to glance immediately in that direction? 'You'll never forgive yourself if you turn this one down, Charlie. I'll find you a mask. All you need to do is decide which one you'll drop in on first.'

He needed my help to manhandle the aluminium skiff over the side. It was very light, but awkward to manoeuvre. Then he found us each a threadbare pair of KD shorts. Mine were two sizes too big and stiff with salt. I climbed down into the rowing boat and he passed a few of the stones down to me – they were heavier than they looked, some sort of marble, I think. He showed me how to place the face mask and adjust the strap to cinch it in tight to my face and under my nose. The old RN black rubber flippers fitted over my feet like gloves.

I was curious about what was to happen next, and that's always been one of my failings – and the idea of being beneath the sea didn't worry me all that much, even though I couldn't really swim. One of the effects of spending a lot of your life in aircraft is that you develop an excessive faith in the laws of physics – what goes up must come down. Now that Tony had explained it, why shouldn't vice versa work just as well? As far as I was concerned a four- or five-million-year-old chunk of rock was going to get me to the floor of the ocean, and then the USAF could get me back up again. I've always liked the Americans.

I hung on the side of the small metal boat alongside a small, moored, blue-glass fishing-net float that I guessed Warboys marked his spot with – you needed to be on top of it to spot it – took three deep breaths to oxygenate my blood, and then a final small one as Warboys handed me down a rock. I held it close to my belly, with one hand at first. It felt hard and cold. Then I let go of the boat, holding my head back the way Warboys had told me. Colder than I expected, but a vertical descent that was no faster than a parachute drop. My legs

dangled below me. Treading water was a natural reflex movement: I didn't even think about it. Looking back above me
I could see explosions of light on the surface. No noise. Very
peaceful. How long does it take to fall through twenty-five feet
of water? Not very long. Far less than a minute, but it seemed
longer. Then my feet were flat on top of something big and
smooth . . . a fine layer of sand moved like dust. I was on a
smooth honey-coloured rock, a couple of yards proud of the
pale sand in a twilight of blue water. Suddenly my breath went,
so I let go of the stone. Looking forward and down as I began
to rise – slowly at first – I realized that I hadn't landed on a
natural rock at all. I had been standing on the belly of a colossal
naked woman, who lay on her back. How large was she? Thirty
feet high at least. An enormous statue. No arms: broken or
unfinished stumps. Serene face. Cold and gentle eyes. These
weren't distinct views. They were like images flashed up fast in
front of me: one after the other. I was rising quickly now,
racing my own bubbles to the surface. And then I was in the
sun, coughing out water and floating on my back. Temporarily
blinded by the light. Warboys was across to me with a couple
of strokes of the short oars. He bent over the gunwale, grabbed
and steadied me. I was gasping.

'OK? You saw her?' he asked. All I could do was nod – I was
filling my lungs with good air. 'You saw the face of Aphrodite.
More than two thousand years old – worth it?' Again, all I
could do was nod. I felt as if something truly momentous had
happened inside my brain, but couldn't begin to explain what.
He said, 'Don't worry about it – she affects everyone, the first
time you see her. The original *It Girl*.' He got a grip on my
Mae West, and pulled me close to the boat. I shook my head;
responding properly at last.

'Another stone,' I finally gasped. 'I've got to . . . go down
again.'

He let me dive on her twice more, but when I turned for the fourth time shouted, 'Enough,' and held me by the hair. I hung on to the stern of the tin boat, and gasped like a spent fish. He rowed me back to the caique, and got me on board. Like a beached fish I lay on my back on the bleached deck planks for twenty minutes before I spoke to him again. It didn't matter anyway. I had made enough images in my mind by then to last a lifetime. In fact, they have: I can still see her now.

He had some bun-like bread, with pieces of olives in it – like stuff you can get in the Italian delis today, but greasier. Swallowed with warm water it suddenly tasted like a feast. Whenever we weren't talking my eyes were drawn to the horizon, as if I had a sudden urge to wander.

I dived on his other find later, and discovered I'd mastered the trick of releasing my stale breath in small nibbles: it won me half a minute's bottom time at least. This treasure hadn't been there two thousand years; more like fifteen. I had the knack, now, of glancing quickly down as I descended, then looking up to balance myself – and I knew a Me-109 when I saw one. An Emil: a German fighter aircraft from my own war. It had lost part of one wing, and its tail had sheared off, but it was otherwise more or less intact – its engine cover was missing, and the prop blades had bent backwards as it hit the water. The guy had probably made a decent controlled ditching, and got away with it.

Except that the canopy was still in place. On the first dive I landed alongside it and stumbled slightly. Fine sand swirled up immediately to waist height. I dropped my weight, and touched the wing briefly as I floated up. Now I knew where it was, and its dimensions, I moved out a few feet before my next drop, and landed on the wing root beside the cockpit. The thin layer of sand on the canopy moved with the current I had created, and for a few seconds I could see inside. The pilot was still hunched in his leathers. Jacket and helmet. Gloved hands resting peacefully on his lap. Those round lens goggles the Jerries used. Skull. I dropped my stone, and ascended with my arms outstretched on either side of me. Flying underwater. I didn't go back. Dead fliers should always be left where they fall, in my opinion.

'He must have been flying from Crete,' I told Tony when we were back on the caique.

'I sometimes wonder if she called to him and brought him here. Like one of the Sirens.'

I knew what he meant: had the pilot seen the statue below him in those last few moments before he hit the sea?

'I know that Emil's not been here long,' I asked him, 'but why is it still so clean . . . and the statue as well . . . so little algae, no weed?'

'We're in fresh water – I don't where from. An underground river, I suppose. You dropped much quicker than you would have done in salt water, and that's why you felt it cold as well – you did notice that?'

'Yes. What next? Back to Kyrenia.'

'Not quite yet, old son. I have to move us along the bay a bit, and closer in for the cabaret. I might even come over the side for that myself.'

I supposed he moved us about two miles, towing his small boat: it's not that easy to judge in a curved bay. We had been there an hour when an open boat powered by a small putt-putt diesel put out from the shore. It looked like a converted ship's lifeboat, and wasn't going anywhere fast. We pulled our skiff up to the caique's counter, climbed down into it, and, still tethered, allowed it to drift out towards the newcomers. A man and two women. They each waved. One of the women stood up, rocking the vessel, blowing extravagant kisses.

'I take it you know them?' I asked Warboys.

'For some time. We became friends when I decided not to report them to the authorities.'

'What for?'

'Looting antiquities. We're parked right over an old wooden shipwreck, and as far as I know no one else realizes it's here. The ship was full of amphorae – terracotta storage jars.'

'I know what they are.'

'Keep your hair on. Most of them contained wine or spiced sauces, but some contained coins. They broke – when it went down, or later, I don't know – and the coins scattered. The girls dive for them with ropes around their waists, like Ama girls diving for sponges in the Pacific – then they sell them piecemeal to visitors and museums. Very against the law, but very profitable.'

'Don't Ama girls dive naked?'

'The GCs learn very fast, I've found. *That* was my idea for them. You'll enjoy this.'

We watched them strip off and dive. The man stayed in their boat, and kept his clothes on. I was glad about that on the whole – he didn't look in the best of condition. Tony showed me how, if I put the Mae West on back to front, I could float face down with my mask in the water, turning and lifting my head for breath. I only did it for ten minutes before I rolled over on to my back, and trudged my flippers until I collided gently with the skiff, then hung there. The girls had looked as graceful as seabirds – their arm and leg movements slow and strong. Their bodies changed colour and shape as their natural buoyancies overcame gravity. That must be what naked women look like in space. When Warboys got back to me we both clung on to the side of the metal boat. It angled up alarmingly but didn't overturn on us.

He asked me, 'What's the matter? Don't you like girls?'

'You know I do. It's just that I feel as if I'm at a strip show – and I've always hated them for some reason. I'm amazed how long they can hold their breath though.'

He reached over, and gently banged a fist on my forehead: a teacher driving home a lesson to a reluctant pupil.

'That, if nothing else, Charlie, should give you cause for thought.' Then he spluttered, because one of the girls suddenly surfaced giggling between us, her rope trailing behind her like a long tail. She lifted in the water, and quickly kissed me on the mouth, dropped back, turned to Warboys and did the same. Then she backed off with little hand movements, treading water and giggling.

'What's your name?' I asked her. She shook her head in incomprehension.

'No English,' Tony told me, and addressed her in Greek Cypo. She smiled at me, and rattled back three or four syllables, then turned away from us, rolled forward and dived. She cut down into the water cleanly. For a moment her white back-side, brown calves and the white soles of her feet balanced high in clear air. Then the sea seemed to swallow her with hardly a ripple. My eyes followed her brown shape away from us, deeper and more shadowy. Gone.

She had looked more at home in the water than many do on dry land. Were these the Sirens? Did women once have the power to turn men into swine? They probably never needed it; look around you in any bar on a Saturday night, and you'll see men turning into pigs without help from anyone.

'She said her name was—' Warboys told me.

'I know. I heard her . . . Aphrodite. Did you know that?'

'Yes, she's an old friend.'

I climbed into the skiff. He put a hand under one of my feet, and helped me scramble up, but made no move to climb in himself. He asked me, 'Can you make it back aboard on your own?'

'Yes, of course. But what about you?'

'Something to do – won't be long.' Then he pulled his mask back on, and dropped away. Before I lost sight of him I saw him turn in the water in the direction the woman had taken. Back on the caique I found my pipe, sat on the gunwale and fired up some smoke. The breeze and the sun dried me.

I saw Warboys and the woman emerge from the water, and walk up the shallows to the beach. They held hands as they crossed the sand. She must have untied her rope, because as she walked the man in her boat pulled it back in; hand over hand, like a fisherman hauling in a fish. He looked over at me, and waved: that was all right then. The other girl stayed in the water, hanging on their boat's side. I saw her reach up and stroke the man's unshaven face. He smiled. That was a nice thing to do. Part of my mind told me that this was what the world could be like, if ever we got our act together.

I was sleeping, sitting on the deck, propped up against the main mast when Tony came aboard. He must have swum from the shore. I don't know how long I'd been asleep. He sat down alongside me, and held out his hand, saying, 'She asked me to give you this.'

A small bronze coin: Roman. I have it yet.

Warboys made the long sweeping turn into Kyrenia harbour in the late afternoon. The sun was already low. When the tide turned, the wind over Kormakiti Point had died with it, and we had driven home in big long seas that failed to distract my stomach. We found the dinghy in which we had rowed out to the caique still at its buoy in the middle of the harbour, swapped the vessels over and rowed ashore. For the first time in my life

I properly experienced that odd feeling of dry land pitching gently beneath my feet: it lasted for a couple of hours.

There was a wiry, barefoot boy lounging at a table outside the restaurant we had eaten at the night before: three empty glasses stood on the table next to him. The wasps and flies around them said they had recently contained something sugary. He jumped up in front of us, and said, 'Hello, Lion.'

Warboys reached out and ruffled his hair; the way you would with any kid.

'Demetrius. Have you been waiting long?'

The owner had been hovering in the doorway. He grunted and said, 'Long enough to drink the juice of nine lemons.' That was the local lemonade. Cloudy and sweet – the bite of the lemons came at the back of your throat as you swallowed it.

'One hour,' the boy said. 'One hour, and seven minutes.' I glanced at his wrist. No watch. That was interesting. 'I have a letter from the priest.' He handed Warboys a grubby envelope. It was old, had been resealed with sealing wax, and contained a piece of lined writing paper folded twice. A short line of Greek letters.

'I can't read that,' I told Warboys.

'It says *a woman*, that's all.'

'She was an old crippled lady,' the boy grinned.

Warboys asked, 'How do you know?' and gave him a coin. The boy tossed the coin from one hand to another several times, and Warboys held out another.

'I saw her when she left the colonel. She was very angry – like Clytemnestra.'

Warboys said, 'Thank you, Demetrius,' and flipped him the second coin. It was all we were going to get. We moved into the cool of the restaurant, and again sat at its rear. The owner brought us a glass of ouzo each, a jug of cold water and a bowl

300

of olives to share. I asked Tony about the boy. Was he EOKA too?

'No, just a courier. He suits the GCs, and he suits me.'

'Won't he give you away one day?'

'I pay him too well for that. With money from Adonis, and money from me, he probably takes home more than his father.'

'And the message was about me.'

'At the moment it doesn't make sense in any other context. The person who asked for your head was a woman . . . an old crippled lady, if what the kid said is right. It's like the story of John the Baptist, isn't it?'

'Does it mean anything else?'

'If they are willing to tell you that much I'd say they've turned her down and taken your bait.'

'You think they killed her?'

'No. They don't do anything face to face, but don't worry, once they've agreed the deal they'll see it through as a matter of honour. I hope you can come up with the money, or they'll be very annoyed.'

'It won't be a problem.'

'Good. Then you'd better leave the delivery of it to me.'

'Only after the dirty deed is done.' I smiled.

After a pause he asked me, 'Do you think this is just some kind of joke?'

This time I wanted to tell him the truth: I wanted him to believe me, so I gave him the eye lock before I answered.

'I think it's *all* a joke, Tony – love, life and everything – and we're the butt of it.'

'If I believed that, Charlie, I'd put my pistol in my mouth.'

'It's because I do, that I don't.' The sentence looks a bit skew-whiff the way I've written it, but Warboys nodded slowly.

He understood me. 'And for your information I can't think of any crippled old ladies I've offended recently.'

But I can think of someone who, if she survived, I might have crippled. But I didn't say that. What *would* Grace do to a man who crippled her?

'Maybe she was only another courier, acting on behalf of someone else. We use so many cut-outs that I sometimes wonder who we're working for,' Warboys said wearily. He didn't want to think about it any more.

'That's happened to me before, as well.' The ouzo tasted good and clean in my mouth, but what I really wanted was a beer.

We passed up on Kyrenia castle. Warboys said we'd been at sea too long, and walked us back up to the UN compound. He examined his truck; had a good poke around underneath, and below the bonnet before he let me anywhere near it. It looked as if my holiday was over.

Bowling back across the plain I asked him, 'Who was that Clytemnestra the boy mentioned?'

'Wife of King Agamemnon. He sacrificed their daughter to get a favourable wind from the gods to blow the Greek fleet to Troy . . . then to add insult to injury as far as his wife was concerned, he came back from there with a new mistress, Cassandra the witch. Clytemnestra, being the good wife she was, greeted her king's return by climbing into his bath with him for a spot of how's-your-father, and whilst engaged in an act of loving congress, cut his throat. That's how I like to think of it happening, anyway. Glorious woman.'

'What happened to her?'

'Killed by Orestes – another Greek hero. They all feature in several Greek tragedies together. Funny bunch, the Greeks. Greek heroes killed a lot of women – their equivalent of Association Football, something to do on a slow Saturday afternoon. We're completely wrong in thinking of Ancient Greece as a peaceful place full of philosophers, mathematicians, writers, musicians and artists – what these people were really interested in was war, incest, human sacrifice, rape and murder. Not much different to their modern descendants, if you asks me.'

'Who should I read?'

'I'd start with Aeschylus, if I was you. Try his *Agamemnon*. When I was sixteen I sat watching it one night with four thousand Greeks in an old open-air theatre – Epidaurus. The place was falling to bits, but from even the highest stone seat you could hear someone whisper on stage. The play opens with a watchman on the walls of Mycenae spotting a signal fire in the east which tells the people in the city that their king is back. That night there were forest fires burning out of control all around us. Smoke and sparks were in the air. It informed my earliest opinions of the Greeks.'

'Which were?'

'Probably the most literate race on earth, but absolutely bloody useless at putting out fires.'

We skirted Nicosia because it was deep in curfew by then anyway. The tarmac hummed beneath our wheels. Occasionally we passed a staff car or a lorry. I almost dozed off. Warboys didn't say much else before dropping me off at my billet in the RAF compound. Then he drove off towards Watson's pavilion. I guess he had to report back.

Pete's gear was still on his bed, and his change of clothes hung in his locker. Neither had been moved so I guessed that he hadn't come back yet, although that didn't mean the hut was untenanted.

Steve sat cross-legged on my bed. She was wearing shorts and a shirt, and had pulled my blanket around her shoulders.

I could see her brown knees. Her face was unreadable. No make-up.

'How did you get in?' I asked her.

'The usual way – I asked someone nicely. That was yesterday. Where have you been?'

'Sightseeing.'

'With Tony?'

'Yes. That's right.'

She sighed, and looked away from me before asking, 'What do you want me to do?'

The song in my head was Hoagy singing 'How Little We Know'. I let it run for a verse and a full chorus, then said it.

'Take your clothes off.'

Our tenderness surprised even me.

Sometime in the small hours I pulled the blanket around us again. I felt cold. When she stirred I kissed her brow, and said, 'I'm hungry.'

'I made you an apple tart.'

'You did what?'

'I made you an apple tart, yesterday. It's on the table – a day old, but probably still OK.'

I got up and brought it back to the bed. We ate a slice each. I brushed the crumbs and sugar from her chin with my hand. She brushed crumbs and sugar from me. When we slid down in the bed she was partly turned away. I wrapped my arms around her the way I had at Salamis. She rubbed a hand slowly up and down one of them, as if reassuring herself I was still there.

I spoke very close to her ear. 'Is this a particularly bad time to tell you I love you?'

She froze for a fraction of a second, relaxed, and murmured, 'Say it in the morning, after you've had me again. That way, if it doesn't work out, I can always tell myself it was just in the heat of the moment.'

I said, 'OK,' bent, and kissed that lovely hollow in a girl's shoulder I've probably told you about before.

I slept eventually. I'm not sure that Steve did. I remember her eyes were open, and her breaths were deep and easy. Just as I was drifting off I think she gave a short, low chuckle – it wasn't a triumphal sound, it was as if she was pleased about something.

'I love you.'

'You're only saying that in the heat of the moment.'

'No, I'm not, but I'll say it in the heat of the next moment, and the one after that, and the one after that if you like.'

She had propped us both up on her elbows.

'You're crazy.'

'Agreed. I was dead meat the first time I woke up and saw you looking at me. My brain boiled, but I'm over that now. I just love you.'

'What are you after, Charlie? A share of the profits?'

'No, I'm after you. Everything else will work itself out, you'll see.'

She smiled like sunshine.

'I think you're nuts.' Silence. Then she added, 'But you can say it again, if you like.'

'I'll need another heat of the moment first.'

'No, Charlie, you have to get up. You have to go to work.' She pushed me out of my bed. We were still on the floor fighting the blankets, when Pat Tobin arrived to get me.

She had left her small car parked behind my hut, which is why I hadn't seen it the night before, and was going to follow Pat through the gate.

Before we split she asked me, 'That woman you told me about – did you mean to do it?'

Pat walked on ahead, and gave us a minute. Steve and I stopped moving, and looked at each other.

'No. It was the last thing in the world I would have wanted.'

'I figured that.'

Chapter Seventeen

Love for Sale

'How long have you been here this time, Charlie?'

'A month? Have I been here longer than a month already?'

'Seven weeks, Fiona tells me. By the way, she's been a bit sweet on you ever since that Kermia trip – I don't know how you do it.'

For the first time since I'd arrived in Cyprus Watson had dropped in to watch me at work. Not that there *was* any. It was a Saturday: the Saudis were having a day off.

'I haven't seen her since then.'

The days had merged into one another it seemed . . . and then the weeks followed them. Eight-hour spells, mainly, of listening to people I'd never met, broken up by regular deliveries of Spam. I had eaten Spam in every form known to man, and a couple that were even less predictable. I reckoned that if the British Army had found a way of compressing Spam into suppositories to shove up your jacksie they would have been on my breakfast plate one morning.

Every eight days I had a long weekend, during which I moved into Yassine's place if Pat thought it was going to be safe. Only once, so far, it hadn't been safe, and I kicked my heels around camp until the library found me a book of Sherlock Holmes stories, and Steve sent me in some fruit to break the monotony.

The fruit box from Steve made me feel like a POW receiving his Red Cross parcel. She used less perfume than any woman I'd met, but even so I caught its muskiness from the wrapping of the parcel, and it made my head spin.

On better days we had a decent gin rummy school going at the hotel – and one of the Danish UN guys had brought a UN Jerry who taught us spoof – a wicked betting game with matches. Every time I looked at him across the bar I would wonder if he and I had been trying to kill each other ten years before.

On the bright side, no one had come to kill me in Cyprus yet. I scanned the English-language newspapers whenever I got my hands on them for news of the dastardly murder of a crippled English lady. Maybe the priest had done a deal with both of us after all, and either we'd both get it – or neither? No, that wouldn't work – they wanted the money, didn't they?

Watson and I sat and sipped iced water in air-conditioned glory. I'd slipped one headphone back so that I could talk to him. From the other I heard the friendly hiss of static. If ever they ask me on to *Desert Island Discs* I shall ask for a recording of radio static. It reminds me of safe, lazy days with little to do. Thirdlow was working one of the sets in the chapel on my left. Occasionally I cast an eye over the partition which divided me from her, and looked at her legs. She had kicked off her shoes, and had worked her skirt back above her knees to expose them to the cool air. They weren't particularly pretty knees, but I had had precious little else to think about for the last two hours. She had a frown of concentration on her face, and was scribbling down one sheet after another. I had been told that the bay she was in was used for monitoring our allies: that was interesting. Occasionally she shot me one of her tight little smiles. That was interesting as well.

Watson asked me, 'Isn't that one of Collins's women?'

'Yes. Her name's Thirdlow.'

'Whose signal is she hooked into?'

'I don't know – you could always ask her.' I knew he wouldn't. 'Are you still happy with my work, sir, or have you come along to have a good old moan?'

'I hate it when you call me *sir*.'

'Didn't you lock me up for *not* doing precisely that when I got here?'

'I was just making a point. I thought it would get us off on the right foot.'

'I always kicked with the left foot when I was at school. I was a leftie.'

'I'll remember that.'

What the hell was the matter with the man? I told him, 'I just gave a perfectly good opportunity to tell me what you wanted, and you muffed it, so now I'll ask you directly. What's the problem?'

He put his glass down.

'The corporal is.'

'Pat?'

'The civvy cops are sniffing round him, and I don't know why.'

'Then ask them.'

'I can't. I made a point of not having anything to do with them. Their operation isn't all that secure – it can't be because they have to work with the island police. Now they won't talk to me.'

'Ask Pat.'

'I can't do that either.'

'Why not?'

Thirdlow glanced over at us, and he'd caught the movement.

He dropped his voice to a whisper, 'Because I don't know where the hell he is. He had at least a week's leave coming, and took it two days ago.'

'Ask your assistant, Fiona.'

'Why should she know if I don't?' Ah. His surprise seemed genuine.

'Just a thought,' I said. 'So, what do you want me to do about it?'

'When's your next rest period?'

'Tomorrow. Monday and Tuesday. Back in this dump on Wednesday.'

'Everything seems to have quietened down again – I thought you could ask about a bit – you know people.'

'Did you know that David Yassine was back in town?'

Watson looked suddenly sheepish. 'We had a row before I left the Canal Zone. We haven't spoken since.'

You didn't need to, I thought. *You got Pat Tobin to do it for you. Now he's gone, you're up the creek.*

'I'll need a car . . .'

'Thought of going down to Akrotiri for a spot of R & R myself. You can have my Humber . . . Ask Fiona.'

'And some spending money.'

He waved his hand as if flapping an imaginary fly away. 'Ask Fiona.'

Then it dawned on me. Watson's well-honed corporate survival instincts were telling him that something decidedly dodgy was in the air, and he was making himself scarce. I'd been here before. He stood up on cue, and picked up his battered blue cap and nasty little swagger stick. When he glanced at Thirdlow she tugged her skirt over her knees. That was interesting.

He said, 'I'll slope off then. Thanks for the help. Volunteer's better than ten pressed men, and all that . . .' Then he left.

Just like that. De Whitt half rose from his chair as he passed, but Watson ignored him. Thirdlow leaned towards me, and lifting one earphone from her head said, 'He gives me the creeps.'

'I think he gives everyone the creeps. That's why I'm glad he's on my side.'

'Are you sure about that?'

She was right, of course. Watson was only ever on Watson's side . . . but once you worked that out, you were usually OK with him.

'Are you staying down here tonight? I could buy you a drink in the mess later.'

She shook her head.

'No. I'm going back to the Keep when I've finished, but thanks for the offer. I'll take you up on it one day.' I know I've said it before, but that was interesting. She was still there four hours later when I signed out.

I hung around outside for five minutes, waiting for Pat's stand-in, Bud Abbott, to come and get me. If things were quietened down that much, why were we still driving everywhere? I could easily have walked the half-mile to the RAF camp, but everyone gave me a very funny look when I suggested it. No one else came from or went into the radio block. If we were monitoring Ibn Saud twenty-four hours a day there must have been at least another three guys working him with me, despite what de Whitt and Watson had tried to fob me off with. The odd thing was I hadn't met one of them yet.

'Do unmarried men think about girls all of the time?' Fiona asked me.

'A *lot* of the time. Will that do?'

'What about married men?'

'We hardly ever think about married men at all.'

'You know what I mean.'

'I don't know, because I've never been married. When I am, I'll give you a call and tell you. What about unmarried women? Do you think about men all of the time?'

'No. It sort of comes and goes. I thought a lot about romantic men when I was a teenager, but I think girls grow out of it.'

'Are you coming or going at the moment?'

I sat on the edge of her desk, and shared her glass of mineral water. The bubbles clung to the inside of the glass. After the first sip I realized that it wasn't water, it was a gin and tonic. Watson had gone. When the cat's away . . .

'I'm definitely going. If I was coming you would have known about it by now.'

'I like you very much,' I told her.

'I like you too, Charlie. You're not as complicated as people make you out to be.'

'So now you can tell me where Pat's gone? The boss is worried about him.'

'So am I. A couple of civvy police came round asking for him yesterday. I don't know where he is. I thought Mr Watson was going to ask you.'

'He did. I don't know either, so I agreed to try to find him. Apparently you're going to give me the keys to his Humber, and a pocketful of money to bribe people with.'

A set of car keys sat on a bulky envelope between us. She said, 'You'll have to account for the money, and don't scratch the car – it's his pride and joy.'

'Cypriot money or sterling?'

'Some of each. A hundred and twenty quid in all.'

'That's not much.'

'It's enough, Charlie. It's wiped out the petty cash until the end of the month, so I'd appreciate it if you brought some back. And bring Pat back too – this place feels not quite under control when he's away. All sorts of odd characters turn up asking for him, but never tell you what they want him for.'

'Give me an example.'

'That American girl who dances at Tony's. She came in the day after he left – and looked pretty glum when she found he wasn't here. Pat really has a way with the ladies.'

'You should know.'

'Don't get catty with *me*, Charlie. I didn't make him any promises.' She made me smile, and gave me a get-out. If I had thought too hard about what business Steve could have with Pat it would probably have wiped the smile from my face too. I scooped up the keys and the envelope – I'd already seen the car parked under a tarpaulin in the side alley outside.

'I'll let you know how I get on. OK?'

Fiona OK'd me back. She was a little distant. Maybe she really was worried.

When I opened the envelope later, and counted the cash, I found I only had a hundred quid's worth. I suppose every bugger was at it.

Watson's Humber Hawk was a curious deserty sandy-pink colour, and wore Cyprus civvy plates. I wasn't that struck on the column gear change, but it went like shit off a shovel. I think someone in Pat's workshop may have breathed on its engine. I had it at over eighty on the road to Famagusta – a flock of sheep in a sunken field fully a hundred yards away panicked and scattered at my approach. The shepherd waved his stick at me in protest. I'm not surprised they wanted the Brits to go to somebody else's island. The Hawk howled the way a proper car is supposed to, and a dust cloud marked my passing. What had Fiona asked me? *Do unmarried men think about girls all of the time?* Nah, sometimes we think about cars.

313

It was an unreasonably happy Charlie who drove to Yassine's Hotel, and scraped one of the car's wings against the stone gatepost. Yassine came out onto the steps smoking one of the long cheroots he favoured. He was wearing a gleaming white dishdash, and a battered red fez. It was odds on he was feeling peculiarly Lebanese again that morning.

'Yah, Charlie.'

'Yah, David.' I had never asked him what *yah* meant, or worked it out for myself. He had several words which were particular to him; I think he made them up.

'Mr Watson's car.'

'Yes. That's right. Where can I buy one?'

'Middle East main dealer in Beirut. He's been sending them to Kuwait, to the oil companies – they are very good in the desert.'

'How much?'

'Four hundred and twenty as a tax-free export. Maybe seventy pounds shipping fee?'

'I want one.'

We were joking of course, but everything David said was likely to be true. He carried money in his head the way other people carry dreams.

'You come for breakfast?'

'Stuffed vine leaves and haloumi?'

'As you wish. Do you want your woman woken?'

'Not yet. Let her lie. Let's go into the garden and talk.'

Yassine looked as stretched out and relaxed as I felt. He must have had a good night.

'What car you drive in England, Charlie?'

'A Sunbeam – a sports tourer.'

'You really want one o' these fat ol' Humbers instead?'

'I rather think I do – I'll see to it as soon as I get home. I'll

314

get married and settle down, be a decent father to my boys . . . probably become a Scoutmaster.' I stretched my feet beneath the table; it was one of those kinds of morning.

'You will die of boredom, my friend.'

'That's a very good thing to die from, David. I've made a lot of money since the war – mainly by following good advice given to me by friends like you. I want to live long enough to begin to spend some of it.'

'I take it that you require some more free advice?'

'No, *help*. I may need to lay my hand on four or five grand without much warning. I have plenty of cash, but no arrangement to access it out here. If I wrote you a cheque for that amount, could you cash it?'

He didn't answer immediately. One of his girls had approached us with coffee, stayed and poured it. I caught a whiff of her as she bent over the cups. Brown and musky. When I flicked a look up I saw her large dark eyes, and a slightly knowing smile. What was that question Fiona had asked me again? When we were alone again Yassine let his face slip into its serious mode.

'Are you in trouble, Charlie?'

'No. I told you the truth – I just may need to lay my hands on a large amount of cash in a hurry. Could you help?'

'Of course. And the cheque is good?'

'Yes. I wouldn't cheat you. I have a bank account in Germany. I bought a house south of Frankfurt just after the war, and the Americans rent it from me for their staff officers. They've had it for ten years now, and pay the rent straight into my bank account by some fancy method or other. The rent goes up every year. I've never taken anything out, so there could be tens of thousands in there.'

'Don't you *know*, Charlie?'

'Not exactly.' That feeling again – as though you were up

in front of the headmaster again, for an offence you didn't know you'd committed. Yassine shook his head ruefully.

'That money should be doing something for you, Charlie.'

'It's going to,' I told him. 'It's going to save my life. You don't want to know the rest.'

Silence. Then a bulbul began to whistle. I could get to like those musical birds.

'OK.' He clapped his hands. 'You ready to eat now?'

'Yes, please.'

'You don't go making no big sheep's eyes at the girl who brings it, OK? I don't want her dropping no more plates.'

'OK.'

We had two conversations over breakfast. One was about that Humber saloon, and the other about a woman.

He told me how to buy my car without the inconvenience of paying purchase tax or car tax. I suppose that there is always a scam if you know who to ask. Yassine proposed that the Beirut dealership buy two cars, one in my name, and one for itself, but only export one. He knew how to fiddle the papers, mix up their identities, so that one remained in the UK tax free.

'How much will I save?'

'Coupla hun'red pound.'

'And you're sure this will work?'

He laughed, and lit another of his cheroots.

'Charlie. The dealer does this all the time for your lords an' ladies back in England. Rolls-Royces and Bentleys. Big Daimlers like the Queen. You want a Daimler? You think they ever pay taxes like an ordinary man? What's the point of being a lord if you pay taxes like an ordinary man? These guys never pay their taxes.'

'Who is this car dealer, David? One of your relatives?'

'No.' I didn't press him. I just waited until he said, 'Is me.'

What I *did* ask him was, 'Are you the richest person I know, David?'

'Dunno, Charlie. How many rich people you know?'

I tried again.

'Are you the richest man in Cyprus?'

He thought about it, and scratched his face. Then he smiled slowly and said, 'Yes. Certainly.'

The second conversation wasn't as easy, because it was about his stake in Steve.

He said, 'Friends shouldn't argue over a woman,' and I didn't get what he wanted to talk about at first.

'Agreed. We didn't argue about Mariam, did we?' She was a girl we'd both known in Egypt – the one who had run off with a weightlifter, and married America. She always got her priorities right.

'But you weren't attached to her. I think you are attached to Stephanie. Are we going to argue about her?'

I pulled my lip. I felt uncomfortable. I felt uncomfortable because I had broken several taboos, and we both knew it. *Thou shalt not fall in love with a prostitute* should have been the eleventh commandment – for either sex. So I told him, 'I'm sorry if I've made things difficult for you. Is it so obvious?'

'To those who know you well, *yes*. I am not worried about the affection you have for her, just that she is no longer my most profitable employee. Now she is just another mouth to feed.'

I wasn't quite sure what he meant.

'Doesn't she still dance for you?'

'Yes, but that's all she does . . . and to be strictly honest, she's not a very talented dancer. Our clients appreciated that her talents lay . . . in other directions.'

'I thought that after she'd danced . . . she was, well . . . self-employed, to coin a phrase.'

'She is. The establishment takes a percentage for facilitating the business contact, and providing a working space.'

'Her bed, you mean?'

'Yes, if you like, and it's become a very peaceful bed when you are not here.'

'Because she's not whoring up to her usual standards, you're not getting your cut. Is that it?'

'Crudely put, Charlie, but exact. I thought I'd mention it. Her regular clients are fretting. I get telephone calls from gentlemen in Nicosia almost every day. They are distraught.'

'What have you told them?'

'That she is ill. That was foolish, because one is a doctor, and now he is demanding to examine her. Some of her other friends are almost as pressing.'

'And how long has this been going on?'

'A week, ten days.'

'What do you want from me?'

'Talk to her, Charlie. All I want is a decision.'

'And if she has decided to . . . take a rest? A holiday?'

'*Fine*, and I mean that – really fine. She can dance for her room as long as she pays her bar bills, and for her food and laundry. It's nothing personal – it's just that I don't want the other girls getting ideas. This is a business, not a charity.'

'Your clubs have always been charities, David. You have always looked after your girls, even given them dowries when they wed.'

'You mustn't be a romantic, Charlie – that too is purely business. The dowries are simple investments, nothing more. Laying up treasure in heaven. When the girls come back to me, and mostly they do, they work even harder to please me. You will talk to Stephanie?'

'Of course I will. What about her clients?'

'The other girls will provide friendly diversions for them. Stephanie's clients are good payers – respectable men. I can arrange that if necessary.'

'Thank you, David. You were right, old friends shouldn't fall out over a woman.'

He leaned forward and supported his chin with a hand.

'Old friends. I like the idea of old friends.'

'So do I, David.' We left it at that.

Bed had not worked, leaving us both feeling vaguely unsatisfied. Getting past that for the first time is a landmark in any relationship. Steve sat across the room from me wrapped in a rumpled sheet. I was turning out the pockets of my jacket, looking for my pipe and tobacco pouch: smoking is something I often do if I want to avoid facing a problem. Steve wasn't that type. She smiled impishly at me without saying anything, until I asked her, 'What happened there?'

'We both did what we thought we ought to be doing, rather than what we wanted to do.'

'What did you want to do?'

'Talk to you about the little things I don't know about you – what's your favourite book, that sort of thing.'

'*Treasure Island.* It's been my book since I was ten. I loved Ben Gunn and John Silver . . .' My mother had read to me until the old man came home from work; then he took over.

It led me to ask her, 'Do you miss them much, your mother and father?'

She looked away; one of those moments of weakness. She blinked the tears back.

'That was cruel, Charlie.'

'Do you?'

'Of course I do, but it's impossible – I told you why.'

'Why don't we go down and visit them – sort it out?

'Are you mad?'

'No, I don't think so. I'll finish up here sooner rather than later, won't I? And you can leave whenever you want. What's the point of me being in the airline business if I can't use my *wasta* to get us tickets down to South Africa and back?'

'Why on earth would you want to meet my family? You might hate them.'

'And I might not. I need to meet your dad anyway, don't I?'

'Why?'

'I'll need his permission to marry you.'

That brought things to an emergency stop.

Steve could unnerve you by staring at you for a long time without saying anything. That's what she did. I filled my pipe, and let the aromatic smell of its burning tobacco lay over the pink perfumes of Steve's room. She got up, and went over to the window trailing the sheet, like a trousseau, I thought. She probably didn't see it that way. When she spoke it was in a whisper so low that I had to incline my head towards her to pick it up.

'Isn't there a girl in England?'

'There have been. But none of them took me seriously.'

'What about you? Are *you* serious?'

'I am this time. Don't ask me why. I just *am*.'

'What about your boys?'

'We'll take them with us. It's about time they saw a bit of the world. London, Mombasa then down to Jo'burg. I think that's the route that BOAC fly. I loved geography lessons when I was at school – it was the only thing I was any good at. I loved the foreign-sounding names of countries and cities.'

I knew that I was gibbering: making noise, not conversation.

I suppose that it was my fault; girls have had more romantic proposals than that, haven't they? Put it down to inexperience

– she was only the third or fourth woman I'd asked. The room seemed unnaturally quiet. A dying fly buzzed itself to death on its back somewhere. The ceiling fan clicked slowly around: why do those damned things always click as they revolve? When my pipe was finished I walked over to join her at the window, and knocked out the pipe ash on the sill. I watched the soft black bones of burned tobacco fall down the face of the outside wall, and into the courtyard. Eventually I couldn't bear her silence, and asked, 'Well? What about it?' although I hope I sounded kinder than it looks on paper. She sighed.

'Let me think about it.'

'You want me to go?'

'Yes, I'll call you.' This time, for some reason, I believed her.

'You won't have to call very loudly. Because I won't be going far. I intended to be around for a couple of days, but I won't crowd you.' She looked doubtful. 'I mean it. I have a few things of my own to do – I'll ask Yassine to let me have a room.'

'What sort of things?'

'Finding Pat Tobin for a start. I was going to ask you where – I know you came to see him a few days ago.' I'd given her the perfect opportunity to tell me why, but she wasn't stupid enough to fall for it.

'I don't know. He spent all night at a table with that German boy from the UN before he left. You could try there.'

'OK.' I'd get round to asking her directly, but not yet. Something held me back.

'And I promised David that I would talk to you. Some of your regular friends have been calling wanting to know where you are.'

'When I am available, you mean.'

'Yes, I suppose so. The choice will always be yours, you know.' I had started to talk about something else. Again she didn't take the bait.

'Tell David that I'm considering my options, and when I get back to business he'll be the second to know.' It sounded as though she was already telling me *no* without using the word. I could hear pots and pans being rattled around in the kitchen. It was getting on for lunchtime, and I wanted a beer.

'I'm going down for a Keo,' I told her. 'Why don't you join me in the bar?'

'OK, sailor. Twenty minutes – I'll take a shower first.' As I reached the door she said, 'Charlie,' again. I turned. She had moved from the window, and the sheet had dropped to the floor. She had a perfectly ordinary body, and I loved every wonderful damned inch of it. I tried not to compare her with other women I had known, but when I did it was like comparing Cinemascope with jerky silent films. Which was stupid. She was half in shadow and half in bright light, like those postcards of women you could buy in Germany just after the war. Then she said very clearly, 'It may be very unfashionable, but sometimes I just long for someone to make a choice for me, Charlie. Remember that.'

'Is that what you want me to do?'

'I don't know. If you try it we'll find out.'

I said *OK*, stepped through the door and shut it behind me. For the first time I looked closely at the rugs in the corridor over the uneven wood floor. I was sure that they were the same pattern as those in Yassine's club in Ismailia.

I had trudged upstairs wanting to get something settled. I trudged downstairs more uncertain than ever.

Yassine intercepted me at the bottom of the stairs before I could get to the bar.

'Don't go out on the street for an hour, Charlie.'

'Why not?'

'Fucking Greeks. Someone's been killed out there.'

'When?'

'Not long ago.'

'Who?'

'A soldier, I think. I have locked the gates – the area will be swarming with police in a few minutes.'

I had heard *pop-pop* sounds while I was wrestling with Steve, but hadn't identified them as gunshots.

'What else do you know?'

It was the first time in our acquaintance that I had seen Yassine truly rattled. He removed his fez, and mopped his face with a handkerchief he carried in one sleeve.

'The woman with the baker's stall said he was a man who came in here a lot. Listen. Here come the police.' Sirens. Bells. The hammering sound of boots on flagged paving. People shouting. A woman sobbing. No requiem for the dead ever gives you the real noises.

Half an hour later I *did* go outside. My nose wasn't bothering me: I just had to make sure it wasn't Pat. Collins sat in a Land Rover parked up behind a civvy police car and an ambulance. Between them they blocked the narrow street. He was smoking a fag, and looked blank. I'd seen that look on his face before after he had shot the boy up in the Troodos, but he risked a small smile when he saw me.

'Where did you spring from?'

'Doing an errand for Mr Watkins.' I nodded at the ambulance, and asked, 'Anyone we know?'

'No. Just some German lad who works for the UN.'

'Was he in his UN clobber?'

'Yes. And I don't understand why they did it. It was a stupid hit . . . it will turn the UN against them, just when EOKA was making some headway over there.'

'Maybe it was nothing to do with politics.'

He took off his cap, and dragged his forearm across his brow:

David Yassine wasn't the only one sweating. He said, 'Charlie, this is Cyprus. *Everything* has to do with politics.'

'Do you know where Pat Tobin went off on leave to?'

'No, and you're not the only one asking for him.'

'Who should I ask next?'

'You could always try praying.' Bloody comedian; they can't bloody resist it, can they? Before I left him I asked, 'I suppose the German guy *was* killed?' It was an afterthought, and one I was still ashamed of days later. It should have been the first thing I asked.

'No. He took one in the back of a knee, and the other shot missed completely. Rank amateurs.'

'He'll be OK then?'

'Apart from being on a stick for the rest of his life. Yes.'

'I wonder what he did to annoy them.'

'That's what I was thinking. Don't hold out on me if you hear anything, Charlie.'

I remembered his sympathy for the girl captured by the GCs.

'No. Of course not. You'll be the first to know.' That was one better than Steve's message to Yassine.

A civvy Brit policeman sauntered towards us like a model on a catwalk. He had *git* written all over his face. He looked me up and down as if I was a piece of dog dirt on his shiny shoe, and asked me, ' 'Elp you, squire?' the way police do. He was telling me to buzz off, of course.

I gave Collins the look, and told the cop, 'No, I was just leaving.'

When I was about ten paces away I heard him ask Collins, 'Who was the titch? Someone you know?'

'Haven't a clue,' Collins said, and that made me smile.

Chapter Eighteen

The Black Spot

When the captains and the kings had departed, taking their ambulances and cars with them, I went out again, but not very far. I remembered the Turkish café to which Pat had taken me soon after I arrived. It seemed like years ago. That's what fear does to you: it makes you remember dangerous places as though you've known them all of your life. Your subconscious is scanning all the time for that little clue which tells you to run. I sat down at the back in deep shadow.

The place was empty at first, and the big man who ran the place came out from a door covered by a beaded curtain, to set a glass of raki – that's what the Turks call the aniseed stuff – a jug of water, and a small black coffee in front of me. A few minutes later a couple of locals came in, and sat at a table near the door. They just had the coffee. Finally a third guy came in, and immediately came over to sit at my table. He said, 'Can we help you?' in good English.

'An English policeman asked me that an hour ago. He didn't mean it either.'

'What did he mean? Your English policeman?'

'He meant me to go away.'

'Maybe I mean that as well. A man was shot near here today – this is a dangerous street.'

'I'm a friend of Pat Tobin's. He brought me here a few weeks ago.'

'We know nobody of that name.'

'Pity. He told me to stay away from you and your friends – that you would start a riot, and blame it on me.'

'He sounds like a sensible man. You could always leave now. My friends will not stop you.'

'Pat took off a few days ago, and nobody knows where he's gone. That is not characteristic behaviour for him, and his friends are worried. I am not here because I wish to compromise you or your colleagues, nor for my health. I am here because I am one of his friends. You are a chance I was willing to take.'

He stared at me for a minute. I could hear flies buzzing against the window. One of the decent things about England is that we're often short of flies. One of those frozen moments until he asked, 'Why are you worried for him?'

'The British police and the Island police are asking questions about him. He probably doesn't know that. I wanted to warn him.' That was about halfway along the road to truth, wasn't it?

'I still do not know him. I am sorry.'

His jacket had been expensive once. Tweed. Its cuffs must have frayed for they had been piped with leather.

'OK. In that case I will not bother you further,' and I leaned forward to stand up.

He held up both his hands, palms towards me. It has probably been a friendship gesture since the Neolithic.

'No, stay. I did not mean to be rude. Have another drink. We are a hospitable people, and this is a friendly town.' He stood up himself, and held his hands up again. This time I noticed his fingers and fingernails were stained by oil: a mechanic of some sort then. He registered my thought processes. 'I have a carburettor to change on the nurse's car. Then I will wash my hands and join you . . . for the *other half*. Isn't that what you British say?'

'Yes, it is, but—'

'You will be safe if you stay here. I promise it . . .'

As he walked out he gestured to the two gorillas at the door. They, too, stood up. One followed him; the other, and larger, came to sit at my table in the chair my interrogator had vacated. He smiled. No teeth.

These Turkish Cypriots talked with their hands. The giant sitting opposite me held his up, but at right angles from his body, and made swivelling movements with them from the wrist, as if describing the heft of a woman's breasts. *This is not my fault*, he was telling me. He grinned when the owner of the joint put an unlabelled bottle of wine on the table between us, and flanked it with two grubby glasses. The owner polished the glasses and the bottle on his pinny for us. To be honest that didn't make much difference. He poured us a decent glass of thin red wine each.

'Comes from a vineyard planted by Attaturk himself,' he told me proudly. That must have been in the 1920s. 'Drink.'

I drank. Old Attaturk could make a fair old bottle of wine. All I could do now was wait, so I might as well enjoy it. I was sure that if I tried to leave I should feel the rough side of my silent companion's mighty hands.

When the mechanic returned he was in his Sunday best, and called for another bottle of wine. I had just discovered that Turkish wines are one of the hidden treasures of the world, so I didn't complain.

'The Lebanese says you are indeed one of Mr Tobin's friends and maybe even one of ours as well.'

'That is less certain. I hardly know you—'

'And you English never kiss on a first date.' He suddenly giggled. It was an odd girlish sound. 'I'm sorry. Pat taught me that joke.'

'You have news?'

'Three days ago he came here and asked to borrow a car. We gave him a small Fiat from the war. They call them Topolinos.'

'Don't worry about what they call them. Where did he go?'

'I don't know. He went to the food shop run by the Englishwoman married to Hayri . . . bought enough supplies for an expedition.'

'To where?'

'I don't know. It's all I can tell you. I am still waiting for my car.'

'Thank you for your help.' I stood up. 'I have used too much of your time already.'

'Sit down, Mr Bassett. We have opened the bottle. It would be impolite to leave before it was empty.'

I did what I was told. So would you. The mechanic had an undefined authority that I wasn't prepared to challenge. I held out my hand, and he shook it.

'I'm Charlie,' I told him. 'What do they call you?'

He smiled, and for the first time looked truly dangerous.

'Now, Mr Bassett,' he said, 'why on earth should I tell you that?'

A proper hero in a proper book would tell you how he rushed home, jumped in his car and set off at once in pursuit. But not me. I was too drunk by the time I got back to Yassine's place to do anything except sleep it off. My new pals must have seen me back; I doubt I could have found the way on my own.

I remember opening my eyes in the late afternoon some-time. Steve was looking down at me. Concerned. She said, 'I'm dancing tonight. Will you wake up in time to watch me?' She didn't seem all that mad at the state I was in.

'Course I will, pet. Just a bit tired.'

'And the rest.'

I shut my eyes again. Love me or leave me. She left me of course.

I was awake, cleaned up and sober again by the time she danced. David Yassine sat with me. He told me, 'I was wrong. She *can* dance. She could give the girls at the Kettle a run for their money. I am very pleased with her.'

'Where do you find your dancers, David?'

'Here and there, old friend, here and there.'

'Where did you find Stephanie?'

'*There*. Didn't she tell you?'

'No.'

'Ask her.'

At the end of her set Steve collapsed on the ground with a dramatic clash of cymbals. Then the stringed instrument pedalled a couple of bars into the darkness, fading away like smoke. Polite applause. She came over to sit with us, and the barman brought her lemonade without being asked. I could smell her perfume evaporating on her body. She was taking deep breaths.

'Tell me,' I asked her. 'What were you doing when you met David?'

'Sitting in a window in Amsterdam,' she flashed back without hesitation. 'He said I could do better than that. How about you?'

'Someone asked me if I'd ever seen a belly dancer, and took me into his club.'

'You sleep with the dancer?'

'It was the quickest way of learning enough Arabic to get by.'

'Excuses, excuses! Does that mean we start square?'

'Yes, of course it does. Is that OK with you?'

'It helps. Give me a cigarette, one of you.'

Yassine was distracted by a new dancer advancing to the small stage. She was a recent addition to his stable. She oozed sexual invitation, but looked young – on the cusp of woman-hood – and that left me a trifle uneasy. When the lights went down for her our table was in darkness. Steve leaned over, and touched my arm. I asked, 'What?'

'I just wanted you to know how happy I am. If my life was always like this I'd want to live for ever.' She squeezed my hand. I suppose I felt something similar, but it was never the sort of thing I could say. I smiled across at her in the half-light. She added, 'But that doesn't mean I've made up my mind about anything.'

My dad once told me there's always a bloody *but*.

When she left us to go and get changed I tugged Yassine's sleeve to get his attention. He didn't take his eyes off the dancer.

'You were wrong, David. The man shot this afternoon wasn't killed. He was just winged. I think it was that Jerry who taught us how to play spoof.'

'I was wrong then, but now I'm right – you slept through the update, Charlie. He died of shock in the ambulance, and they didn't bring him back. The UN is furious and is threatening to pull out . . . The Governor's calling a special parliament tomorrow. Apparently the poor young man survived three years in a concentration camp, only to be murdered in our dirty little backwater, by silly little schoolboys who can't tell the difference between a German and an Englishman. They've already arrested the shooters – they are both thirteen.'

'And they will become martyrs of the fucking revolution. Their classmates will post pictures of them up in the village squares, and volunteer to follow them into battle – and so it will go on for ever. What a bloody mess we've made of things.'

'You British?'

'No, my generation. You and me. All of a sudden I can't wait to go home.'

Yassine took a minute to consider his response before he said, 'You swear too much, Charlie, did you know that? You should clean up your language.' Then he stood up and walked away.

I kept my word to Steve: I took a room of my own. In the small hours I couldn't sleep, and lay awake digesting the implications of what Yassine had told me.

I'd complained for years that the Palestinians and Israelis had no place fighting each other, because they were both Arab tribes with identical concerns and needs. There was nothing they did apart that they couldn't do better together. You could say the same for the Pakistanis and the Indians. And you know what I've said about the Greeks and the Turks – can anyone tell them apart in the dark? Now David had told me that the German guy had copped it because no outsider could tell the difference between a Brit and a Jerry at six feet. So why did we spend six years murdering each other in the 1940s? Suddenly that didn't make so much sense.

Yassine's new dancer put her head round my door before breakfast. She was a cleaner in the morning and a dancer at night, and looked even younger without the blue eye make-up they danced in.

'Just checking. I'll clear the room up later if you like.' Her accent put her in the bullseye of England.

I asked her, 'Where are you from?'

'Halifax. You?'

'God only knows these days. Sometimes I feel as if I'm from bloody everywhere. I have a house in a place called Bosham, down on the south coast. Will that do for now?'

'What's your name?'

'Charlie Bassett.'

'I've heard people talk about you.'

'Nothing good, I hope. What's your name?'

'Jessie, but Mr Yassine calls me Reem – because of my white skin.'

'What does it mean?'

'White antelope.'

'It's a pretty name,' I told her firmly, 'but I prefer Jessie.'

'So do I, but he pays my wages.'

'How old are you, Jessie?'

Her next smile was the smile of a thirty-year-old.

'Old enough, so don't go fathery on me.'

'OK. I'll remember that. You can tell the kitchen I'll be down in five minutes.'

Yassine was in a foul mood; cursing the kitchen staff, and following the cleaners around the bar quality-checking their work. Everyone looked jumpy.

'What's the matter with you?' I asked him.

'You bloody British are.'

'What have we done now?'

'Some delegation of English schoolteachers is calling for martial law. It was on the radio.'

'How will that matter?'

'Because a bastard of a military governor will ratchet up the

332

state of emergency, and take powers to control the prices of everything. Everything! That's what military governments do. How can a businessman expect to take his profit when the army is in charge?' He stood with his feet planted apart, and his hands on his hips. His stomach stuck out in front of him like a barrage balloon straining to break free.

'Is that all, David?'

'What do you mean, *is that all*? Isn't it enough?'

'It won't happen. Believe me.'

'You are suddenly an expert on politics?'

'No, but I know the British ruling class, and it does not trust its armed forces – never did. After Oliver Cromwell dissolved parliament on the end of a pike, things were never the same for them. Our politicians will never put the army in charge of anything if they have a choice. They don't trust it.'

'Do they have an alternative?'

'Bound to have. And another thing . . .'

'Yes?'

'We Brits distrust schoolteachers even more than we fear the army – and no one ever pays any attention to anything they suggest. Too much flogging and pederasty. The day that teachers start being elected to parliament will be the day my country dies.'

'And you really believe this.'

'I'm willing to bet you fifty quid it will come to nothing. You can stop kicking the staff about now, and join me for breakfast.' He probably didn't need breakfast. He was half the size again, larger than the Yassine I had met three years earlier. He shrugged – but the tension went out of him. Then he smiled. It was like the sun coming out after a squall.

'I take your word for it.'

Over the fresh orange juice I scouted around him for the

places that Pat might have taken off for, but David didn't know either . . . or if he did, he wasn't saying. I asked him about the girl Jessie. 'She says you've given her a new name.'

'I've given her more than that – she rides like a champion jockey. They are wonderful when they are young.'

'You're a dirty old man.'

'So are you. I been to your club in Berlin, remember? Just because you don't handle the money don' make you a saint, Charlie.'

I sat back in my chair. I thought the coffee was especially good that morning. The golden smell of fresh bread. He broke into a bread roll, and tapped his forehead with a fat finger. 'You think I debauched a nice English rose too young for this sort of life, right?'

'Maybe.'

'Think again. She's been on her back since she was twelve, and was wanted for killing a man in Hamburg. She gutted him with a skinning knife. I smuggled her here in a fishing boat – a friend did that for me. I saved her life so far. But I don't live it for her, an' she wouldn't thank you for trying.' There was a *so there* inflection in his last words. The girl had told me more or less the same herself, hadn't she?

'OK, David. I'll take your word for it.'

'Take my wager instead, Charlie. I'll bet you fifty pound that your Stephanie dumps you . . . jus' like all the rest did. More coffee? It's good this morning.'

I looked out through the arches of the covered walkway behind the dining room, and into the garden. A pair of bulbuls was drinking at the fountain. I'd always thought Yassine a good judge of women. I wondered if Steve had spent the night alone, and knew I wouldn't ask her.

*

I sat in the garden and smoked a pipe, wondering which direction to head in, or who to telephone next. Steve must have come up behind me very quietly. She bent, and put her arms about me. I could feel her breasts against my shoulders through my shirt. She kissed me beneath my right ear – Grace had done that once – and said, 'It might be quite nice to be your Old lady one day.'

'Quite nice? Only that?'

She nuzzled me. There's little point to sexual desire when they're in that sort of mood.

'Quite nice. Don't get greedy – I'll think about it while you're away.'

They're bloody psychic, but I suppose you knew that already.

Jessie came out to us. Barefoot. It made her seem even younger.

'A kid just ran in with a message for you, Charlie, and then ran away again. The boss said he was a Greek kid, but I don't know how he tells the difference.'

'What was the message?'

'He said you should go to church more often.'

I suddenly remembered what Collins had said, and click, click, click. I've told you before; you get these messages all of the time, but often you're listening to the wrong stations.

I called Collins's office from the phone on the bar. They said he was somewhere else and gave me another number. A woman answered the telephone. I thought I knew her voice, but couldn't place it. Another Brit anyway.

'How did you get this number?' Cool. Distant.

'I'm not going to say. Tell him it's Charlie Bassett. He knows me.'

She put the phone down, and although I could hear murmurings in the room they didn't coalesce into sounds I could interpret.

Eventually Collins's voice asked, 'Yes?' He sounded wary. I supposed that he was working somewhere. Probably turning over some poor sod's quarter.

'It's Charlie. I need some information.'

'Only if I can.'

'I need to contact Tony Warboys, but he moves about all the time, and I don't have a number for him.'

'Wait one.'

More shadowy murmurings. What was he doing? Checking his address book? Thinking about it? Consulting?

Eventually he came back and said, 'Give me the number you're at, and don't go away. Wait for a call.'

I read out the number on the circle of round paper on the telephone cradle. He asked, 'Is that Yassine's place?'

'Yes.'

'OK. Wait there until he calls you.' He put the phone down.

Ten minutes later Warboys had not called, and I began to get impatient. Then I remembered that Collins wasn't the only one with a line on him. I called Watson. Fiona answered the phone, and said he was away.

'I know he's away. He must have left you a contact number.'

'Only for emergencies.'

'This is one – my glass is getting empty. Give it to me now, love . . . please.' She gave me another telephone number I didn't recognize. I asked her, 'Where is he?'

'I can't tell you that, Charlie.'

I didn't push it. As long as I could speak to him I didn't need to know where he was.

It all turned into déjà vu. I dialled the number, and again a woman answered. The first thing she asked was, 'How did you get this number?'

'I can't tell you that. Tell Mr Watson a Liquorice Allsort wants to talk to him, and put him on.'

'A Liquorice Allsort?'

'Yeah, you know – one of those sweets that come in boxes.'

'Is that cockney rhyming slang?'

'It might be. Please tell him . . .'

I heard her lay the receiver down. Murmurings. Maybe laughter in the background. My imagination added clinking glasses. If it was Watson then he had to be in a bar. His voice came over loud and clear.

'Hello, Charlie. Have you made some progress?'

'Not really, sir. I need Tony Warboys's telephone number, and I thought you probably had it.' I thought I'd better give him the *sir*; I wanted something from him after all. He was quiet for so long I thought I'd lost the line. I did the Duke and 'Caravan', and got as far as the chorus. Then he just barked at me.

'What are you bothering me for? You just asked somebody else for it.'

Silence. My jaw probably dropped.

'How did you know that?'

'Because someone was listening, of course, dear boy. Wake up, Charlie! Finish your beer and be patient, just like the man told you.' And he hung up. Watson always loved being one up on me, and I bloody hated it. I'd have to get him back before the end of this tour.

I held my hand up to the bar boy, and he reached for another bottle of beer. I could get used to this stuff. No wonder returning squaddies were known to smuggle it back home in their kit. I had to wait for an hour; sat in the garden and took my book out again. The *Pequod* had just been hailed by another whaling ship looking for a lost boy: and the great white whale was in a foul temper. I could understand that. I'd met a few great white whales myself . . . even worked for them.

I didn't mince words when Warboys called.

'I want to see your tame priest. A safe meeting.'

'He may not want to see you. Is this about the offer you sent him away with?'

'No. It's about something else altogether.'

'He still may not want to see you.'

'Use your charm.'

'What's in it for me?'

'I'm not sure, but I suspect it will save you a lot of work in the long run.' Then I added, just to dot the i and cross the t, 'I don't suppose you know where Pat Tobin is, do you?'

'No, but you're not the only one who's asking. The civvy police are asking questions about the cargo of a coastal oil tanker – can you imagine what that's worth? This isn't anything to do with that, I suppose?'

Trick or treat? Lie or truth?

'Could be.'

'OK, but don't get mixed up with the civil authorities, Charlie. They hate both Collins and your boss with a passion. Nobody will be able to get you out of trouble once you get in – not even me.'

'Don't worry, Tony, I consider myself properly warned. What happens next? Will you call me?'

'Someone will.'

It was one of those days when people are always putting the phone down on you. It pissed me off, but there was nothing I could do about it. I'd already drunk enough beer, so I called for some coffee. A very beautiful girl dressed in something not unlike a silk sari of swirling greeny colours walked into the bar. She travelled in a mist of invisible thin blue perfume; maybe it was an aphrodisiac, because it made my head swim. She smiled and I smiled. I wish I could stop myself doing that. I said, 'I remember you. You're Laika, aren't you?'

'Yes. Alison's upstairs changing. We got in an hour ago.'

I've told you before, you lose some . . . and you lose some. Story of my life. But for once I knew which girl I really wanted, so I made myself scarce until I had rehearsed my lines.

That night I sat at the same table near the dance floor, but with Alison, Laika and the three men flying with them – a pilot, co-pilot and radio operator. That left them one short by my reckoning.

'Where's your engineer?'

'That's me, mate,' the co-pilot told me. 'Co-pilot and engineer rolled into one – just like a Marine's a soldier and sailor too. They're getting rid of the radio ops next year. It won't be long before the bloody things fly themselves, and we can all go home.' He held his hand out for the manly shake. He had a grip of iron. A bloody Kiwi. 'Jonathan Crane.'

'Charlie Bassett.'

'Someone said you were a radio man, out here on a government contract. Any jobs going for the likes of me?' That was the radio operator: Maurice Kacik. They called him Little Mo because he was small, like me. If you don't understand that one you'll have to get out your book of sporting heroes and heroines of the 1950s: she's in there somewhere.

'I can give you a couple of telephone numbers. The job's shite, but the money's not bad.' I tore the top from his fag packet and scribbled the two numbers I had for Watson on it with my lucky pencil. Watson would be livid at getting a call from an unvetted outsider to his private sanctum. Their skipper had been introduced to me as Brome. I didn't know if that was his first or last name, but he wanted to keep the conversation.

He asked me, 'I know you're a sort of sparks out here, but what do you do back home?'

'I run an airline. They released me for six months to help the Queen.'

I could see that that set him back a peg or two. He leaned closer.

'Which airline?'

'Halton. We're at Panshanger now.'

'Christ, skipper!' That was Crane. 'Aren't they the bastards who've nicked half our War Office work?' This was how I found out that Old Man Halton had kept himself busy while I was away.

'Come and see me when I get back, 'I told them. 'We've always got room for talent.' I was grandstanding, of course – probably showing off in front of the girls. I had never taken on anyone personally in my life, except Bozey and Randall: the old man did the hiring and firing all himself.

Someone once told me the old man recruited the women who worked with us by touch – that instead of interviewing them for positions, he tied a scarf around his eyes and stretched out his hands. That sounded like company legend to me, but it might explain why most of our female colleagues had busts to die for. I thought suddenly of Elaine back at Panshanger now, and wondered if he'd recruited her that way: I could have watched the sun come up over her tits for the rest of my life, as long as I never had to commit to anything. Which is why I had one of those *eureka*! moments there and then – with Alison's crew all around me. I realized that I could commit myself to Steve without feeling trapped. That was interesting.

It became even more diverting halfway through the evening when she came out to dance: for a start Crane and Brome's eyes came out on stalks. Then every time she came close to our table she shot me, and the girls with us, a mean eyeful of daggers. You'll agree, that was interesting too. Alison grabbed for my hand under the table; I'm sure that was what she was aiming for, and anyway that was all she got.

Steve finished with a flourish, and stalked off the small dance area with applause ringing in her ears. People stood for her. I didn't see her again that night, and spent it alone. When I awoke in the morning someone had pushed a small sheet of white paper, with a big black spot inked on it, under my door. Why the hell had I ever told her about *Treasure Island*?

Chapter Nineteen

Chasing the Dragon

The same kid. I reckoned we were about sixty miles from where I'd last seen him, so he covered the ground. I was taking breakfast in the garden on my own when he marched through Yassine's hotel as if he owned the place, and then stood in front of me not saying a word. When I looked up he said, 'You can finish eating if you wish, sir. I am not in a hurry – no school today.'

'But you're hungry, I'll bet?'

'I'm always hungry.'

'Go to the kitchen and get yourself something. Tell them I sent you. Then come back here.'

He came back with a bowl of cornflakes, swimming in milk and liberally buried in Golden Syrup, a sausage sandwich and a glass of orange – all precariously balanced on a tray.

'The English lady said I needed fattening up,' he told me. Jessie.

'You and I both, chum. Did you bring me a message from the Lion?'

He looked mystified.

'No. I brought you a letter from Father Adonis.'

'Let me see it. I'll read while you eat.'

The priest had agreed to meet me mid-afternoon, and gave

me directions to a ruined church on the Karpas peninsula. That was more than seventy miles distant.

'Would the priest have had a problem coming to Famagusta?' I asked the boy.

'More than you will have getting to Agios Filion.'

'I thought you didn't read the letters you carry?'

'I don't, sir . . . but I wrote this one with him. I check his English writing sometimes, my English is better.'

'You go to school at TES, I take it?'

His face split with delight.

'How did you know that?'

'I didn't. I guessed.'

The only thing that worried me was that I'd asked Warboys for a *safe* meeting, and the letter said nothing about safety. The kid studied my face.

'You're worried for your personal security?' That was a bit of a mouthful for a kid of that age, but he had been spot-on in his assessment. I reckoned he'd be a psychologist practising in Athens before he was twenty-five.

'Yes, I am.'

'Do not be, sir. When the father gives his word he keeps it.'

'Why can't he come here?'

'Because he is wanted by the police.'

'What for?'

'You will ask him that yourself.'

'Yes, I will. Am I supposed to give you money?'

'The father said I should ask for five shillings English, but I hoped for more. My little sister needs new shoes.' I gave him two crumpled ten-bob notes for which he thanked me gravely; he carefully smoothed them out before pocketing them. 'Thank you, mister.'

'My pleasure. Make sure you buy your sister's shoes one size too big, so she will grow into them.'

'You have a family?'

'Two sons. One is about your age.'

'Tell them Demetrius sends them a greeting — when next you see them.' Unless he was an ace little liar, at least *he* thought I would live long enough to see them again then.

'I shall.'

I don't want you to think I'm a complete dummy. I phoned Collins to check out the security situation. He said, 'There's a hell of a hoo-ha going on over the UN killing, so it could be OK for a few days. EOKA will probably keep its head down, and wait to see what happens next — they overstepped the mark, and they ruddy well know it. Why? Thinking of going sightseeing?'

'Yes. I was going to take a drive along the Karpas peninsula — take in a few old churches. What do you think?'

'It's your funeral, squire, but as long as you take your side arm and are prepared to use it, you should be OK. There hasn't been a problem up there for months — not that that means anything, of course.' It's been my experience that policemen frequently change from being comedians into manic depressives with nothing in between to warn you.

'Thanks. I'll bear everything you've said in mind.'

'Do that, and check in this evening, just in case.' The poor sod actually sighed as he put the phone down.

I bought two jerrycans of petrol from David, and topped up the Humber's great tank from one of them. The other one went in the boot. I had bloody nigh eighty miles to cover, and precious little time to do it.

This time there was no table groaning with food waiting for me at the end of the rainbow. Just a ruined church in honey-coloured stone. It was overgrown by native climbing plants, and looked like one of those follies the nobs once planted at the ends of their gardens. The Pre-Raphaelite Brotherhood would have loved it. I didn't, because I was hungry and thirsty, and it had too many nooks and crannies to hide anyone who bore me ill will.

Father Adonis sat in a deckchair in a square of daylight in the ruined nave. There was another alongside him. Light was pouring into the place through great open gashes in its walls and roof. It actually didn't look that safe a building to me. We shared the place with several lazy goats, which dined from the shrubs and scrub threatening to engulf the structure. He had put out the chairs to catch the rays through most of a missing gable end. He was dressed differently. Still as a priest, but not a black-skirted fusilier. He looked less like a giant bat in a top hat than the last time we had met. I flopped alongside him and asked, 'Is that your walking-out gear? Priest in mufti?'

'No, Mr Bassett. Not today. Today I am just an ordinary Catholic. You do not arrest Catholics. Why did you need to see me? If you wished to withdraw your offer, you are too late. It has already been accepted.'

'No. I'm happy about that. I wanted to ask you about something else. One of my army colleagues has taken a few days' leave, and gone away without telling anyone where he went. That is worrying. The police are asking questions about him, and that is even more worrying. When I made my own enquiries yesterday one person told me that perhaps I should pray, and another that I should go to church more often. I thought I could see a connection between the two, and decided to ask the only dodgy priest I know.'

'Me?'

'Precisely. I'm sure you know Pat Tobin — every crook around here does. Do you happen to know where he's buggered off to?'

Father Adonis, however, was still catching up.

'You think I'm a *dodgy* priest?'

'Exceptionally, and one of the few people on this bloody island who seems to know what's going on. So help me now — and put me in your debt.' He gave that a minute's silence for solemn thought, like Armistice Day, before he responded.

'Are you thirsty?'

'Very.'

'I have some beer.' He reached down alongside, to a new-looking galvanized iron bucket that had six bottles of Keo in it sitting in iced water. I'd been wondering when he was going to mention that. My tongue was hanging out. He opened a bottle for each of us. I said, 'Thank you,' but ungraciously added, 'I didn't think Orthodox priests drank alcohol.'

'Why not, Mr Bassett? We're not Muslims. You British have very odd notions about foreigners, you know.'

'I'm sorry, and I'm *Charlie*, if that's all right with you.'

'Perfectly.' He shut his eyes, and sat in apparent peace for a minute. Then he said, 'I love the sun on my face and my arms. I couldn't live anywhere else.'

'Surely, no one could make you.'

He shrugged.

'My superiors could send me wherever they pleased, even to your benighted country. But the Turkish Cypriots could have us all out long before then.'

'Surely not? There's five times as many of you, as there are of them — the maths is against it.'

'I think you'll find you should have said *math* — but even so mainland Turkey is poised to invade the moment we and you Brits turn our backs. Life for an Orthodox priest won't be easy here then.'

'But you didn't join up for an easy life, did you?'

He actually smiled before he replied.

'No. I became a priest because my mother wanted it.'

'I joined the RAF despite my mother's wishes. She was sure that I would be killed over Germany. As it turned out she died in an accident before I even got there. Her and my sister both. Why am I telling you this?'

'Because I am a priest. It is in our nature to be listeners. Go on, if you wish. Do you miss them, your mother and sister?'

'Of course I do. Time doesn't help.'

'Why would you think it should? If you love someone time is meaningless.'

The most surprising people teach you the things about life you should have worked out for yourself.

He gave me another bottle of beer. I thanked him. We drank in silence for a while, and then I asked, 'I'm sorry to return to the reason for this meeting, but—'

He interrupted before I got any further: 'He had a small Fiat car liberated from the Italians after the war, filled up with enough food and water to last two men a week . . .'

'Where did he go?'

'Up into the Troodos. You Brits can't seem to stay away.'

'Why? What for?' Never ask another question until you get an answer to the first one, Charlie: one of my interrogation trainers taught me that.

'To find your lost army pilot, of course. No one else is going to.'

'Why would he do that, if everyone else has given up on the man?'

'Because they were cousins, brought up in the same street. They went to school together, like Tony and I. Didn't you know that?'

'No.' Neither did any other bugger, I suspected. 'But thank you for telling me, anyway. Do you know even roughly where he went?'

'Up around Kampos, that's a big village a long way south or south-west of Lefka – very bad country. The man had been seen there, or if not him, some other wandering soldier. I told Pat that myself.' I think that was the first time he admitted directly that he knew Tobin.

'How far am I behind him?'

'Three days. He may not welcome pursuit – you know that?'

'That's a chance I'll have to take . . . And thank you again for telling me.'

'It's a favour I'm doing for Tony. It's the way things work out here.'

'It's the way things work anywhere, believe me.'

'Shall we have the last beer? The air will get colder shortly – the tide is about to turn.'

Metaphor, I suppose. It took another fifteen years, the way things ran out in Cyprus. Adonis was right about the Turkish invasion . . . and the tide still hasn't turned.

Eventually we stood, and folded the deckchairs like two old pensioners on Margate beach. Adonis picked up his bucket as well, which now contained six upturned empty bottles. I asked him, 'What do the police want you for?'

'How well do you know your history, Charlie?'

'Try me.'

'Henry the Second and Thomas à Becket.'

'The turbulent priest?'

'That's me, of course.' He smiled, and looked younger.

'Surely you don't think we'd murder you for it?'

'Why not? You have form for it, after all. Isn't that the phrase your policemen use?'

The slang had sounded incongruous, coming from him.

As we shook hands and parted, I said, 'If I can help at all . . . ?' It was probably a rash offer to make.

'I'll remember, Charlie,' and that was it. I'm sure that he

had minders around us during the meeting, but they were very good. I didn't get a sniff of them.

Four hours later I stood under a tepid shower at the hotel David Yassine had called Tony's just to confuse everyone. I washed off a hundred and fifty miles of road dust, and changed into clean duds. Then I went downstairs to phone Collins. It was half past seven in the evening and he was still at his desk.

'Mr Watson asked me to find out where Corporal Tobin has scuttled off to,' I told him.

'I thought it could be something like that. Did you find him?'

'He's gone up into the Troodos to find that pilot. On his own.'

'Then he's off his head, isn't he? We'll end up burying both of them.'

'I'm going after him in the morning.'

That provoked a nice peaceful silence. I began to hum that Sidney Bechet number '*Petite Fleur*'.

'OK. What do you want?'

'A decent gun in case I mess it up. I usually talk my way out of trouble but I can't speak Cyppo.'

I thought that Collins's silence meant that he was trying to work out how best to say *no*. In fact he was making a technical judgement.

'A silenced Sterling and fifty rounds? That do you?'

'Thank you.'

'I'll get it delivered early tomorrow, and if you fuck up we'll say you stole it.' He was taking a big chance, and Red Caps don't usually take chances. He asked, 'What transport are you using?'

'Watson's Humber.'

'That's as good as you'll get. Let me know how you get on.'

'Of course.'

'Good luck, Charlie.'

Steve was behind me; she had whispered up in bare feet. I turned and kissed her cheek as I replaced the telephone. It seemed the most natural thing in the world to do. She must have heard our sign-offs, because she asked, 'Good luck doing what?'

'Oh, nothing. I have to meet someone tomorrow, and Collins is worrying about it already. He's an old worry guts.'

'It's because he's a worry guts that he lived long enough to get old.'

'I'll remember that.'

Her arm was curled lightly around my waist, and mine hers. Neither was a mark of possession . . . something more like reassurance. Like the way a cat rubs up against you as it passes, in order to say *I'm here*.

'Why did I get the black spot?' I asked her. 'Not that it counts – it wasn't a proper black spot.'

'Why wasn't it?'

'In the book they cut it from the flyleaf of a Bible – which is about a million years' worth of bad luck. I wouldn't wish that on you anyway.'

'Thanks. You got it because I saw you holding hands under the table with that goofy air hostess.'

'Don't worry. I've known Alison since she was sixteen – friend of the family. Her stepfather's a sumo wrestler. He'd tear me to pieces if I hurt her.'

'I know. We spent an hour together in the garden this morning, deciding what's best for you. You know she loves you, don't you?'

'But not in a way that adds up to marriage and babies. I think I sort of grew into her elder brother without noticing it. Is that what you think?'

'Yes. We both do. You can give me the black spot back now – it's changed its mind.'

We had got as far as the bar, and hopped up on stools. Jessie was behind it. She put a bottle of Keo in front of each of us: no glasses.

'What did you decide was best for me?'

Steve took a long contemplative swig at her bottle, and said, '*I* am, apparently, but I'm still not convinced.'

'Are you dancing tonight?'

'No.'

'Then why don't you take me out to your favourite restaurant, then let me spend the rest of the night convincing you.'

Full bloody circle. It had been the sort of thing I'd say to a girl when I was back on the squadron: we would all come on to them with heavy lines. Don't get me wrong; I was always sure that I was going to make it – was going to be one of the survivors – but still frightened that I mightn't be. Talking to the old guys these days I realize that most of us felt the same, although at the time I thought I was the only one scared stiff every time I climbed up into an aircraft.

I was a lucky man. Steve was probably the only good-time girl in Cyprus who knew where to find an old-fashioned English fish-and-chip shop. The proprietors were second-generation Cypriot Italian, and there were chequered oil-cloth tablecloths and brown vinegar shakers on the small tables. The radio was tuned to an Italian long-wave station, and the music drifted in and out with the signal – like waves on a shore. '*Amami se vuoi*' was one of the songs. I asked Steve, 'Do you know what that means?'

'Yes. *Love me if you want to.*'

Perfect answer. It made me laugh. She didn't laugh back. One of those odd serious moments that can embarrass you both.

'Can you speak Italian?'

'Yes, and French and Afrikaans. You?'

'I can't even speak English.' That wasn't quite true: I've always been good at picking up languages on the trot. I don't know why I lied, except that it seemed important to identify things she could do better than me. I can't remember the rest of the songs. We followed our supper down with more beer, then went back to the hotel and went to bed.

Someone was asleep on the back seat of the Humber when I went out to it in the morning. That was odd because I was sure that I'd left it locked the night before. And I still had to unlock it to get in. There were two Sterlings in the passenger-side wheel well and neither sported a mag, although one was silenced. I wondered what sort of mob would use a silenced sub-machine gun anyway. A big pack of heavy-duty canvas stuffed with magazines and ammo left precious little space for a passenger's feet. That didn't worry me because I didn't intend to take a passenger anyway.

Thirdlow sat up, smiled and yawned. And stretched. She had small breasts, but they still jiggled.

'Seen enough, or shall I do it again?' she asked coldly.

'Sorry. At this time of the morning my brain stops whenever I'm this close to a very beautiful woman.' I couldn't think of another get-out and, thankfully, she liked it and smiled. She wasn't very beautiful, of course, and we both knew it – but she liked being told. 'How long have you been out here?'

'Since six. You don't start early, do you?'

'I thought a big civvy saloon driving around up in the mountains might attract too much attention early in the morning. At least there might be a bit of traffic now.' She nodded and bit her lip.

'You could be right. We don't want to broadcast our presence.'

'We?'

'You and I. Captain Collins thought you'd be better off with someone who can use a Sterling, as well as the gun itself.'

'I *can* use it. I had a course three years ago.'

'And they thought you were useless. I know – we looked at your papers last night.'

'Were you ordered, or are you a volunteer?'

'Bit of both. If I hadn't suggested it Captain Collins would have said he was coming along himself, so I volunteered to stop that.'

'Why?'

She pushed a strand of blonde hair away from her forehead.

'Army business, Charlie – not yours. Are we going to sit here discussing military policy all day, or are we going to get your pal?'

She had a nice determined, straight mouth. I also thought she had the look; was probably a better soldier than most of the men I'd met. And there was no arguing with her, so it was an easy decision to make.

'You coming up front, or going back to sleep?'

'Give me a second, and I'll be with you.'

The Hawk had an automatic choke, so she was a great starter. I toyed with the idea of driving off whilst Thirdlow was changing seats, but for all I knew she had a girl's gat in her khaki shoulder bag, and would shoot out the tyres before I moved ten yards. Besides, the old Humber had a great big bench seat of polished, slippery leather across the front – it would be interesting to see how she coped with sliding along it every time we changed direction. That was my excuse, anyway.

The first time I made a hard right she almost ended up in my lap, snorted with laughter but didn't make the same mistake again. I noticed her hand as she reached for the car radio, and tuned it for a talkie programme – maybe she didn't do music. Her fingers were small and slim. Fingernails short and perfectly manicured. Killer's hands. Maybe things would be OK.

More than two hours later, as we crossed a humpy bridge over the Setrachos river she taught me a lesson I'd never forget as long as I live. I'd slowed for the bridge, and then accelerated away from it past a wide T-junction on our left. The random shots also came from our left – a scattering of them; maybe half a dozen. One smacked into the boot, and I hoped it hadn't found the jerrycan of petrol I had stowed there. I shouted out, 'Bastards!' and floored the throttle pedal. I've already told you the Humber could shift when she felt like it.

Thirdlow was already bending to clip a mag on the silenced Sterling. When she saw a field entrance ahead – we were probably still just in sight of our ambushers, or at least our dust plume was – she shouted, 'Stop! Turn here!'

I stopped because I was too stunned by the power of command to do anything else.

'What?'

'Turn. Go back.'

'Don't be daft.'

'Do as you're bloody well told, Charlie!'

She was the one with the gun in her hands, so I did what I was bloody well told. If you shout loudly enough at me it works every time.

The shots had come from an olive grove raised away from the road above a low stone wall. The twisted old trees were not much bigger than bushes. One guy was already on the road, and three were scrambling down to join him. Thirdlow launched herself over the back of our seat and into the back. It's funny what your mind notices and remembers when it's going flat out: her knickers were a creamy yellow. I heard her frantically winding the window down on the side of the car nearest the olive grove. Then she leaned out of the window, and swept them away with a full burst of nine mil. It was a controlled summary execution: she got all three, and none got up again. One rolled out of the raised grove and into the road. The man already on the road had turned to face us as I drove towards him. He crouched, and aimed a big automatic pistol at us. I crouched down myself, reasoning that the big Humber engine block between us would give me a chance. I didn't need one as it happened, because he never pulled the trigger. He rose up again as he saw his three pals go down, and jumped for the side of the road. I must have been doing seventy when I hit him. I think he was thrown at least ten feet in the air by the impact of the car, and my brain made those little photographs we wished we could forget, and never can. Even in the air I could see that his body was fundamentally broken: that was before he came down across a dry-stone wall.

I reckon the Humber made half that height when we took off over the highest ridge of the bridge. I kept the wheels centred. I had never been in a flying car before, and it seemed to be the right thing to do. We hit the road the other side with a hell of a thump, the boot lid flew open, and it took me about thirty yards to pull her up. I hadn't even stalled the engine. I was quite proud of that. Thirdlow got out, and slammed the boot shut. She needed two goes at it.

When she got back up alongside me she said, 'Your petrol can hasn't leaked, and the tyres still look OK.'

I was looking ahead, but seeing nothing. My hands, clamped to the steering wheel now, were trembling. I said, 'Fuck!'

'Turn the car round again, Charlie. Go back there.'

'You're a fucking lunatic!'

'Yes, but I'm still the one with the gun in her hands, so turn the bloody car round. We have to get their guns.'

I took us back to where the shooting had occurred. I've told you before that the most shocking thing about violence is the speed with which it occurs, and the speed with which it's over. I stayed in the car still gripping the steering wheel. My knuckles were literally white. I hadn't seen that before. Thirdlow clipped a fresh mag onto the silenced Sterling and got out. I could hear the guy I'd hit groaning, still lying across the wall. She walked up to him, and I heard a small *pop*. He twitched, and then relaxed; stopped moving. She picked up his pistol, and moved on to the others. I heard no more pops so I guess they'd had it. She came back a few minutes later with two pistols, and an old Italian military rifle. She put them on the back seat, then climbed back in beside me.

'OK, you can go on now, Charlie. We're finished here.'

I didn't speak at first. I put the bus into first and let her roll, picking up speed. Probably after a minute I said, 'You're a bloody murderer.'

It's funny that I'd lost sight of the ghosts which would be knocking on *my* door when my *Christmas Carol* came round, isn't it? She sighed, and looked away from me out of the passenger-side window, her arm leaning on the sill and catching the breeze.

'Murderess. OK, if you like, Charlie. But don't worry, it doesn't make me unreliable.'

After a minute I think I began to laugh; out of pure relief, I'm sure. Then she started to laugh as well. A low little chuckle. She had a nice laugh to go with her nice stretch and nice hands. One of us must have turned off the radio as the action started. She reached forward and turned it on, and found some music this time.

I said, 'I can't believe that the car and us came through that with barely a scratch.'

She smiled and replied, 'They make them good in England, Charlie.'

Some time later she asked me, 'Let me get this right. Your plan, if I can call it that, is to ride into Kampos like the cowboy with the white hat, and ask the priest at the local church where Pat Tobin and Will Carney are?'

'Will Carney?'

'Warrant Officer Wilson Carney, the Army Air Corps pilot. You didn't even know his name, did you?'

'It may not be as simple as that. As far as I can gather Kampos is a bit bigger than your average mountain village. It may have more than one church. I'll pick the biggest. And I'm not going to go knocking on the priest's door – I thought I'd just go and sit in the church, and wait to see what happens. Sooner or later someone's going to get curious.'

'Why the priest?'

'Because the best info we've had so far came from a priest. They're the black mafia out here – if anyone's heard anything, they have. Whether they'll tell me about it, is another thing. I was going to make an appeal to their better nature – the bit God talks to. I'm willing to listen to better suggestions if you have them.'

She hadn't, but did ask me, 'Why are you doing this, Charlie?'

'Because Pat Tobin looked after me when I arrived in the Canal Zone three years ago. I might not have survived it without the advice and help he gave me then. I don't like to think of him out here on his own, without anyone to back him up.'

'He chose to go out on his own. A couple of National Service boys took a week's leave last year at the height of the killings, and hiked right across the island to see the sights. They got away with it, why shouldn't he?'

'And I chose to do the same . . . until you turned up. Why *are* you here?'

'I chose to as well, didn't I?'

'Stupid.'

'Thanks.'

'Don't mention it.'

A few miles on I asked her, 'Can you fill and light a pipe for me?'

'Yes. I used to do that for my grandfather.'

'You'll find everything in my small pack, under your seat.'

She had a good couple of puffs herself before she handed it over. A nice-looking woman smoking an old straight billiard briar looks very exotic. The Humber had one of the quietest engines of any car I had driven. She had been right: they made them well in England.

It was like a bloody ghost town. We found two churches, and both were shut. You should always have a Plan B, shouldn't you? Unfortunately that's never been my strongest suit.

An old woman, led by a boy of about ten, came from a small house surrounded by chickens in the small, dusty square in front of the second of the churches. Thirdlow and I sat on the wide church steps, by the Humber. The passenger door was open so Thirdlow could get at her armoury if she needed to. We'd switched the courtesy light off – the one that came on as soon as a door was opened; I didn't want to drain the battery. The woman addressed us in formal but not unfriendly Cyppo. The boy translated.

'She says you are not welcome here. She says you would

have been welcomed here before you started killing our men, and sided with the Turks.'

'Tell her I am on nobody's side. I wanted to speak with a priest.'

'She says the priests have all gone to the Mother of God monastery at Kykkos for the festival, and asks why you wanted them. Do you and the lady wish to be married?'

'No. We do not wish to be married. A brother was lost in the Troodos some weeks ago. I was hoping for some news.'

The old lady crossed her hands at lap level, and said nothing for some time. When she spoke again she addressed Thirdlow directly.

'She asks if you are the Lion's woman.'

Thirdlow said, 'Tell her *yes*. I am a friend of the Lion.'

The old woman nodded, and fell silent again. If I ran a tune in my head it was a hymn. One of those nice harvest festival ones. It seemed appropriate. When the old woman spoke again she was still looking at Thirdlow.

'She says there is a small church where a hermit lives.' The boy had a shrill piping voice. He was proud to be able to translate the conversations. 'On the back road to Varisia. Perhaps five or six English miles. You take the right-hand fork alongside the river – it runs north.'

'Yes?' Thirdlow asked him.

'Your brother is probably dead. She says a lot of brothers have died – yours and ours. She says ask there.'

The old lady sought the boy's hand with one of hers. I noticed for the first time that her eyes were milky: she was nearly blind. He took her back to the house from whence they had come. The shutting of its door came as a clear sound in the clean air. The birds and the insects, which had fallen silent, started sounding off with an almost shocking suddenness.

359

Thirdlow shrugged. 'No point in hanging about here.'

We got back in the Humber, and continued south and deeper into the Troodos, looking for the junction that would lead us back to the north, and the tree-smothered river valleys.

Once we were rolling something occurred to me.

'I wonder if we have to go back the same way, or can cut south or east?'

'Why?'

'We're hardly going to be welcomed with open arms once they realize what we did this morning. Holding up our hands, and bleating *not our fault*, isn't going to satisfy anyone.'

'It *wasn't* our fault.'

I thought about it.

'I'm not so sure. We could have kept on driving.'

'And they would have shot up the next unarmed civvy car that came along,' she retorted. 'If ever I have to talk to God about that fight I think you'll find we came out morally ahead.'

'You've got it all worked out, haven't you?'

'My job.' She had our map on her lap. She read it like a man. 'We want the next road on the right. It will probably be a dry track, but wide and firm enough for us.' I wondered if she ever lost her focus, and decided that she probably didn't. What had Collins said a hundred years ago? *God help any man who ends up with her.* He must have had a reason for saying it.

An hour later we found the small stone chapel. It had a pigsty built onto one side of it. I'd seen other buildings in Cyprus which couldn't make up their minds whether they were residences for humans or animals, but they had all been farms or smallholdings. This was the first church with a split person-ality I'd encountered so far. There were chickens, and even a scraggly turkey, pecking in the dirt around the chapel door.

We parked the Humber up under the trees across the road.

When we got out, stiff from the bouncing the track had given us, Thirdlow reached back in and grabbed her Sterling, which she looped over her shoulder by its carrying strap, and held out in front of her as we advanced on the building. Thirdlow was always ready for anything; I'll bet she never even went out without an emergency pack in her handbag.

We both saw the movement in the pigsty at the same time. An aimed pistol, I thought, attached to a sunburned hand and arm, over the dry-stone wall. I fumbled for my own pistol, but was far too slow of course: one day I'll learn. Thirdlow didn't hesitate. Four rounds maybe . . . five. *Pop, pop* . . . pop, pop, pop. The impact of the bullets threw the man back into the pigsty. I heard a pig squeal. When we reached it, and looked over the wall, the man lying spreadeagled in the shit and the blood was Pat Tobin. His gun, an old-fashioned service revolver, had fallen on my side of the wall. I picked it up. No bullets. I had been behind Thirdlow. Maybe he just hadn't recognized us. Balls.

He was still alive. His short-sleeved KD shirt already saturated, wet and red. I reckoned he'd taken three slugs at least. He made eye contact with me, and, although his grave facial expression did not change, something softened in his eyes just before he died. He was probably just pleased someone he knew was there to see him off. His lower lip quivered, almost as if he was about to cry, and then he died. It was one of those moments when I felt like crying myself. It was over so quickly.

When I looked at Thirdlow her eyes were as dead as his had become. All she said as she turned away was, 'Silly beggar. He only had to shout.' She had no doubts about herself. Where do people like that come from?

To tell you the truth, I felt like pulling the trigger on her myself. They call that sort of thing 'friendly fire' these days, to make the relatives feel better. Let me tell you something:

there's nothing friendly about a fucking bullet. Never was, never will be – except maybe the one that comes out of the pistol you've put in your mouth to kill the pain you can no longer bear. I can see that one coming one day; when I'm old.

The door of the small church was open. We stepped inside. Thirdlow's weapon carried the smell of burned propellant with it. The priest, praying on his knees on the packed-earth floor before the small altar – a crucifix on a table below an illumin-ated painting of Christ's face – finished his prayer, before he stood and faced us. Did he think we were going to kill him as well? He was tall and thin, had an immense unkempt beard and a dirty cassock. Maybe that's what hermits are supposed to look like. He spoke first in Greek, and then, when we failed to respond, in English.

'So, you are beginning to kill each other now. You did kill him, I suppose?'

I took on the White Man's Burden. I nodded.

'I'm afraid we did. It was an accident. He didn't identify himself.'

The priest studied the earthen floor of the chapel. He was barefoot, and his feet were the same colour. He looked up.

'He was actually a good man. He came here to help another – did you know that?'

'Yes, we did. We followed to help him.'

'But killed him instead. That was very unfortunate.'

'I told you . . . it was an accident.'

'Yes.'

Thirdlow spoke to him for the first time. A couple of candles guttered. I could smell the red scent from her gun again.

'You are in no danger. We will not harm you.'

I was learning about her: learning fast. So I wondered about that. I wondered if she would leave a witness alive.

All he said was, 'Yes.'

She persisted, 'It is sad, but an accident. He came here to help yet another man . . .'

'His cousin, yes.'

'Do you have news of him?'

'You will kill him too?'

'No. We told you. We came to help.'

He turned away from us, and snuffed one of the candles between a finger and thumb.

'I hope I never have to ask you to help me.'

I asked his back, 'Is the pilot alive?'

'Yes, he is alive and well, and is being recovered. I will not tell you how, but you need not concern yourself any longer. Go home.'

'Did the dead man know his cousin was being rescued?'

'Yes. I told him this morning when he arrived. He had been driving around in the mountains for days looking for him. Everyone knew – and the wolves were gathering. I doubt that he would have escaped unharmed anyway. You saved the patriots a bullet, that's all. If you stay here they will come for you too.'

I suppose that the priests had a hard line to draw. Priest or patriot? Which comes first? I won't make the cheap point of observing that it's odd how often different elements of the Christian religion use their faith to justify murders. Except that I just did.

We got into our next battle in a village, and for once you have to believe that it wasn't my fault. The place was built around a farmyard and named Agios Nikolaos Something-or-other. When the Orthodox Greeks set out to name their saints they promoted enough of them to raise a battalion, and St Nick was just one of them. We had dropped down on to the southern foothills of

363

the Troodos after a five-minute stop to swallow the last of the water, and top up the Humber from my jerrycan. I had to watch the car's water temperature; the gauge kept on stealing into the red. No one had pointed a weapon at us for at least an hour, so things were looking up. I'd given the hermit a handful of money to say prayers for Pat Tobin, and clean his body up, and told him someone would come to collect it later. I didn't want to think about Pat yet . . . I knew that would come later, and anyway, in my book the days of the British not abandoning the bodies of their dead were long gone. I didn't want him in the car with us. Thirdlow reckoned I was making a mistake, but didn't argue her case that strongly.

The road south ran through the farmyard, and when we arrived it was like the Lincoln County War down there. Pat Garrett and Billy the Kid must have been just around the corner. We heard the gunshots from a mile away, and I coasted the car down towards them with the engine switched off, the way you still could in the fifties.

I stopped on a bend in the track which called itself a road, looking down on a farmyard and a huddle of buildings. I told you already that I reckoned Thirdlow was prepared for any-thing; she proved it by opening her bag and producing a dinky set of Zeiss binoculars. She scanned the scene below us and said, 'There's an army Bedford in front of the house – flat tyres. British soldiers in the house and the animal sheds. The terrorists are in a grove of trees and on the hillside opposite. They look fairly evenly matched.'

'And you want to join in?'

'That's the general rule – we don't walk away from fights out here. What do you think?'

'The road goes between the two sides, right?'

'Right.'

'We'd never make it. It turns sharp left the other side of the farmyard. I'd have to slow for the corner – we'd be a sitting duck.'

'Agreed. We could always stay back, and see what happens. If that squad has a functioning radio they're bound to have called in the cavalry.'

'But you don't want to do that . . .'

'No. When the GCs pull out they could come in this direction, in which case you and I will be stuffed. I think there are about twenty of them dug into that hill.'

'What do you want to do?'

'Hide the car, and work our way down to the edge of the yard. Then we'll throw a light barrage down on the GCs, hope some squaddy realizes that there's a third element to the fight, and lets us in when we race for the farmhouse door. I can see it's open.'

I gave her proposition a microsecond's thought and said, 'OK. I'm with you.'

'You're not going to argue?'

'Why should I? You're trained to do this – I'm not. I'm only any good at aircraft, and I can't see any of them around at present . . . so you're in charge.'

Watson's Humber was beginning to look the worse for wear. We had lost a front wing somewhere along the line, and the rear window was lying on the back seat in a million tiny pieces. The boot smelt strongly of petrol – maybe the tank had been nicked – and on both flanks the paintwork was gouged down to the undercoat. It didn't take more than a couple of minutes to run it into a bank of juniper scrub on the side of the track. Then I accepted the Sterling she handed me, shouldered the ammo pack, and followed her down the road to the farm. We stayed ducked under crumbling stone walls, and more straggly junipers and vines. Common sense told me we were well concealed. Funk told me that every EOKA man on the island had his sights on me.

From behind a stone drinking trough near the yard gate Thirdlow started to lay bullets on what looked to me like an empty hillside. The empty hillside shot back at us. Its bullets ricocheted off the trough the way they do in Richard Widmark Westerns. Like *Warlock*: did you ever catch that? I managed half a mag before the damned gun jammed. She changed hers, and gave them another scattered burst before I'd cleared it. I think the rest of my bullets went everywhere. I think I shot the sky. I hoped the sky wasn't offended; it was where I made my living, after all, and I wouldn't feel happy up there if it was holding a grudge.

As I started to change the magazine she hoiked me to my feet by my elbow, and got us sprinting for the farmhouse door. Now I knew why she always wore low lace-ups on her feet: she had hoisted her skirt, and ran like Emil Zátopek, beating me to the door by six clear feet. The mad cow was actually laughing as we bundled through it. A tough-looking sod from the Lancashires booted it half-shut behind us. We careered clear to the other side of the room. I saw a scared family hunkered down behind a heavy overturned table, and Tony Warboys trying to tie a narrow bandage around one of his biceps, pulling the knot tight with his teeth.

Thirdlow said, 'I'll do that,' and crawled on hands and knees to help him.

He grinned at me, and waved the other hand. A bullet came in through an already glass-free window, and smashed a piece of plaster from the wall. A small child behind the table cried out in fear. Then half a dozen ill-aimed rounds of automatic fire; they seemed to hit the roof tiles. A lot of noise. That smell of burned propellant in the air. Gun smoke visible in the blocks of light coming through the window. Fights are like that: your brain absorbs thousands of impressions in split seconds, and when you try to remember them afterwards, you can't believe you've seen so much in so short a time.

There was a child's rag doll lying in some spilt wine on the floor, its arms and legs akimbo. Pat Tobin had looked like that when I'd last seen him. I put that thought out of my mind and sat on the floor with my back against the stone wall one side of the door. The Lancs squaddy was on the other side. He raised an eyebrow in enquiry.

'Charlie Bassett,' I told him. 'Thanks for asking me to your party.' At least that raised a few grins. 'Who's in charge?'

'Sar'nt Chatto. Don't give him any lip.'

I nodded, and asked, 'Where is he?'

'Upstairs wiv the radio. Our radio op copped it after he sent out our situation.'

'Can I get up there?' The staircase was at the back of the room, but it had a ruddy great square of sunlight shining on the bottom steps which meant they could be seen from the outside.

'I'll cover you if you like, son, but what makes you think he'll welcome you?'

'I'm another bloody radio op,' I snarled. 'God's just sent you his second choice.' I wasn't being brave or manly. I was being unpleasant. Most of the men I know tend to get very unpleasant when they are as scared as I was. I got up to a squatting position, my back still against the wall, and when he bounced half a dozen rounds along the hillside overlooking the yard – the best he could do, because no one could see who they were shooting at – I dived for the stairs.

And, like a clot, tripped over the bottom one.

I sprawled flat out across them in the sunlight, which just about saved my bloody life. The bullet from the sniper, sighted on that square of visible stair, went a foot above my head, and

I was up, and around the curve of the stairs before he could get another in. He tried though. The top of the staircase emerged directly through the floor into a bedroom. I didn't see much of it initially because I was mesmerized by the muzzle of a big ugly service automatic grasped in the big ugly hand of a big ugly man. It was about a foot from my forehead.

'Name?' he shouted.

'Bassett, sarge. Radio operator.' In one word he'd taken me straight back to my basic training in 1943. *Name?* . . . Name, rank and number. He moved the pistol out of my line of sight, and I heard a click. The bastard thing had been cocked and ready to go. I collapsed, still on the stairs, and let my chin rest against the floor.

'Get up 'ere then, son. See what you can do wi' that. It took a whack – so did Charlie.'

I looked at Charlie. Another proper Charlie; another radio man, like me. He was propped up against a wall. His uniform was cut about and torn at its right shoulder. Bloodstained. A lot of blood. A field dressing had been competently applied to his shoulder, and he was holding it compressed in place with his other hand. He smiled and nodded, but didn't speak. His face was as pale as a swan's back.

The hit the radio had taken wasn't all that serious. These big, heavy army portables were built like tanks anyway, but the mic, which the operator held up to his mouth – the new one looked like a small, curved inverted speaking trumpet – was the weak point. They smashed far too easily. The damaged radio was leaning against the wall alongside damaged Charlie, and the mic had taken the second bullet – which had blown it apart. I picked up the earphones.

'I can hear their signals,' Chatto said, pointing to the earphones, 'but I can't respond.'

'Give me a minute,' I said, and crawled over to it. I smashed the mic off completely, and freed up the wires. The sergeant frowned. Who *was* this bastard destroying army property? I could see it in his face. Then I put on the headphones and began crossing the wires, sending a sparky kind of Morse. How long I could keep it up would depend on what was left in the batteries. It only took the army operator on the other end about thirty seconds to realize he was getting Morse, and another fifteen to begin to read it.

'What do you want to know, Sarge?' I asked the big man. 'And what do you want me to send?'

He grinned a slow grin and said, 'Ask them where t'hell they've been, an' how long we have to wait 'ere?'

I translated that into Service-ese, and when the guy came back told him, 'Twenty minutes, Sergeant. They can hear the gunfire, but they're on foot now coming over the hill behind the enemy. They hope to sandwich the insurgents between them and you, and take a few prisoners.'

'*Insurgents?*'

'That's what he called them. He asks you to fire a few rounds every five minutes, so they can orientate on you.'

'*Orientate?*'

'That's what he said. What's the matter?' The sergeant had suddenly looked pained.

'Those long words. It must be the Mad Major. It's all right for you lot, but I'll have to ride back with him, and listen to him all the way back to camp.' But I could see he was chuffed really. He asked, 'You got a first name, Bassett?'

'Charlie, Sergeant, same as his.' I nodded at his wounded man, who smiled again, but still didn't attempt to speak.

'Well, Charlie Bassett . . .' Chatto suddenly reached for a Sten he had under one hand, pointed it over his shoulder and out of the window, and fired off three rounds. Half a dozen came back by return. Plaster dust exploded around us. 'Well,

Charlie Bassett, which regiment did you have the honour to serve before you put on the funny clothes?'

'None, Sergeant. I'm a RAF operator, or was. Lancasters.'

'I'll be damned . . .'

'What?' I asked him.

'You seem too clever for that.'

Warboys's voice called from below, 'Mr Chatto, what's your situation?'

'Under control, sir. Major Cussiter will be here in fifteen minutes. Then we can hammer the bastards.' I didn't like the little bit of American history that sprang to mind, but it was Cussiter, not Custer, so that was all right.

'You OK, son?' Chatto asked his proper Charlie.

'Yes, Sar'nt.'

'Just stay put. We'll soon have you out of here. Right as ninepence.' I'd often wondered what was particularly right about ninepence. This time all the boy did was nod. He looked about eighteen years old. Chatto turned his attention on me.

'Well, Charlie. What shall we talk about while we wait then? You fond of music?'

'Yes, Sergeant.'

'I like a touch of Edmundo Ros. You like Edmundo Ros?'

Another bullet bounced off the tiles above our head. I winced. I could hear gunfire, but most of it was no longer coming in our direction.

Then it stopped.

It stopped because the EOKA men outside must have been as surprised as us when a naked man on a racing bicycle freewheeled through the farmyard, carrying the United Nations flag raised on a stick in one hand.

Less than a minute later another four or five naked people on cycles followed him through, and out of sight. In the middle of the bunch was a tandem, and the man on the back of the tandem gave me an idea I couldn't get rid of. Most of the cyclists were as pale skinned as proper Charlie's blood-drained face. The guy on the tandem wasn't. He had a suntanned face, forearms and calves. He had spent a lot of time in short sleeves and shorts out in the sun. It didn't take me long to work it out, and it won't you either.

The firing didn't resume. We waited another quarter of an hour before a dusty file of soldiers came in from the south. Trailing them was a small ambulance, and a Champ mounting a heavy-cal machine gun. They must have left their heavy transport down the hill. That didn't surprise me. I've always been impressed by the way the Brown Jobs are willing to shoulder loads that would crush the average market porter, and then walk ten miles with them.

I was stiff when I stood up, and went downstairs. Getting older, Charlie. Thirdlow was standing by a window. Warboys was with the GC family, jabbering away in their lingo, and helping them set the place to rights, as much as a farmhouse that's just been shot up can be set to rights. The table was back on its feet, and I heard the farmer laugh at one of Warboys's jokes. The small girl hugged the rag doll, as if she had thought she would never see it again. I went over to Thirdlow.

'Do you want to travel back with them?'

She still looked out of the window, not at me. 'No. I always go home with the man who takes me to the dance, Charlie. One of my rules.'

'OK. Shall we walk up and get the car?'

'I already asked the corporal to recover it.'

'I have the key.'

'Don't worry, he'll manage.'

Then I remembered that she'd managed as well. She had

been in the car when I had come down that morning. That morning: it seemed like weeks away already.

I drove her back, tailing the small convoy. We had had to wait for an armed one-tonner to crawl up into the hills and back, recovering Pat's body, which meant, of course, that we finished the journey in the dark. As we settled into the bench seat of the battered Humber she said, 'I can't quite believe what's happened. It wasn't long ago that we were all drinking with Pat – it seems like months ago – don't you remember?'

'No.' It was my turn.

'A party at Pat's place. After that stupid girl was brought back.'

'Did I behave badly?'

'No, I think you went to sleep. Pat was very happy that night. He was a good organizer.'

'What did the civvy police want him for?'

'Loads of things – sleeping with the enemy.'

'Christ, was that all? We all do that sooner or later.' The faces of all the women I'd known went briefly and bitterly through my mind. It didn't take long, because there weren't that many of them. But, then again – maybe she'd meant something different.

'Did Collins send you up here to kill him?'

'No, of course not. It was an accident. I saw the gun and reacted the way I've been trained. I would have helped you to get him out if I could.'

'Will you get into trouble?'

'Mm . . . I expect so. Court-martial job.' She didn't sound all that concerned. 'Some smart little boy from the Solicitor General's office will try to prove I've got finger trouble . . .'

'Sorry?'

'Trigger happy. Even if I get away with it they'll send me home.'

'Then don't argue with them. Anywhere's better than here.'

She laughed, and I asked her, 'What's so funny?'

After a pause she said, 'You ever been to Aldershot, Charlie?'

I expected her to get off at Wayne's Keep with the rest of them, but she stayed put, and on the road back to Famagusta we were flagged down by a cop car. The British policeman who walked back to us sounded like a west coast Scot. Firm, prepared to be friendly, but not prepared to take any shit. He explained that the lights on the Humber did not pass muster. We'd lost the driver's-side front wing and its lights with it, and the one on Thirdlow's side was flapping up and down like a WAAF's sneakies.

'We were in a shoot-out with EOKA, Constable. The car got hit.'

'Then you should have left it where it was, laddie, and found an alternative means of transport.' The last few words came out as if he had learned them by rote. Then he started writing me a ticket. Life must go on, I suppose, even when you're in the middle of a bloody civil war.

The RAF regiment corporal in charge of the gate detail at the RAF compound gaped when he saw the state of Watson's car. I knew I'd get it in the neck in the morning. Wasn't that stupid? I had already forgotten about Pat, and was worried about the car. We unloaded the small arsenal we seemed to have collected into my hut.

Thirdlow said, 'I'm going to bunk here tonight, but don't get any ideas. OK?'

'Too tired for ideas. I want a shower, and I want to go to sleep, and wipe today from my memory.'

'That sounds good. Do you have anything to eat?'

'Pete usually keeps something in his locker for emergencies.' I pointed out Pete's bed. It still hadn't been slept in. She found a tin of Fray Bentos, and we split it. Then I showered. When I came back into the bunk room she was already in Pete's bed. Her shirt and skirt were folded neatly on a chair, and her dirty shoes were tidily beneath it. I turned out the light, and unfurled the mosquito net around my bed. Then I did hers: maybe they didn't have insects on her part of the island. As I climbed into my bed it creaked, and she said, 'Thank you.'

I turned on my side so that my back was to her even though we were fifteen feet apart. 'Goodnight, Ann.' Using her first name sounded odd, but I was too tired to talk about it. I wondered if Watson already knew what a hash I'd made of things this time.

'Goodnight, Charlie.'

I had an odd final thought that I was sleeping in the same room as a mass murderess, which was quickly replaced by the realization that anyone who knew what I'd been up to over Germany in 1944 probably felt the same about me. The fan on the ceiling clicked. It moved the mosquito nets as if people were brushing past them. I went to sleep, and dreamed that I was on a sunny slope somewhere, lying down alongside my lioness.

Chapter Twenty

Last Orders, Please

Watson handed me a hefty glass of cheap Greek brandy. I'd glimpsed over his shoulder: he had at least a dozen bottles in his cupboard, and I asked myself where they had come from. In case you're wondering, it tastes like silver polish. Thinking about it, being handed a glass of something heavily spirituous by Mr Watson had been the prelude to most of the good or bad events of my life. But it was barely 0830, and this was going it some, even by his standards.

'Sit down, Charlie.'

I sat. He sat. He looked uncomfortable. It was possible that he was about to explode.

'I'm sorry about your car . . .' I said.

He did explode.

'Bugger the car. It's only a fucking car.'

I was too surprised to be surprised.

'And I'm sorry about Pat . . . Corporal Tobin.'

'Ah.' He held the glass up to the light, and squinted through the amber liquid. That's something that men, in particular, do when they don't know what to say next. Women don't have that problem.

'Yes. Poor Pat. He's been with me since Suez.'

'I know. I was there with you.'

'So you were . . . so you were. Did you see the GC who got him?'

I picked up the clue fairly quickly. Watson and Collins must have cooked up a story between them.

'No, we were just getting out of the car when it happened. It was over in seconds. Collins's woman got a few rounds off in the general direction. I don't think she hit anyone, although she's very good.'

'I know . . . and this hermit chappie? Involved?'

'No, nothing like. He fought for Pat's life afterwards.' I've told you before. When you lie to someone you like, it's important to do it well.

'Did Corporal Tobin say anything?'

I cast my mind back for anything Pat had ever said to me.

'He wanted to say sorry to someone called Mary Walters, but I think in his mind he had gone back to being a teenager again. We'd better forget it.'

'Fine by me. Both parents deceased, no siblings, so it will be a service funeral at Wayne's Keep in a few days. You'll be there?'

'Of course. My duties permitting.'

'Your duties will permit. From now on you won't have much more to do. You can clock on to Ibn Saud occasionally so we can verify that the system's up and running. Apart from that, Cyprus is your oyster, as long as you keep out of trouble. I plan to send you home in a few weeks anyway. Cheers.' He drained a quarter-pint of brandy in a oner.

'Cheers, sir.' I sipped mine. What I was thinking was, *That was quick*. All of a sudden they wanted to get rid of me. Get me off the island perhaps, before anyone started asking questions. I sipped my drink because Watson looked determined to get drunk, and that worried me. Just as the words *the system* had worried me. You noticed them of course. He splashed himself another drink. Something else was coming.

'You have a son Carlo, don't you? Mother called Grace? Grandfather Lord So-and-So-Something-Baker, the arms manufacturer? Trust you to keep bad company.' I half rose from the chair, but Watson said, 'Bloody well sit down, Charlie, and now do what you're told. Swallow your drink.' I did both. He poured me another whopper.

When I had my breathing back under control, and decided that I didn't need to cry until I was on my own, I asked him, 'What?' And then, more sensibly, 'What's happened to Carlo?'

These events happen to all of us, don't they? It's the ordained way of things. I'm sure you've been there. A million things tear through your mind all at once, and there's usually a face in the middle of them. Grief hits you like an atom bomb.

'Nothing. Nothing at all.'

'What then?'

'His mother's been killed.'

Time stops.

'Grace?'

'Yes.'

It was as if all of the air had been squeezed from my lungs, then pumped in, and then squeezed out again. I felt almost physically sick. Words, facts began to slot together in my head.

'Not Carlo?'

'No. Grace.' He looked confused.

I had a few sips of the brandy. Didn't taste it. Then I said, 'Thank God for that,' and immediately felt like the worst kind of traitor.

Watson said, 'You look a bit pale, old man. Would you like to get some air? Come back in a min?'

'Yes. Good idea.'

I walked up and down the dusty road outside his ridiculous wooden cabin. Fiona came out and walked with me, not saying a word. We must have looked odd because she towered over me.

For three years I'd feared I might have shot and killed Grace Baker. I had loved her, but she got mixed up with the Stern Gang in Israel and we'd ended up on opposite sides. Funnily enough it had been quite like Thirdlow's shooting of Pat. Grace had shot at me, and I returned fire almost without thinking about it. She'd got two shots in at me first, and had winged me. What had Thirdlow said about the scrap at the bridge? Something like, *If I have to talk to God about that fight I think you'll find we were morally ahead.* Is that what I was supposed to believe?

Finding out she'd been alive all this time, but was now dead, was like being a child who'd been offered something wonderful, only for it to be snatched back when I reached for it. Don't get me wrong: I didn't want her. I just didn't want her dead. I'd always harboured the hope that I could introduce Carly to his mother one day.

Back inside, I sat in front of Watson again, and was prepared to listen.

'First of all, are they sure it's her?' I asked. 'Grace can be a bit of a slippery fish.'

'Yes. They're sure. Her parents identified her – there's no mistake. It was Lord Baker who asked the Foreign Office to find and notify you. It's taken a few days, I'm sorry about that.'

'How did it happen?'

'She was in Greece. No one knows what she was doing there. The signal hinted she had kept some pretty rum company in the last few years. She married some sort of gangster in Israel – did you know that?'

'She did it to get a passport, and divorced him a year later.'

'Anyway, she was shot and robbed in an old open-air theatre

she was visiting. It was late evening, and the other tourists had left. They shot her in the back, and ransacked her bag. If it helps, it must have been over very quickly.'

Why do people always say that? I've told you it *doesn't* bloody help. It can't. It never will.

'So how did the authorities know it was Grace?'

'The killers left her passports. She had three. A valid Israeli one, an expired British one in her own name . . . and a forged British passport in another name. I think that's why Baker insisted you be told.'

'I'm sorry. I don't understand.'

'The name in the bogus passport was Grace Bassett, and she listed you in it as husband, next of kin, and *person to be informed* . . . You know the drill. It was a very good forgery.'

I had a couple more sips of the jungle juice, and said, 'I think I'll go outside again.'

This time Fiona let me do it alone.

As I paced up and down in the dust I remembered that Warboys's little courier had said the person who had offered to pay for my murder was a crippled old lady. He was about ten, wasn't he? Did he look on me as *old*? What would he have thought of Grace?

When I went back for the third time I told Watson, 'I'm not sure I can believe it. I thought she was dead a couple of times. She always manages to come back.'

'Not this time, old boy. Anyway, I thought you might say that, so I pulled a few strings, and had a couple of snaps flown over. The camera never lies.'

'From the Foreign Office?'

'No, from the police chief's office in Athens – much more reliable.'

'I thought we were *persona non grata* with the Greeks at the moment, over this Enosis business.'

379

'We are, we are . . . it's just that some of us are still a bit more *grata* than the rest, believe me. Gregori owed me a favour. You don't have to look at them if you don't want to.'

I thought, and had a couple more sips before reaching for them. My glass was miraculously empty, and so was Watson's bottle. He opened another, and threw the cap away.

The photographs had obviously been taken in daylight, and therefore the next morning. One was of her face; a remorseless close-up. Grace's elfin features had taken on that marbled immobility of death. Her mouth was a little open – she always did that when she was surprised – and her eyes heavy lidded, but not quite shut. She often looked like that after we had made love. The other photograph was of her body *in situ*, taken from above. Her arms and legs made her look as if she was running: I had seen a body like that somewhere before, and couldn't remember where. Although she had been shot in the back, she had twisted over to see the sky as she went. That was Grace all over. I hoped that there had been a million million stars for her. A walking stick lay close to her right hand.

'Was the walking stick hers?' I asked Watson.

'Yes. Her right hip had been smashed up by a pistol bullet years ago. They found it still there when they autopsied her – small-calibre job. Too much information – sorry . . .'

'No. Go on.'

'Apparently it must have completely crippled her. The pathologist said she would have walked like an old woman.' All the words came back together.

I stood up, and walked to the window. I left my back to him.

'Do they know how it happened?'

'She was found the next morning down near one of the exits by the stage. The police theorize she was trying to get away. She might have made it if she hadn't been slowed down by her old injuries.'

'You said *they* when talking about who killed her . . .'

'At least two – two different makes of bullet. What with the one in her hip, it must have been like the death of Caesar.'

I slopped my drink around in its glass, and tried to think. I couldn't. I could just believe that Grace would want me dead; she didn't leave jobs unfinished. But that meant that I . . .

'Has anyone told Carlo yet?'

'No. We rather thought you'd want to do that yourself when you got back. He didn't ever meet her, did he?'

'Apart from the moment of birth, no – I don't think so.'

'No point in him being at the funeral then. What about you? I could always speed things up, and fly you home in time. It's going to be a quiet affair, I understand – at the family pile in Cambridgeshire.' *Bedfordshire*, I thought, but didn't correct him.

I remembered Grace there the morning a Lanc had crashed nearby; she'd found the body of a crew member. That was virtually the only time I'd seen her cry. Did I want to go to her funeral, and finish it? It was another thing I had to think about before replying, and then I used almost the same words.

'No. I don't think so. I'll see her later.'

Watson walked over to the door which hid Fiona's territory.

I heard him say, 'Sandwiches, please, dear. Cheese, bags of mustard and a bit of cress. And once you've brought them, take the rest of the day off. Switch off the phones, and lock the door on us. Charlie and I are going to get drunk.'

I don't understand how these things work. Grace was murdered at a place called Epidaurus; a huge old Greek theatre. I'd seen one in Egypt so I knew what they looked like. I hadn't even heard of it until a week or so before, when Warboys had spoken of it, of course – so I already had a helpful picture in my head when Watson described the scene to me. We call these things coincidences, shrug and turn away. But what they are like are

381

echoes. Echoes from the past or from the future . . . or from both at the same time: it doesn't matter. They aren't really anything, except little reminders, perhaps, that life is nothing like we think it is.

We drank all day and I still wasn't properly drunk when I went to bed. I told Watson Grace's story, and we talked about Pat, and the people we had known who were no longer around. I put Watson to bed at about eleven, and then just walked around the camp for hours in the dark. Drunk but not drunk. I was challenged twice.

Each time I was challenged I stopped, and my phantom lioness pacing alongside me also stopped, and sat down in the dust. Once I rested my hand on her head. Silky. Warm. Nobody else saw her, so she wasn't really there of course.

Eventually I looked up, and it was dawn. Someone was standing in front of me. It was Pat's man who looked like Bud Abbott. He looked how Bud Abbott would have looked if he had been crying. He was the man who had promised to look after me because I was a comrade. I remembered that now. He said, 'Why don't I take you back to your hut, Mr Bassett?'

'Yes, that's a good idea.'

He didn't notice the lioness, even though she walked between us, right up to the wooden steps.

I don't think you need to know any more. Nothing is neat at the end. The things that you do and the people you know . . . they all unravel. All you are left with are the hollow spaces they made inside you.

A month later I kicked along a beach with Carly. The sea was a deep dark blue, with heavy rollers which had come all the way from Brazil or Argentina. A large sailing ship bent its white sails on the horizon. The darkness of the blue made the caps of the long waves gleam and flash sharp in the sun. Steve and her mother had taken Dieter off to visit a Zulu kraal. The Zulu women were beautiful. They were bound to make fun of him, and turn his head. Steve's father had brought Carly and me out in his car, and was sitting in it at the head of the beach, reading the *Cape Times*. Carly put his hand in mine. He was small for his age. A pocket battleship, like me. We had talked about Grace for an hour.

'You're sure she's dead? She was pretty adventurous, wasn't she? Maybe it wasn't her.'

'I'm sure, son. She was good at getting into scrapes, and getting out of them. But this time she didn't get out. I think there were too many men against her. It was her last fight.'

'That was unfair.' I felt his hand tighten.

'Yes. It was unfair.'

'When I'm older I'm going to find the men responsible, and kill them all.' He had that vehemence which kids can find from somewhere inside them.

'Are you?'

'Yes. I promise.'

I glanced over my shoulder. Our barefoot tracks in the sand bridged the line between wet and dry golden sand. Not another soul. Seabirds. He said, 'When Dieter goes to college we'll miss him.'

'Yes. We will.'

He picked up a piece of seaweed shaped like a lion's tail, and flicked it at the sand.

'Just me, you and Miss Stephanie then?'

It wasn't that bad a prospect.

'Hang on – I haven't asked her father yet.'

'Let's ask him now. He's sitting in the car waiting for you to do it . . . I'll ask him, if you're scared. He can only say *no*.'

Epilogue

Last Words . . .

I am an old man, and old men doze in the garden when the sun is high. Yesterday I was disturbed by the sound of an aircraft. No matter what I am doing, I always stir and turn to an aircraft. It was the Twin Otter on its way to landfall at the airstrip on the beach at Barra at low tide. It's good to know that somewhere in the country real flying is still going on.

The lioness was sitting on her haunches beneath the old copper beech tree. Autumn again: my life never seems to get further than autumn. The leaves on the tree are starting to curl, and crisp to that thick gingery brown which smells of woodsmoke.

Grace was sitting alongside the lioness with her arm looped around its shoulders, and she wore that same old mocking smile which said she'd won after all. Even though she's been gone for thirty years or more she can still reach right inside my chest and give my heart a squeeze. I see her around more often than I see the others. Sometimes she walks right up and touches me, and her touch feels as real as that of a living person. She always looks the same – just as she was in 1947. She must have been thirty or thirty-one then. Like my other ghosts she speaks occasionally – or I hear her voice inside my head, which is the same thing. Last week she came up behind me when I was sitting on this very bench, lightly touched my scalp and observed that I was balding. She sounded amused, light hearted – but I know her well enough to know she still holds a grudge. Maybe we can sort it out when we meet for good.

Anyway, the lioness lifted herself onto her four legs, stretched the way cats do, and stalked off into the shrubbery. Grace pulled up one knee and hugged it, and we sat there smiling at each other, watching each other until dusk. Maybe twenty feet between us. When the old lady switched on the lights in the kitchen I knew it was time to go in.

The Watsons came to stay last week, and one night he and I sat drinking in the study until the small hours, talking about Pat Tobin. We killed a bottle of 'Morangie from the distillery at the bottom of the hill. That was when I realized that he didn't actually know what had happened to Pat – Collins had peddled him the official line, and Watson had chosen not to question it. He cried when I told him. That's another thing that old men do. He proposed that the four of us go back to Cyprus in the spring, and visit Pat in his grave in the Wayne's Keep cemetery. I said *yes*, but I didn't mean it. I didn't tell him that I'd been back alone a few years ago, and that Pat's grave is no longer marked.

Neither Carly nor Dieter has married yet. Was that my fault, I sometimes ask myself? Dieter sends us postcards from ports around the world. The old lady has a world map on a cork board in the kitchen and she tracks his progress with coloured pins. I never did get round to telling Carly that I had a leading part in how Grace died. Every time I tried the conversation seemed to drift away from me, and eventually I gave up. He comes up to stay whenever he gets leave, and plays golf at the Royal Dornoch. I consider that my biggest failure of his upbringing. Often we take my small pistol and shoot targets behind the house: I'm not ashamed of the fact that it was one of my sons who finally taught me to shoot straight.

Carly has proofread each of the volumes of my memoir – he corrects the manuscripts before you get a look at them. He's in the house now, having sat up all night with the book you've just read, and in a few minutes will walk from the porch carrying our gun, and a box of bullets. Half an hour on the targets before we go in to supper. There is just a little darkness in Carly; when the ghosts crowd round, and Carly has a pistol in his hand, it is almost as if he knows them as well as I do.

I wanted

The Last Post

Although our misadventure in Cyprus from the mid nineteen fifties onwards wasn't the last time an incompetent British government sent conscript soldiers to other lands with guns in their hands, it was one of our last attempts to apply serious military pressure to the politics of the Mediterranean and the near Middle East for colonial purposes . . . mind you, the Aden crisis was only just around the corner, and then there was Oman.

As with the previous Charlie Bassett novels, it has been National Service veterans who were actually there who have given me the background material for the story, and generously allowed me to see ten weeks in Cyprus during the Emergency through their eyes: they put the frame around my picture. But don't blame them if you have spotted a mistake or two, or an inaccuracy – that will have been my fault. It was one of them who told me that two young soldiers had taken a week's leave during a lull in the EOKA insurgency, and had hiked from one side of the island to the other, staying with hospitable Greek Cypriot families along the way. It puts an entirely different meaning on that delightful invitation – 'take a hike'. Either they were lucky, or it can't always have been all love and bullets over there.

I borrowed the Foreign Office mandarin, Carlton Browne, from Terry Thomas, who gave us so many wildly comic creations in the Fifties and Sixties. He is among the most underrated of British comic actors – I still have his films as DVDs, and drag them out to cheer me up when I'm blue. I don't know why he professionally outlasted his contemporaries like Norman Wisdom and Ronald Shiner, but between them they taught us to laugh again – and, as importantly, to laugh at ourselves. We owe them a large debt: I'm sure the small classic cinemas will rediscover them one day, and start to run film festivals based on their uniquely British comedies.

There was a real Inspector Robert Fabian – 'Fabian of the Yard'. He was a master thief taker of the 1940s who became famous for the successful investigation of high profile murders. After he retired he pumped up his pension with frequent contributions to the national newspapers: if a quotation was needed to round off a juicy murder report then Fabian was your man . . . and, you might have guessed it, one of the earliest successful Police dramas on TV was 'Fabian of the Yard', in which he was portrayed by the wonderful Indian-born Scots actor, Bruce Seton – actually Major Sir Bruce Lovat Seton of Abercorn. Bruce made his first film in 1935, and was still facing the cameras in 1961. Charlie loves these survivors.

There was once also a real *Steve*, although, as far as I know she didn't evolve to become a belly dancer in a seedy Cyprus hotel. Steve was the second girl with whom I fell in love – I was probably 12 or 13. She was older, gentle, more intelligent and (in my memory) very, very tall. Although at different schools, for part of a magic year we travelled daily on the same bus between Rose Hill and Carshalton. My pals made fun of me, and called her 'Tarzan' behind her back. Boys can be cruel, can't they? I lost touch with her, and my school, at roughly the same time – one of my former classmates recently described me as a 'serial absconder' – and sadly, now, can't even remember her family name. I hope she made it.

It was about that time that I began to knock around with Alan Miller, the boy next door. He was maybe four years older than me, and one of those people born with a wrench or a screwdriver in their hands; the Great Architect had meant him to be a motor mechanic from the start. His first car was a pre-war Hillman open tourer. He rebuilt it completely on a piece of dead ground at the end of his garden, and coach painted it a vivid leaf green. We used to drive out in it on Sundays (I was usually working on a Saturday – most of my peers had Saturday jobs), spot a family group taking a walk, coast the car up silently behind them and shout the strange word 'Mackeson!' as loudly as we could. Consternation, shouts and screams usually ensued; Alan would then bang the car into gear, and we would race away looking for another victim. That memory is the reason I feel I can't complain about the 'boy racers' who make the Edinburgh streets lively places to walk on Saturday nights. I suppose one would be arrested for doing that sort of thing today, and if there is anyone still alive on whom we played that trick, let me take this opportunity to apologize. It was Alan's car that Dieter was driving, of course . . . and you know what Charlie would say: *what goes around comes around*.

I hope I haven't offended the 1956 Suez veterans too much by describing the Anglo–Franco–Israeli attempt to seize the Canal Zone as one of the most successful, least effective, invasions carried out by the British Army. As usual the Army, Navy and RAF played their parts well – gave their all – and the politicians made a mess of it. Although there is one story that I would like to verify: one Canberra pilot in Cyprus allegedly raised the undercarriage of his aircraft, and dropped it on the ground, rather than bomb unsuspecting Egyptians. If he took his decision for the right reason that action must have taken a lot of courage. It doesn't appear in any of the official histories, but the veterans will tell it all the same: truth, or just another Suez myth?

The way the Americans and the UN saw us off in 1956 was as humiliating for Britain as was the Cuban Missile Crisis to the Soviets a few years later. Washington took the high ground over Suez, and said that if it was opposing the Soviet invasion of Hungary, it was damned if it would let us do the same in Egypt. It was actually nothing to do with what was happening in Hungary, of course. International relations are essentially a competition for resources, and consequently the US and UN stance on Suez was absolutely nothing to do with the morality of the British action: morality and politics are words I have difficulty in working into a single sentence anyway. I'm certain the US saw its pressure on Britain at the time of Suez as a way to clip British wings for ever, and make sure we could never compete with them successfully on the world stage again. And we never have.

. . . and who paid the bill? Mostly the soldiers, sailors, airmen and their families of course . . . although you've been paying for it through your petrol ever since. It's been the same since Thermopylae; we never seem to bloody learn.

In 1950s London one of the places to be seen was The Savoy Grill, off The Strand. When I contacted the nice people who have it now, to ask them what it was like at that time, their archivist responded with e-mailed photographs, menus and a seating plan which detailed the favourite tables of the celebrities of the period. I never fail to be impressed by the people and organizations which go out of their way to help me get the detail of my stories right. But I had a sentimental reason for setting scenes at The Savoy hotel: I spent my last night as a bachelor there – then my first night as a married man – in September 1965. I remember sitting in what seemed to be an enormous bedroom, reasoning that if a chimney sweep's son could make it to The Savoy, then anything could happen! It has recently re-opened after a major refurbishment – I must stay there again at least once more before I go, and see what they've made of the old lady . . . and in case you are wondering, the film star sitting at the next table to Charlie and Robert Fabian was Lauren Bacall – the place still has very fond recollections of her.

Now I have to comment on the very last sentence that Charlie wrote for you in the body of this book, because this book may – just *may* – be *The Last Post* for Charlie Bassett. If you didn't pick up on what might have happened, just go back and read the last four or five pages again: I'm sure you'll get it. The publisher doesn't want another Charlie Bassett book at present, and I'm sure Charlie is getting tired of me picking over his bones anyway, so unless you kick up hell and bully Pan Macmillan into it, you probably won't be hearing from him again.

Am I sad? In a way; but also very grateful for having been given the opportunity to put his stories in front of you in the first place.

One last word: if you want to *see* Charlie, just look around you. He is the man alongside you now: every man with a small 'e'. He and his people are composites – I think they draw their characteristics and textures from all of the ordinary people I have ever met, and what he has taught me is that I have *never* known an ordinary person . . . just hundreds and hundreds of extraordinary ones: there is a little bit of Charlie and Grace in each of you.

And I am rather proud to have marched with you.

DAVID FIDDIMORE
Edinburgh
30 October 2010

extracts reading groups

competitions books new

discounts extracts extracts

competitions

books new

events books

extracts new reading groups

interviews

discounts

new books events

events new

discounts extracts discounts

www.panmacmillan.com

extracts events reading groups

competitions books extracts new